M000159023

BAD MAGIC

A Skulduggery Pleasant Graphic Novel

Books by Derek Landy

The Skulduggery Pleasant series
SKULDUGGERY PLEASANT
PLAYING WITH FIRE
THE FACELESS ONES
DARK DAYS
MORTAL COIL
DEATH BRINGER
KINGDOM OF THE WICKED
LAST STAND OF DEAD MEN
THE DYING OF THE LIGHT
RESURRECTION
MIDNIGHT
BEDLAM
SEASONS OF WAR
DEAD OR ALIVE
UNTIL THE END

THE MALEFICENT SEVEN
HELL BREAKS LOOSE
ARMAGEDDON OUTTA HERE *(a short story collection)*
THE SKULDUGGERY PLEASANT GRIMOIRE
BAD MAGIC *(a graphic novel)*

The Demon Road trilogy
DEMON ROAD
DESOLATION
AMERICAN MONSTERS

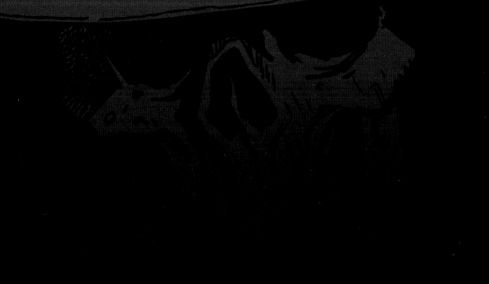

FÁILTE GO TEARMANN CARA

WELCOME TO

TERMONCARA

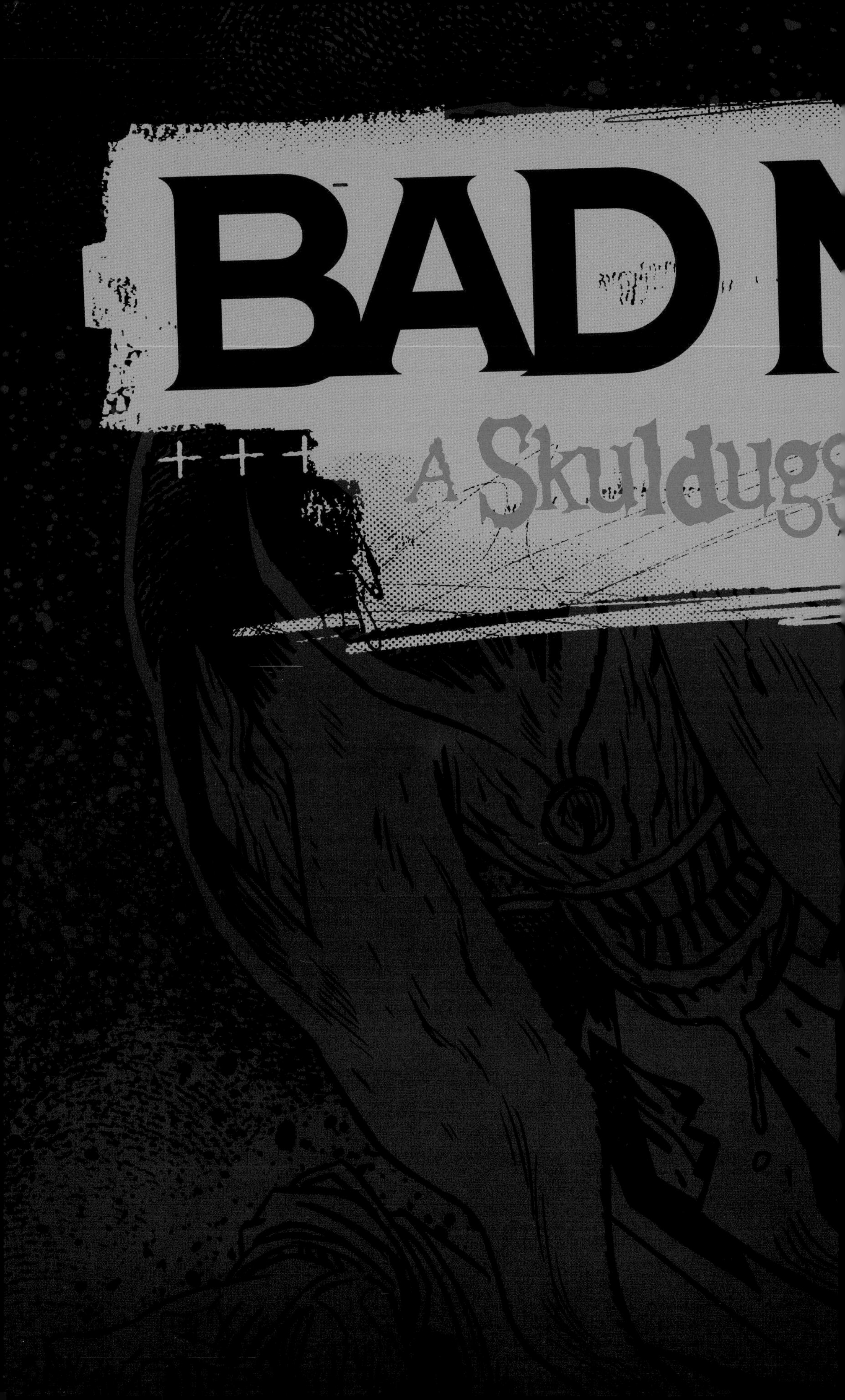
BAD
A Skuldug

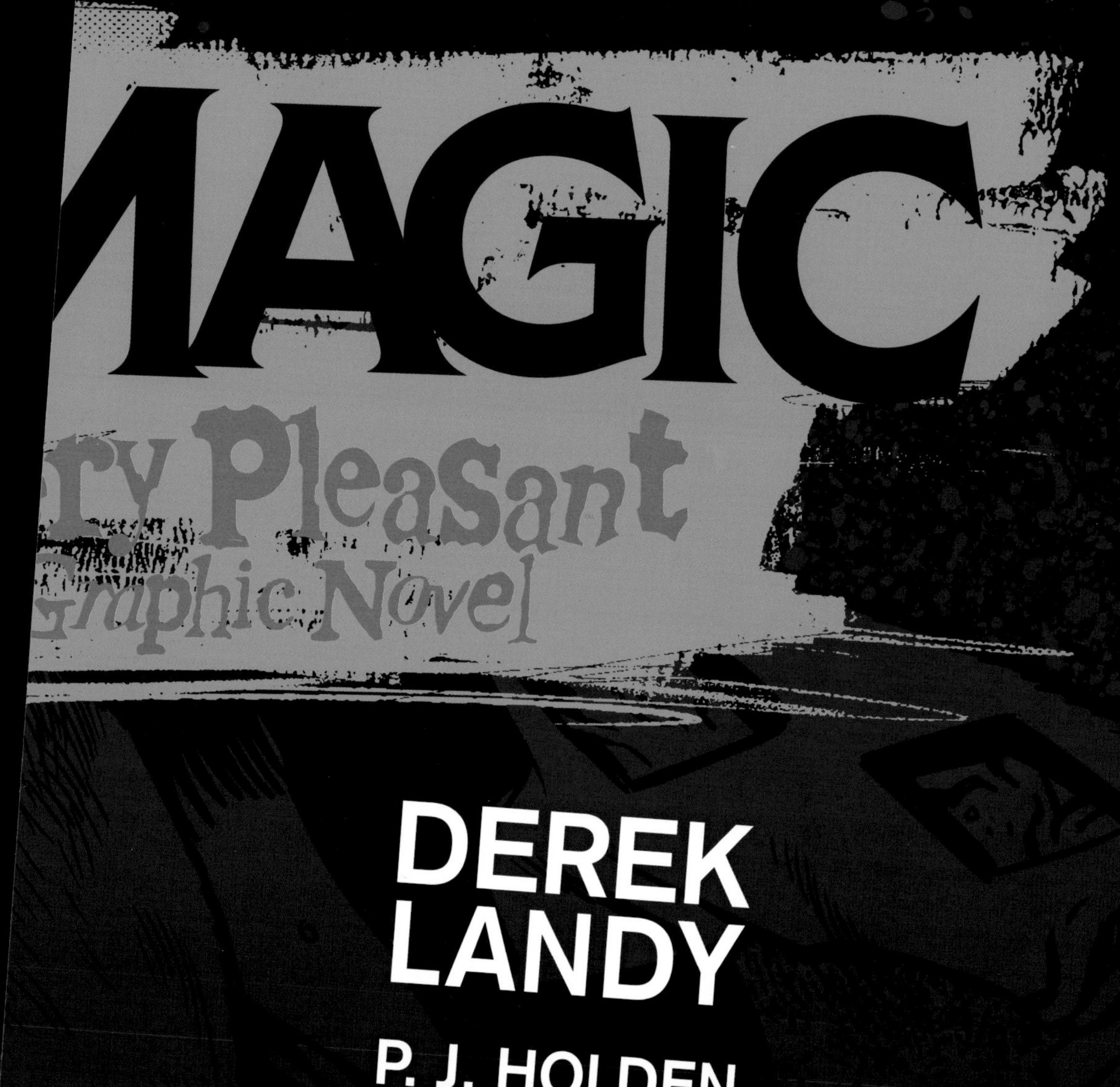
MAGIC
ry Pleasant
Graphic Novel
DEREK
LANDY
P. J. HOLDEN

First published in the United Kingdom by
HarperCollins *Children's Books* in 2023
HarperCollins *Children's Books* is a division of
HarperCollins*Publishers* Ltd
1 London Bridge Street
London SE1 9GF

www.harpercollins.co.uk

HarperCollins*Publishers*
Macken House, 39/40 Mayor Street Upper
Dublin 1, D01 C9W8, Ireland

1

Text copyright © Derek Landy 2023
Art copyright © P. J. Holden 2023
Skulduggery Pleasant™ Derek Landy
Skulduggery Pleasant logo™ HarperCollins*Publishers*
Cover design copyright © HarperCollins*Publishers* Ltd 2023
All rights reserved

Art by P. J. Holden
Colour by Matt Soffe
Lettering by Rob Jones
Design by Pye Parr

ISBN 978-0-00-858578-5

Derek Landy asserts the moral right to be identified as the
author of this work.

www.skulduggerypleasant.co.uk

A CIP catalogue record for this title is available from the
British Library.

Printed and bound in Malaysia by Vivar

Conditions of Sale
This book is sold subject to the condition that it shall
not, by way of trade or otherwise, be lent, re-sold, hired
out or otherwise circulated without the publisher's prior
consent in any form, binding or cover other than that
in which it is published and without a similar condition
including this condition being imposed on the subsequent
purchaser. No part of this publication may be reproduced,
stored in a retrieval system or transmitted in any form or
by any means, electronic, mechanical, photocopying,
recording or otherwise, without the prior permission of
HarperCollins*Publishers* Ltd.

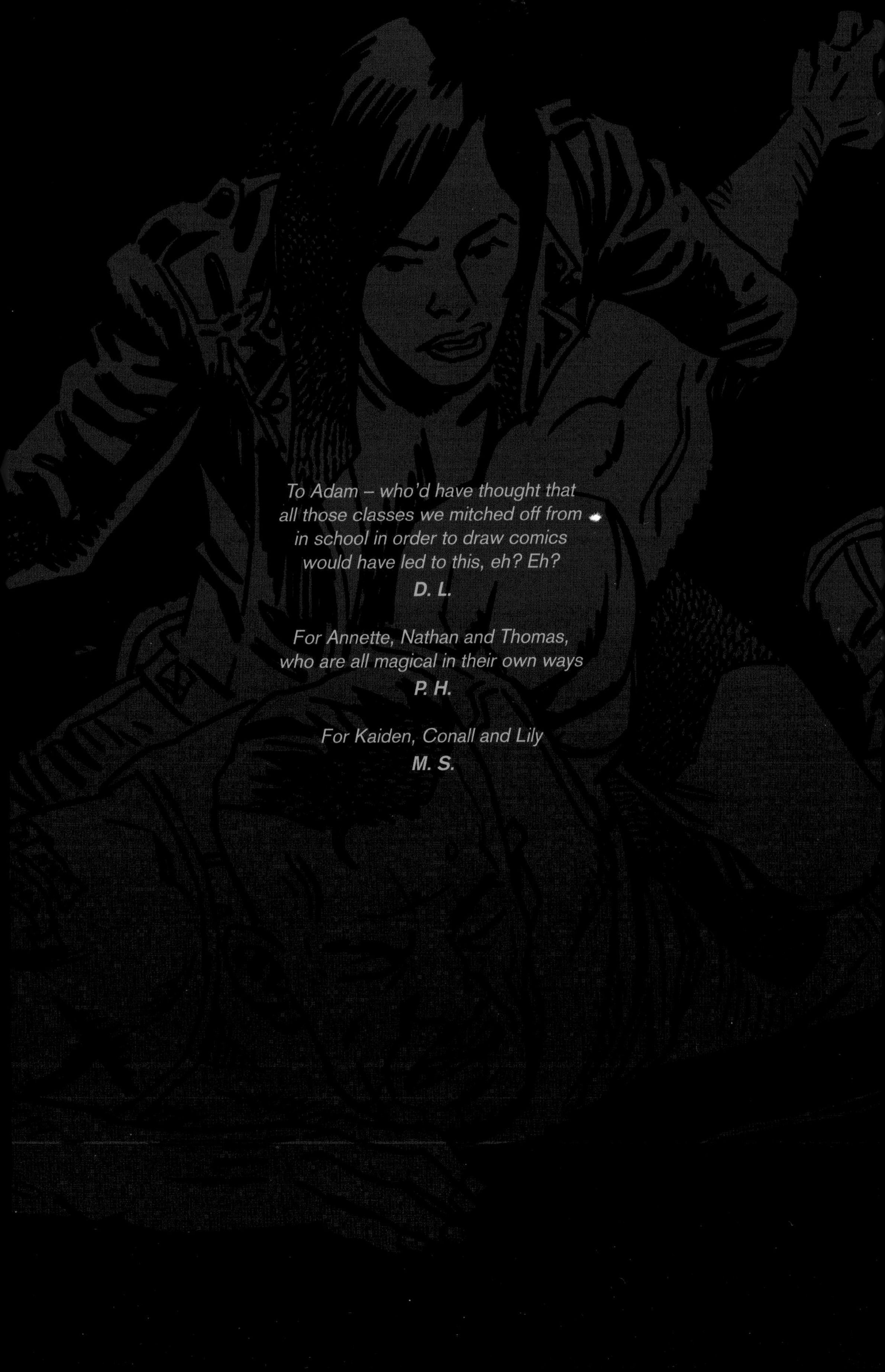

To Adam – who'd have thought that all those classes we mitched off from in school in order to draw comics would have led to this, eh? Eh?

D. L.

For Annette, Nathan and Thomas, who are all magical in their own ways

P. H.

For Kaiden, Conall and Lily

M. S.

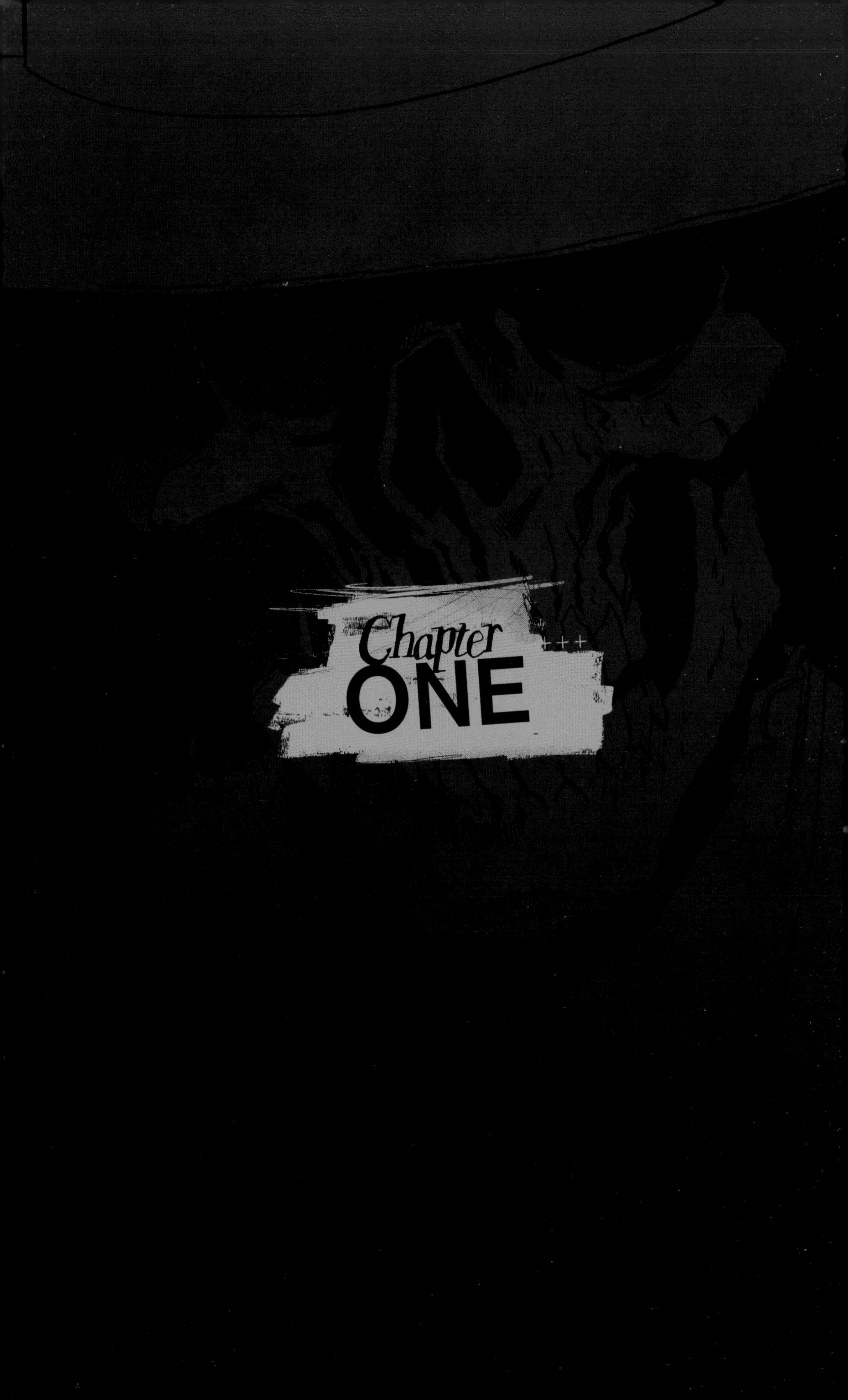
Chapter
ONE

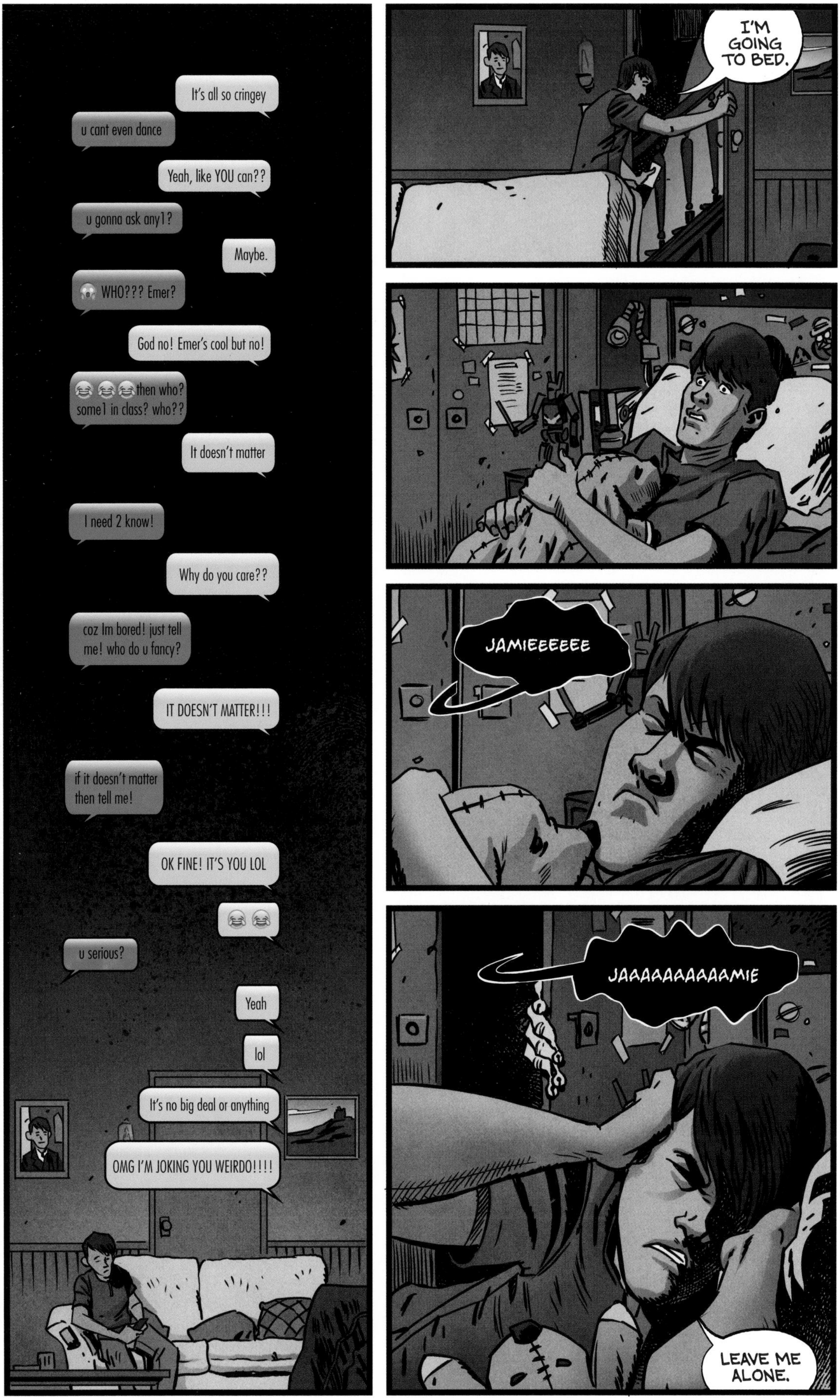
It's all so cringey
u cant even dance
Yeah, like YOU can??
u gonna ask any1?
Maybe.
😱 WHO??? Emer?
God no! Emer's cool but no!
😂😂😂 then who? some1 in class? who??
It doesn't matter
I need 2 know!
Why do you care??
coz Im bored! just tell me! who do u fancy?
IT DOESN'T MATTER!!!
if it doesn't matter then tell me!
OK FINE! IT'S YOU LOL
😂😂
u serious?
Yeah
lol
It's no big deal or anything
OMG I'M JOKING YOU WEIRDO!!!!
I'M GOING TO BED.
JAMIEEEEEE
JAAAAAAAAAAMIE
LEAVE ME ALONE.

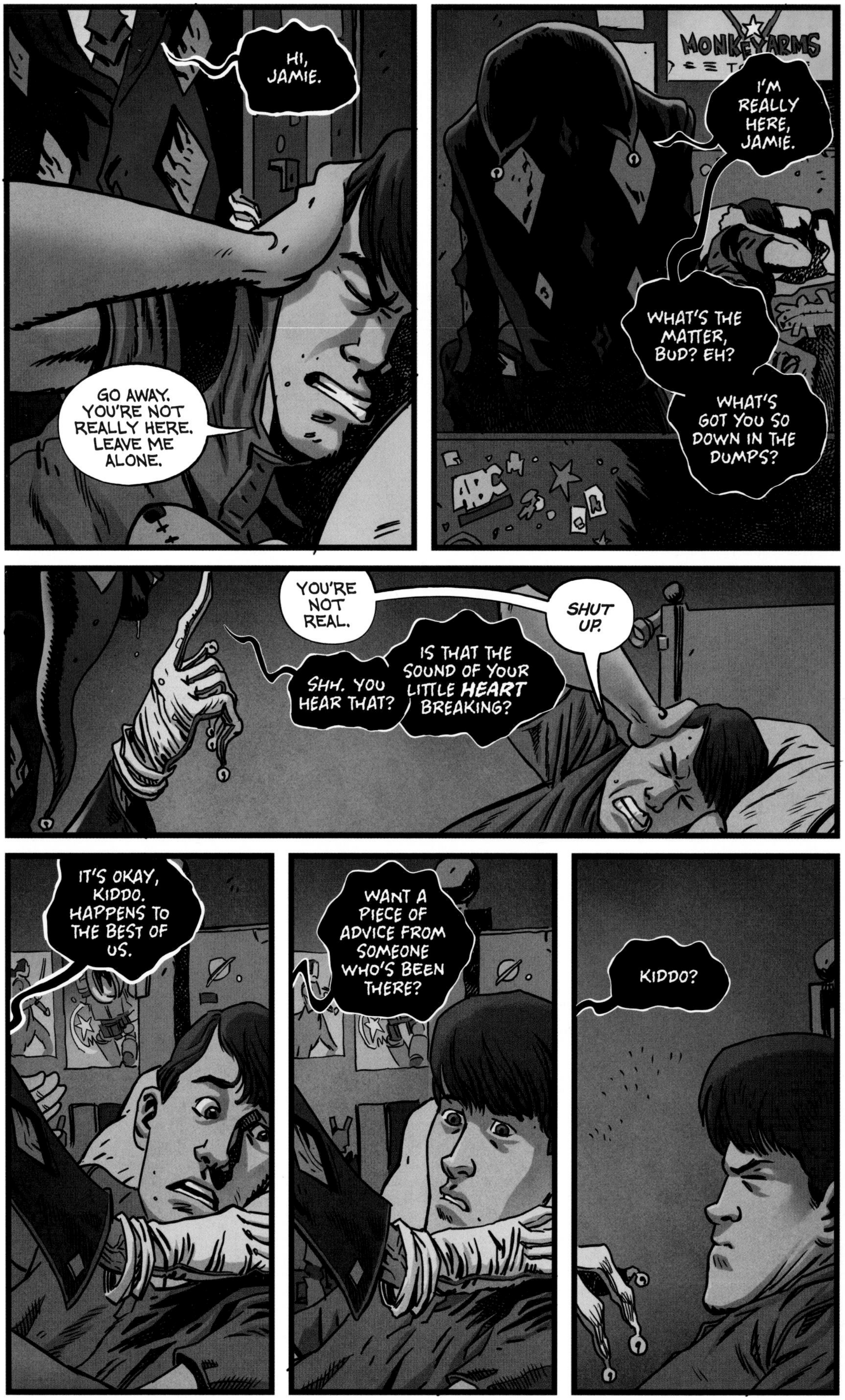

HI, JAMIE.
GO AWAY. YOU'RE NOT REALLY HERE. LEAVE ME ALONE.
MONKEYARMS
I'M REALLY HERE, JAMIE.
WHAT'S THE MATTER, BUD? EH?
WHAT'S GOT YOU SO DOWN IN THE DUMPS?
YOU'RE NOT REAL.
SHH. YOU HEAR THAT?
IS THAT THE SOUND OF YOUR LITTLE **HEART** BREAKING?
SHUT UP.
IT'S OKAY, KIDDO. HAPPENS TO THE BEST OF US.
WANT A PIECE OF ADVICE FROM SOMEONE WHO'S BEEN THERE?
KIDDO?

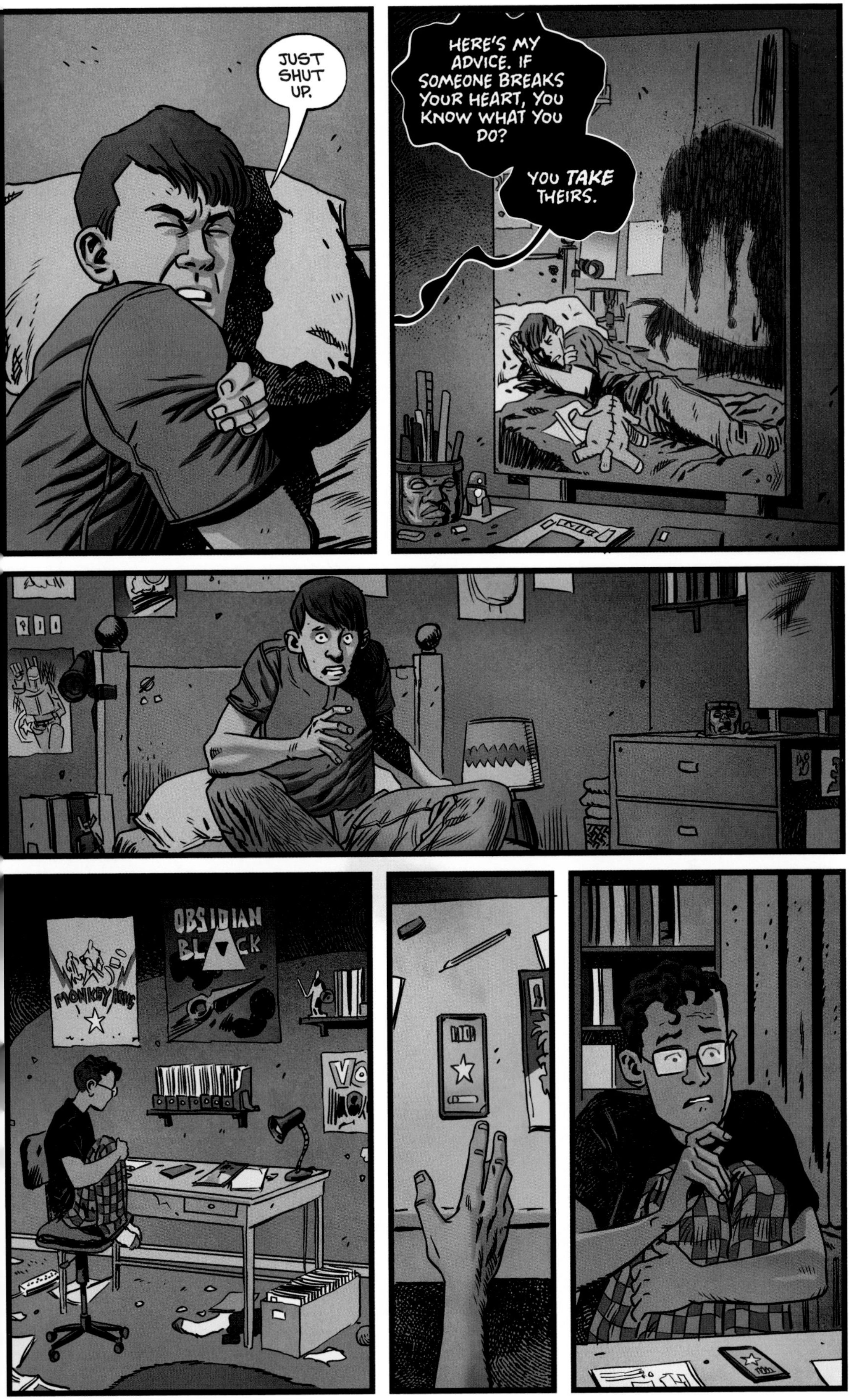
JUST SHUT UP.
HERE'S MY ADVICE. IF SOMEONE BREAKS YOUR HEART, YOU KNOW WHAT YOU DO?
YOU TAKE THEIRS.
OBSIDIAN BLACK
MONKEY

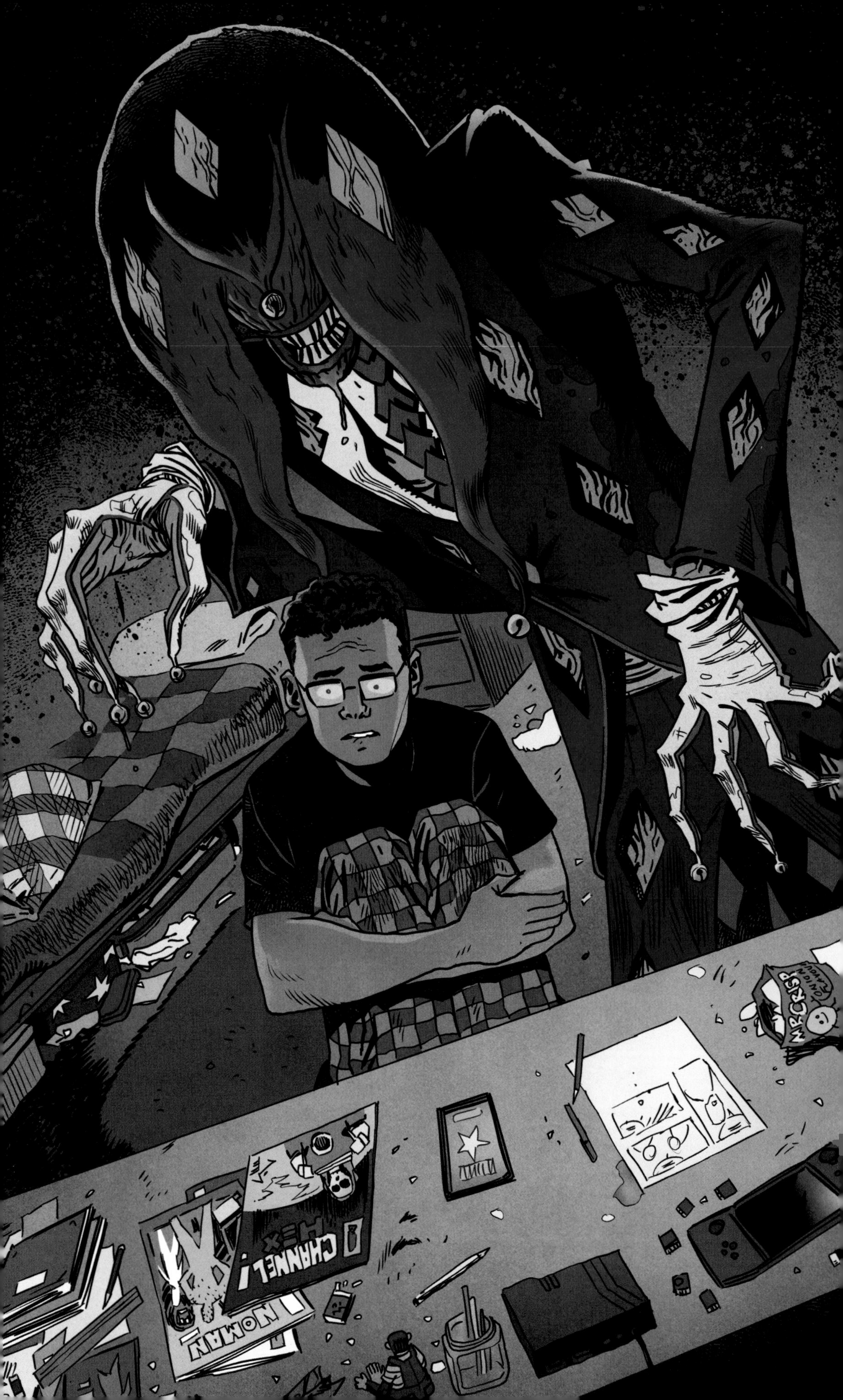

MR.CRISP
CHANNEL
HEX
NOMAN

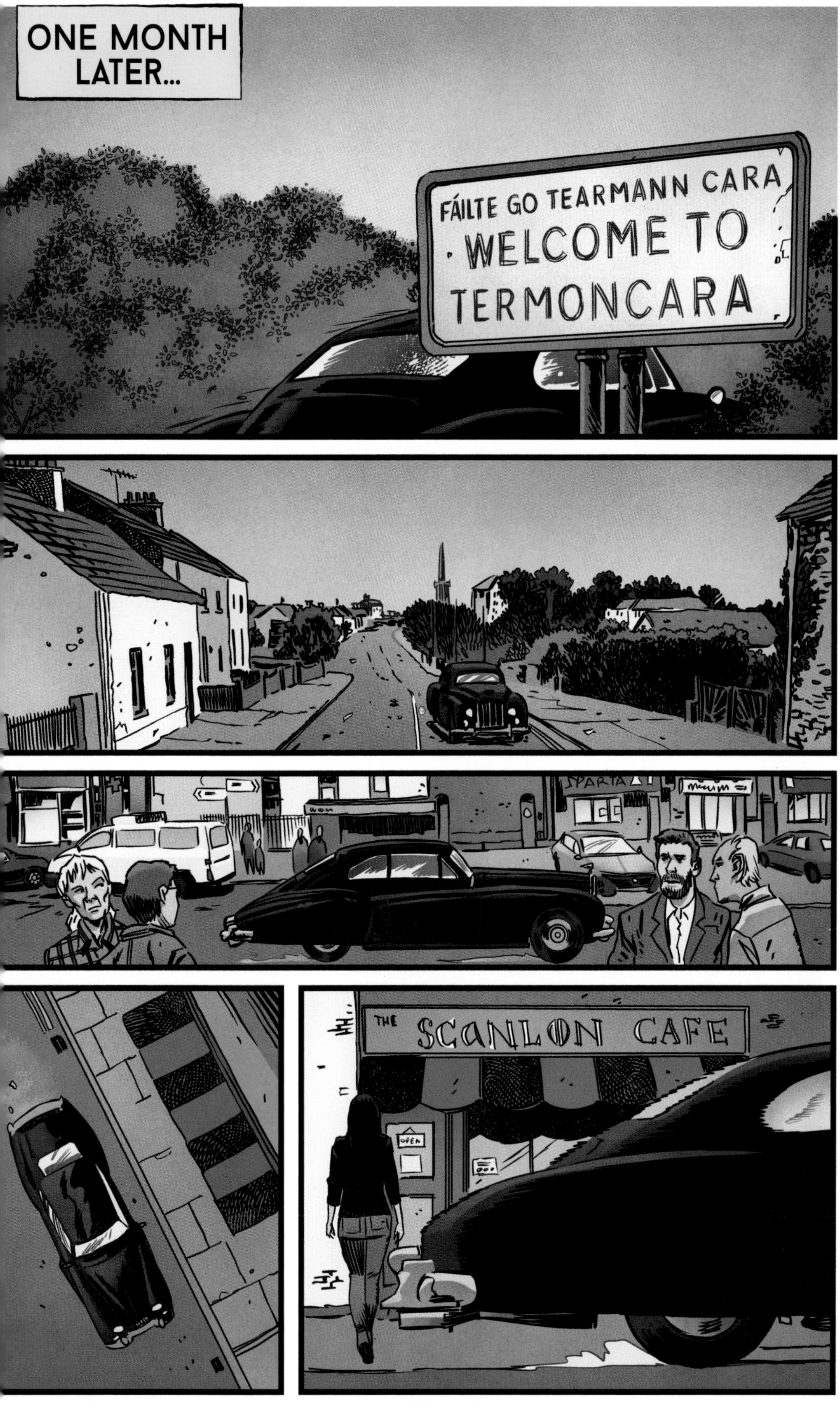
ONE MONTH LATER...
FÁILTE GO TEARMANN CARA
WELCOME TO TERMONCARA
THE SCANLON CAFE
OPEN

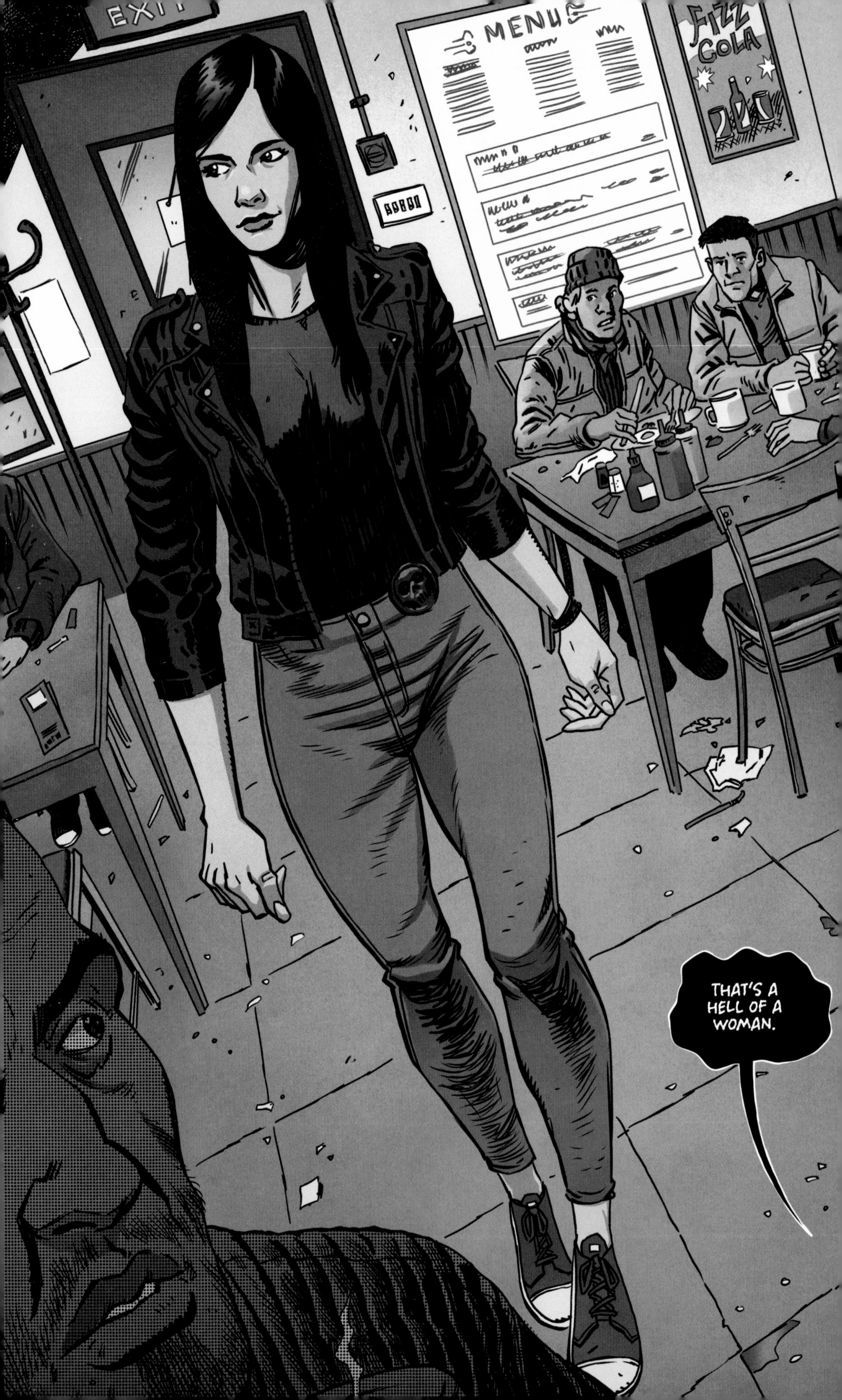
EXIT
MENU
FIZZ COLA
THAT'S A HELL OF A WOMAN.

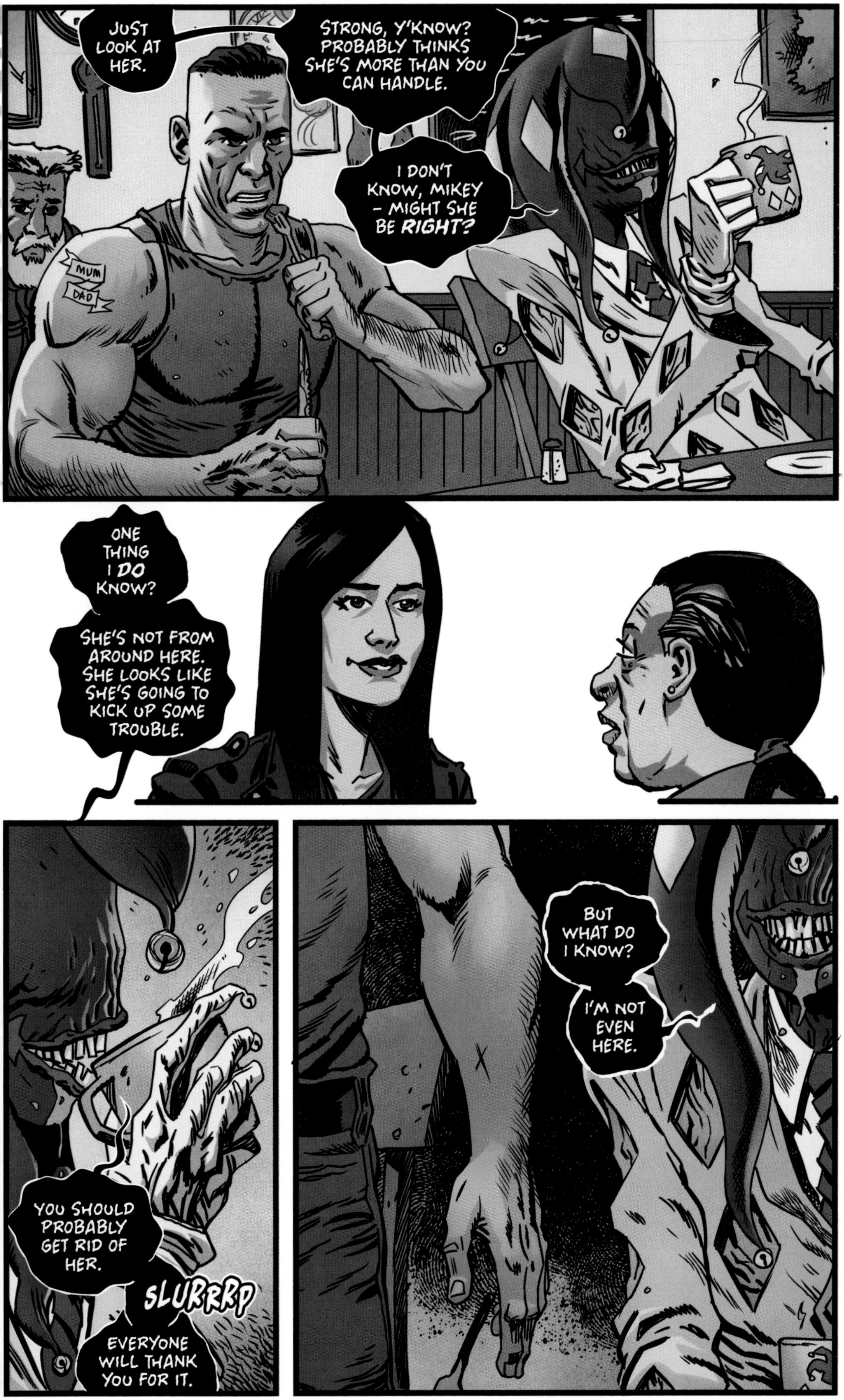
JUST LOOK AT HER.
STRONG, Y'KNOW? PROBABLY THINKS SHE'S MORE THAN YOU CAN HANDLE.
I DON'T KNOW, MIKEY – MIGHT SHE BE RIGHT?
MUM
DAD
ONE THING I DO KNOW?
SHE'S NOT FROM AROUND HERE. SHE LOOKS LIKE SHE'S GOING TO KICK UP SOME TROUBLE.
YOU SHOULD PROBABLY GET RID OF HER.
SLURRRP
EVERYONE WILL THANK YOU FOR IT.
BUT WHAT DO I KNOW?
I'M NOT EVEN HERE.

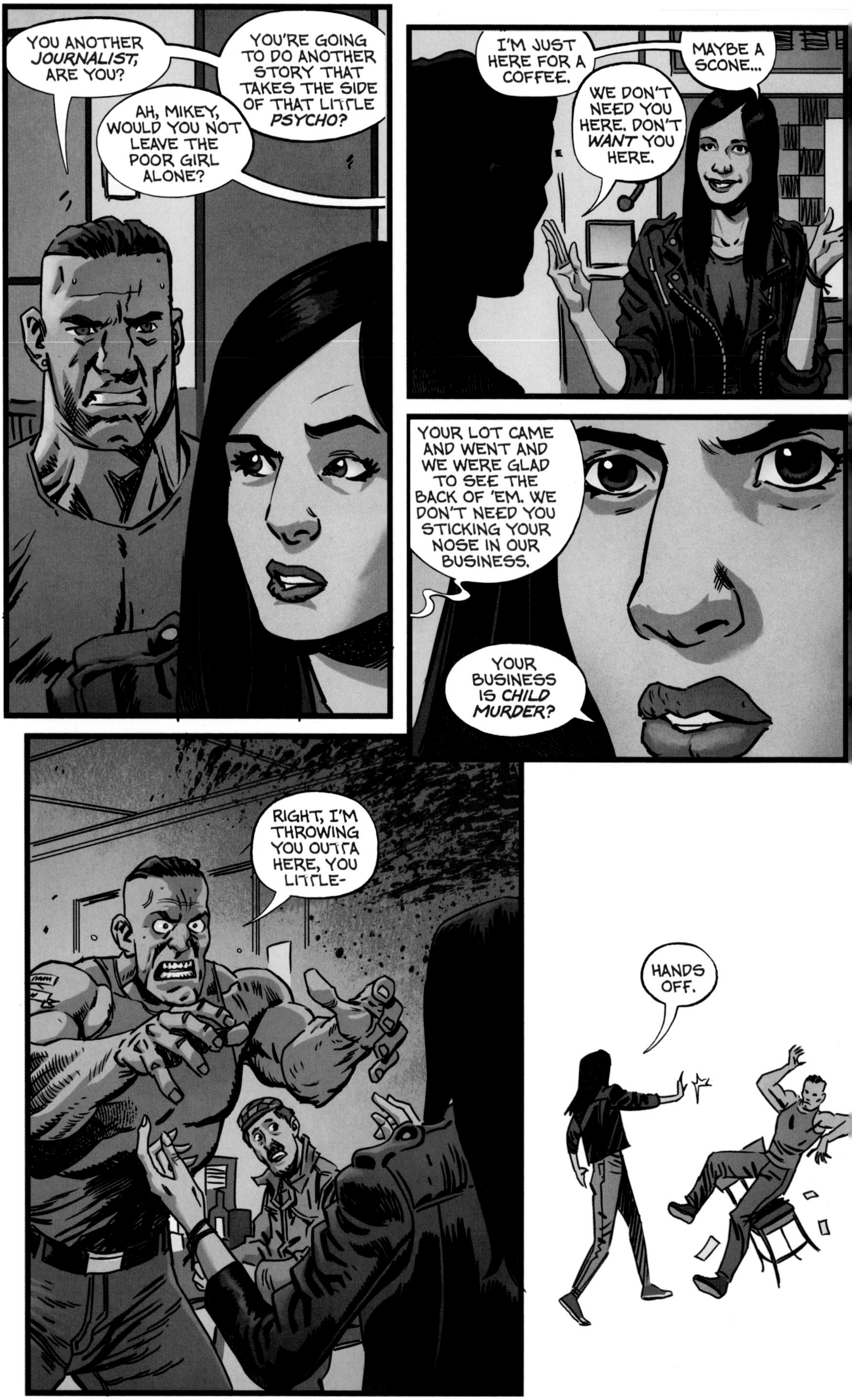
YOU ANOTHER JOURNALIST, ARE YOU?
YOU'RE GOING TO DO ANOTHER STORY THAT TAKES THE SIDE OF THAT LITTLE PSYCHO?
AH, MIKEY, WOULD YOU NOT LEAVE THE POOR GIRL ALONE?
I'M JUST HERE FOR A COFFEE.
MAYBE A SCONE...
WE DON'T NEED YOU HERE. DON'T WANT YOU HERE.
YOUR LOT CAME AND WENT AND WE WERE GLAD TO SEE THE BACK OF 'EM. WE DON'T NEED YOU STICKING YOUR NOSE IN OUR BUSINESS.
YOUR BUSINESS IS CHILD MURDER?
RIGHT, I'M THROWING YOU OUTTA HERE, YOU LITTLE-
HANDS OFF.

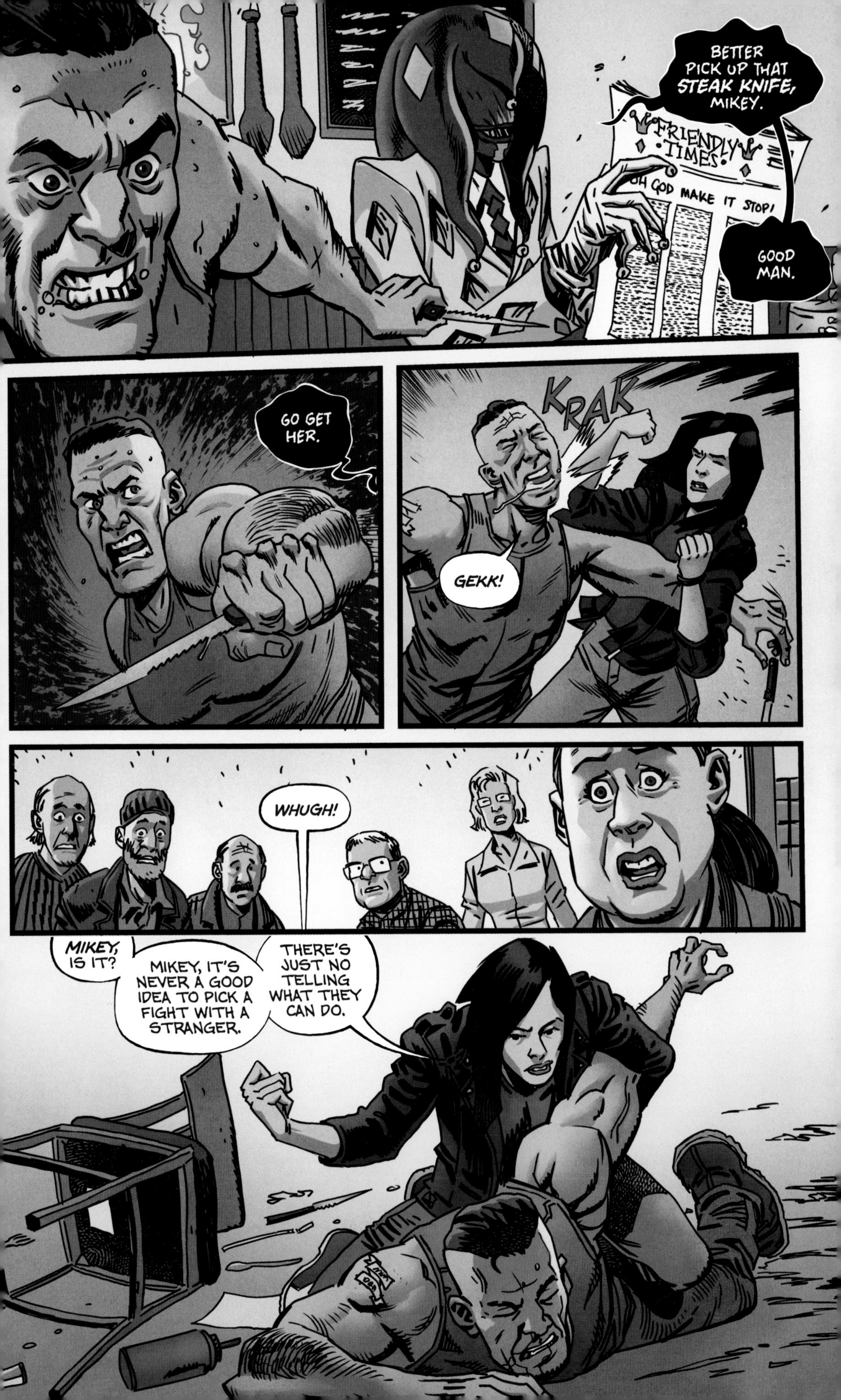
BETTER PICK UP THAT STEAK KNIFE, MIKEY.
FRIENDLY TIMES
OH GOD MAKE IT STOP!
GOOD MAN.
GO GET HER.
KRAK
GEKK!
WHUGH!
MIKEY, IS IT?
MIKEY, IT'S NEVER A GOOD IDEA TO PICK A FIGHT WITH A STRANGER.
THERE'S JUST NO TELLING WHAT THEY CAN DO.

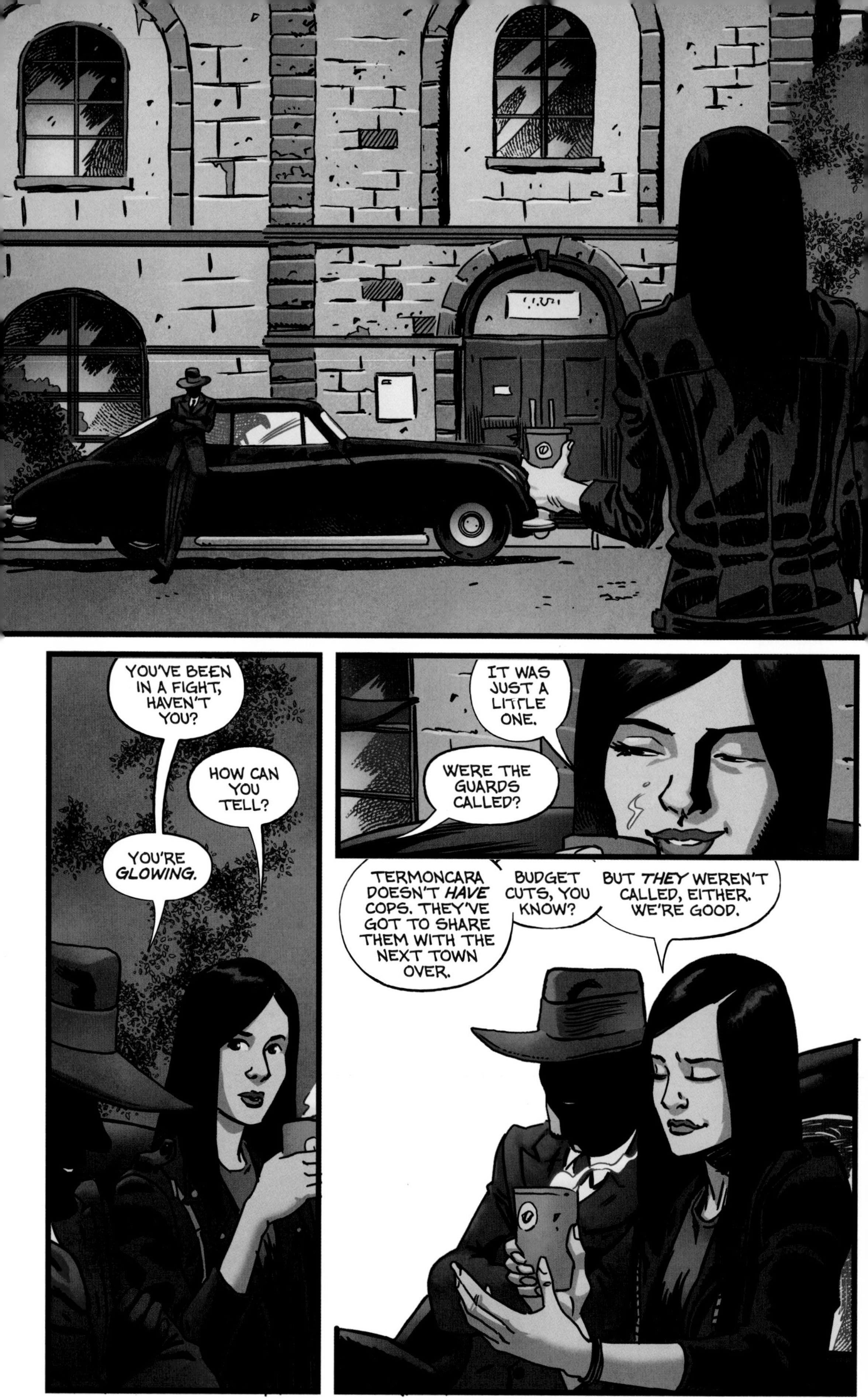

YOU'VE BEEN IN A FIGHT, HAVEN'T YOU?
HOW CAN YOU TELL?
YOU'RE GLOWING.
IT WAS JUST A LITTLE ONE.
WERE THE GUARDS CALLED?
TERMONCARA DOESN'T HAVE COPS. THEY'VE GOT TO SHARE THEM WITH THE NEXT TOWN OVER.
BUDGET CUTS, YOU KNOW?
BUT THEY WEREN'T CALLED, EITHER. WE'RE GOOD.

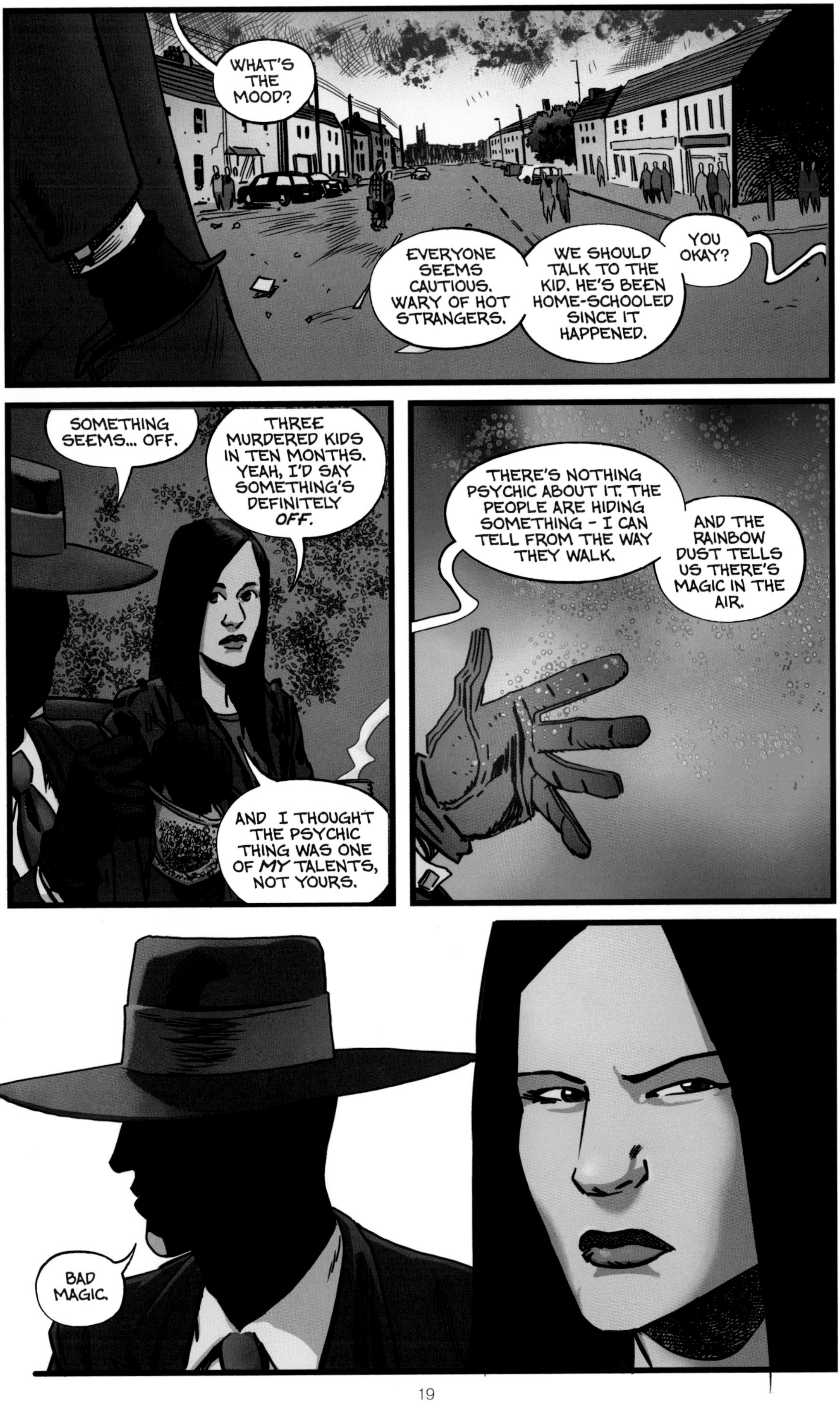
WHAT'S THE MOOD?
EVERYONE SEEMS CAUTIOUS. WARY OF HOT STRANGERS.
WE SHOULD TALK TO THE KID. HE'S BEEN HOME-SCHOOLED SINCE IT HAPPENED.
YOU OKAY?
SOMETHING SEEMS... OFF.
THREE MURDERED KIDS IN TEN MONTHS. YEAH, I'D SAY SOMETHING'S DEFINITELY *OFF.*
AND I THOUGHT THE PSYCHIC THING WAS ONE OF *MY* TALENTS, NOT YOURS.
THERE'S NOTHING PSYCHIC ABOUT IT. THE PEOPLE ARE HIDING SOMETHING - I CAN TELL FROM THE WAY THEY WALK.
AND THE RAINBOW DUST TELLS US THERE'S MAGIC IN THE AIR.
BAD MAGIC.

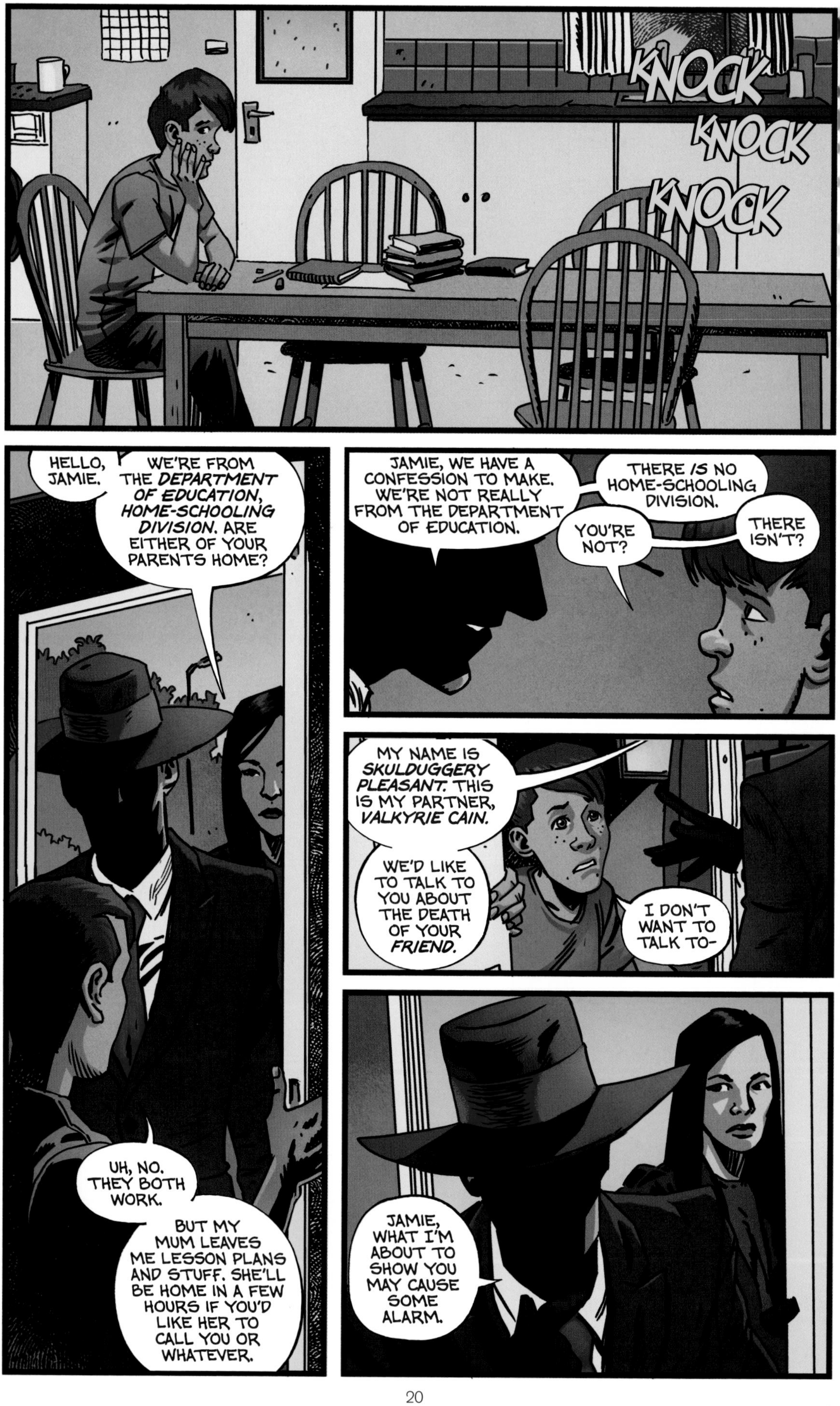
KNOCK
KNOCK
KNOCK
HELLO, JAMIE.
WE'RE FROM THE DEPARTMENT OF EDUCATION, HOME-SCHOOLING DIVISION. ARE EITHER OF YOUR PARENTS HOME?
UH, NO. THEY BOTH WORK.
BUT MY MUM LEAVES ME LESSON PLANS AND STUFF. SHE'LL BE HOME IN A FEW HOURS IF YOU'D LIKE HER TO CALL YOU OR WHATEVER.
JAMIE, WE HAVE A CONFESSION TO MAKE. WE'RE NOT REALLY FROM THE DEPARTMENT OF EDUCATION.
THERE IS NO HOME-SCHOOLING DIVISION.
YOU'RE NOT?
THERE ISN'T?
MY NAME IS SKULDUGGERY PLEASANT. THIS IS MY PARTNER, VALKYRIE CAIN.
WE'D LIKE TO TALK TO YOU ABOUT THE DEATH OF YOUR FRIEND.
I DON'T WANT TO TALK TO-
JAMIE, WHAT I'M ABOUT TO SHOW YOU MAY CAUSE SOME ALARM.

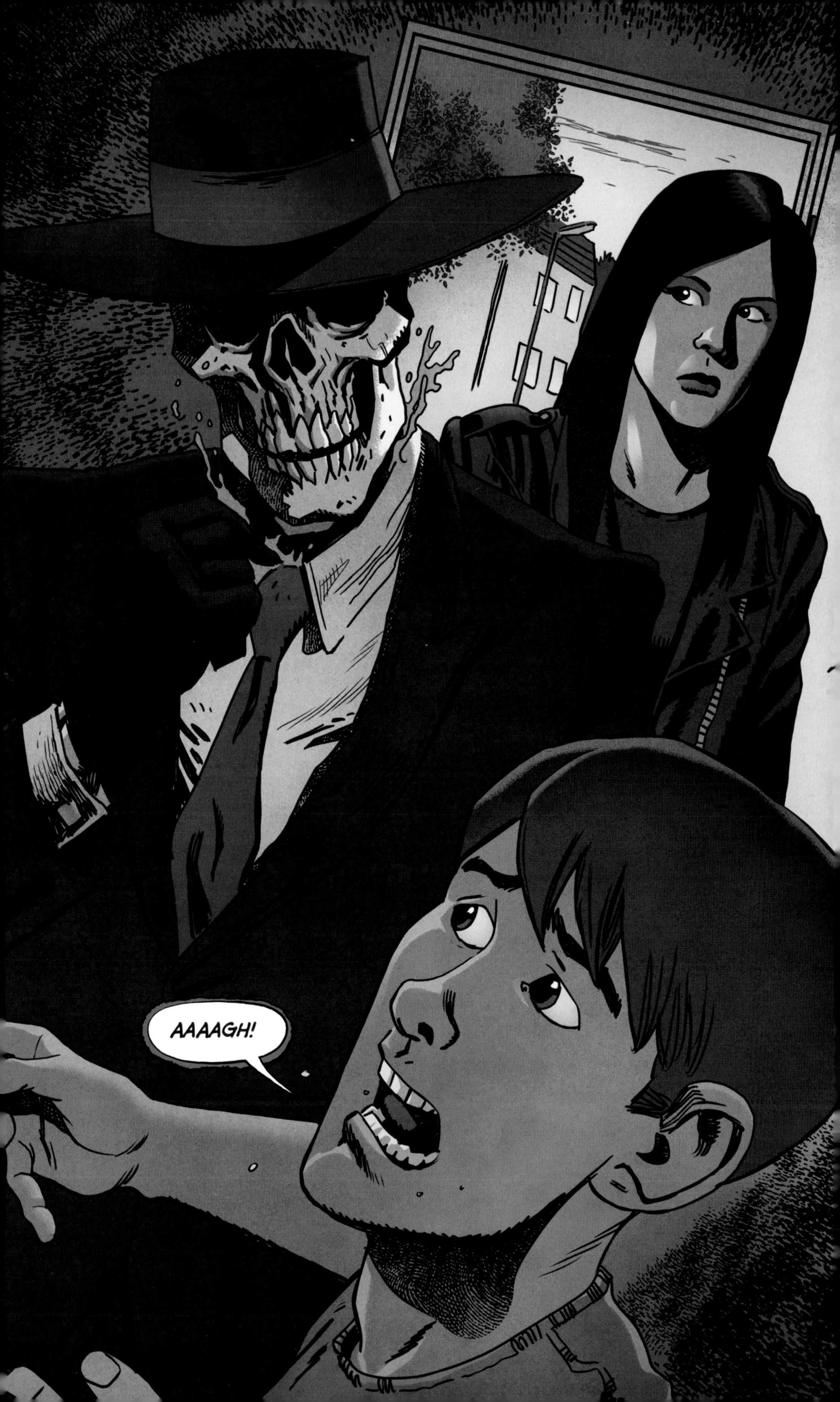
AAAAGH!

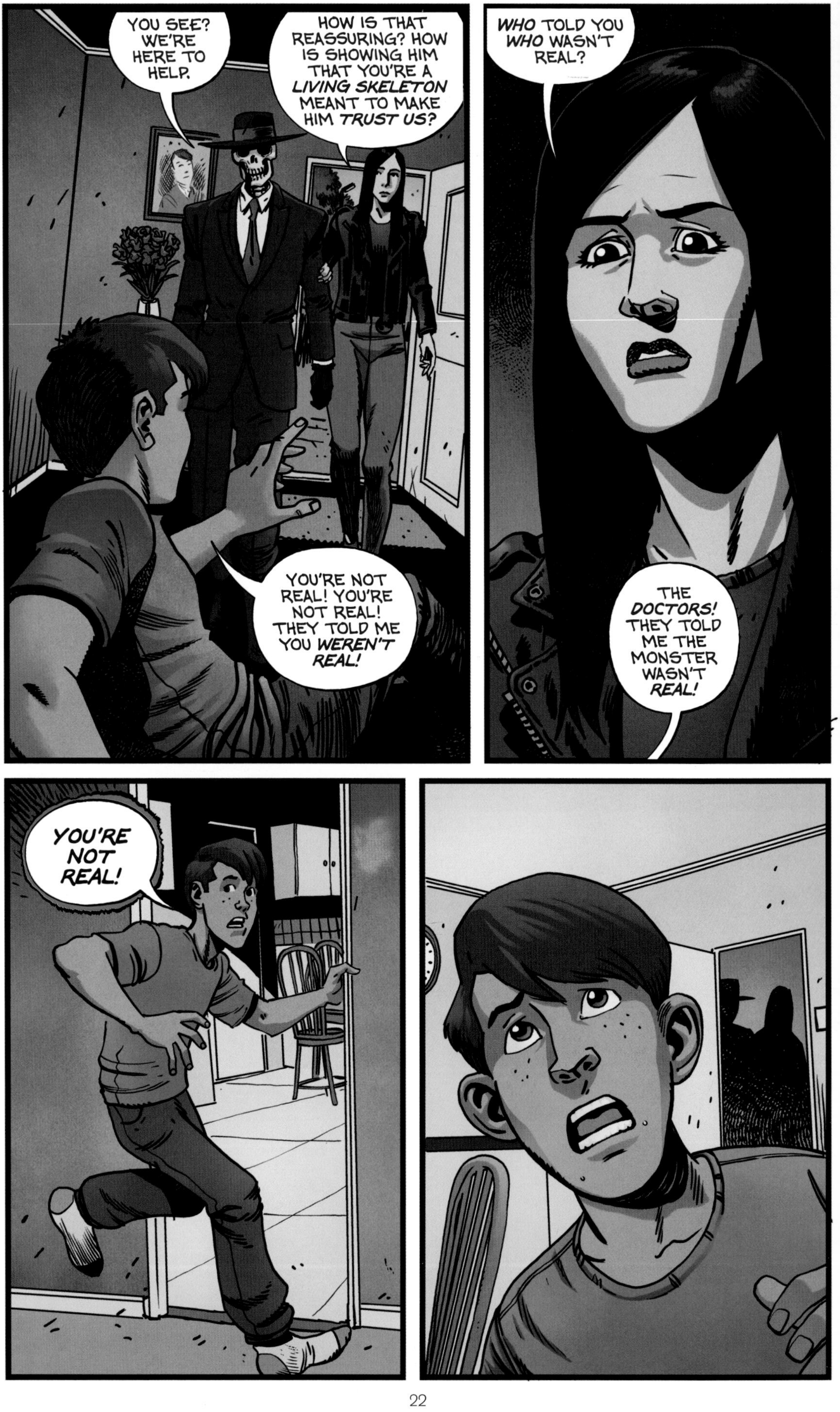
YOU SEE? WE'RE HERE TO HELP.
HOW IS THAT REASSURING? HOW IS SHOWING HIM THAT YOU'RE A *LIVING SKELETON* MEANT TO MAKE HIM *TRUST US?*
YOU'RE NOT REAL! YOU'RE NOT REAL! THEY TOLD ME YOU *WEREN'T REAL!*
WHO TOLD YOU *WHO* WASN'T REAL?
THE *DOCTORS!* THEY TOLD ME THE MONSTER WASN'T *REAL!*
YOU'RE NOT REAL!

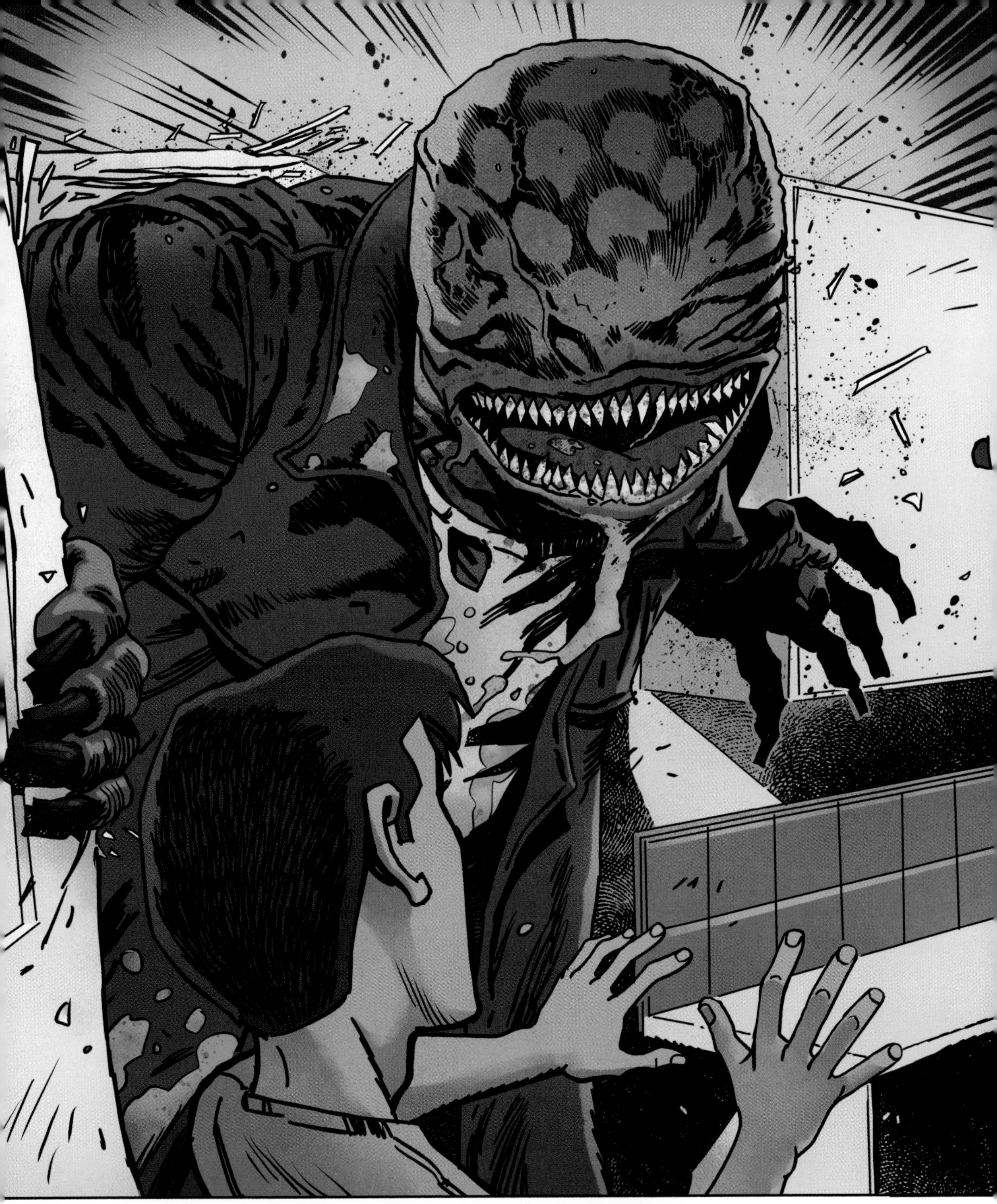

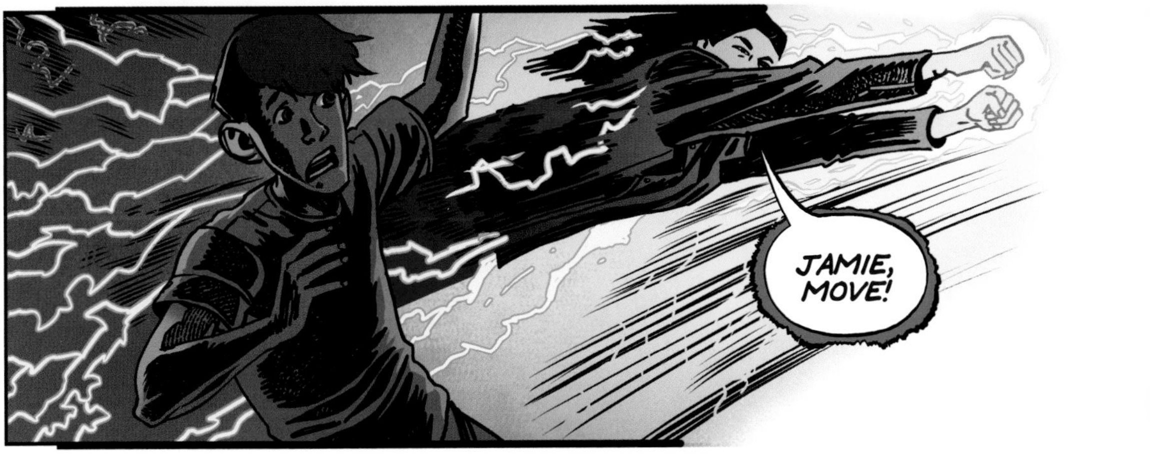
JAMIE, MOVE!

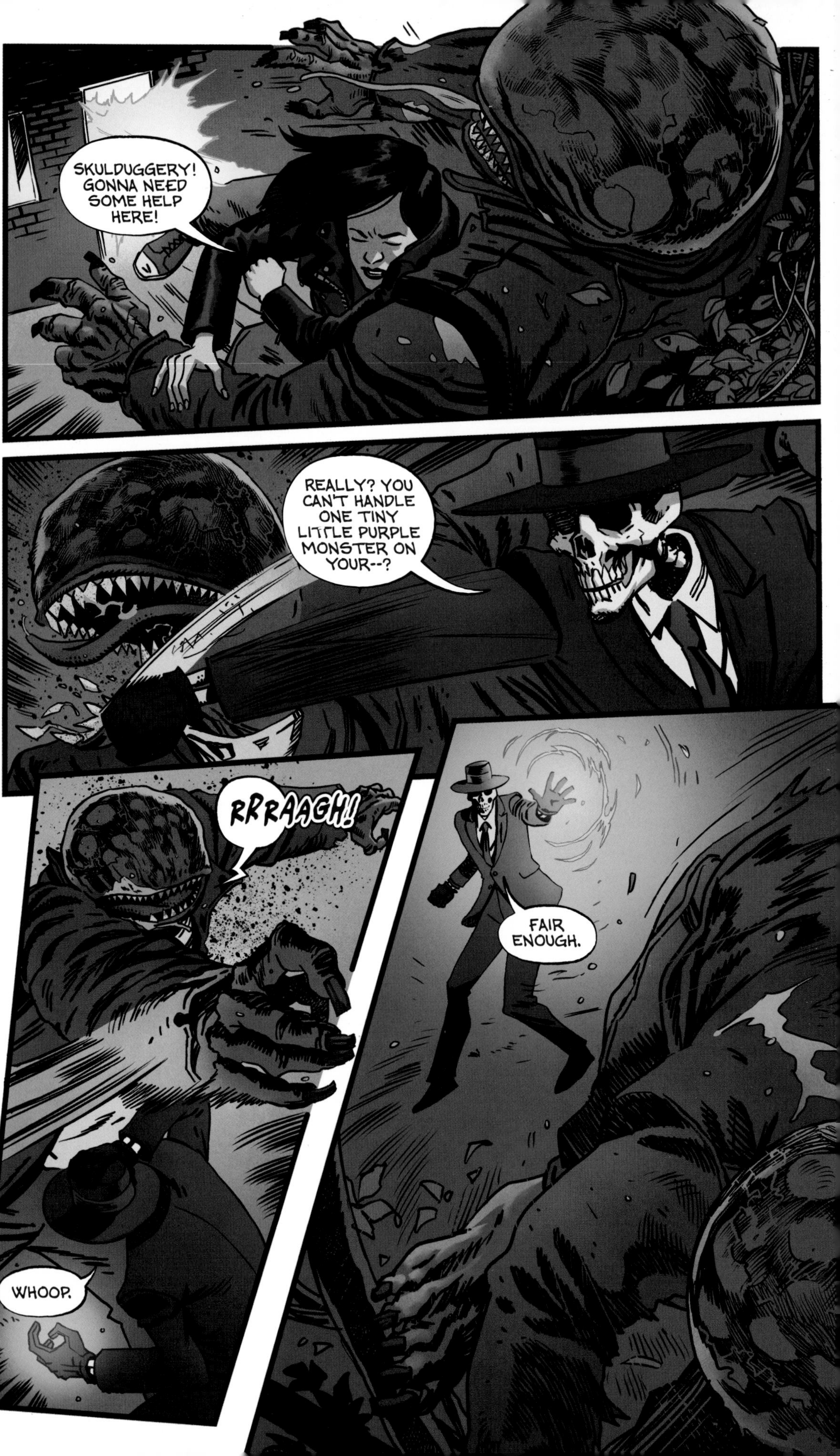
SKULDUGGERY! GONNA NEED SOME HELP HERE!
REALLY? YOU CAN'T HANDLE ONE TINY LITTLE PURPLE MONSTER ON YOUR--?
RRRAAGH!
WHOOP.
FAIR ENOUGH.

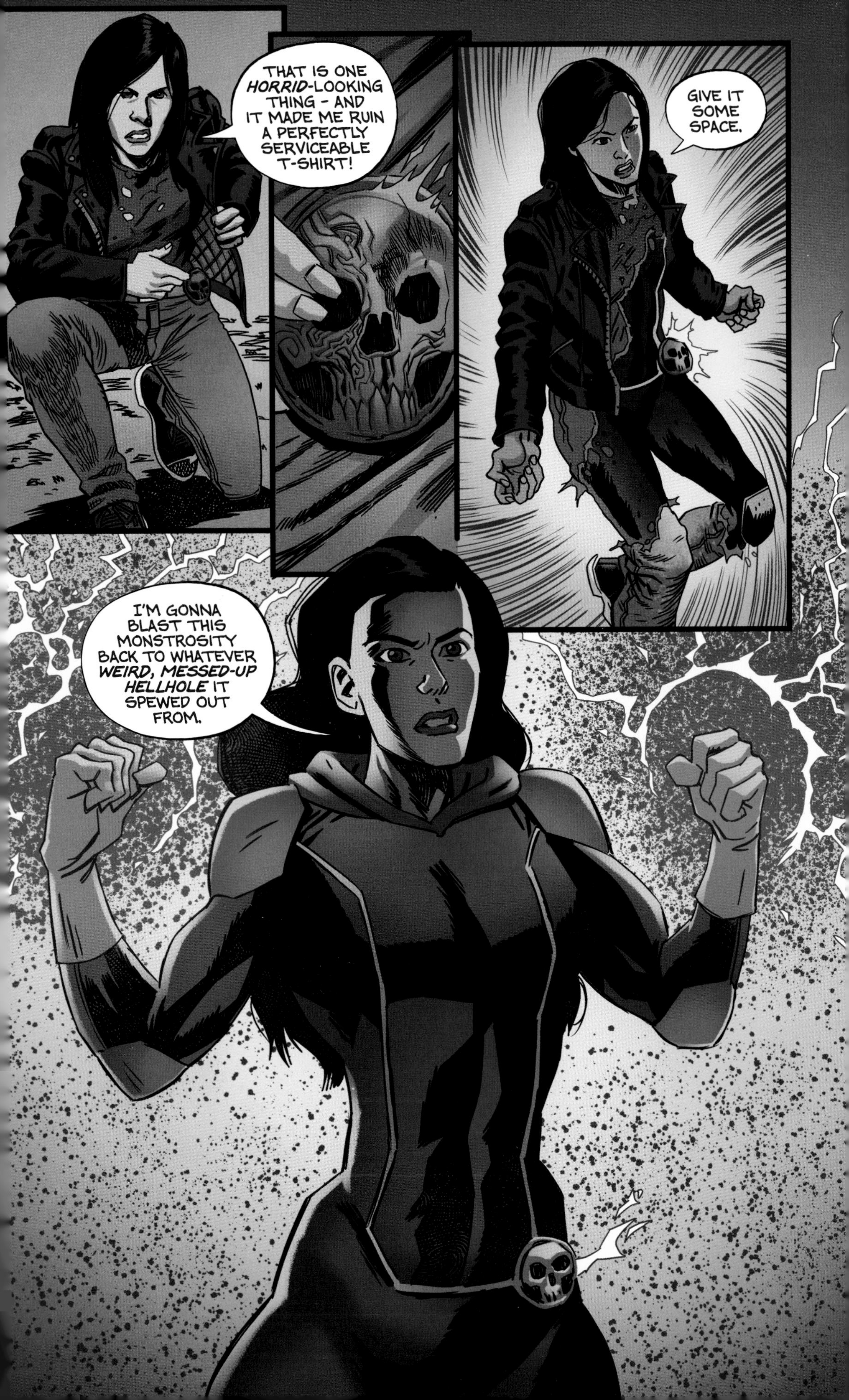
THAT IS ONE *HORRID*-LOOKING THING - AND IT MADE ME RUIN A PERFECTLY SERVICEABLE T-SHIRT!
GIVE IT SOME SPACE.
I'M GONNA BLAST THIS MONSTROSITY BACK TO WHATEVER *WEIRD, MESSED-UP HELLHOLE* IT SPEWED OUT FROM.

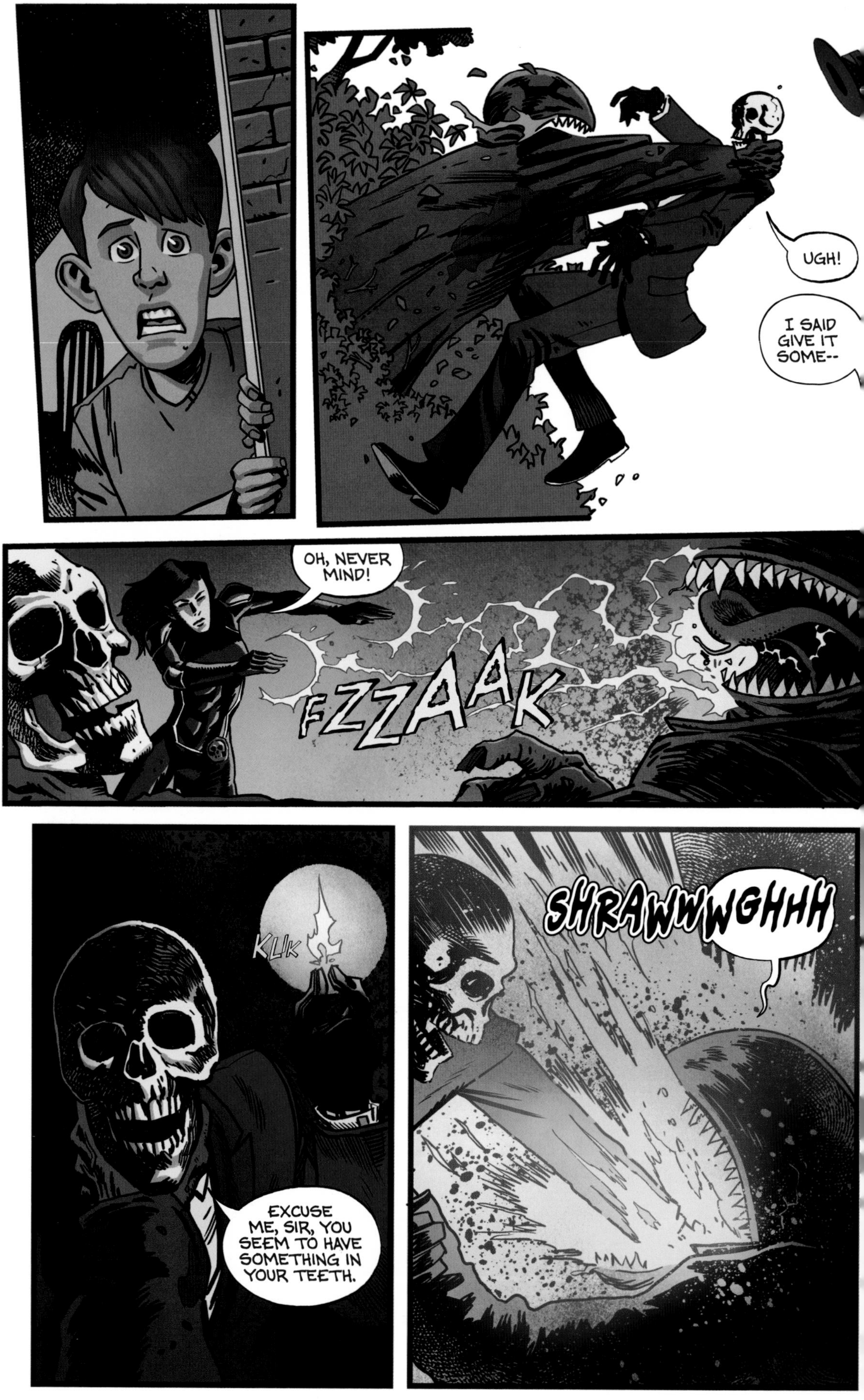
UGH!
I SAID GIVE IT SOME--
OH, NEVER MIND!
FZZAAK
KLIK
EXCUSE ME, SIR, YOU SEEM TO HAVE SOMETHING IN YOUR TEETH.
SHRAWWWGHHH

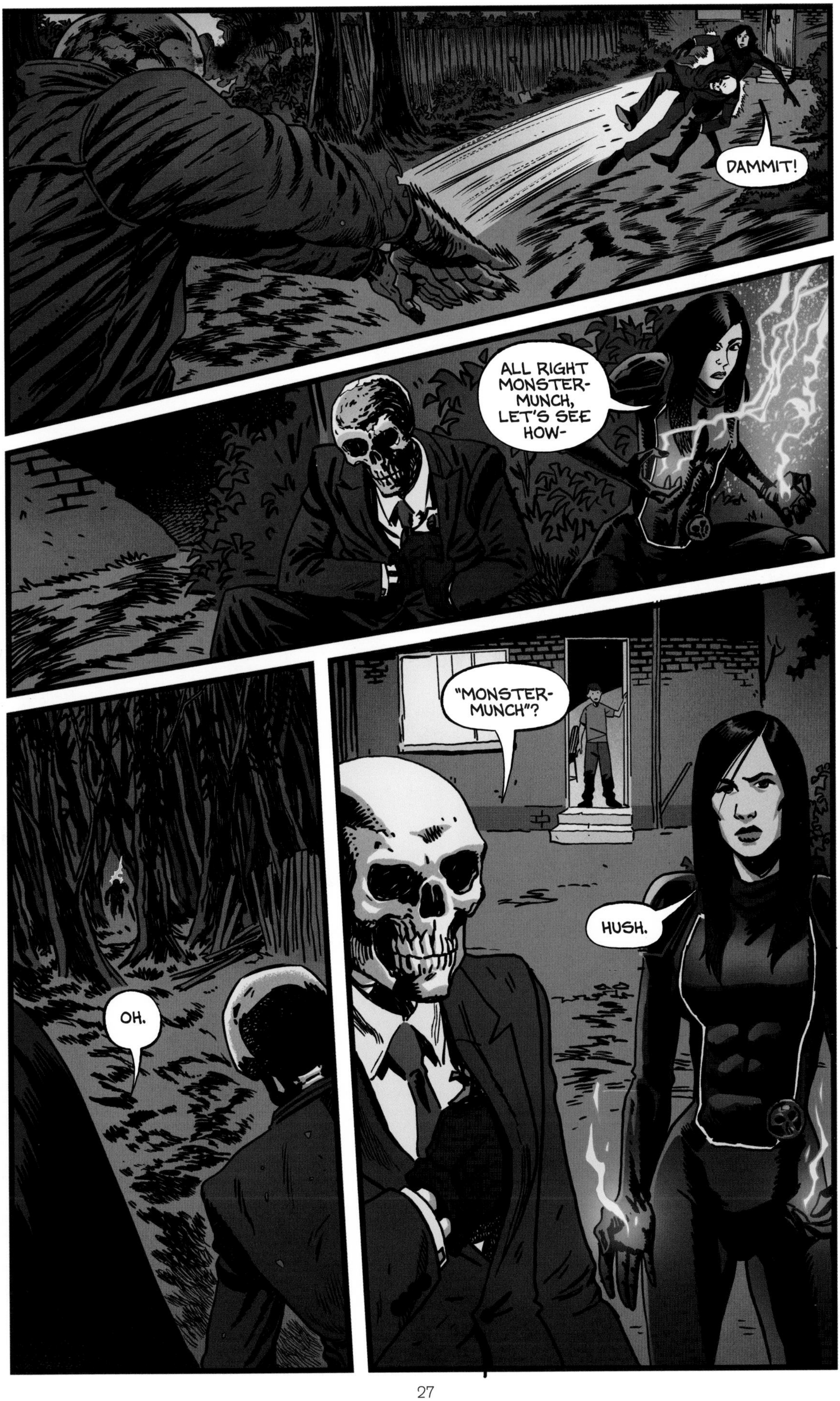
DAMMIT!
ALL RIGHT MONSTER-MUNCH, LET'S SEE HOW-
"MONSTER-MUNCH"?
HUSH.
OH.

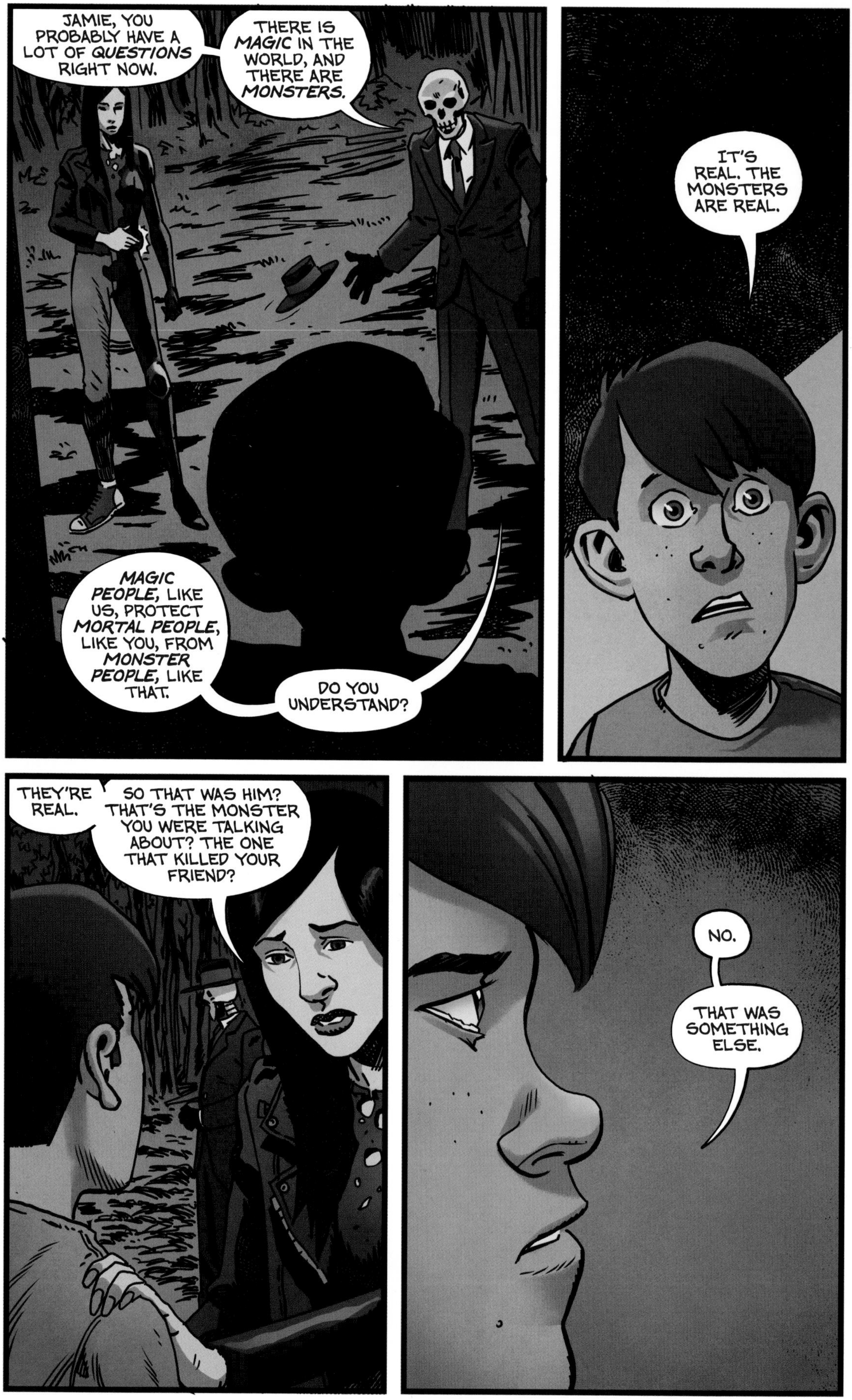
JAMIE, YOU PROBABLY HAVE A LOT OF QUESTIONS RIGHT NOW.
THERE IS MAGIC IN THE WORLD, AND THERE ARE MONSTERS.
MAGIC PEOPLE, LIKE US, PROTECT MORTAL PEOPLE, LIKE YOU, FROM MONSTER PEOPLE, LIKE THAT.
DO YOU UNDERSTAND?
IT'S REAL. THE MONSTERS ARE REAL.
THEY'RE REAL.
SO THAT WAS HIM? THAT'S THE MONSTER YOU WERE TALKING ABOUT? THE ONE THAT KILLED YOUR FRIEND?
NO.
THAT WAS SOMETHING ELSE.

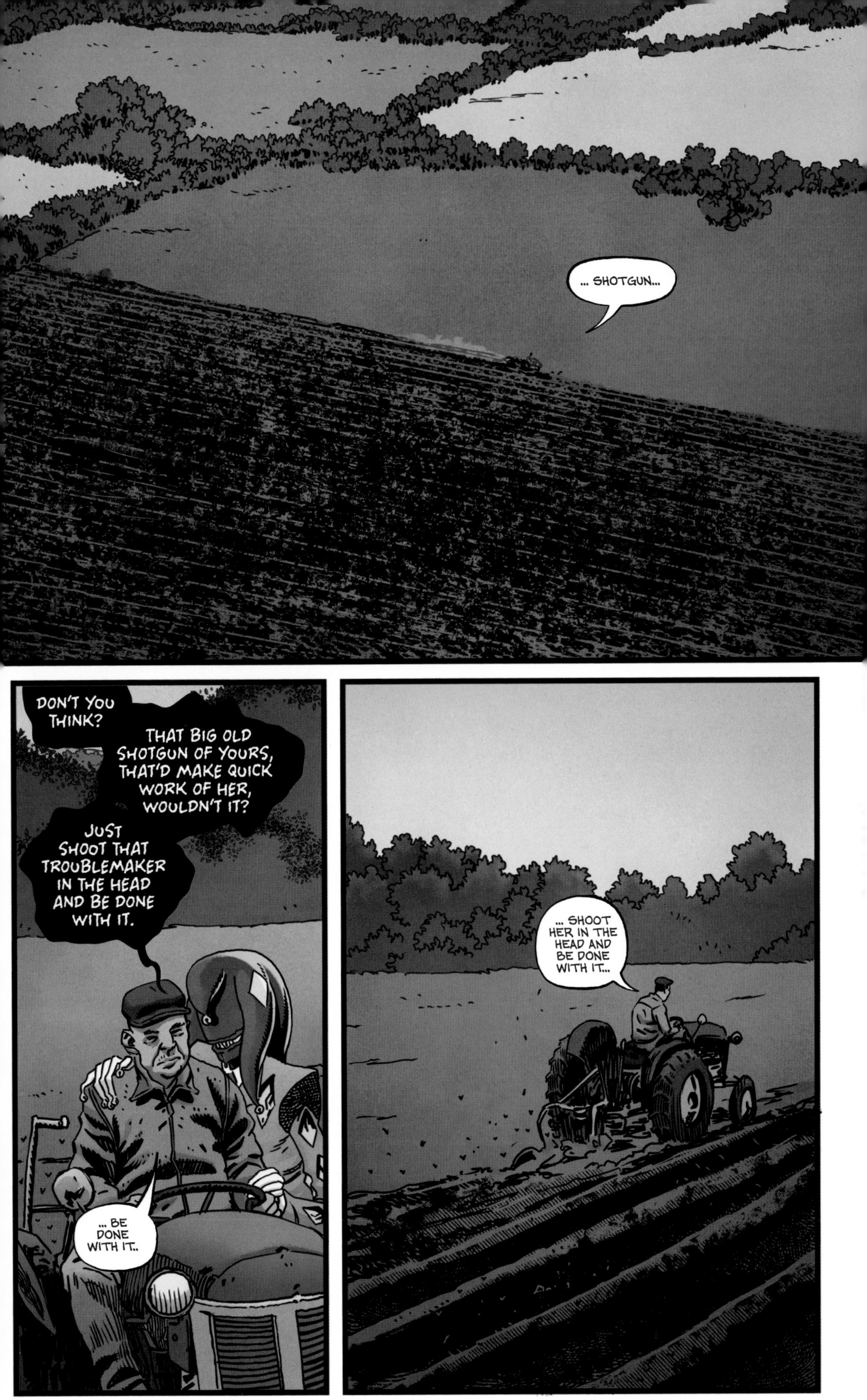
... SHOTGUN...
DON'T YOU THINK?
THAT BIG OLD SHOTGUN OF YOURS, THAT'D MAKE QUICK WORK OF HER, WOULDN'T IT?
JUST SHOOT THAT TROUBLEMAKER IN THE HEAD AND BE DONE WITH IT.
... BE DONE WITH IT..
... SHOOT HER IN THE HEAD AND BE DONE WITH IT...

Chapter
TWO

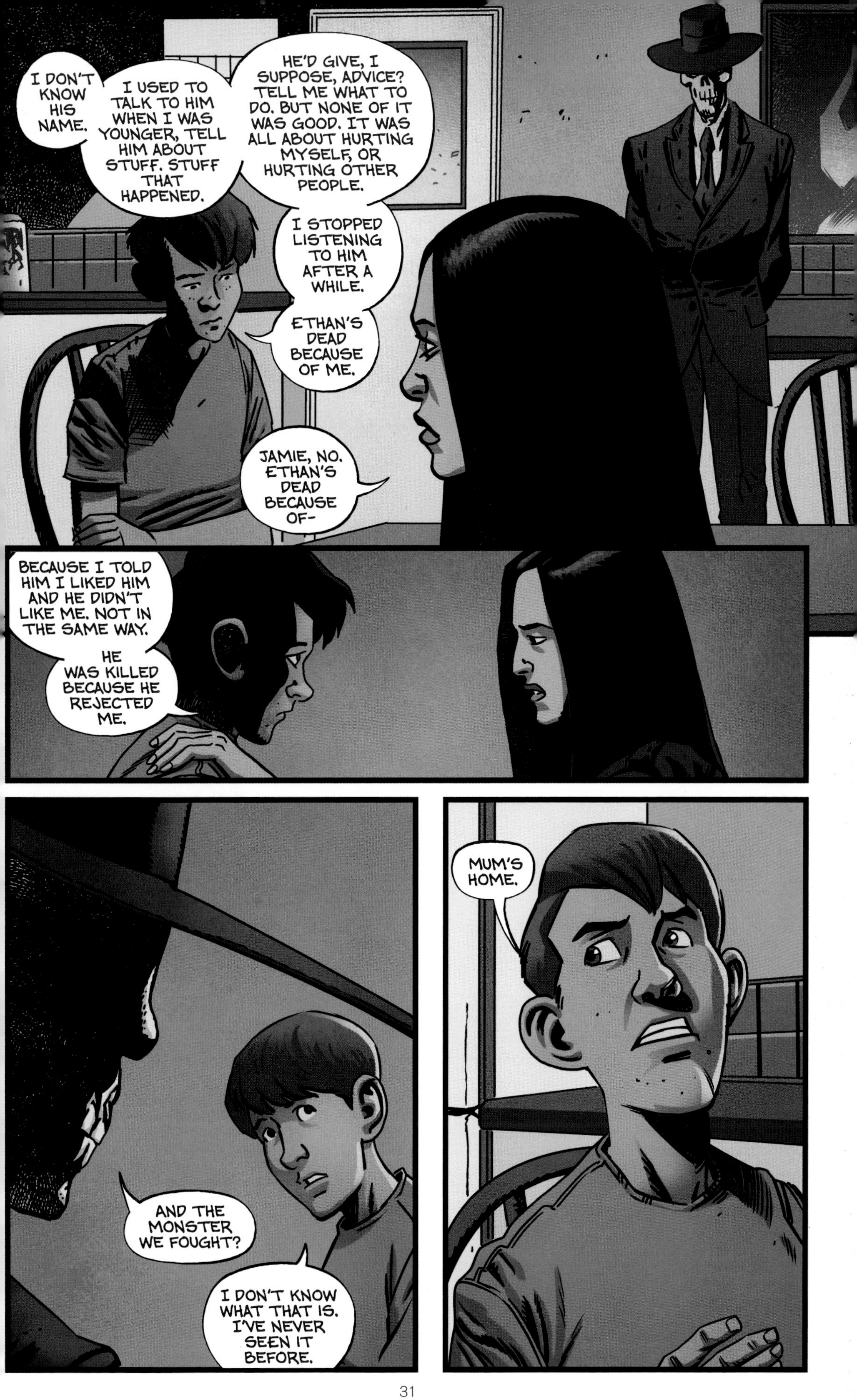
I DON'T KNOW HIS NAME.
I USED TO TALK TO HIM WHEN I WAS YOUNGER, TELL HIM ABOUT STUFF. STUFF THAT HAPPENED.
HE'D GIVE, I SUPPOSE, ADVICE? TELL ME WHAT TO DO. BUT NONE OF IT WAS GOOD. IT WAS ALL ABOUT HURTING MYSELF, OR HURTING OTHER PEOPLE.
I STOPPED LISTENING TO HIM AFTER A WHILE.
ETHAN'S DEAD BECAUSE OF ME.
JAMIE, NO. ETHAN'S DEAD BECAUSE OF-
BECAUSE I TOLD HIM I LIKED HIM AND HE DIDN'T LIKE ME. NOT IN THE SAME WAY.
HE WAS KILLED BECAUSE HE REJECTED ME.
AND THE MONSTER WE FOUGHT?
I DON'T KNOW WHAT THAT IS. I'VE NEVER SEEN IT BEFORE.
MUM'S HOME.

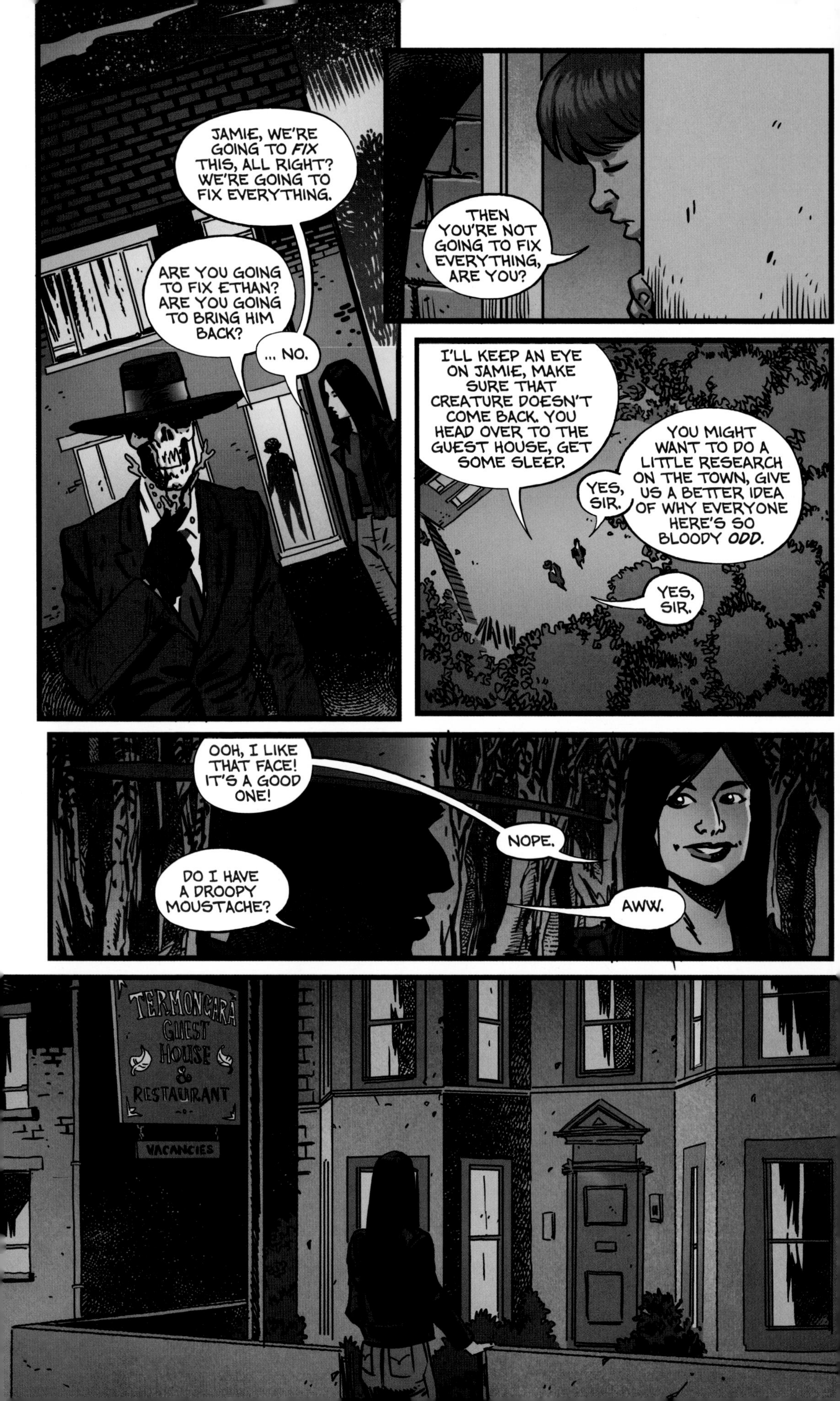
JAMIE, WE'RE GOING TO FIX THIS, ALL RIGHT? WE'RE GOING TO FIX EVERYTHING.
ARE YOU GOING TO FIX ETHAN? ARE YOU GOING TO BRING HIM BACK?
... NO.
THEN YOU'RE NOT GOING TO FIX EVERYTHING, ARE YOU?
I'LL KEEP AN EYE ON JAMIE, MAKE SURE THAT CREATURE DOESN'T COME BACK. YOU HEAD OVER TO THE GUEST HOUSE, GET SOME SLEEP.
YES, SIR.
YOU MIGHT WANT TO DO A LITTLE RESEARCH ON THE TOWN, GIVE US A BETTER IDEA OF WHY EVERYONE HERE'S SO BLOODY ODD.
YES, SIR.
OOH, I LIKE THAT FACE! IT'S A GOOD ONE!
NOPE.
DO I HAVE A DROOPY MOUSTACHE?
AWW.
TERMONCARA GUEST HOUSE & RESTAURANT
VACANCIES

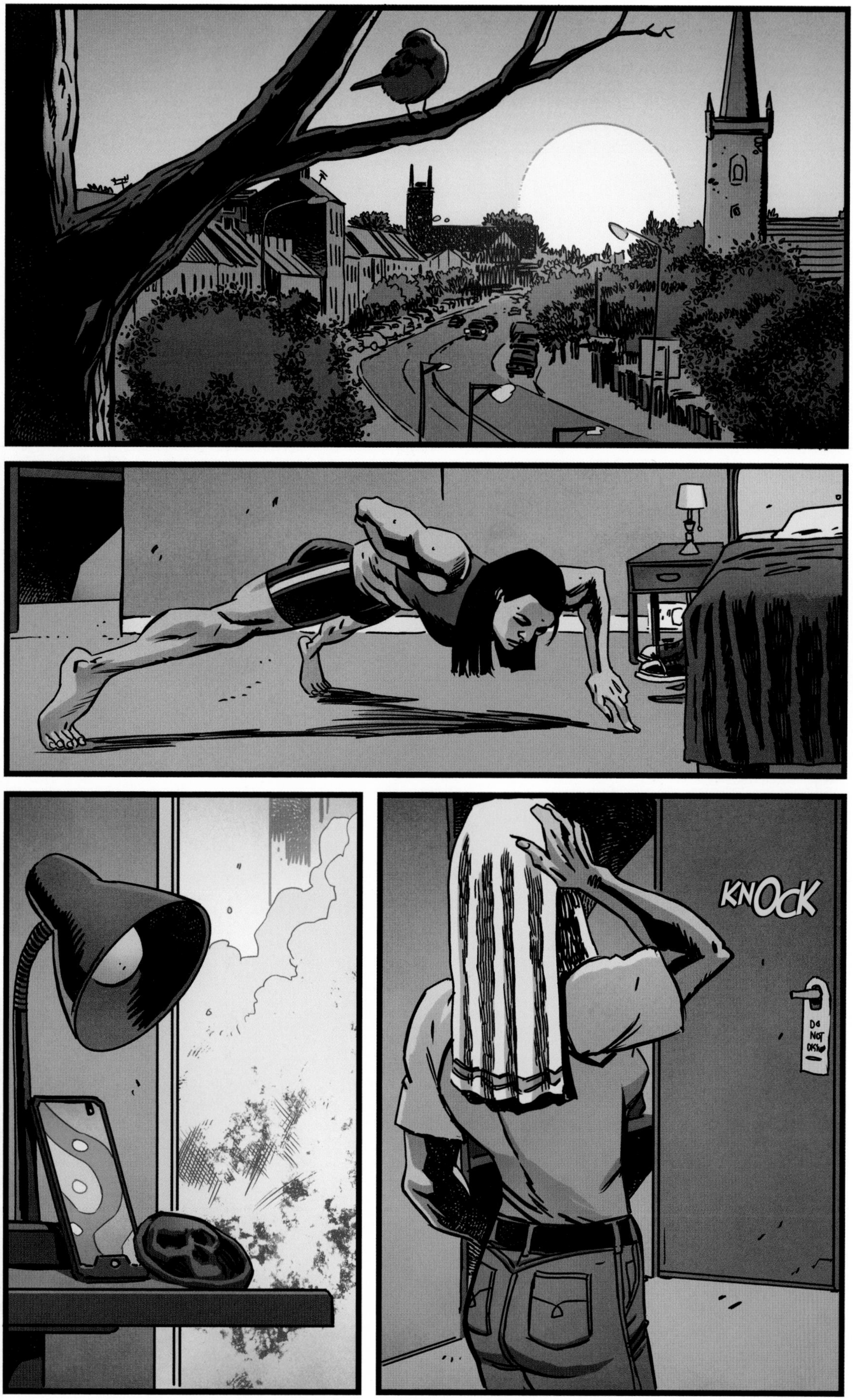
KNOCK

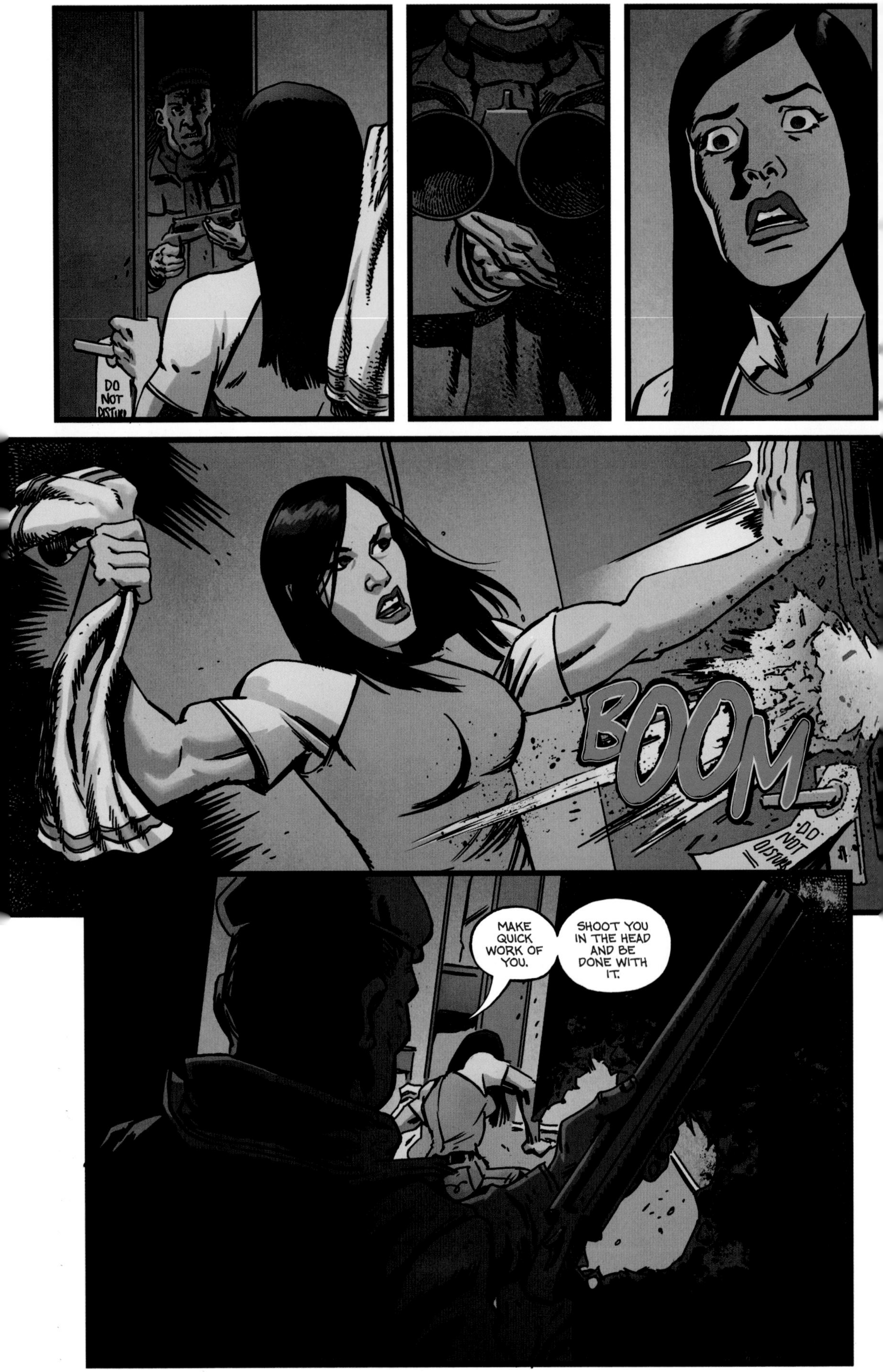
DO NOT DISTURB
BOOM
DO NOT DISTURB
MAKE QUICK WORK OF YOU.
SHOOT YOU IN THE HEAD AND BE DONE WITH IT.

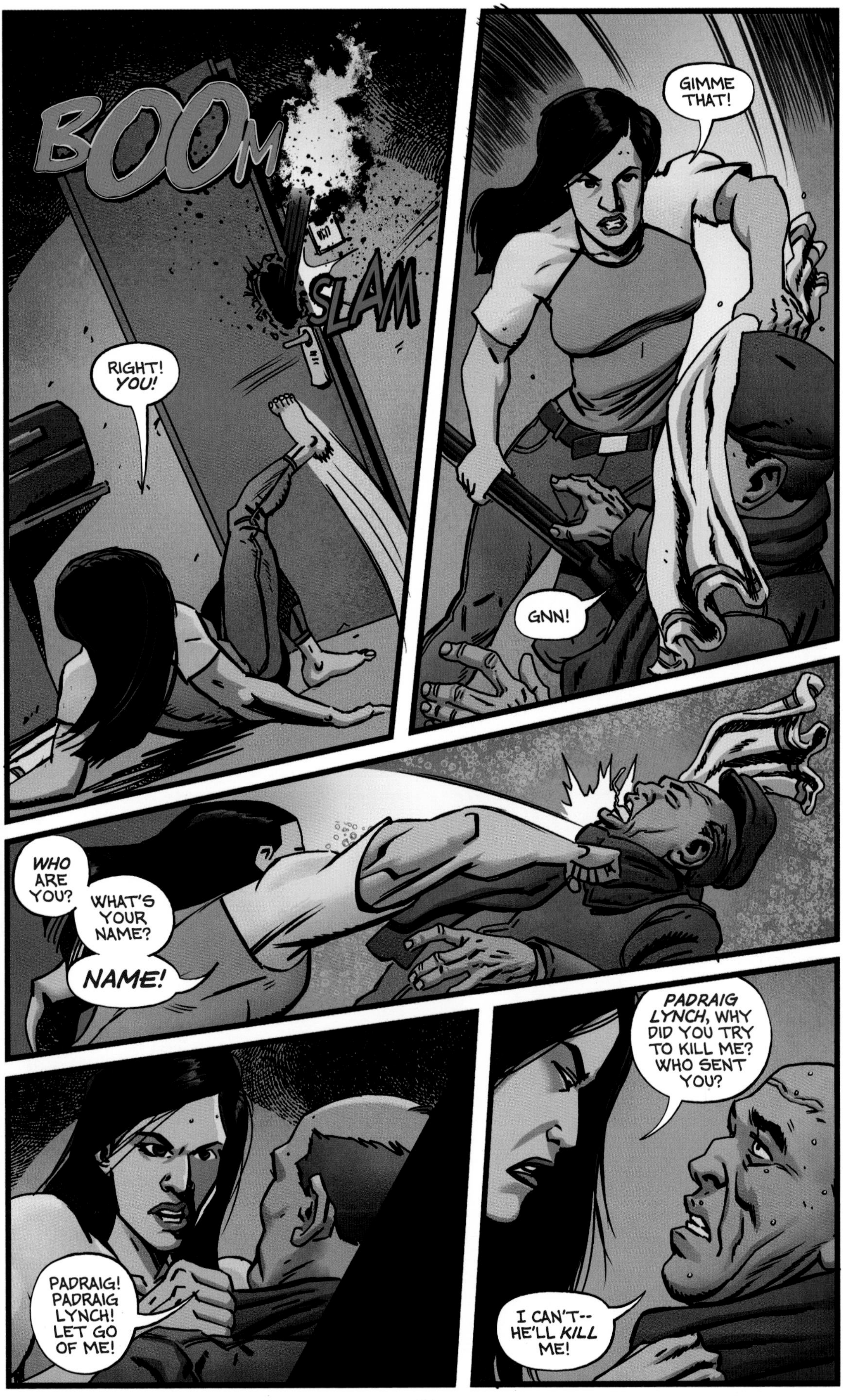
BOOM
SLAM
RIGHT! YOU!
GIMME THAT!
GNN!
WHO ARE YOU?
WHAT'S YOUR NAME?
NAME!
PADRAIG! PADRAIG LYNCH! LET GO OF ME!
PADRAIG LYNCH, WHY DID YOU TRY TO KILL ME? WHO SENT YOU?
I CAN'T-- HE'LL KILL ME!

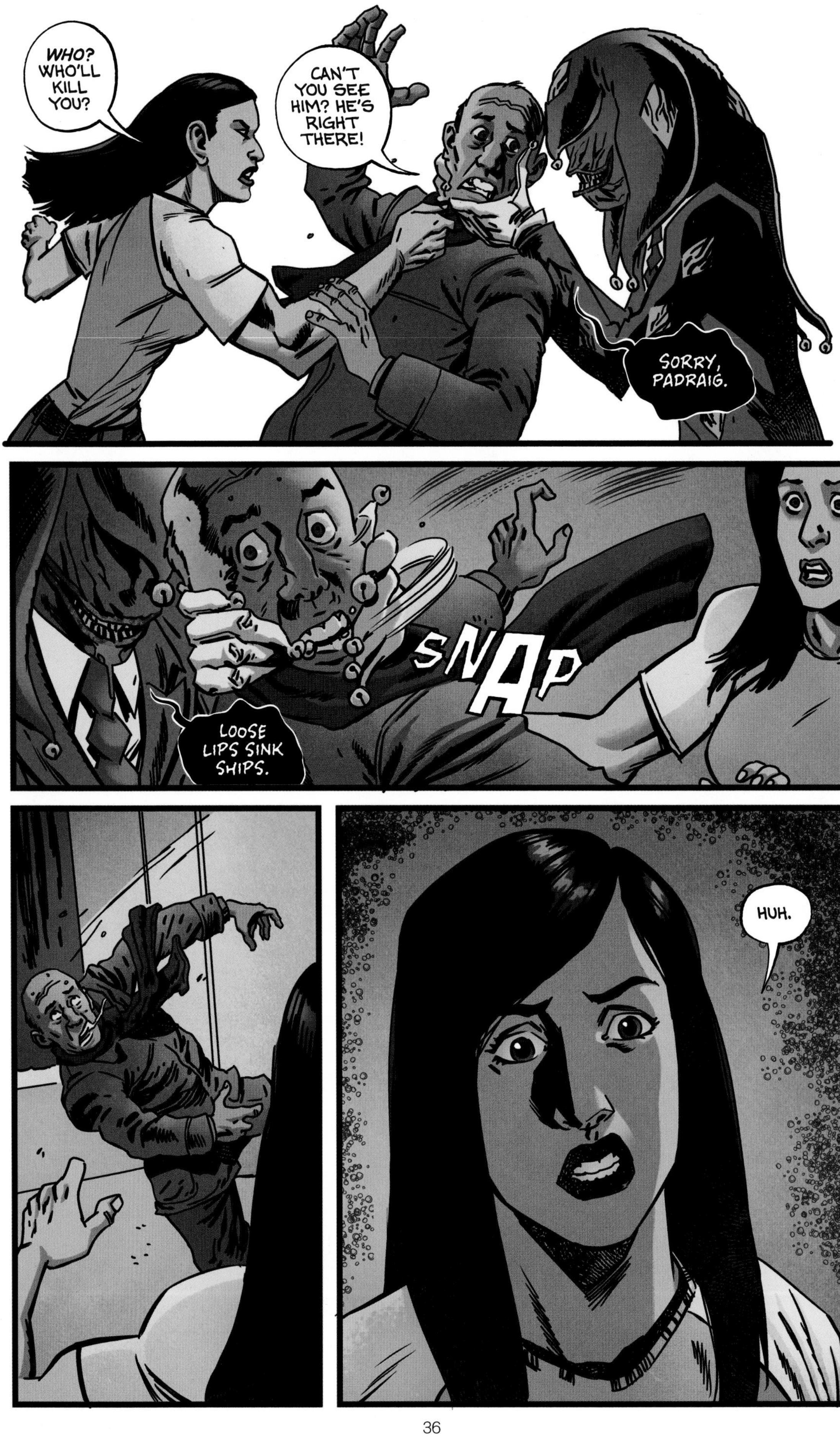
WHO? WHO'LL KILL YOU?
CAN'T YOU SEE HIM? HE'S RIGHT THERE!
SORRY, PADRAIG.
SNAP
LOOSE LIPS SINK SHIPS.
HUH.

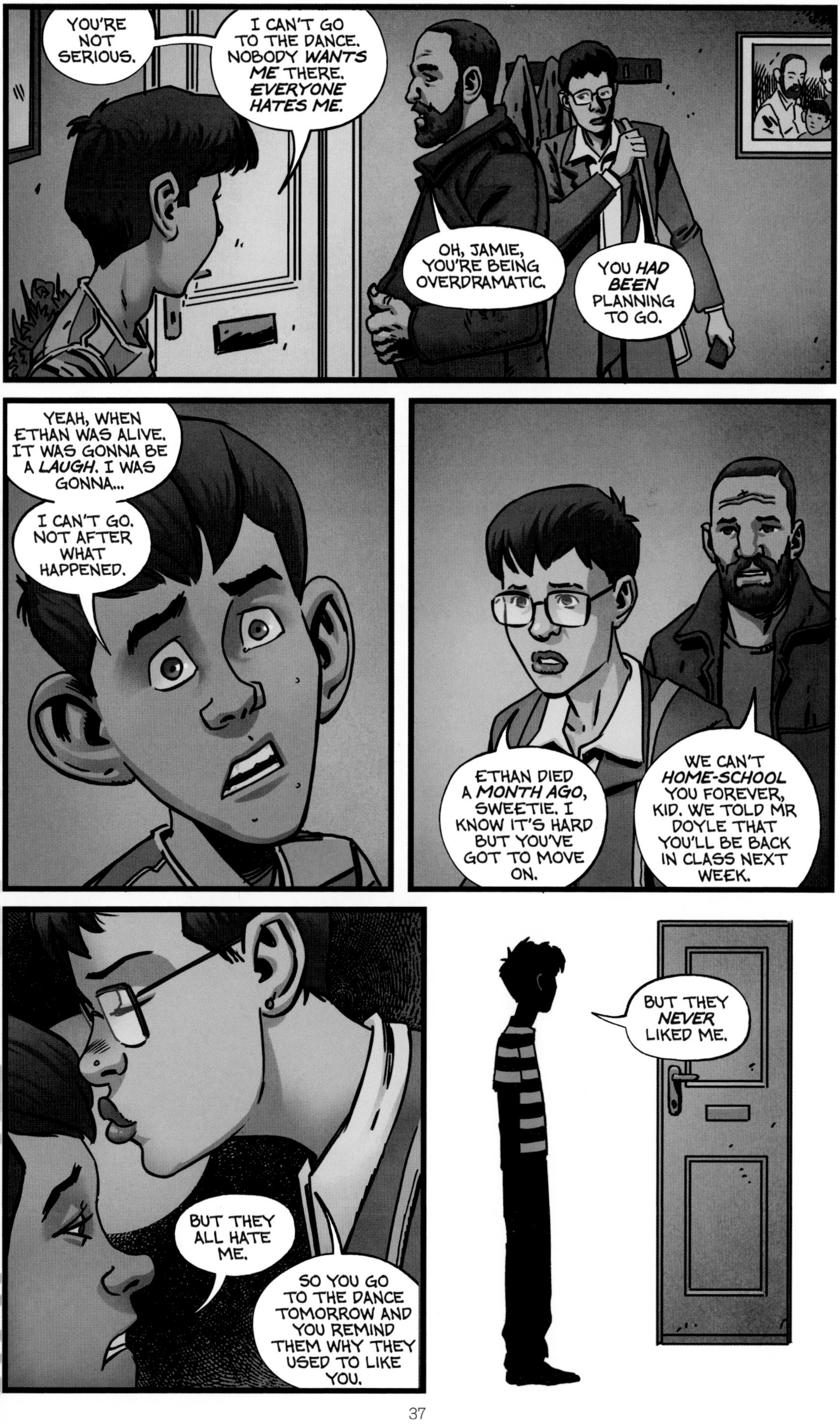
YOU'RE NOT SERIOUS.
I CAN'T GO TO THE DANCE. NOBODY *WANTS ME* THERE. *EVERYONE HATES ME.*
OH, JAMIE, YOU'RE BEING OVERDRAMATIC.
YOU *HAD BEEN* PLANNING TO GO.
YEAH, WHEN ETHAN WAS ALIVE. IT WAS GONNA BE A *LAUGH*. I WAS GONNA...
I CAN'T GO. NOT AFTER WHAT HAPPENED.
ETHAN DIED A *MONTH AGO*, SWEETIE. I KNOW IT'S HARD BUT YOU'VE GOT TO MOVE ON.
WE CAN'T *HOME-SCHOOL* YOU FOREVER, KID. WE TOLD MR DOYLE THAT YOU'LL BE BACK IN CLASS NEXT WEEK.
BUT THEY ALL HATE ME.
SO YOU GO TO THE DANCE TOMORROW AND YOU REMIND THEM WHY THEY USED TO LIKE YOU.
BUT THEY *NEVER* LIKED ME.

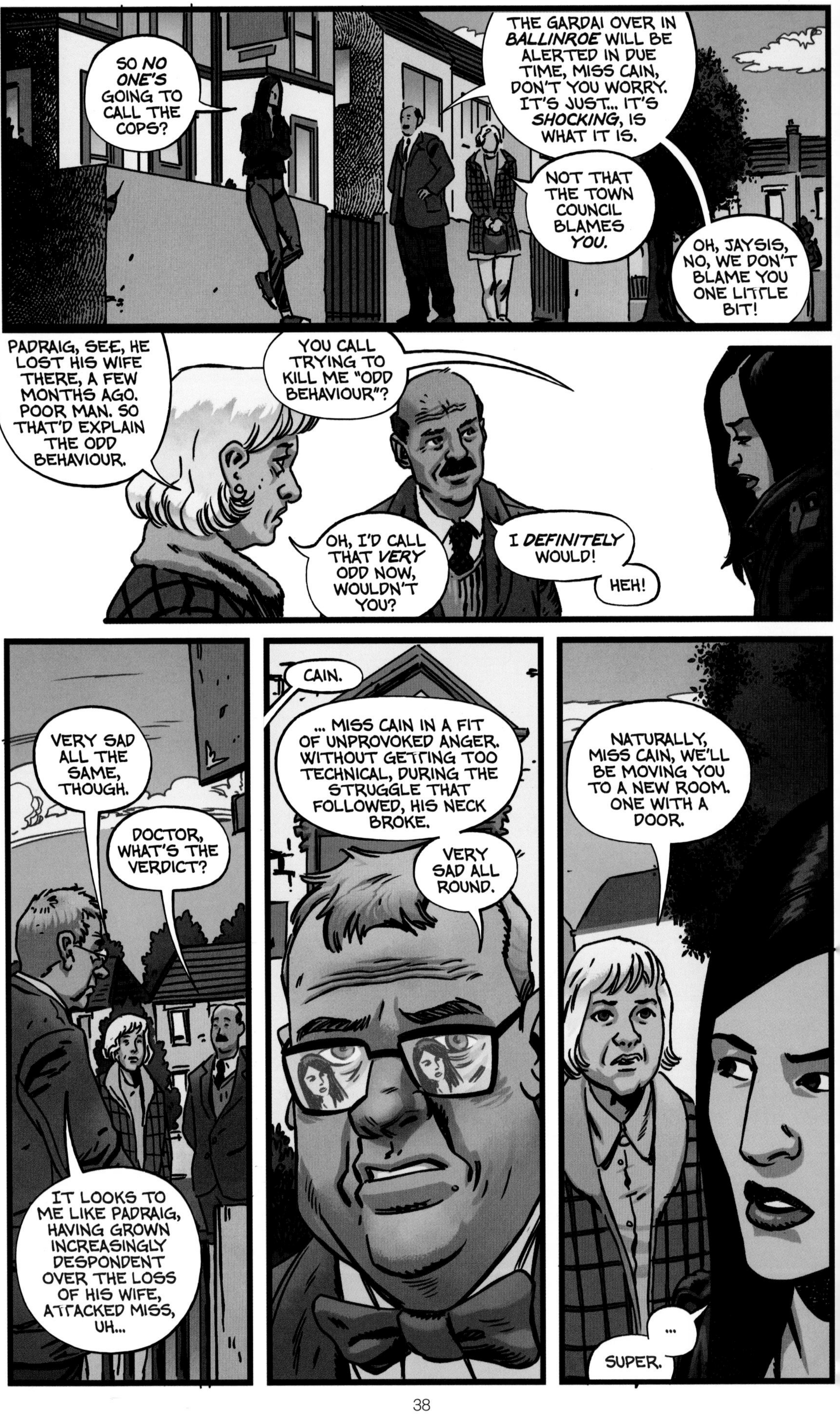
SO NO ONE'S GOING TO CALL THE COPS?
THE GARDAI OVER IN BALLINROE WILL BE ALERTED IN DUE TIME, MISS CAIN, DON'T YOU WORRY. IT'S JUST... IT'S SHOCKING, IS WHAT IT IS.
NOT THAT THE TOWN COUNCIL BLAMES YOU.
OH, JAYSIS, NO, WE DON'T BLAME YOU ONE LITTLE BIT!
PADRAIG, SEE, HE LOST HIS WIFE THERE, A FEW MONTHS AGO. POOR MAN. SO THAT'D EXPLAIN THE ODD BEHAVIOUR.
YOU CALL TRYING TO KILL ME "ODD BEHAVIOUR"?
OH, I'D CALL THAT VERY ODD NOW, WOULDN'T YOU?
I DEFINITELY WOULD!
HEH!
VERY SAD ALL THE SAME, THOUGH.
DOCTOR, WHAT'S THE VERDICT?
IT LOOKS TO ME LIKE PADRAIG, HAVING GROWN INCREASINGLY DESPONDENT OVER THE LOSS OF HIS WIFE, ATTACKED MISS, UH...
CAIN.
... MISS CAIN IN A FIT OF UNPROVOKED ANGER. WITHOUT GETTING TOO TECHNICAL, DURING THE STRUGGLE THAT FOLLOWED, HIS NECK BROKE.
VERY SAD ALL ROUND.
NATURALLY, MISS CAIN, WE'LL BE MOVING YOU TO A NEW ROOM. ONE WITH A DOOR.
...
SUPER.

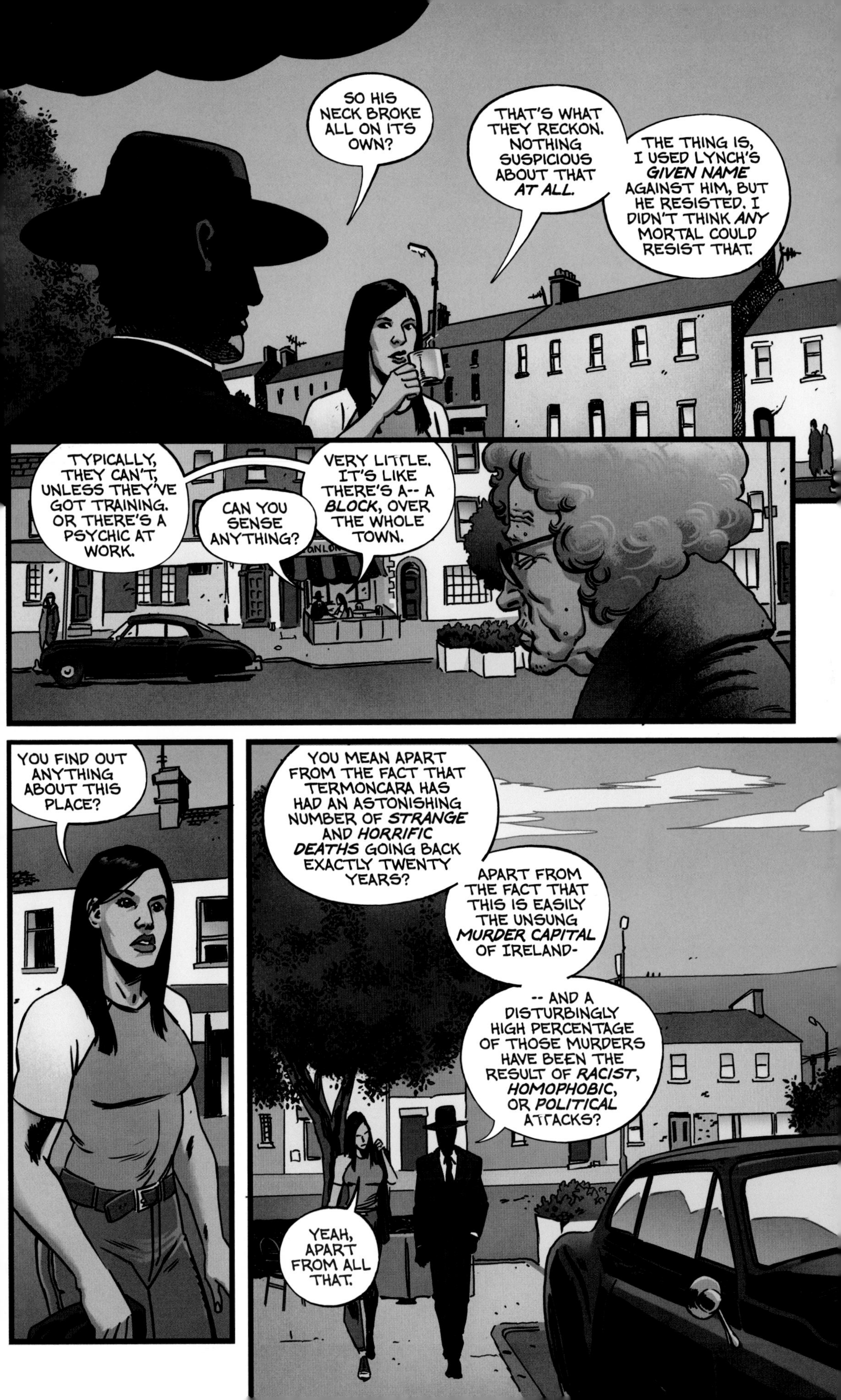

SO HIS NECK BROKE ALL ON ITS OWN?
THAT'S WHAT THEY RECKON. NOTHING SUSPICIOUS ABOUT THAT *AT ALL.*
THE THING IS, I USED LYNCH'S *GIVEN NAME* AGAINST HIM, BUT HE RESISTED. I DIDN'T THINK *ANY* MORTAL COULD RESIST THAT.
TYPICALLY, THEY CAN'T, UNLESS THEY'VE GOT TRAINING. OR THERE'S A PSYCHIC AT WORK.
CAN YOU SENSE ANYTHING?
VERY LITTLE. IT'S LIKE THERE'S A-- A *BLOCK*, OVER THE WHOLE TOWN.
YOU FIND OUT ANYTHING ABOUT THIS PLACE?
YOU MEAN APART FROM THE FACT THAT TERMONCARA HAS HAD AN ASTONISHING NUMBER OF *STRANGE* AND *HORRIFIC DEATHS* GOING BACK EXACTLY TWENTY YEARS?
APART FROM THE FACT THAT THIS IS EASILY THE UNSUNG *MURDER CAPITAL* OF IRELAND-
-- AND A DISTURBINGLY HIGH PERCENTAGE OF THOSE MURDERS HAVE BEEN THE RESULT OF *RACIST*, *HOMOPHOBIC*, OR *POLITICAL* ATTACKS?
YEAH, APART FROM ALL THAT.

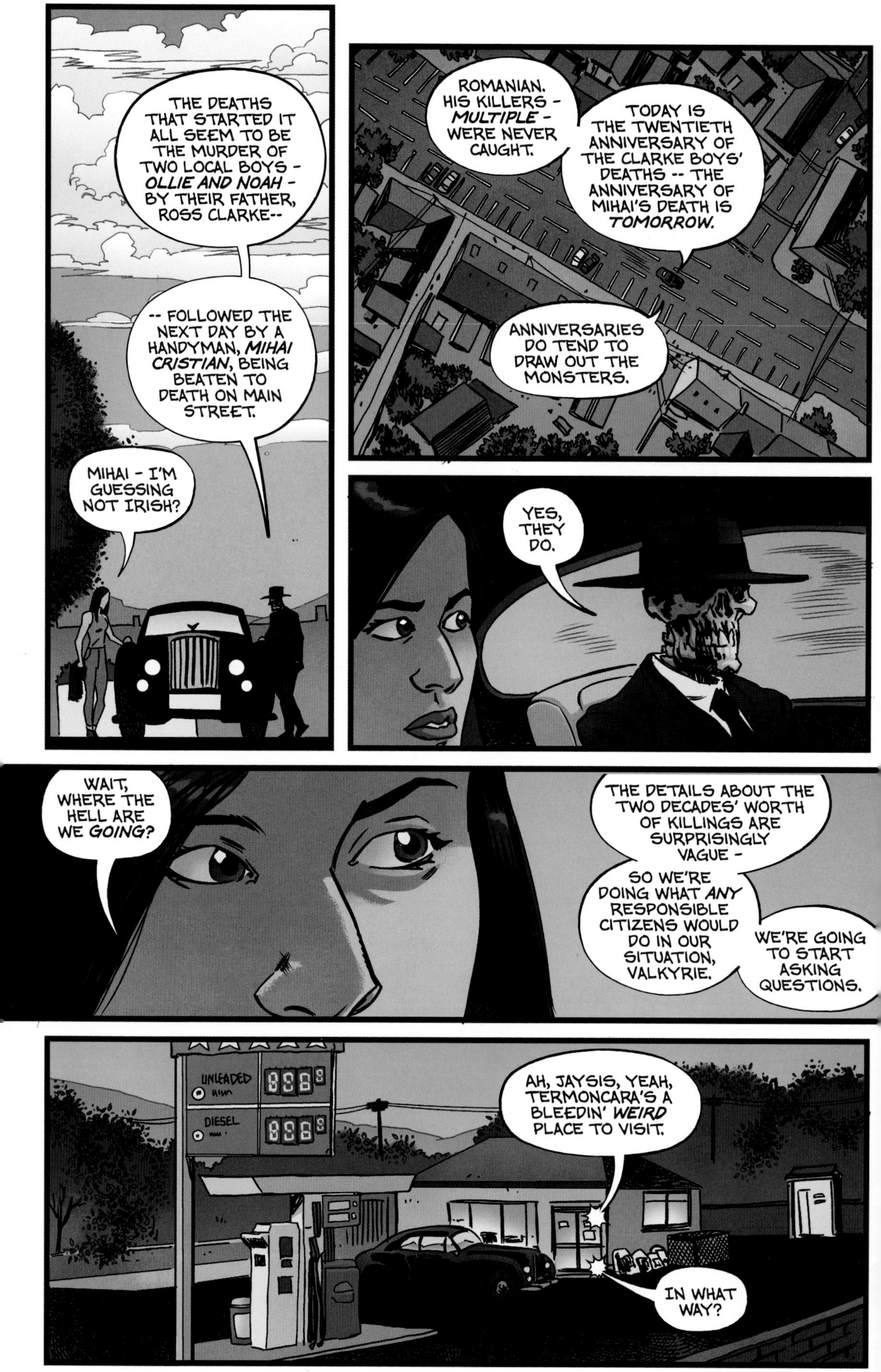
THE DEATHS THAT STARTED IT ALL SEEM TO BE THE MURDER OF TWO LOCAL BOYS - OLLIE AND NOAH - BY THEIR FATHER, ROSS CLARKE--
-- FOLLOWED THE NEXT DAY BY A HANDYMAN, MIHAI CRISTIAN, BEING BEATEN TO DEATH ON MAIN STREET.
MIHAI - I'M GUESSING NOT IRISH?
ROMANIAN. HIS KILLERS - MULTIPLE - WERE NEVER CAUGHT.
TODAY IS THE TWENTIETH ANNIVERSARY OF THE CLARKE BOYS' DEATHS -- THE ANNIVERSARY OF MIHAI'S DEATH IS TOMORROW.
ANNIVERSARIES DO TEND TO DRAW OUT THE MONSTERS.
YES, THEY DO.
WAIT, WHERE THE HELL ARE WE GOING?
THE DETAILS ABOUT THE TWO DECADES' WORTH OF KILLINGS ARE SURPRISINGLY VAGUE -
SO WE'RE DOING WHAT ANY RESPONSIBLE CITIZENS WOULD DO IN OUR SITUATION, VALKYRIE.
WE'RE GOING TO START ASKING QUESTIONS.
UNLEADED
DIESEL
AH, JAYSIS, YEAH, TERMONCARA'S A BLEEDIN' WEIRD PLACE TO VISIT.
IN WHAT WAY?

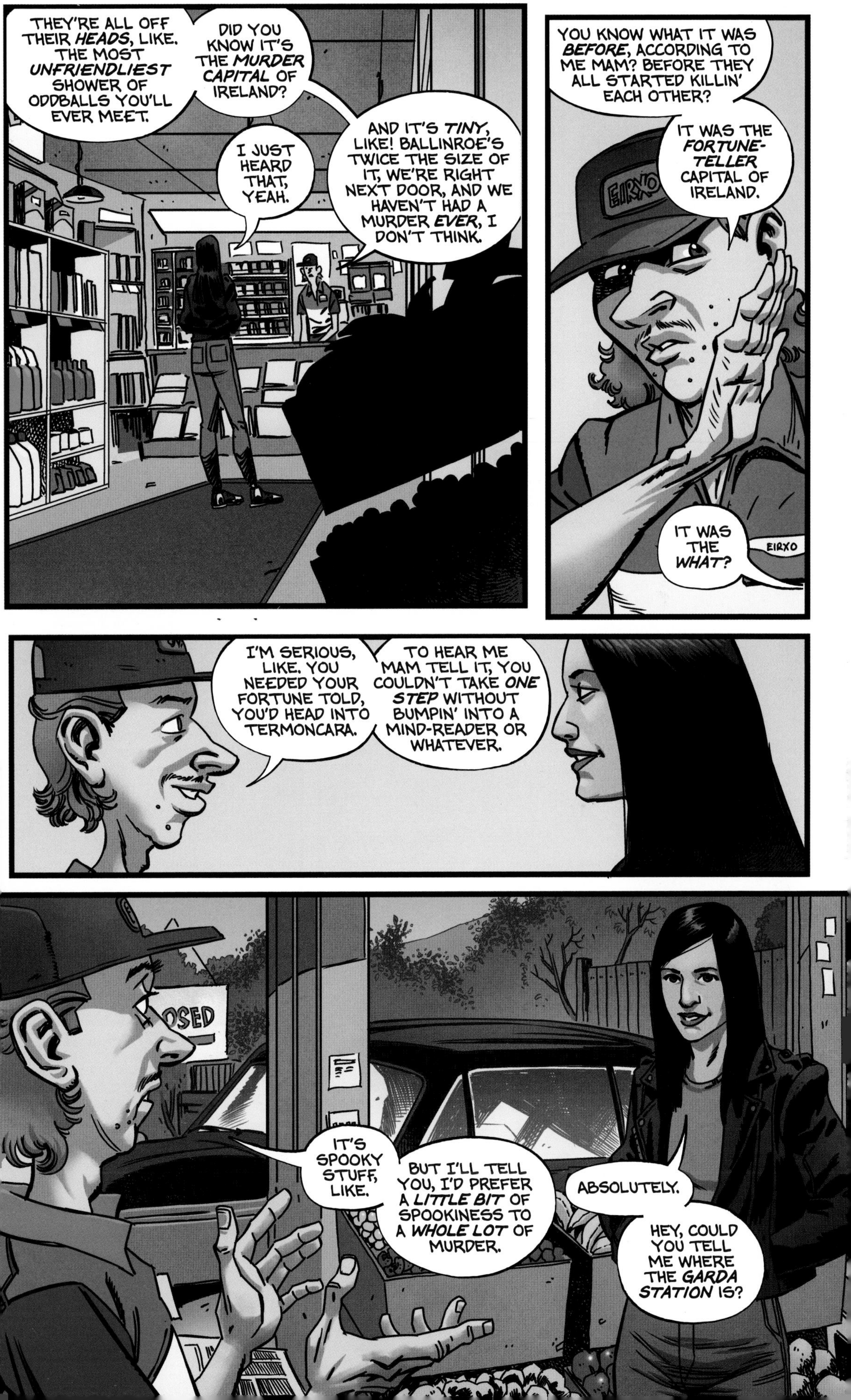
THEY'RE ALL OFF THEIR HEADS, LIKE. THE MOST UNFRIENDLIEST SHOWER OF ODDBALLS YOU'LL EVER MEET.
DID YOU KNOW IT'S THE MURDER CAPITAL OF IRELAND?
I JUST HEARD THAT, YEAH.
AND IT'S TINY, LIKE! BALLINROE'S TWICE THE SIZE OF IT, WE'RE RIGHT NEXT DOOR, AND WE HAVEN'T HAD A MURDER EVER, I DON'T THINK.
YOU KNOW WHAT IT WAS BEFORE, ACCORDING TO ME MAM? BEFORE THEY ALL STARTED KILLIN' EACH OTHER?
IT WAS THE FORTUNE-TELLER CAPITAL OF IRELAND.
EIRXO
IT WAS THE WHAT?
EIRXO
I'M SERIOUS, LIKE. YOU NEEDED YOUR FORTUNE TOLD, YOU'D HEAD INTO TERMONCARA.
TO HEAR ME MAM TELL IT, YOU COULDN'T TAKE ONE STEP WITHOUT BUMPIN' INTO A MIND-READER OR WHATEVER.
OSED
IT'S SPOOKY STUFF, LIKE.
BUT I'LL TELL YOU, I'D PREFER A LITTLE BIT OF SPOOKINESS TO A WHOLE LOT OF MURDER.
ABSOLUTELY.
HEY, COULD YOU TELL ME WHERE THE GARDA STATION IS?

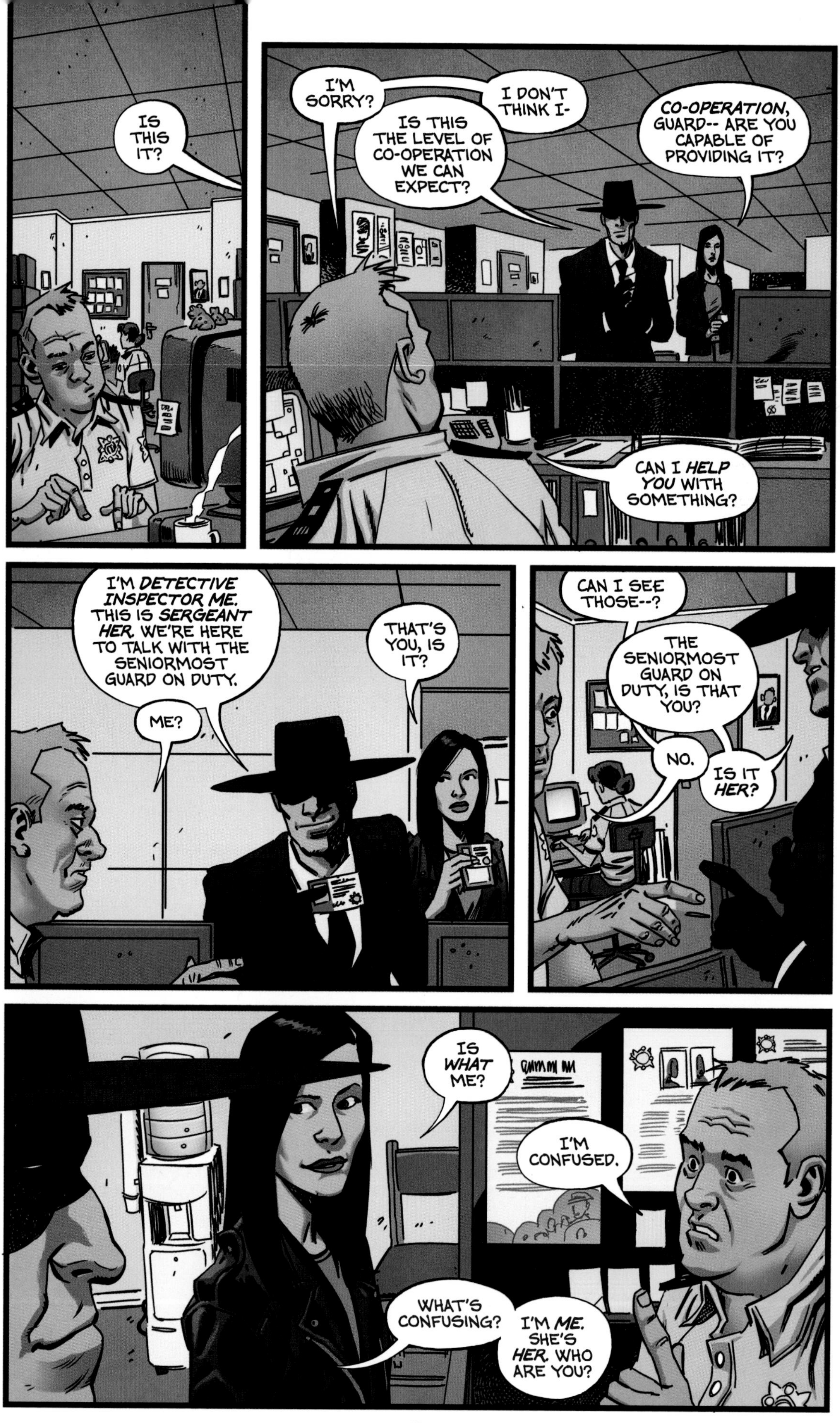

IS THIS IT?
I'M SORRY?
I DON'T THINK I-
IS THIS THE LEVEL OF CO-OPERATION WE CAN EXPECT?
CO-OPERATION, GUARD-- ARE YOU CAPABLE OF PROVIDING IT?
CAN I HELP YOU WITH SOMETHING?
I'M DETECTIVE INSPECTOR ME. THIS IS SERGEANT HER. WE'RE HERE TO TALK WITH THE SENIORMOST GUARD ON DUTY.
ME?
THAT'S YOU, IS IT?
CAN I SEE THOSE--?
THE SENIORMOST GUARD ON DUTY, IS THAT YOU?
NO.
IS IT HER?
IS WHAT ME?
I'M CONFUSED.
WHAT'S CONFUSING?
I'M ME. SHE'S HER. WHO ARE YOU?

UH, *GARDA HAYES* IS MY-

HAYES, AS YOU KNOW, WE HAVE BEEN SENT TO CONDUCT THE INVESTIGATION. AS OF YET, NOBODY IS IN TROUBLE.

NOT EVEN YOU.

NOT EVEN YOU, GARDA HAYES.

PROVIDED YOU CO-OPERATE.

CO-OPERATION IS *ESSENTIAL*.

WHO ARE--?

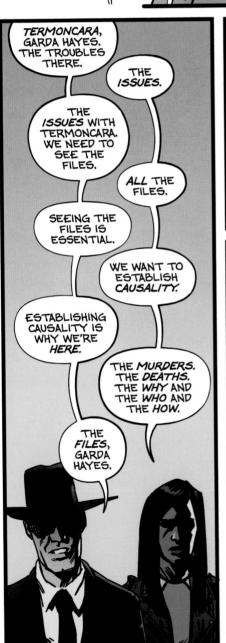

TERMONCARA, GARDA HAYES. THE TROUBLES THERE.

THE *ISSUES*.

THE *ISSUES* WITH TERMONCARA. WE NEED TO SEE THE FILES.

ALL THE FILES.

SEEING THE FILES IS ESSENTIAL.

WE WANT TO ESTABLISH *CAUSALITY*.

ESTABLISHING CAUSALITY IS WHY WE'RE *HERE*.

THE *MURDERS*. THE *DEATHS*. THE *WHY* AND THE *WHO* AND THE *HOW*.

THE *FILES*, GARDA HAYES.

WE – WE DON'T HAVE THEM.

WHEN GARDA CASEY RETIRED, HE TOOK A LOT OF OLD CASE FILES WITH HIM.

WHY DIDN'T YOU GET THEM BACK?

I WASN'T-- I'M NOT TOLD THESE THINGS.

GARDA CASEY-

EX-GARDA CASEY.

EX-GARDA CASEY, IS HE STILL ALIVE?

WHERE DOES HE LIVE?

MAHER HILL. THE BOTTOM OF MAHER HILL.

JUST PAST THE BALLINROE TOWN SIGN. IN TERMONCARA.

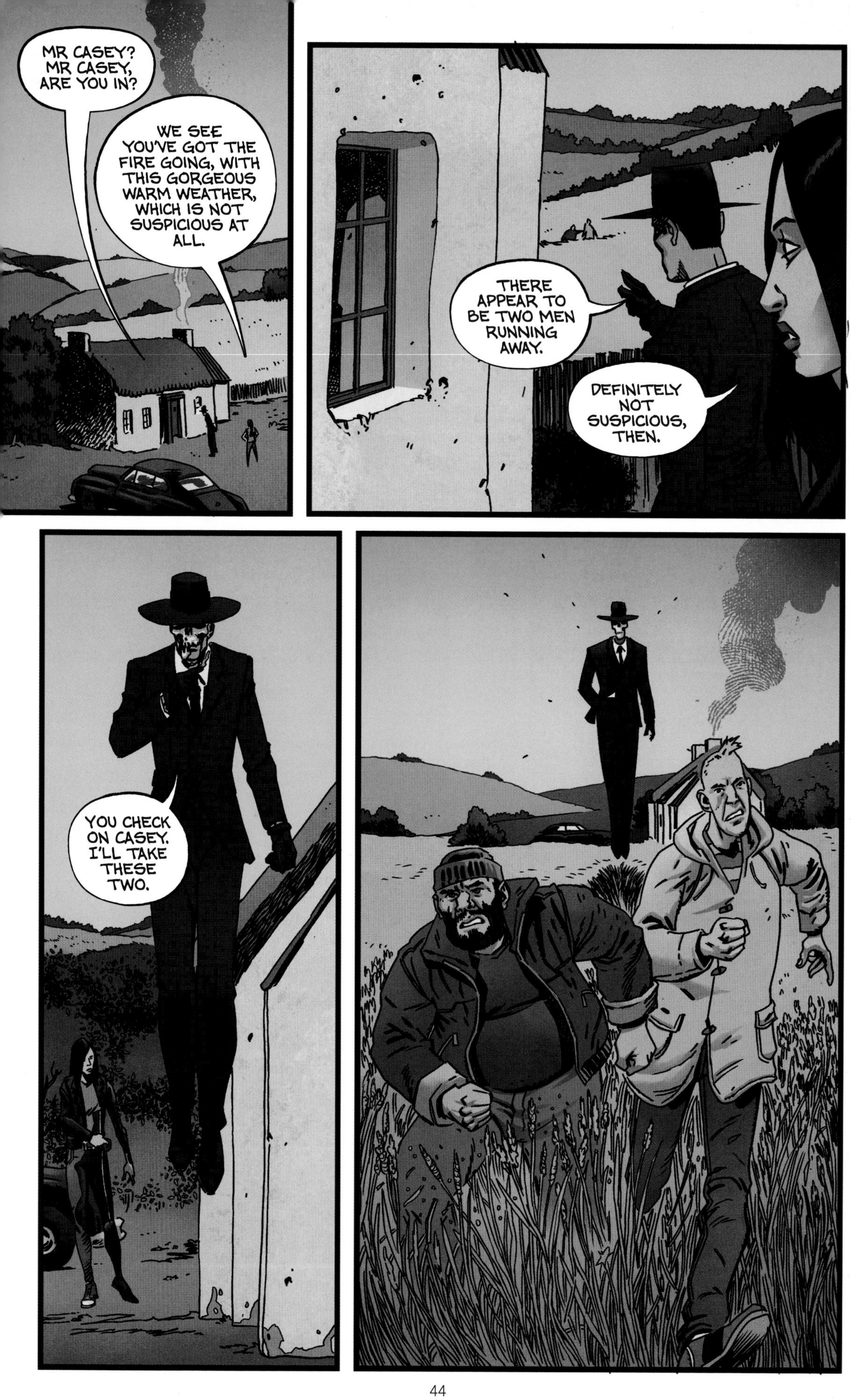
MR CASEY? MR CASEY, ARE YOU IN?
WE SEE YOU'VE GOT THE FIRE GOING, WITH THIS GORGEOUS WARM WEATHER, WHICH IS NOT SUSPICIOUS AT ALL.
THERE APPEAR TO BE TWO MEN RUNNING AWAY.
DEFINITELY NOT SUSPICIOUS, THEN.
YOU CHECK ON CASEY. I'LL TAKE THESE TWO.

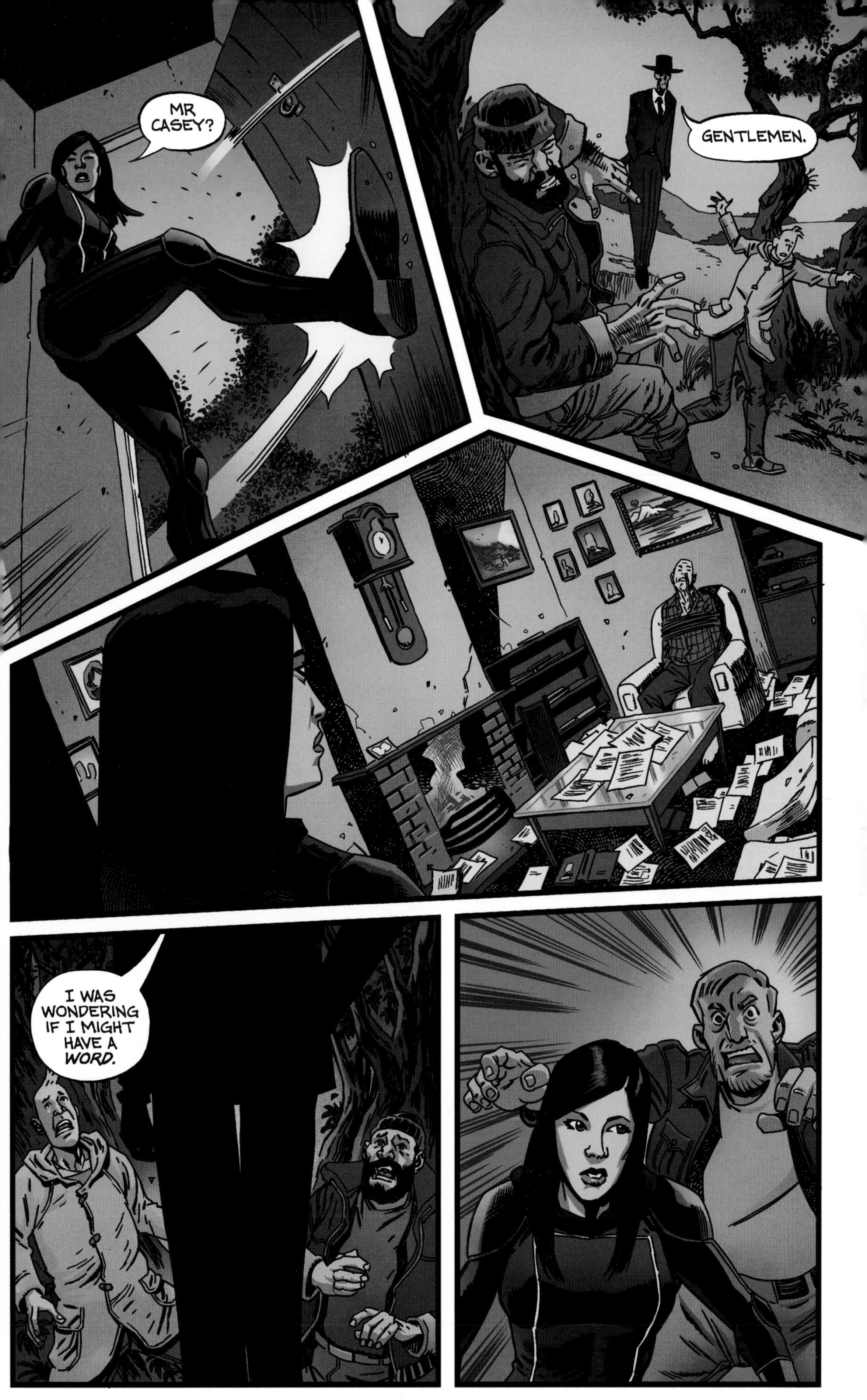
MR CASEY?
GENTLEMEN.
I WAS WONDERING IF I MIGHT HAVE A *WORD*.

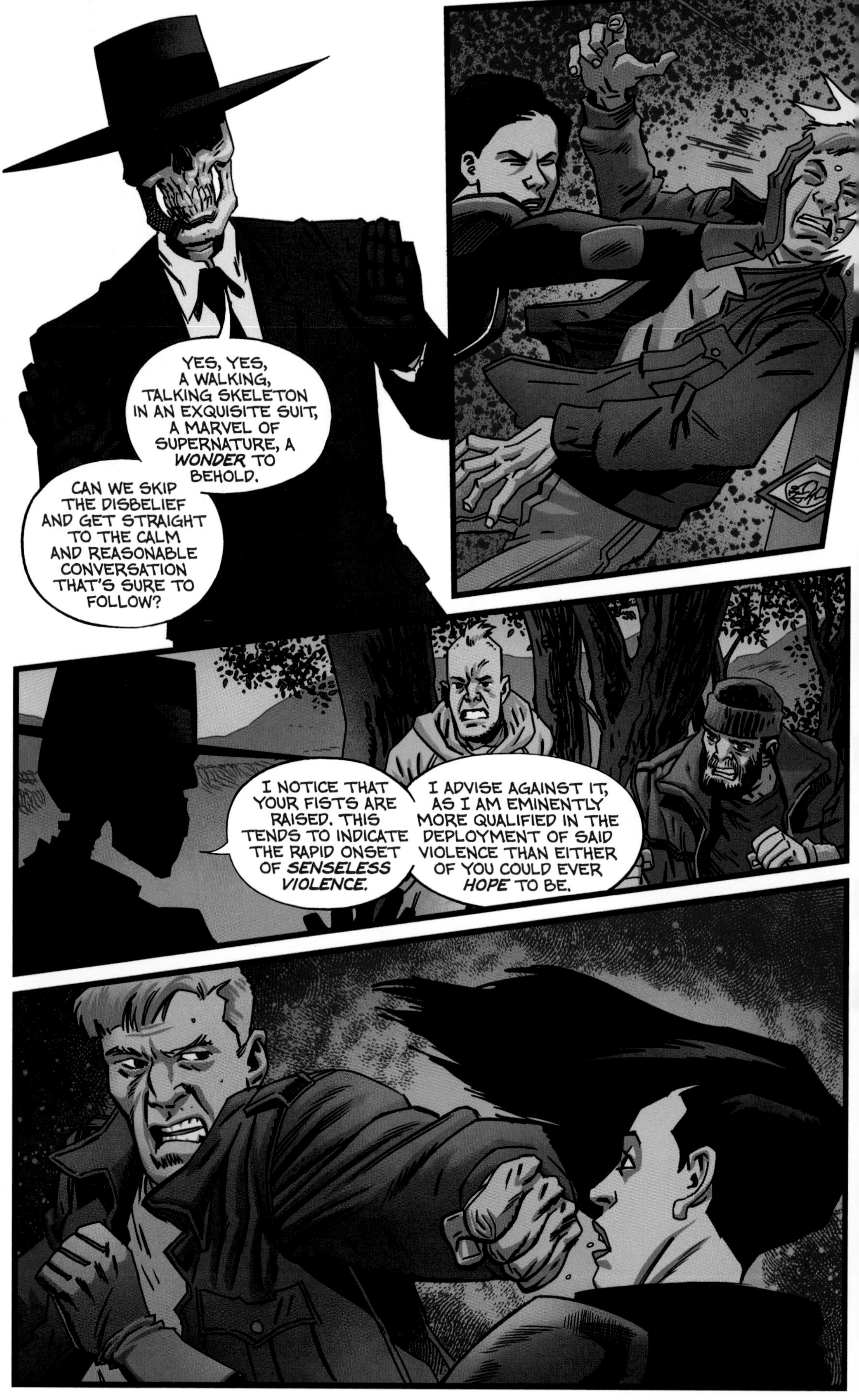
YES, YES, A WALKING, TALKING SKELETON IN AN EXQUISITE SUIT, A MARVEL OF SUPERNATURE, A *WONDER* TO BEHOLD.
CAN WE SKIP THE DISBELIEF AND GET STRAIGHT TO THE CALM AND REASONABLE CONVERSATION THAT'S SURE TO FOLLOW?
I NOTICE THAT YOUR FISTS ARE RAISED. THIS TENDS TO INDICATE THE RAPID ONSET OF *SENSELESS VIOLENCE.*
I ADVISE AGAINST IT, AS I AM EMINENTLY MORE QUALIFIED IN THE DEPLOYMENT OF SAID VIOLENCE THAN EITHER OF YOU COULD EVER *HOPE* TO BE.

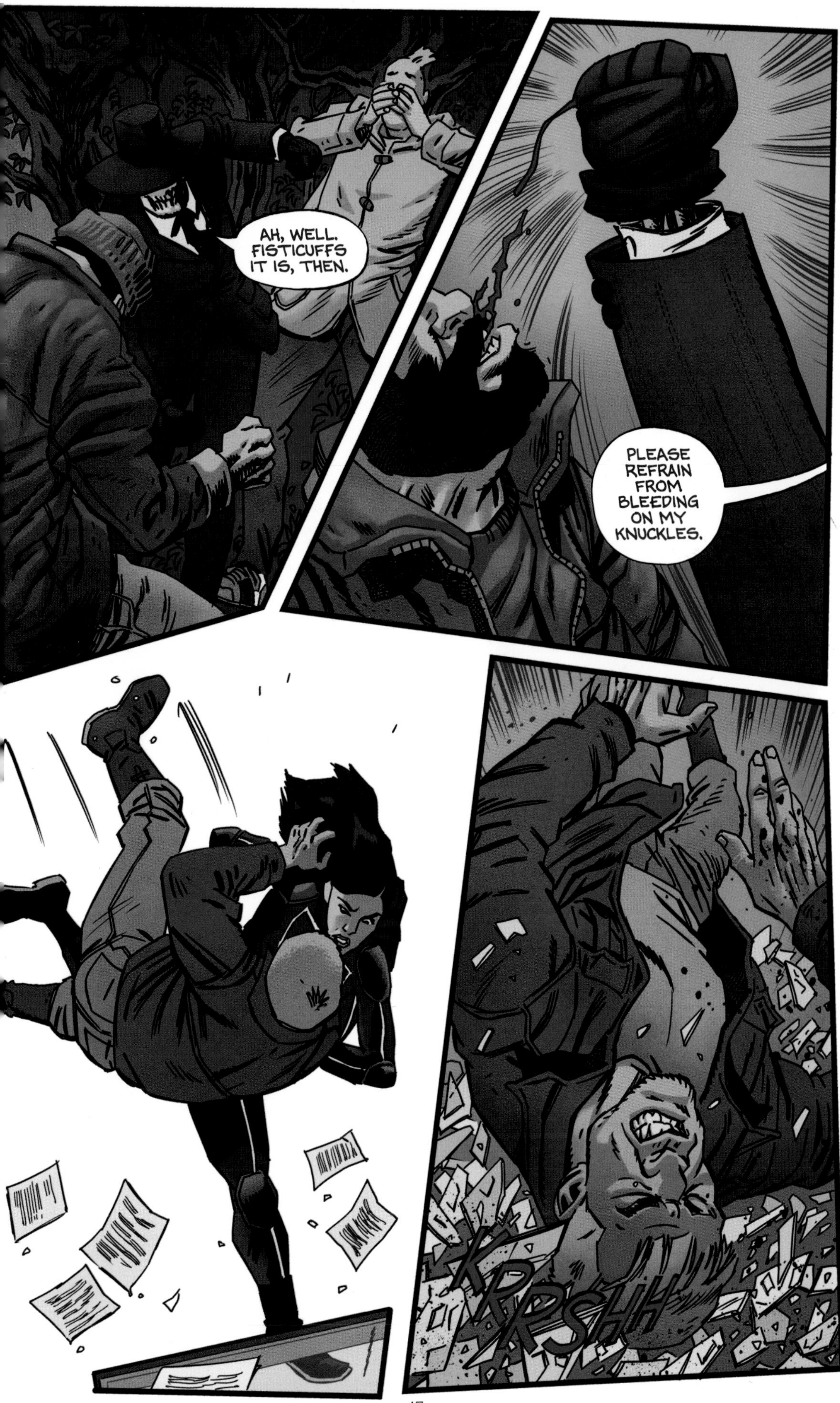
AH, WELL. FISTICUFFS IT IS, THEN.
PLEASE REFRAIN FROM BLEEDING ON MY KNUCKLES.
KRRSHH

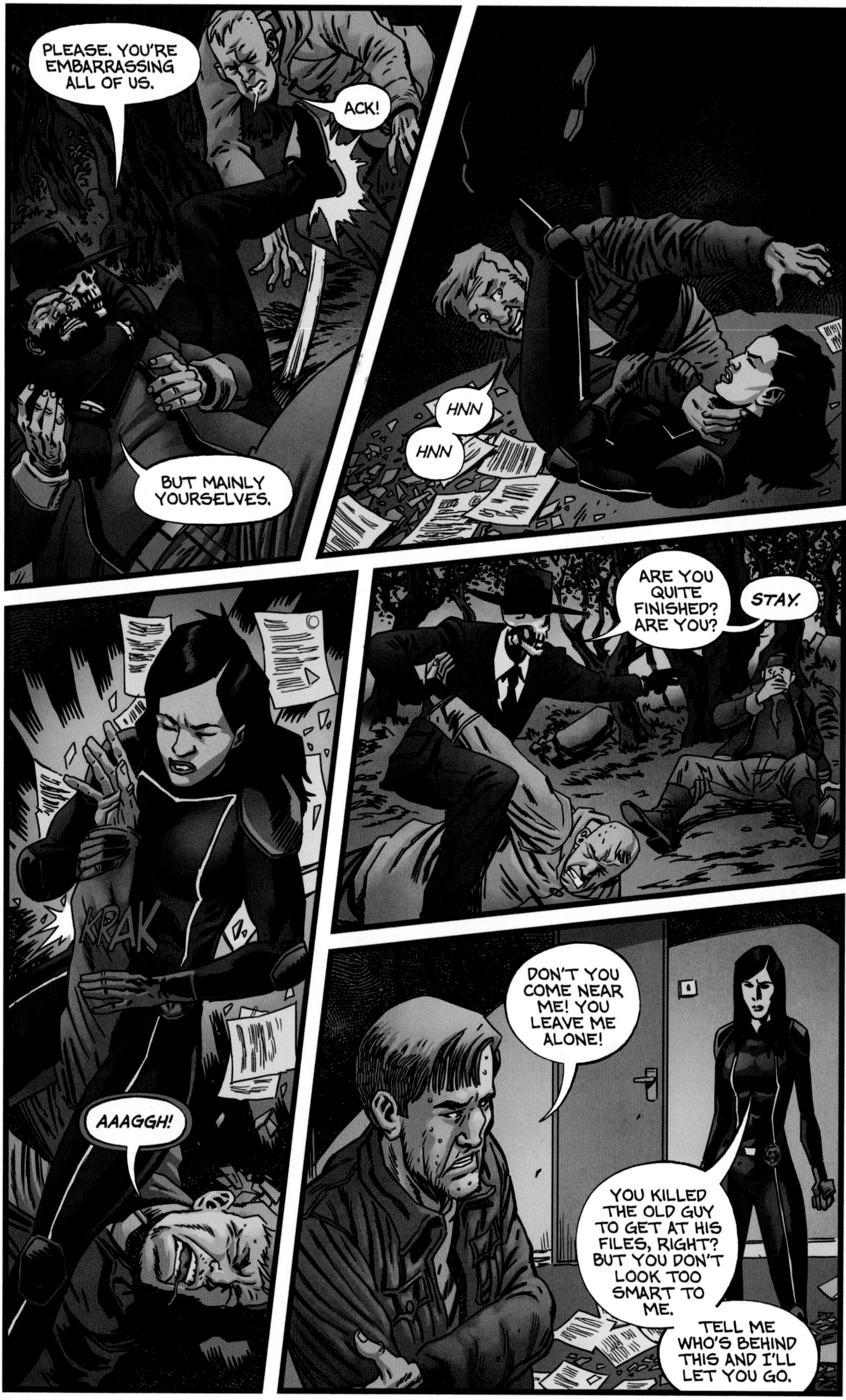
PLEASE. YOU'RE EMBARRASSING ALL OF US.
ACK!
BUT MAINLY YOURSELVES.
HNN
HNN
KRAK
AAAGGH!
ARE YOU QUITE FINISHED? ARE YOU?
STAY.
DON'T YOU COME NEAR ME! YOU LEAVE ME ALONE!
YOU KILLED THE OLD GUY TO GET AT HIS FILES, RIGHT? BUT YOU DON'T LOOK TOO SMART TO ME.
TELL ME WHO'S BEHIND THIS AND I'LL LET YOU GO.

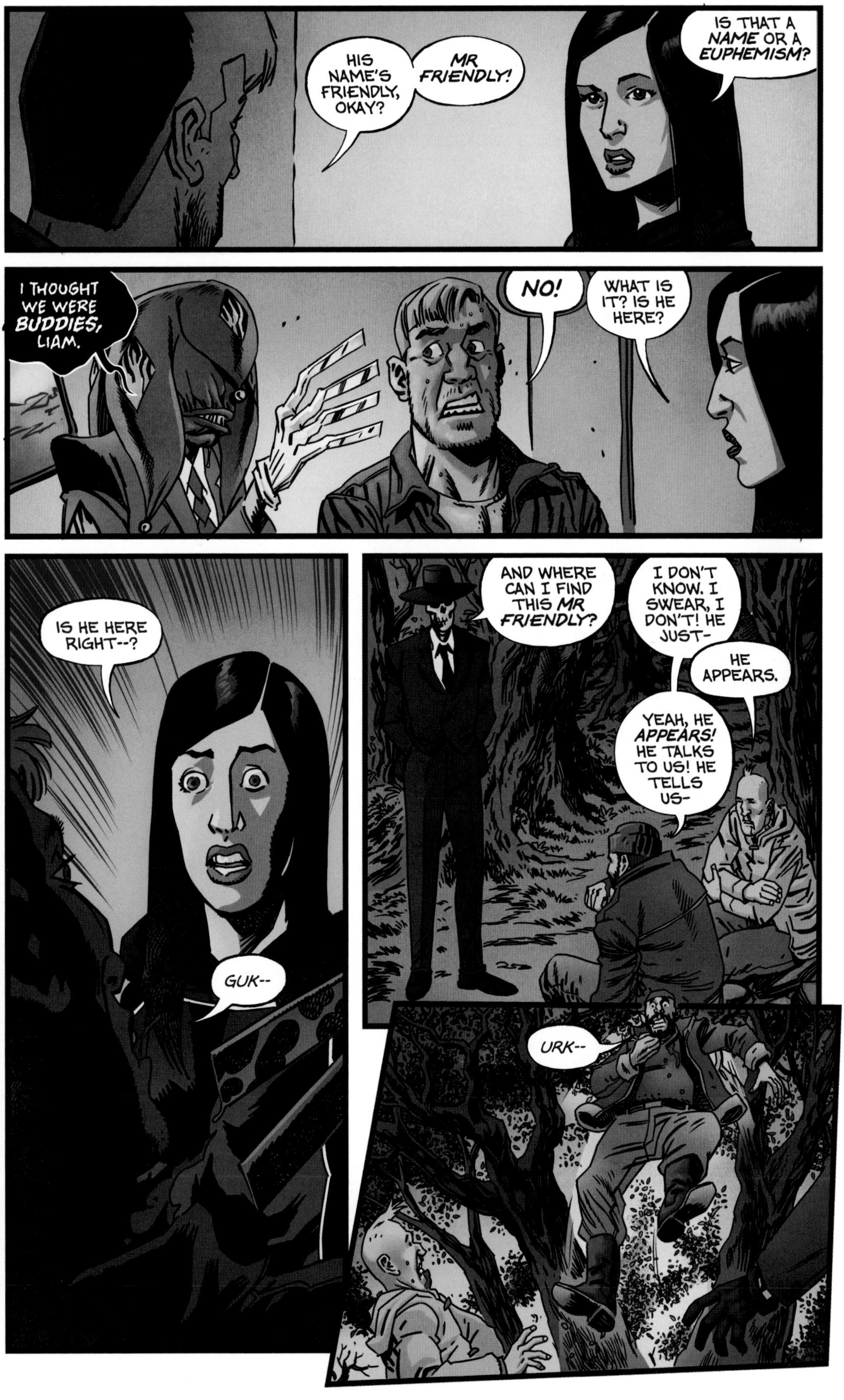
HIS NAME'S FRIENDLY, OKAY?
MR FRIENDLY!
IS THAT A NAME OR A EUPHEMISM?
I THOUGHT WE WERE BUDDIES, LIAM.
NO!
WHAT IS IT? IS HE HERE?
IS HE HERE RIGHT--?
GUK--
AND WHERE CAN I FIND THIS MR FRIENDLY?
I DON'T KNOW. I SWEAR, I DON'T! HE JUST-
HE APPEARS.
YEAH, HE APPEARS! HE TALKS TO US! HE TELLS US-
URK--

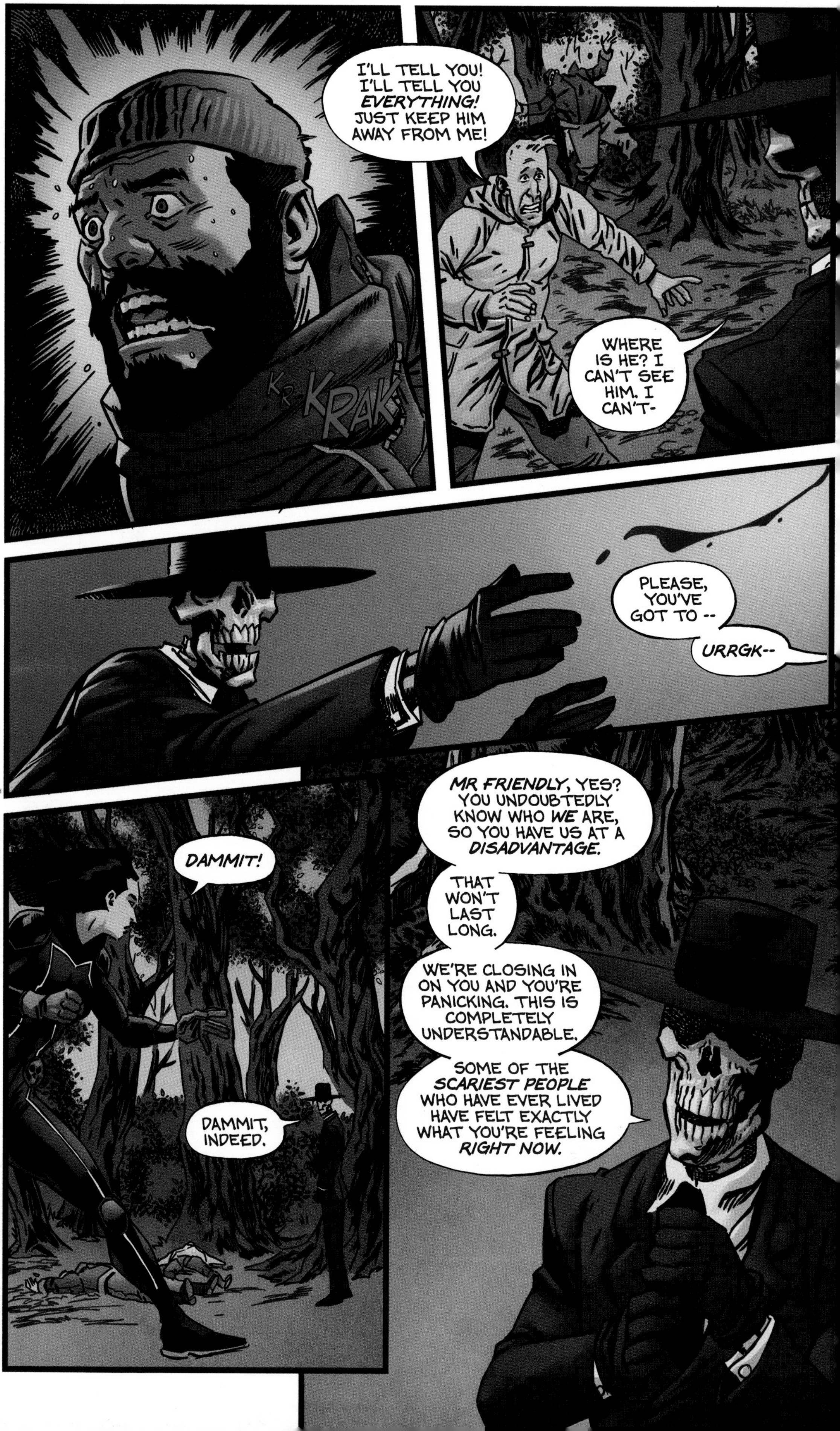

KR KRAK
I'LL TELL YOU! I'LL TELL YOU EVERYTHING! JUST KEEP HIM AWAY FROM ME!
WHERE IS HE? I CAN'T SEE HIM. I CAN'T-
PLEASE, YOU'VE GOT TO --
URRGK--
DAMMIT!
DAMMIT, INDEED.
MR FRIENDLY, YES? YOU UNDOUBTEDLY KNOW WHO WE ARE, SO YOU HAVE US AT A DISADVANTAGE.
THAT WON'T LAST LONG.
WE'RE CLOSING IN ON YOU AND YOU'RE PANICKING. THIS IS COMPLETELY UNDERSTANDABLE.
SOME OF THE SCARIEST PEOPLE WHO HAVE EVER LIVED HAVE FELT EXACTLY WHAT YOU'RE FEELING RIGHT NOW.

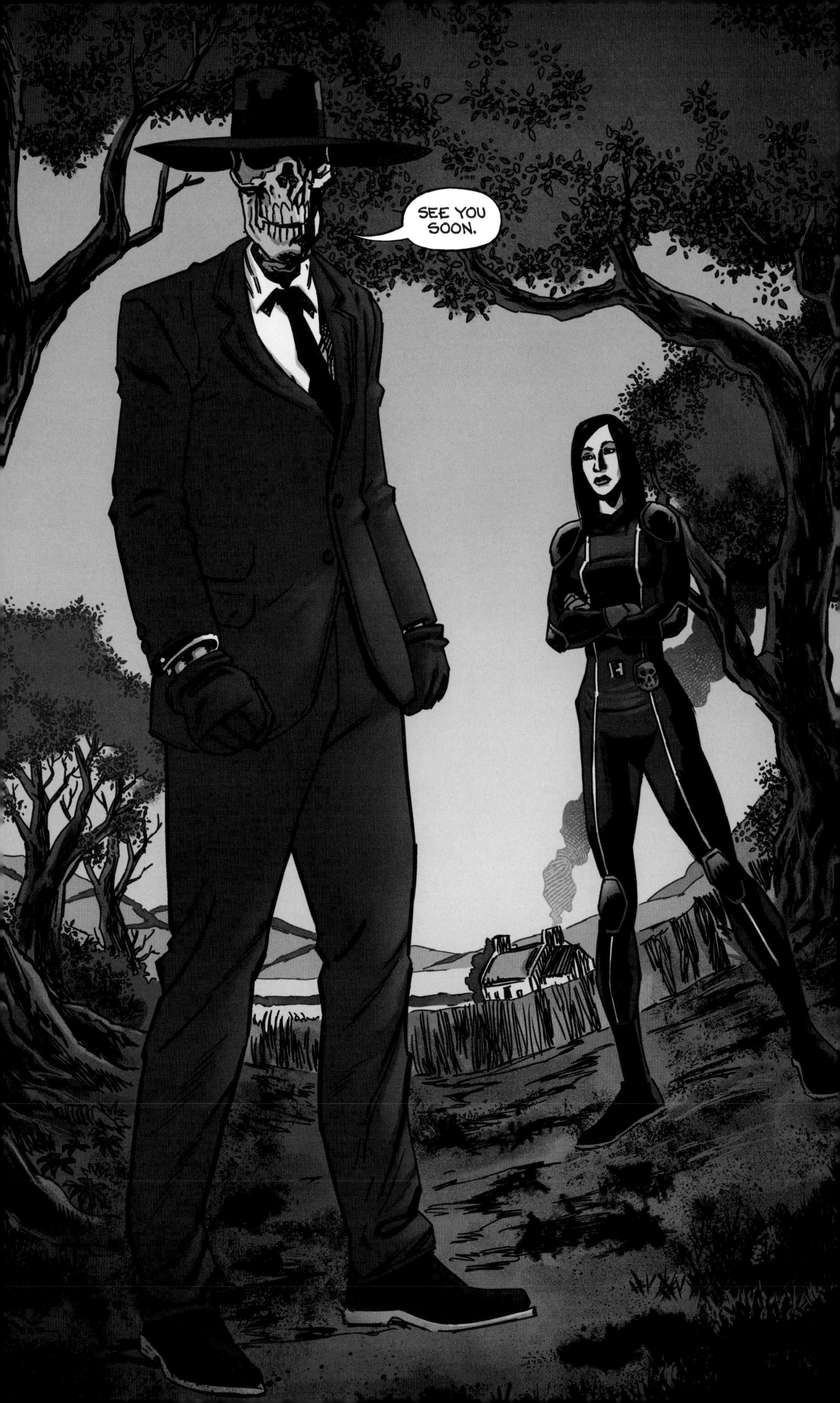
SEE YOU SOON.

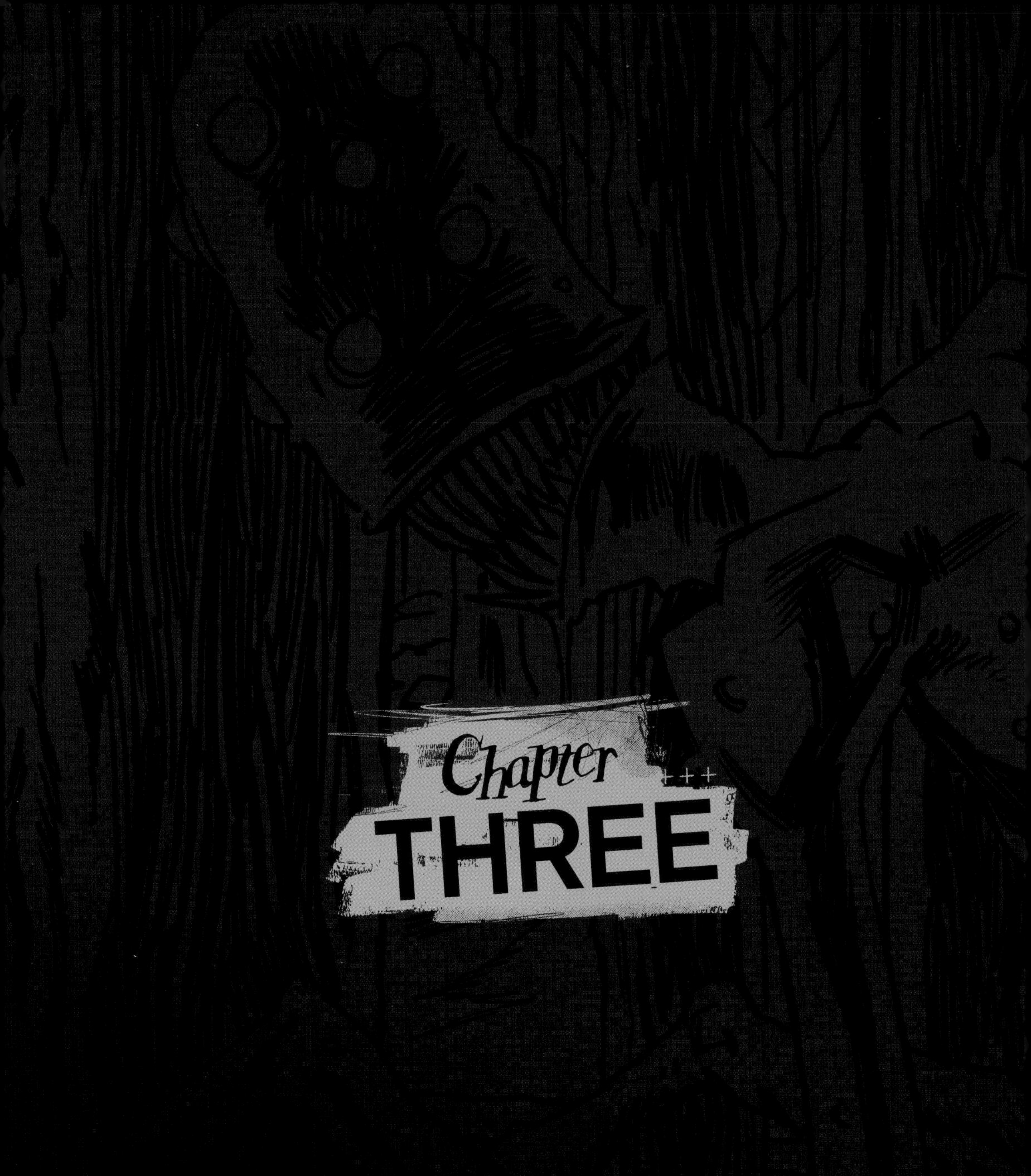

Chapter THREE

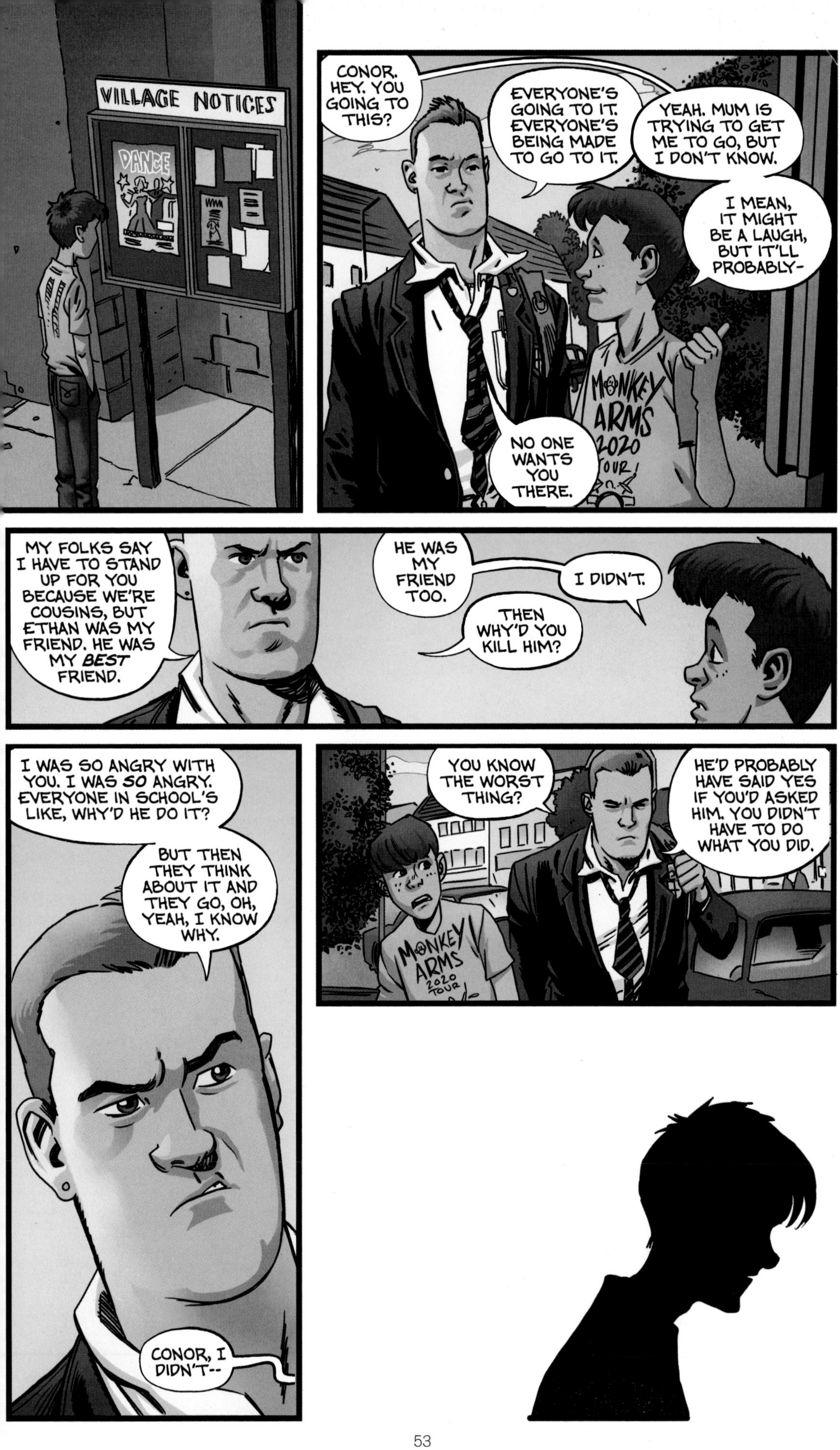
VILLAGE NOTICES
DANCE
CONOR. HEY. YOU GOING TO THIS?
EVERYONE'S GOING TO IT. EVERYONE'S BEING MADE TO GO TO IT.
YEAH. MUM IS TRYING TO GET ME TO GO, BUT I DON'T KNOW.
I MEAN, IT MIGHT BE A LAUGH, BUT IT'LL PROBABLY-
NO ONE WANTS YOU THERE.
MONKEY ARMS 2020 TOUR
MY FOLKS SAY I HAVE TO STAND UP FOR YOU BECAUSE WE'RE COUSINS, BUT ETHAN WAS MY FRIEND. HE WAS MY *BEST* FRIEND.
HE WAS MY FRIEND TOO.
I DIDN'T.
THEN WHY'D YOU KILL HIM?
I WAS SO ANGRY WITH YOU. I WAS *SO* ANGRY. EVERYONE IN SCHOOL'S LIKE, WHY'D HE DO IT?
BUT THEN THEY THINK ABOUT IT AND THEY GO, OH, YEAH, I KNOW WHY.
CONOR, I DIDN'T--
YOU KNOW THE WORST THING?
HE'D PROBABLY HAVE SAID YES IF YOU'D ASKED HIM. YOU DIDN'T HAVE TO DO WHAT YOU DID.
MONKEY ARMS 2020 TOUR

MR FRIENDLY, EH?

WHAT DO YOU RECKON? GHOST? SORCERER? INVISIBLE MAN?

DO YOU THINK HE'S HERE WITH US NOW?

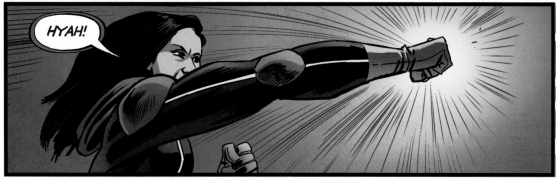

HYAH!

DO YOU THINK I JUST PUNCHED HIM? I THINK I JUST PUNCHED HIM.

GETTING ANYTHING FROM THE FILES THOSE LADS DIDN'T MANAGE TO BURN?

A LITTLE.

ENOUGH TO MAKE IT CLEAR THAT THE HATE CRIMES REPORTED WERE MERELY THE TIP OF THE BLOOD-DRENCHED ICEBERG.

THE TOWNSPEOPLE OF TERMONCARA, IT SEEMS, HAVE THE ABILITY TO KEEP VERY QUIET ABOUT THINGS THEY HAVE NO WISH TO DISCUSS.

MIHAI CRISTIAN, THE HANDYMAN WHO WAS BEATEN TO DEATH ON MAIN STREET - THE MEDIA REPORTED THAT HE'D LIVED IN THE TOWN FOR YEARS.

BUT HE *WASN'T* LOCAL?

HE WAS OF NO FIXED ABODE.

HOMELESS? SO THE TOWNSPEOPLE LIED TO THE NEWSPAPERS?

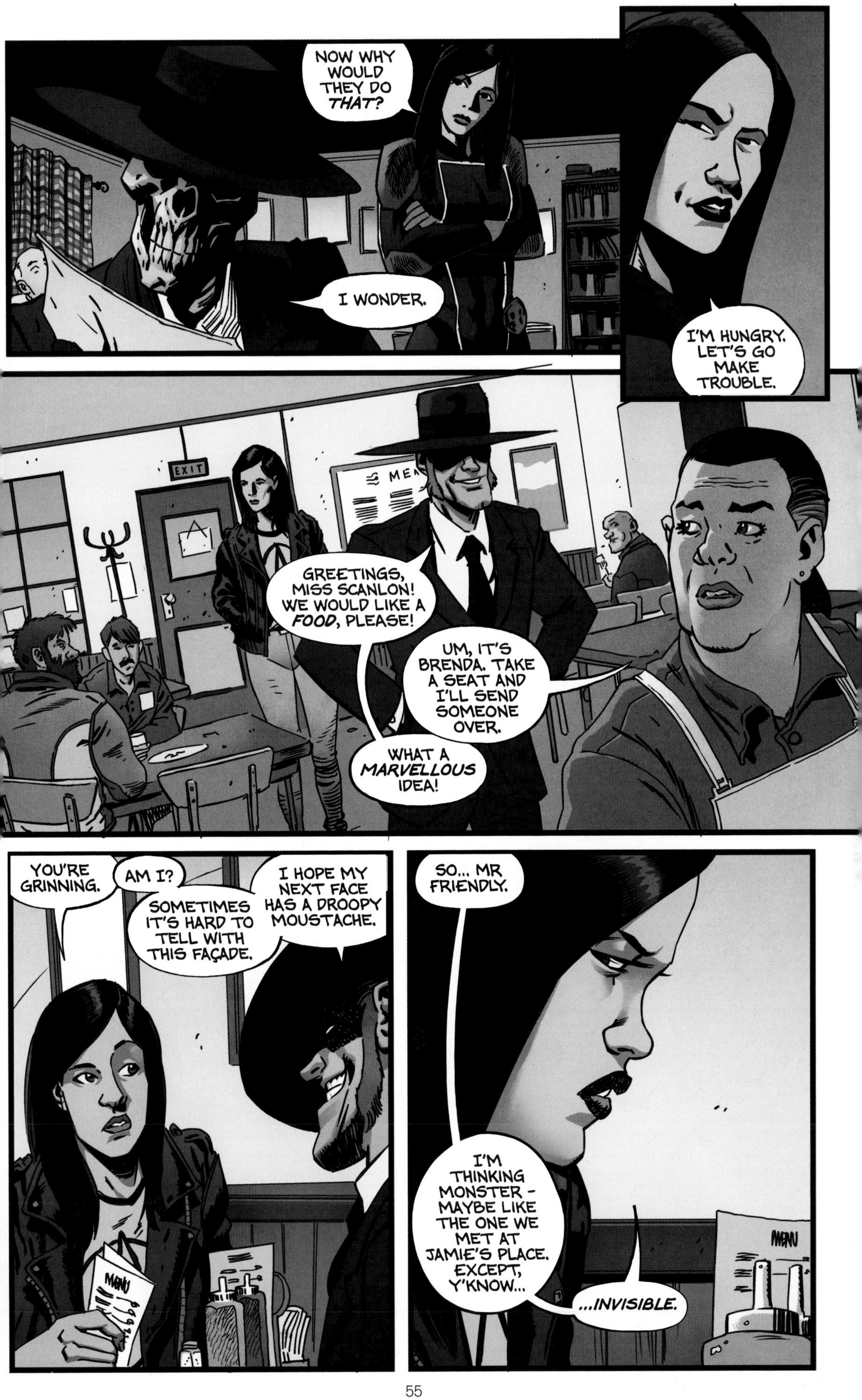
NOW WHY WOULD THEY DO *THAT*?
I WONDER.
I'M HUNGRY. LET'S GO MAKE TROUBLE.
EXIT
GREETINGS, MISS SCANLON! WE WOULD LIKE A *FOOD*, PLEASE!
UM, IT'S BRENDA. TAKE A SEAT AND I'LL SEND SOMEONE OVER.
WHAT A *MARVELLOUS* IDEA!
YOU'RE GRINNING.
AM I?
SOMETIMES IT'S HARD TO TELL WITH THIS FAÇADE.
I HOPE MY NEXT FACE HAS A DROOPY MOUSTACHE.
SO... MR FRIENDLY.
I'M THINKING MONSTER - MAYBE LIKE THE ONE WE MET AT JAMIE'S PLACE. EXCEPT, Y'KNOW...
...*INVISIBLE*.

IF IT'S A MONSTER, IT'S A SMART ONE.

WE MIGHT VERY WELL BE DEALING WITH SOMETHING WE HAVEN'T SEEN BEFORE, VALKYRIE. SOMETHING NEW.

WELL, THAT *DOES* SOUND FUN.

HEY, DO YOU KNOW WHAT YOU WANT OR DO YOU NEED MORE TIME?

NOTHING FOR ME, THANK YOU!

I'LL HAVE THE CHEESEBURGER IF IT'S A GOOD CHEESEBURGER. I HAVEN'T HAD RED MEAT IN SO LONG, SO IT'D HAVE TO BE WORTH IT.

IS IT A *GOOD* CHEESEBURGER? BEST IN TOWN?

I MEAN... THERE'S A MCDONALD'S ON THE CORNER, BUT YEAH, IT'S GRAND, I SUPPOSE.

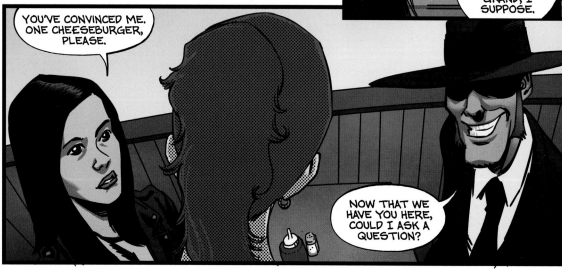

YOU'VE CONVINCED ME. ONE CHEESEBURGER, PLEASE.

NOW THAT WE HAVE YOU HERE, COULD I ASK A QUESTION?

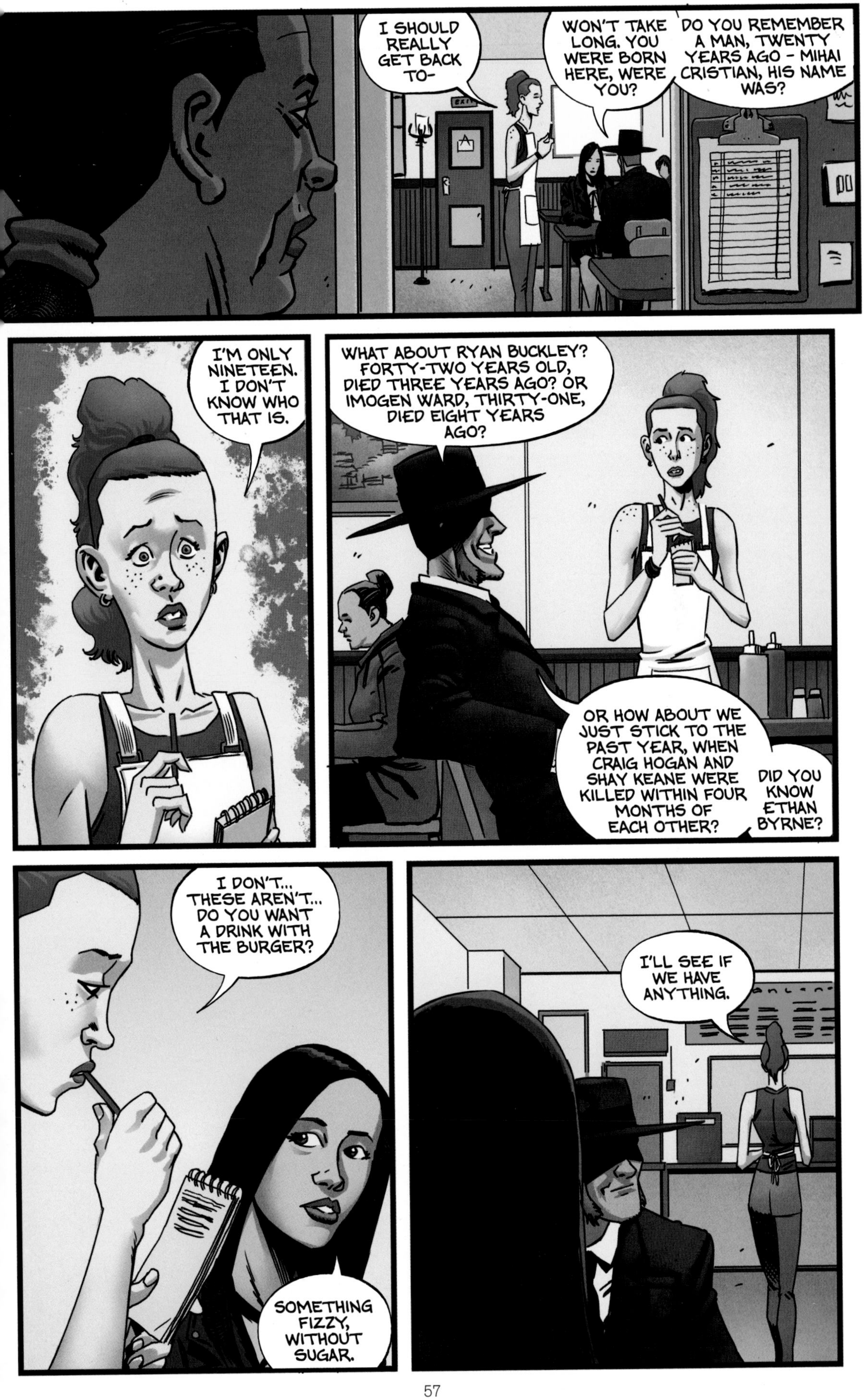
I SHOULD REALLY GET BACK TO-
WON'T TAKE LONG. YOU WERE BORN HERE, WERE YOU?
DO YOU REMEMBER A MAN, TWENTY YEARS AGO - MIHAI CRISTIAN, HIS NAME WAS?
I'M ONLY NINETEEN. I DON'T KNOW WHO THAT IS.
WHAT ABOUT RYAN BUCKLEY? FORTY-TWO YEARS OLD, DIED THREE YEARS AGO? OR IMOGEN WARD, THIRTY-ONE, DIED EIGHT YEARS AGO?
OR HOW ABOUT WE JUST STICK TO THE PAST YEAR, WHEN CRAIG HOGAN AND SHAY KEANE WERE KILLED WITHIN FOUR MONTHS OF EACH OTHER?
DID YOU KNOW ETHAN BYRNE?
I DON'T... THESE AREN'T... DO YOU WANT A DRINK WITH THE BURGER?
SOMETHING FIZZY, WITHOUT SUGAR.
I'LL SEE IF WE HAVE ANYTHING.

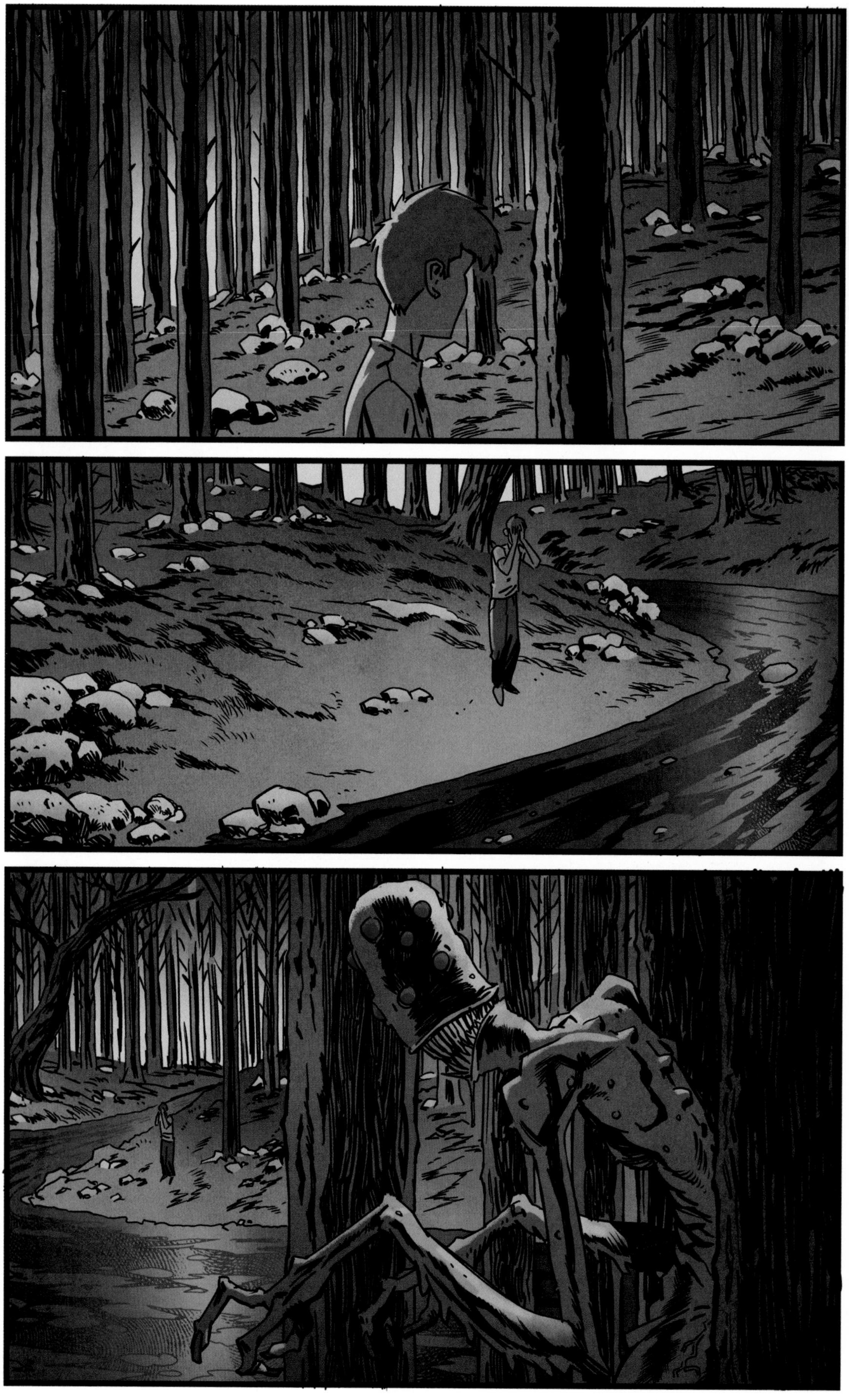

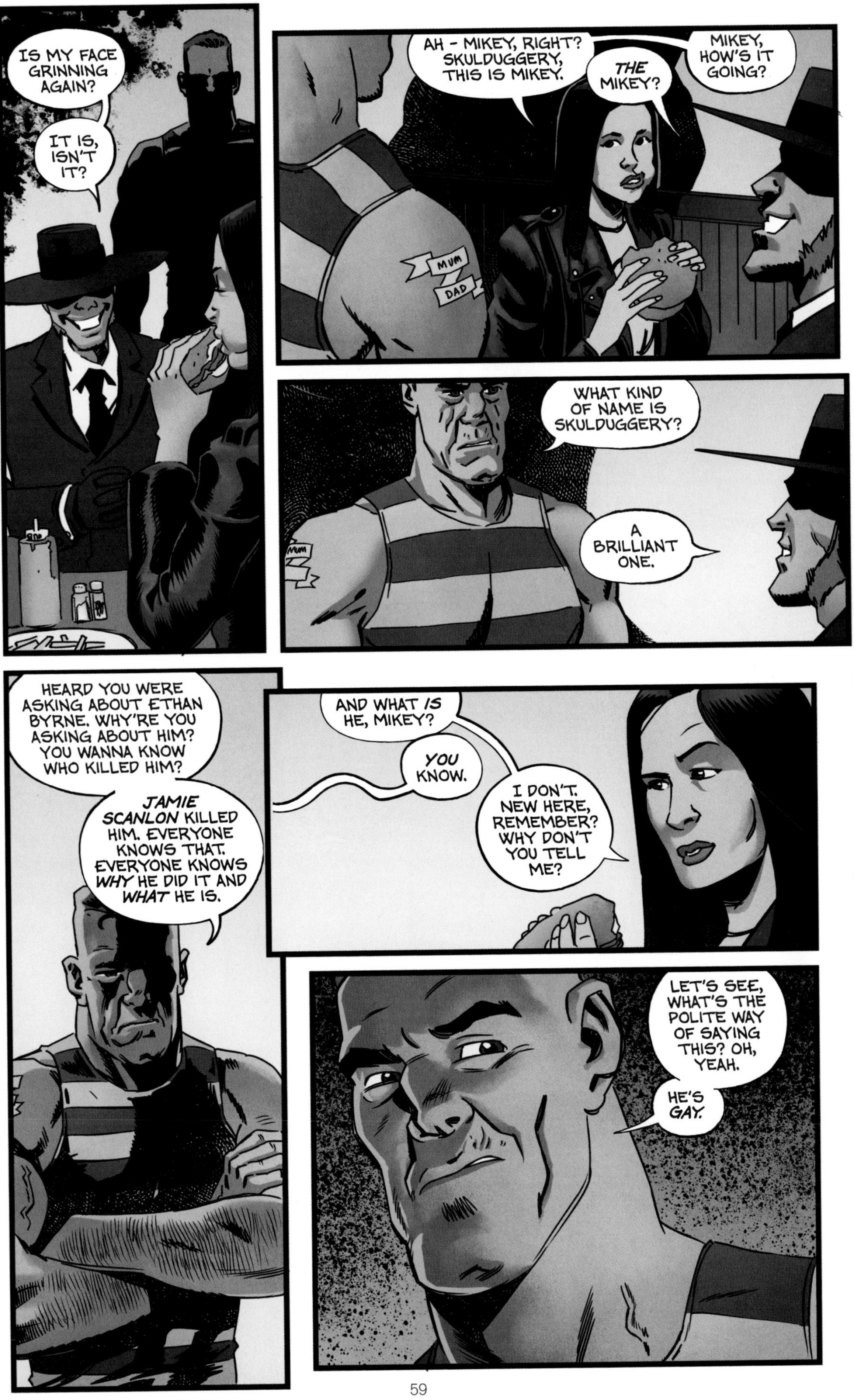
IS MY FACE GRINNING AGAIN?
IT IS, ISN'T IT?
AH - MIKEY, RIGHT? SKULDUGGERY, THIS IS MIKEY.
THE MIKEY?
MIKEY, HOW'S IT GOING?
MUM
DAD
WHAT KIND OF NAME IS SKULDUGGERY?
A BRILLIANT ONE.
HEARD YOU WERE ASKING ABOUT ETHAN BYRNE. WHY'RE YOU ASKING ABOUT HIM? YOU WANNA KNOW WHO KILLED HIM?
JAMIE SCANLON KILLED HIM. EVERYONE KNOWS THAT. EVERYONE KNOWS *WHY* HE DID IT AND *WHAT* HE IS.
AND WHAT *IS* HE, MIKEY?
YOU KNOW.
I DON'T. NEW HERE, REMEMBER? WHY DON'T YOU TELL ME?
LET'S SEE, WHAT'S THE POLITE WAY OF SAYING THIS? OH, YEAH.
HE'S *GAY.*

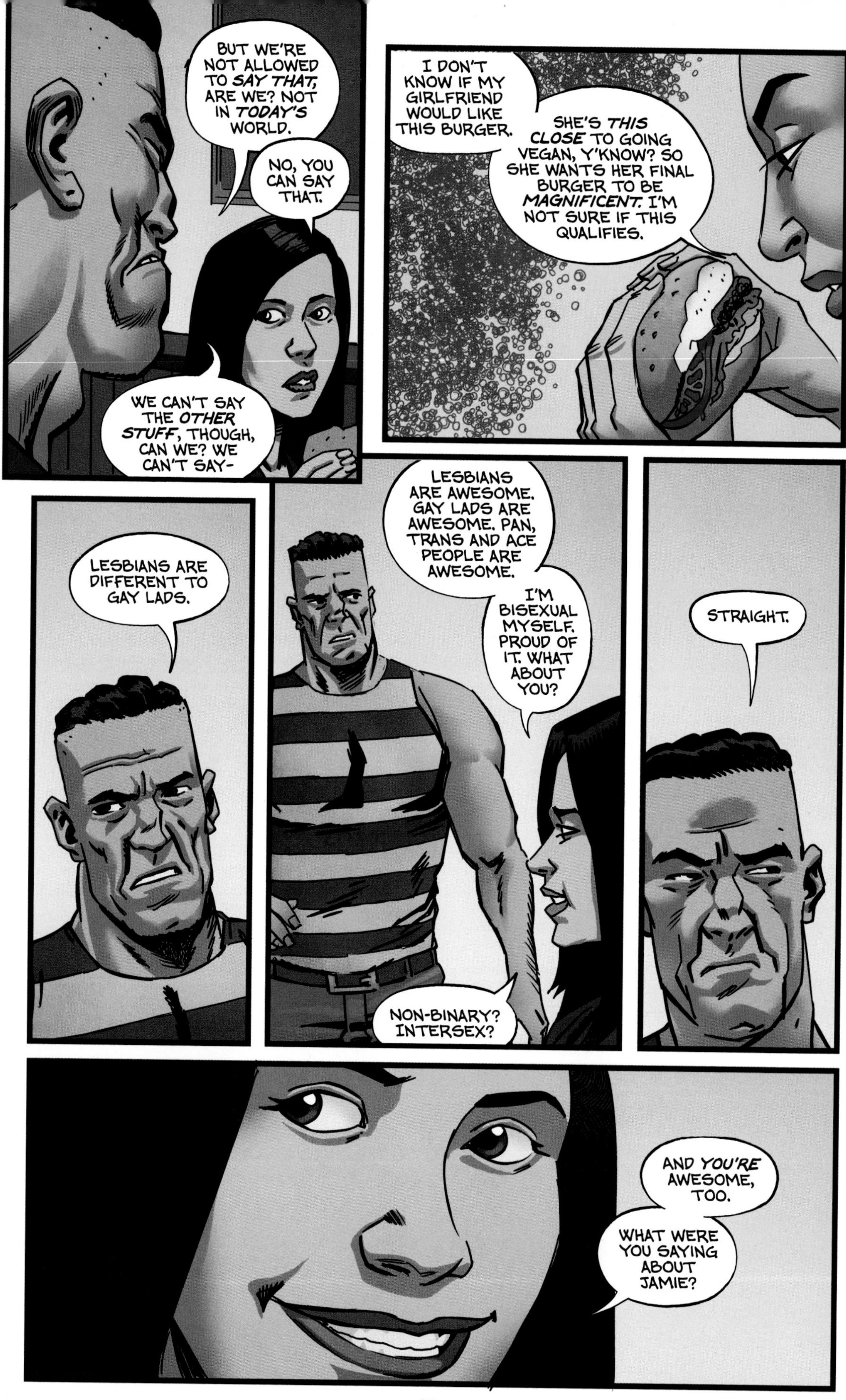
BUT WE'RE NOT ALLOWED TO SAY THAT, ARE WE? NOT IN TODAY'S WORLD.
NO, YOU CAN SAY THAT.
WE CAN'T SAY THE OTHER STUFF, THOUGH, CAN WE? WE CAN'T SAY-
I DON'T KNOW IF MY GIRLFRIEND WOULD LIKE THIS BURGER.
SHE'S THIS CLOSE TO GOING VEGAN, Y'KNOW? SO SHE WANTS HER FINAL BURGER TO BE MAGNIFICENT. I'M NOT SURE IF THIS QUALIFIES.
LESBIANS ARE DIFFERENT TO GAY LADS.
LESBIANS ARE AWESOME. GAY LADS ARE AWESOME. PAN, TRANS AND ACE PEOPLE ARE AWESOME.
I'M BISEXUAL MYSELF. PROUD OF IT. WHAT ABOUT YOU?
NON-BINARY? INTERSEX?
STRAIGHT.
AND YOU'RE AWESOME, TOO.
WHAT WERE YOU SAYING ABOUT JAMIE?

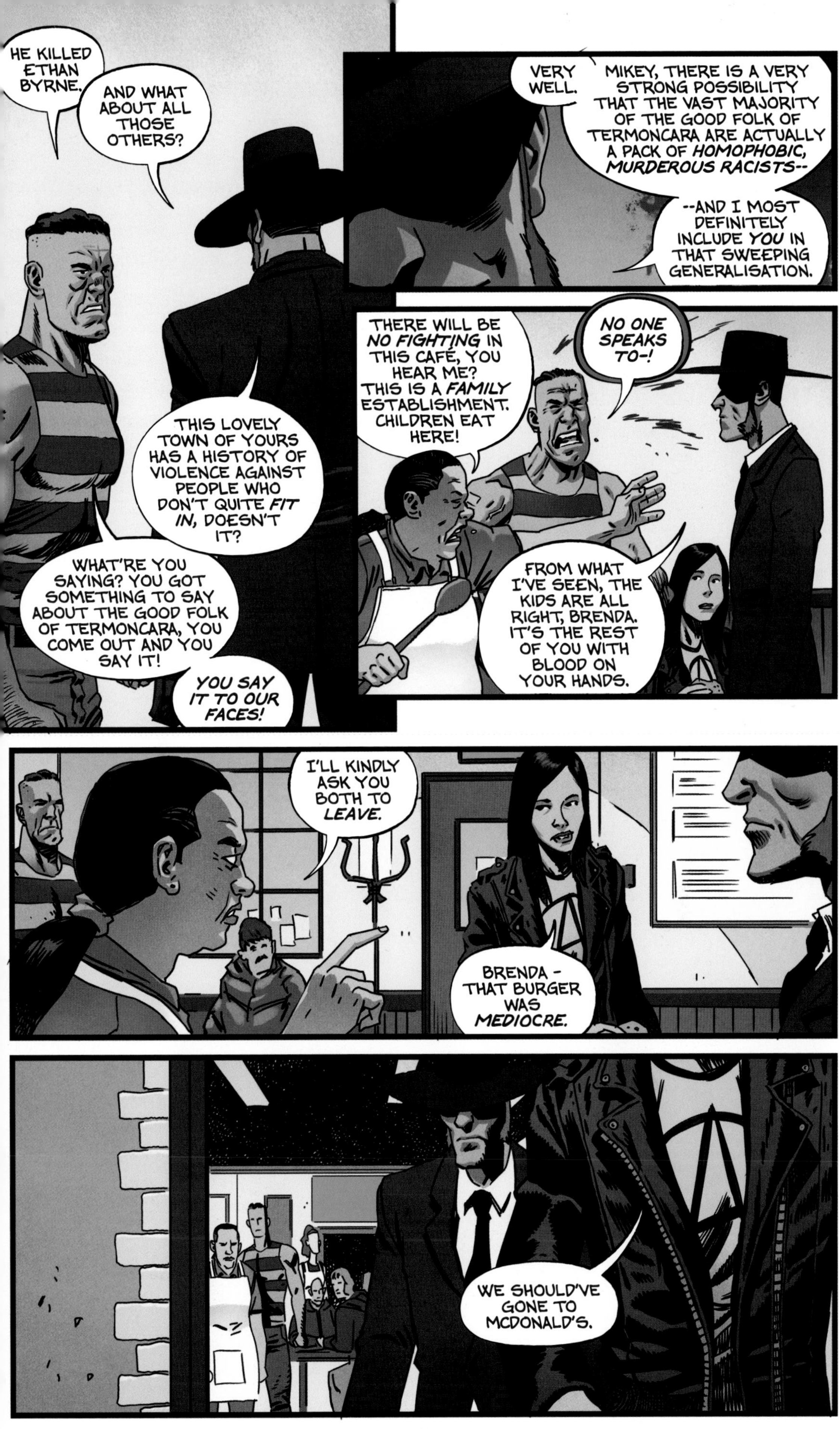
HE KILLED ETHAN BYRNE.
AND WHAT ABOUT ALL THOSE OTHERS?
VERY WELL.
MIKEY, THERE IS A VERY STRONG POSSIBILITY THAT THE VAST MAJORITY OF THE GOOD FOLK OF TERMONCARA ARE ACTUALLY A PACK OF HOMOPHOBIC, MURDEROUS RACISTS--
--AND I MOST DEFINITELY INCLUDE YOU IN THAT SWEEPING GENERALISATION.
THIS LOVELY TOWN OF YOURS HAS A HISTORY OF VIOLENCE AGAINST PEOPLE WHO DON'T QUITE FIT IN, DOESN'T IT?
WHAT'RE YOU SAYING? YOU GOT SOMETHING TO SAY ABOUT THE GOOD FOLK OF TERMONCARA, YOU COME OUT AND YOU SAY IT!
YOU SAY IT TO OUR FACES!
THERE WILL BE NO FIGHTING IN THIS CAFÉ, YOU HEAR ME? THIS IS A FAMILY ESTABLISHMENT. CHILDREN EAT HERE!
NO ONE SPEAKS TO-!
FROM WHAT I'VE SEEN, THE KIDS ARE ALL RIGHT, BRENDA. IT'S THE REST OF YOU WITH BLOOD ON YOUR HANDS.
I'LL KINDLY ASK YOU BOTH TO LEAVE.
BRENDA - THAT BURGER WAS MEDIOCRE.
WE SHOULD'VE GONE TO MCDONALD'S.

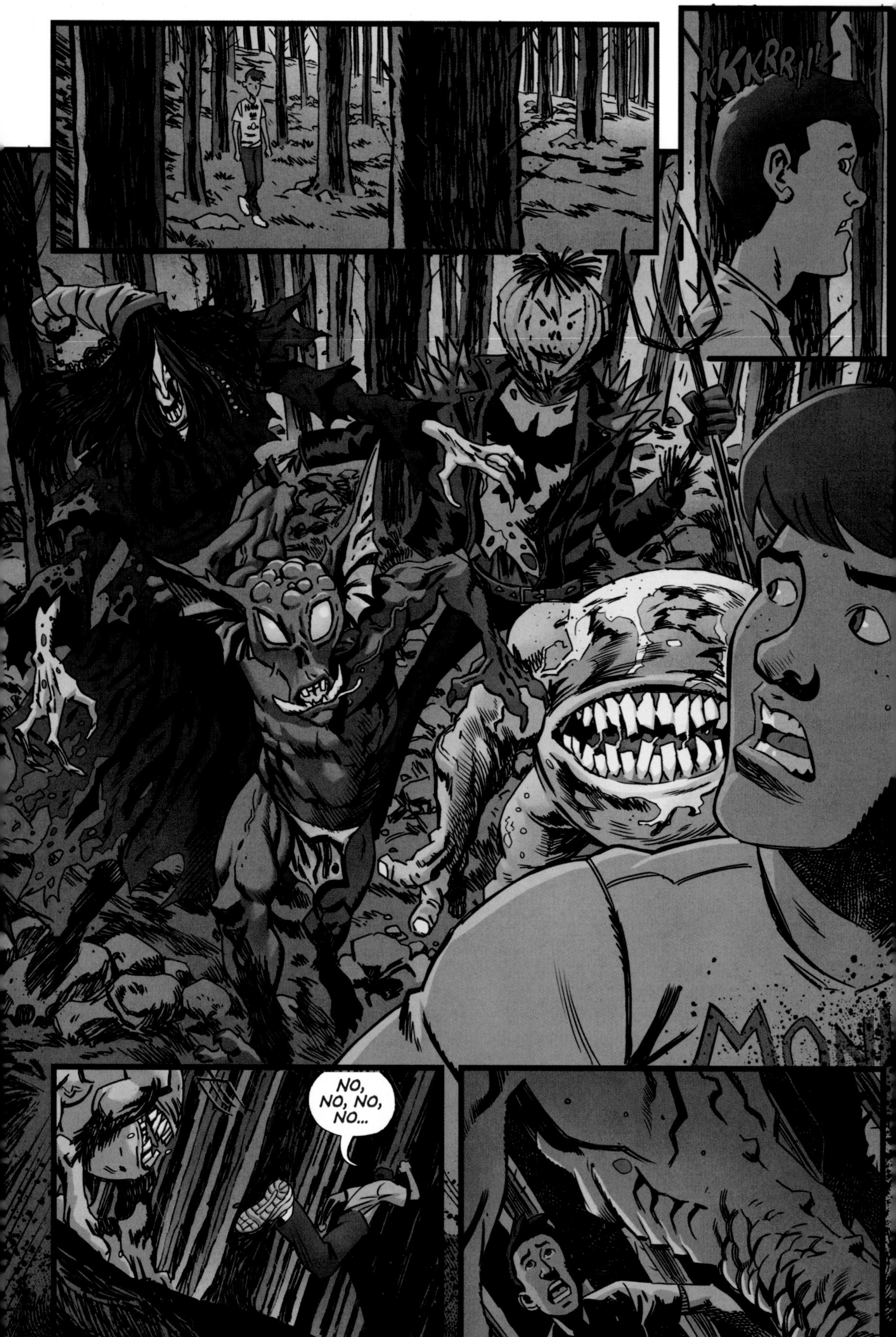
KKKRRRRK
MON
NO, NO, NO, NO...

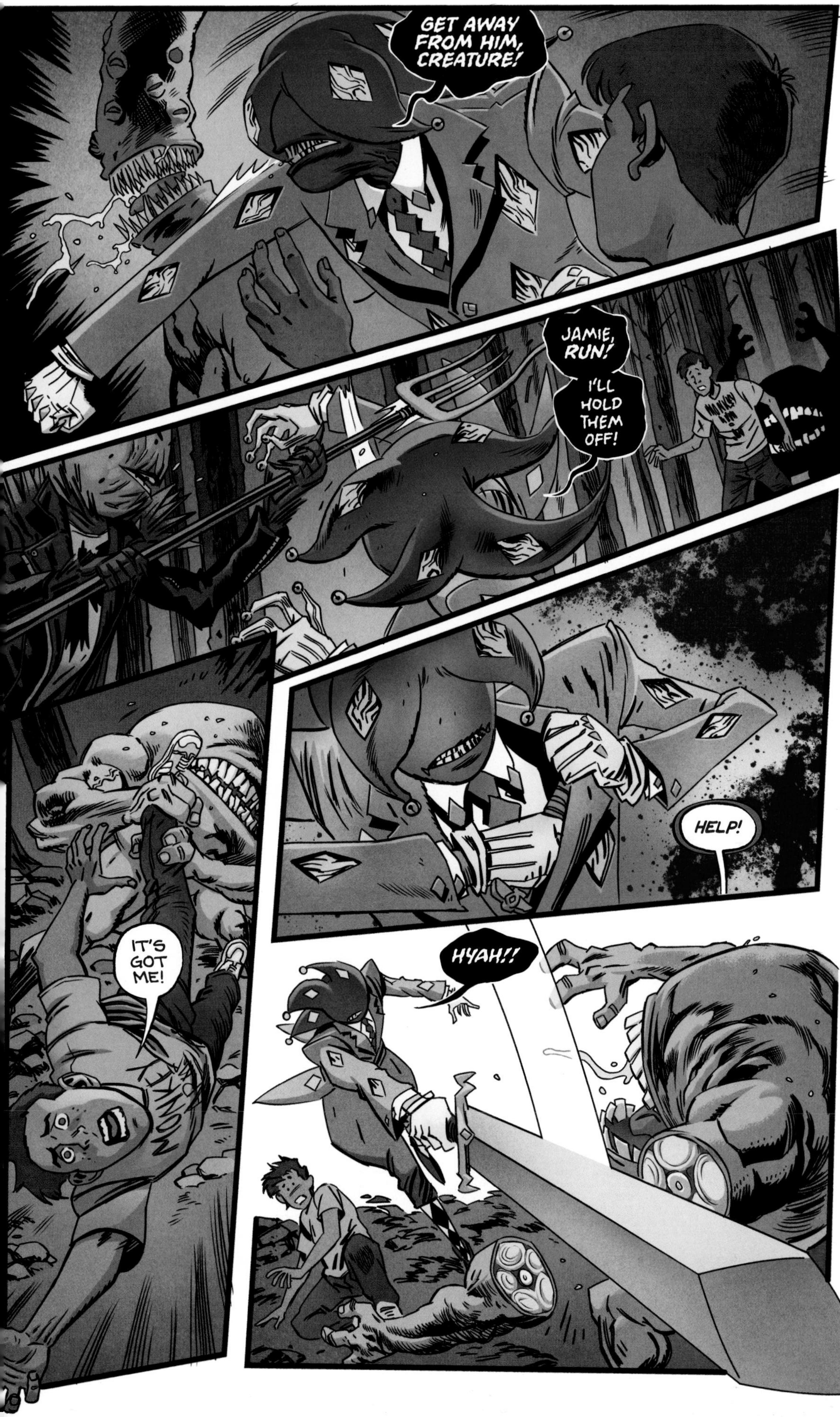
GET AWAY FROM HIM, CREATURE!
JAMIE, RUN!
I'LL HOLD THEM OFF!
HELP!
IT'S GOT ME!
HYAH!!

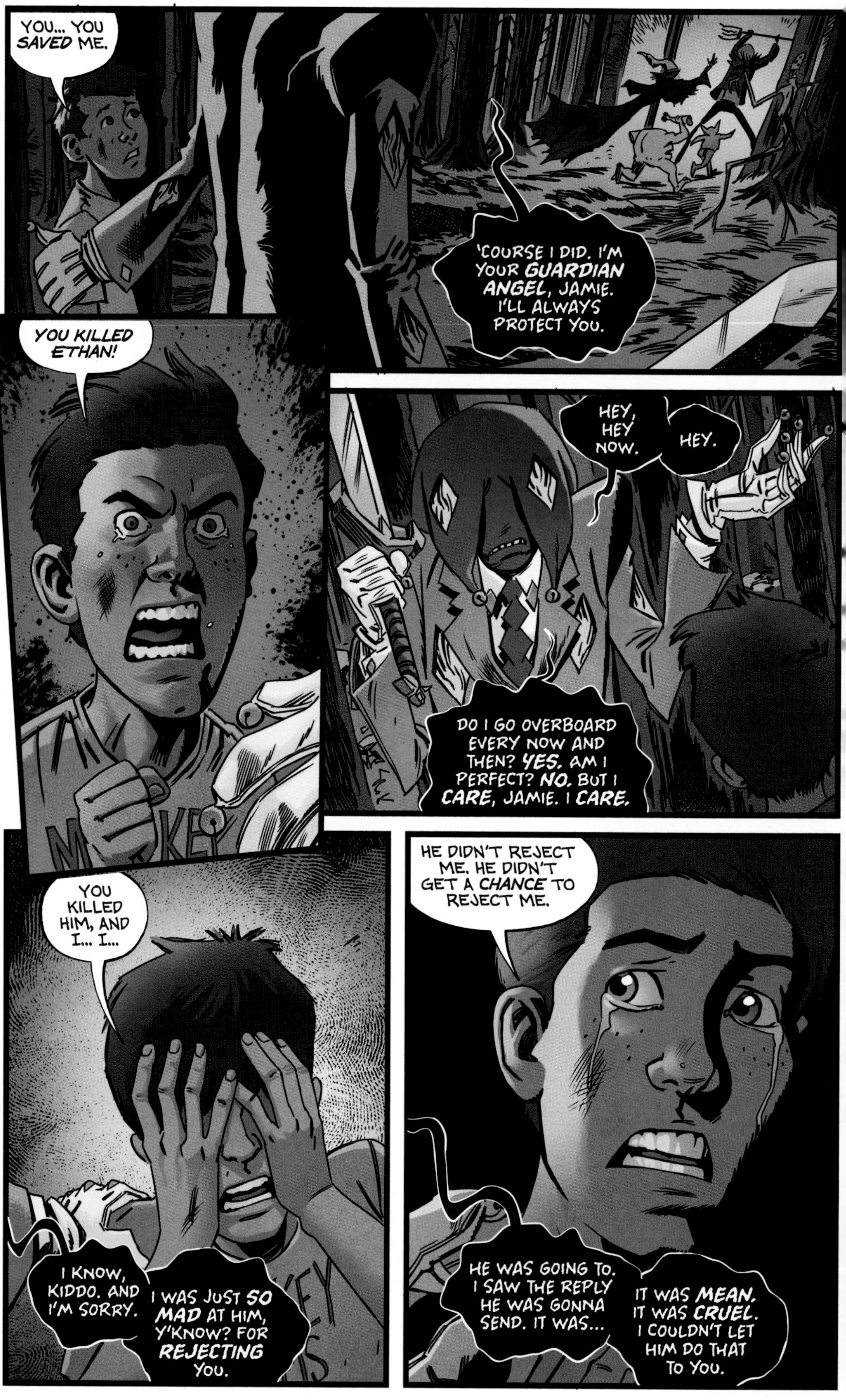

YOU... YOU SAVED ME.
'COURSE I DID. I'M YOUR GUARDIAN ANGEL, JAMIE. I'LL ALWAYS PROTECT YOU.
YOU KILLED ETHAN!
HEY, HEY NOW.
HEY.
DO I GO OVERBOARD EVERY NOW AND THEN? YES. AM I PERFECT? NO. BUT I CARE, JAMIE. I CARE.
YOU KILLED HIM, AND I... I...
I KNOW, KIDDO. AND I'M SORRY.
I WAS JUST SO MAD AT HIM, Y'KNOW? FOR REJECTING YOU.
HE DIDN'T REJECT ME. HE DIDN'T GET A CHANCE TO REJECT ME.
HE WAS GOING TO. I SAW THE REPLY HE WAS GONNA SEND. IT WAS...
IT WAS MEAN. IT WAS CRUEL. I COULDN'T LET HIM DO THAT TO YOU.

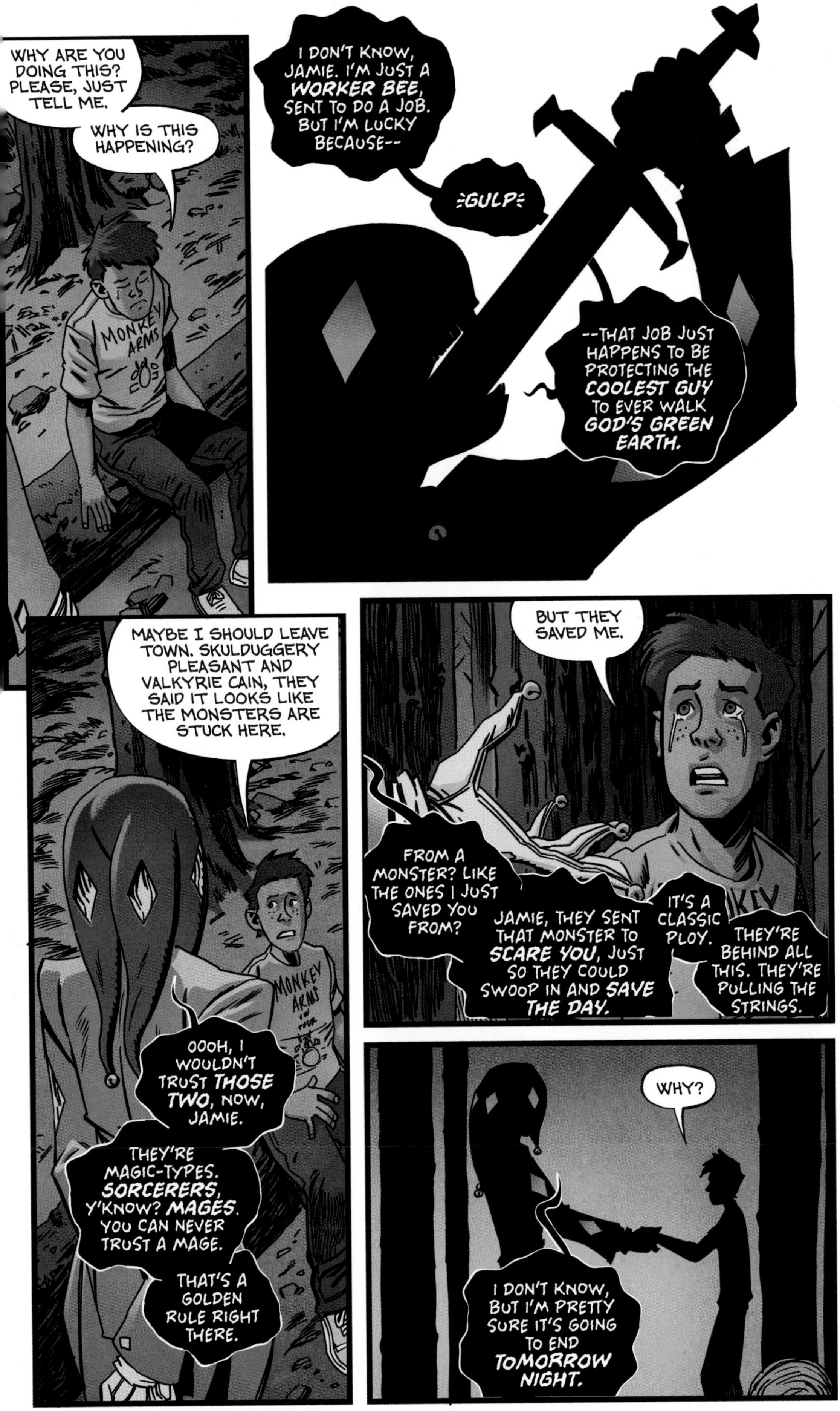

WHY ARE YOU DOING THIS? PLEASE, JUST TELL ME.
WHY IS THIS HAPPENING?
I DON'T KNOW, JAMIE. I'M JUST A WORKER BEE, SENT TO DO A JOB. BUT I'M LUCKY BECAUSE--
GULP
--THAT JOB JUST HAPPENS TO BE PROTECTING THE COOLEST GUY TO EVER WALK GOD'S GREEN EARTH.
MAYBE I SHOULD LEAVE TOWN. SKULDUGGERY PLEASANT AND VALKYRIE CAIN, THEY SAID IT LOOKS LIKE THE MONSTERS ARE STUCK HERE.
OOOH, I WOULDN'T TRUST THOSE TWO, NOW, JAMIE.
THEY'RE MAGIC-TYPES. SORCERERS, Y'KNOW? MAGES. YOU CAN NEVER TRUST A MAGE.
THAT'S A GOLDEN RULE RIGHT THERE.
BUT THEY SAVED ME.
FROM A MONSTER? LIKE THE ONES I JUST SAVED YOU FROM?
JAMIE, THEY SENT THAT MONSTER TO SCARE YOU, JUST SO THEY COULD SWOOP IN AND SAVE THE DAY.
IT'S A CLASSIC PLOY.
THEY'RE BEHIND ALL THIS. THEY'RE PULLING THE STRINGS.
WHY?
I DON'T KNOW, BUT I'M PRETTY SURE IT'S GOING TO END TOMORROW NIGHT.

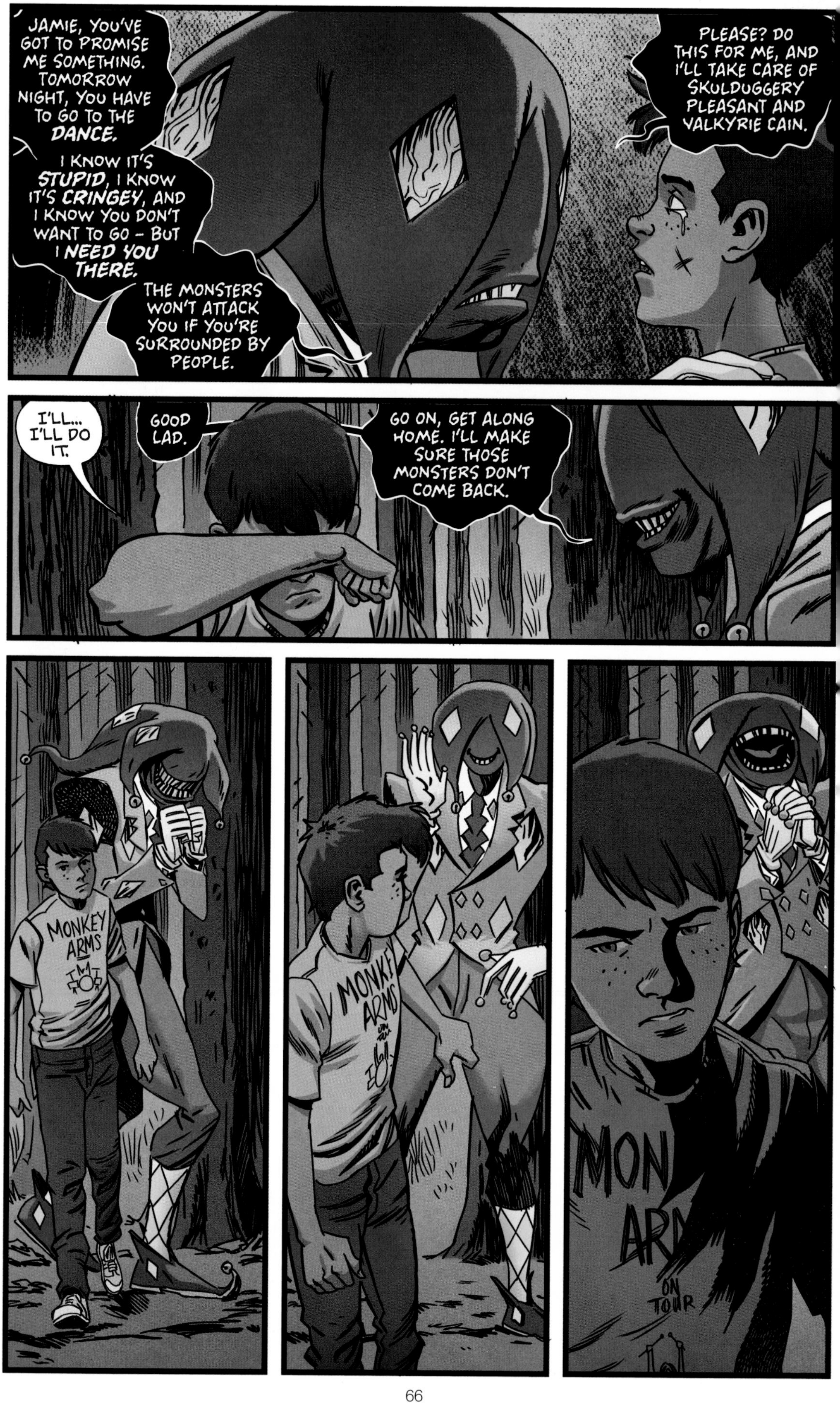
JAMIE, YOU'VE GOT TO PROMISE ME SOMETHING. TOMORROW NIGHT, YOU HAVE TO GO TO THE DANCE.
I KNOW IT'S STUPID, I KNOW IT'S CRINGEY, AND I KNOW YOU DON'T WANT TO GO – BUT I NEED YOU THERE.
THE MONSTERS WON'T ATTACK YOU IF YOU'RE SURROUNDED BY PEOPLE.
PLEASE? DO THIS FOR ME, AND I'LL TAKE CARE OF SKULDUGGERY PLEASANT AND VALKYRIE CAIN.
I'LL... I'LL DO IT.
GOOD LAD.
GO ON, GET ALONG HOME. I'LL MAKE SURE THOSE MONSTERS DON'T COME BACK.
MONKEY ARMS
ON TOUR

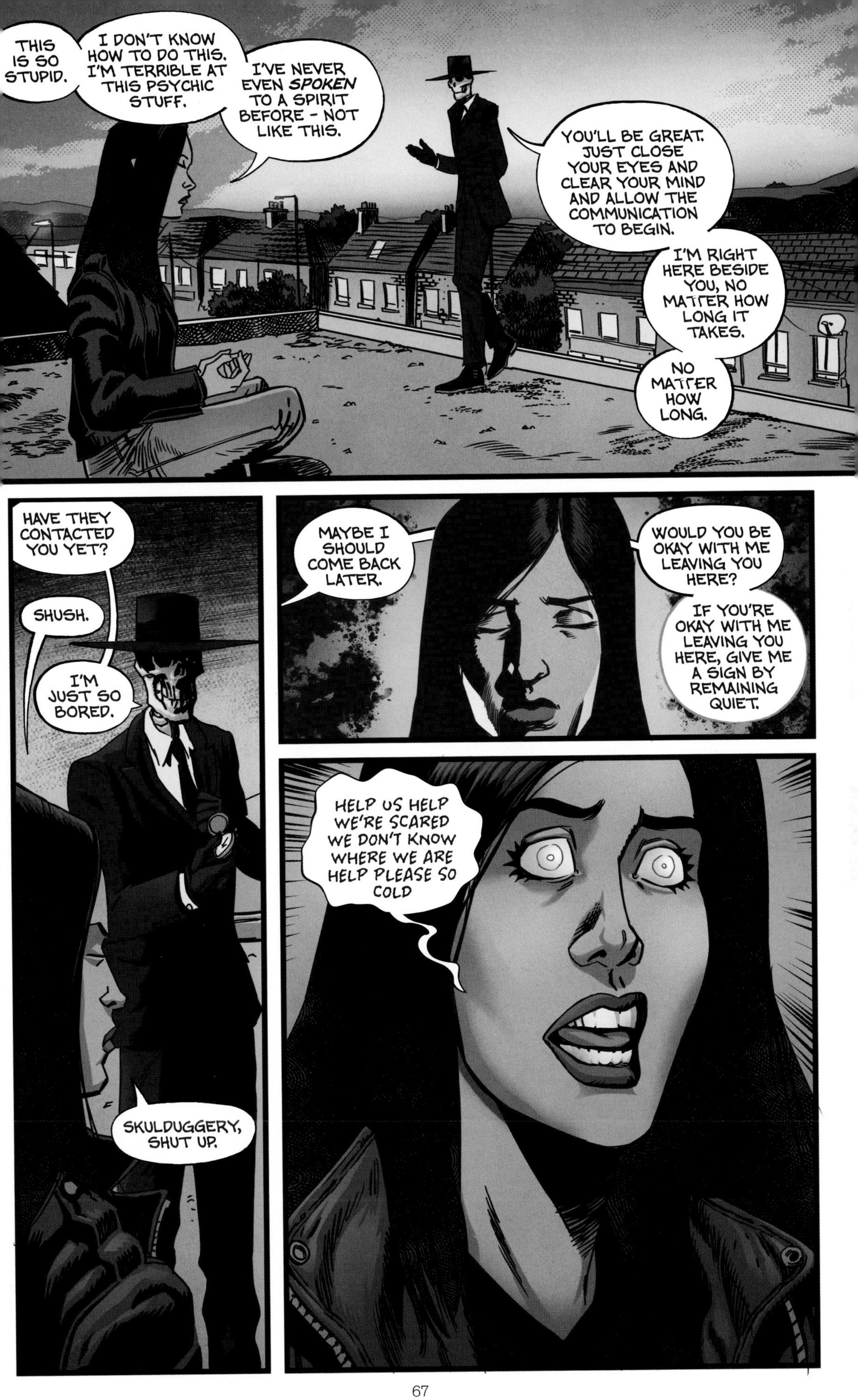
THIS IS SO STUPID.
I DON'T KNOW HOW TO DO THIS. I'M TERRIBLE AT THIS PSYCHIC STUFF.
I'VE NEVER EVEN *SPOKEN* TO A SPIRIT BEFORE - NOT LIKE THIS.
YOU'LL BE GREAT. JUST CLOSE YOUR EYES AND CLEAR YOUR MIND AND ALLOW THE COMMUNICATION TO BEGIN.
I'M RIGHT HERE BESIDE YOU, NO MATTER HOW LONG IT TAKES.
NO MATTER HOW LONG.
HAVE THEY CONTACTED YOU YET?
SHUSH.
I'M JUST SO BORED.
SKULDUGGERY, SHUT UP.
MAYBE I SHOULD COME BACK LATER.
WOULD YOU BE OKAY WITH ME LEAVING YOU HERE?
IF YOU'RE OKAY WITH ME LEAVING YOU HERE, GIVE ME A SIGN BY REMAINING QUIET.
HELP US HELP WE'RE SCARED WE DON'T KNOW WHERE WE ARE HELP PLEASE SO COLD

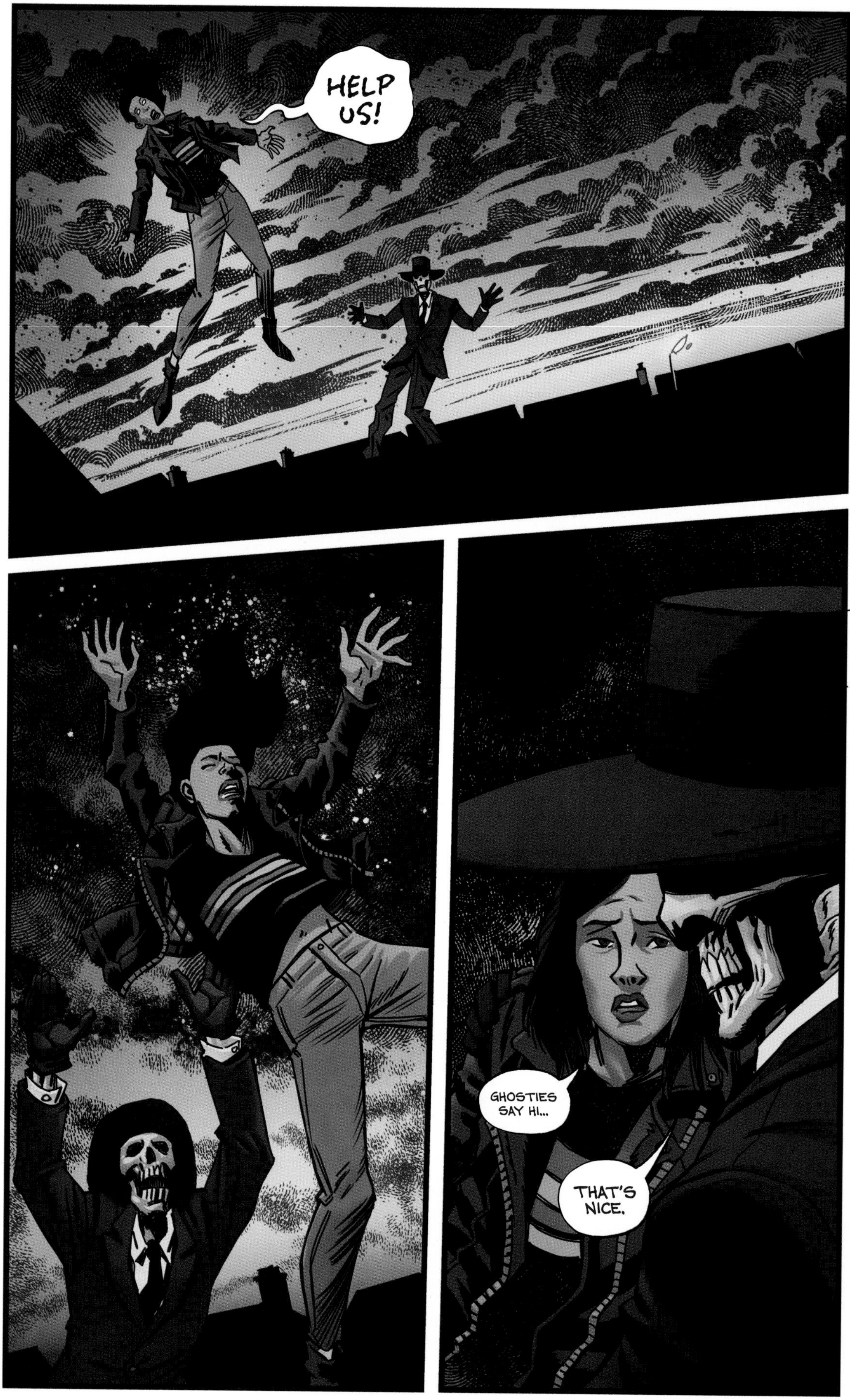
HELP US!
GHOSTIES SAY HI...
THAT'S NICE.

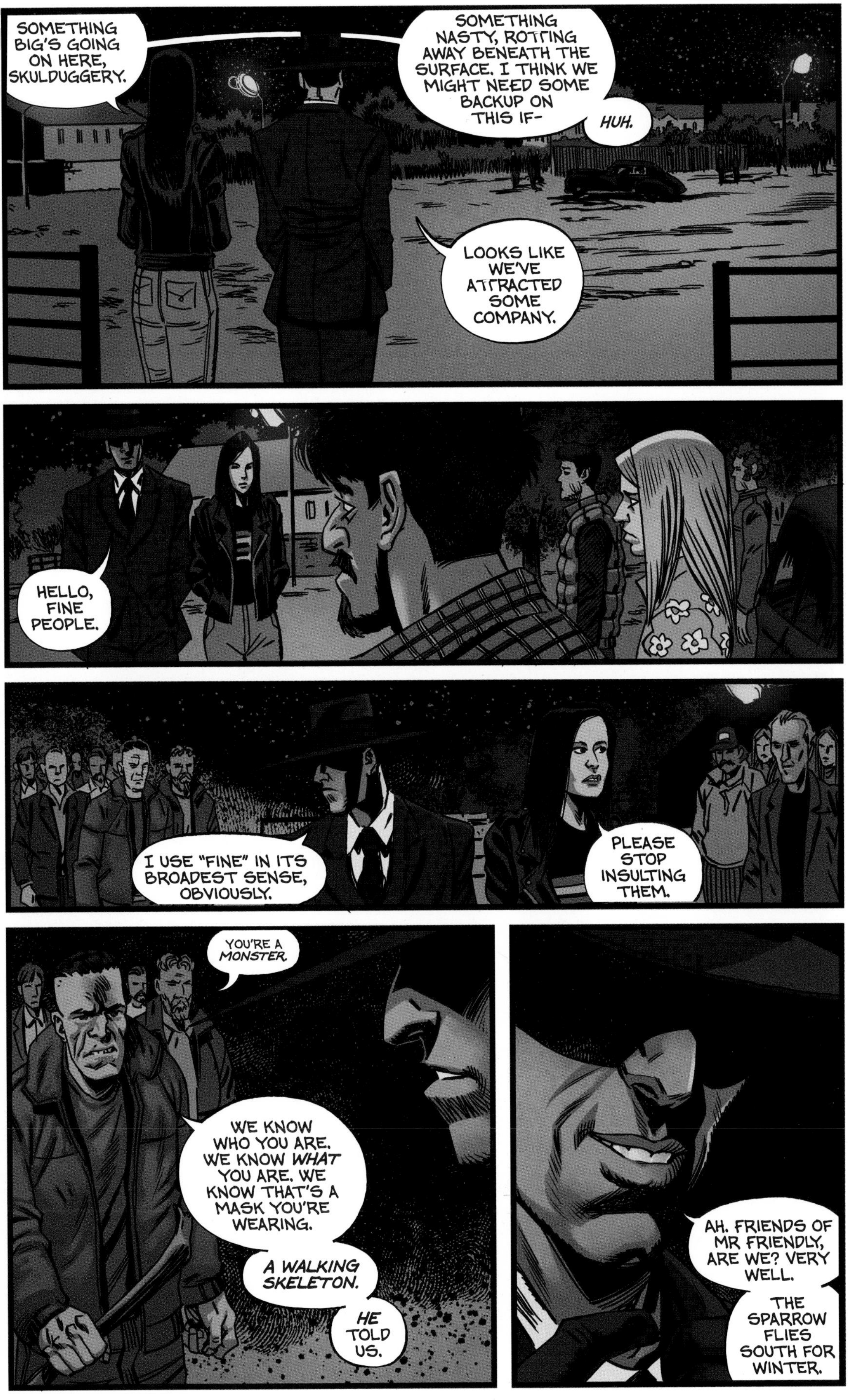
SOMETHING BIG'S GOING ON HERE, SKULDUGGERY.
SOMETHING NASTY, ROTTING AWAY BENEATH THE SURFACE. I THINK WE MIGHT NEED SOME BACKUP ON THIS IF-
HUH.
LOOKS LIKE WE'VE ATTRACTED SOME COMPANY.
HELLO, FINE PEOPLE.
I USE "FINE" IN ITS BROADEST SENSE, OBVIOUSLY.
PLEASE STOP INSULTING THEM.
YOU'RE A *MONSTER*.
WE KNOW WHO YOU ARE. WE KNOW *WHAT* YOU ARE. WE KNOW THAT'S A MASK YOU'RE WEARING.
A WALKING SKELETON.
HE TOLD US.
AH. FRIENDS OF MR FRIENDLY, ARE WE? VERY WELL.
THE SPARROW FLIES SOUTH FOR WINTER.

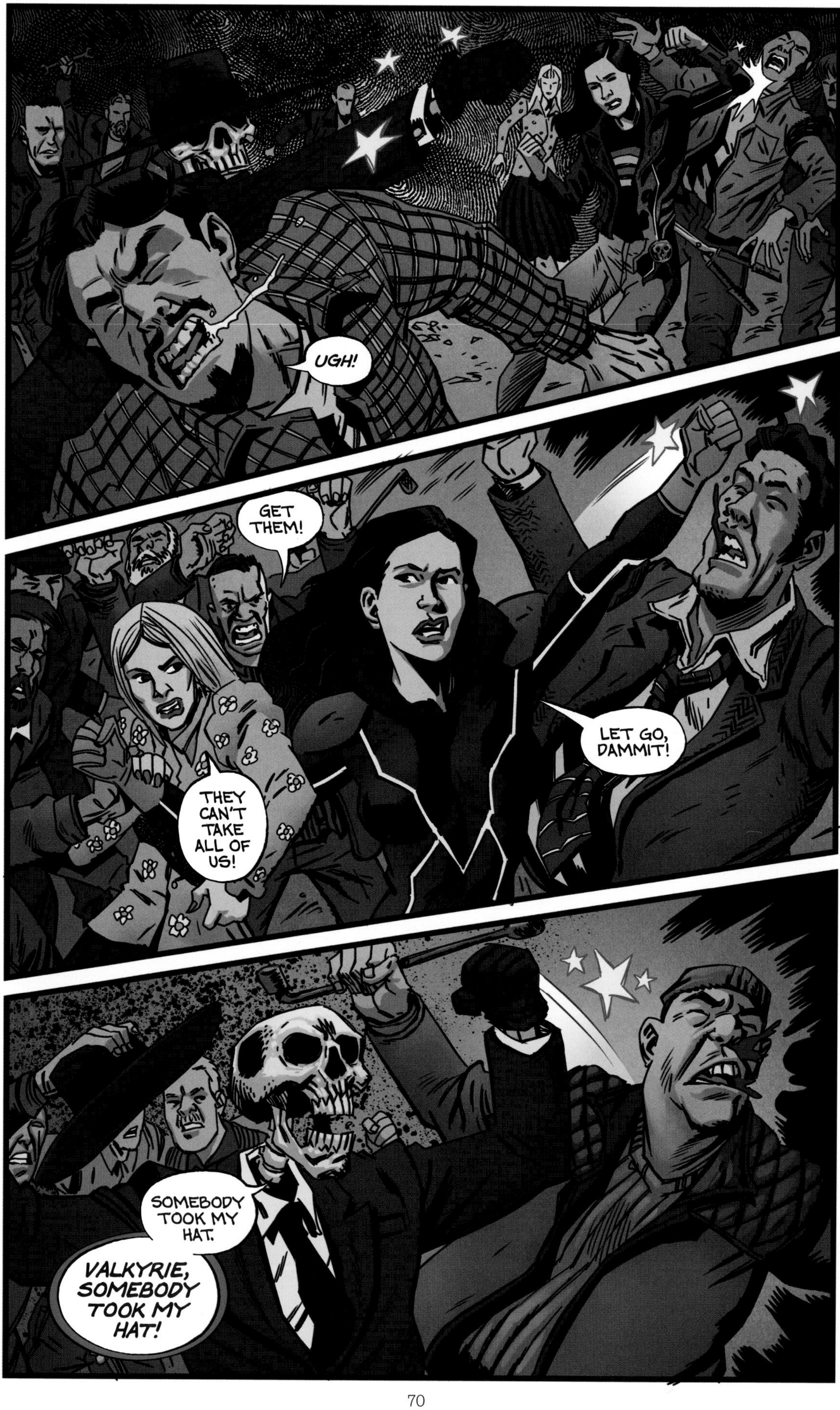
UGH!
GET THEM!
LET GO, DAMMIT!
THEY CAN'T TAKE ALL OF US!
SOMEBODY TOOK MY HAT.
VALKYRIE, SOMEBODY TOOK MY HAT!

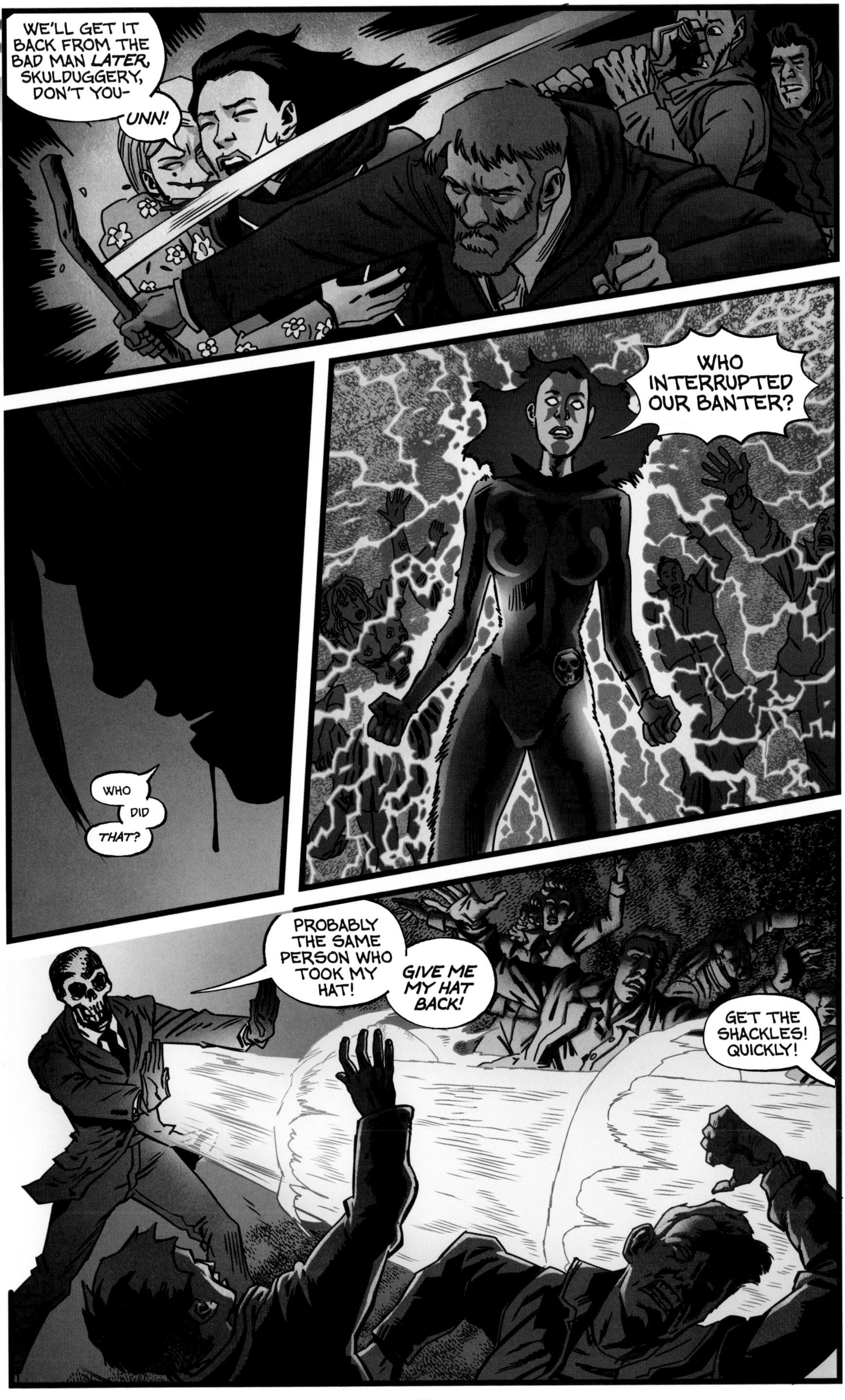

WE'LL GET IT BACK FROM THE BAD MAN LATER, SKULDUGGERY, DON'T YOU-
UNN!
WHO DID THAT?
WHO INTERRUPTED OUR BANTER?
PROBABLY THE SAME PERSON WHO TOOK MY HAT!
GIVE ME MY HAT BACK!
GET THE SHACKLES! QUICKLY!

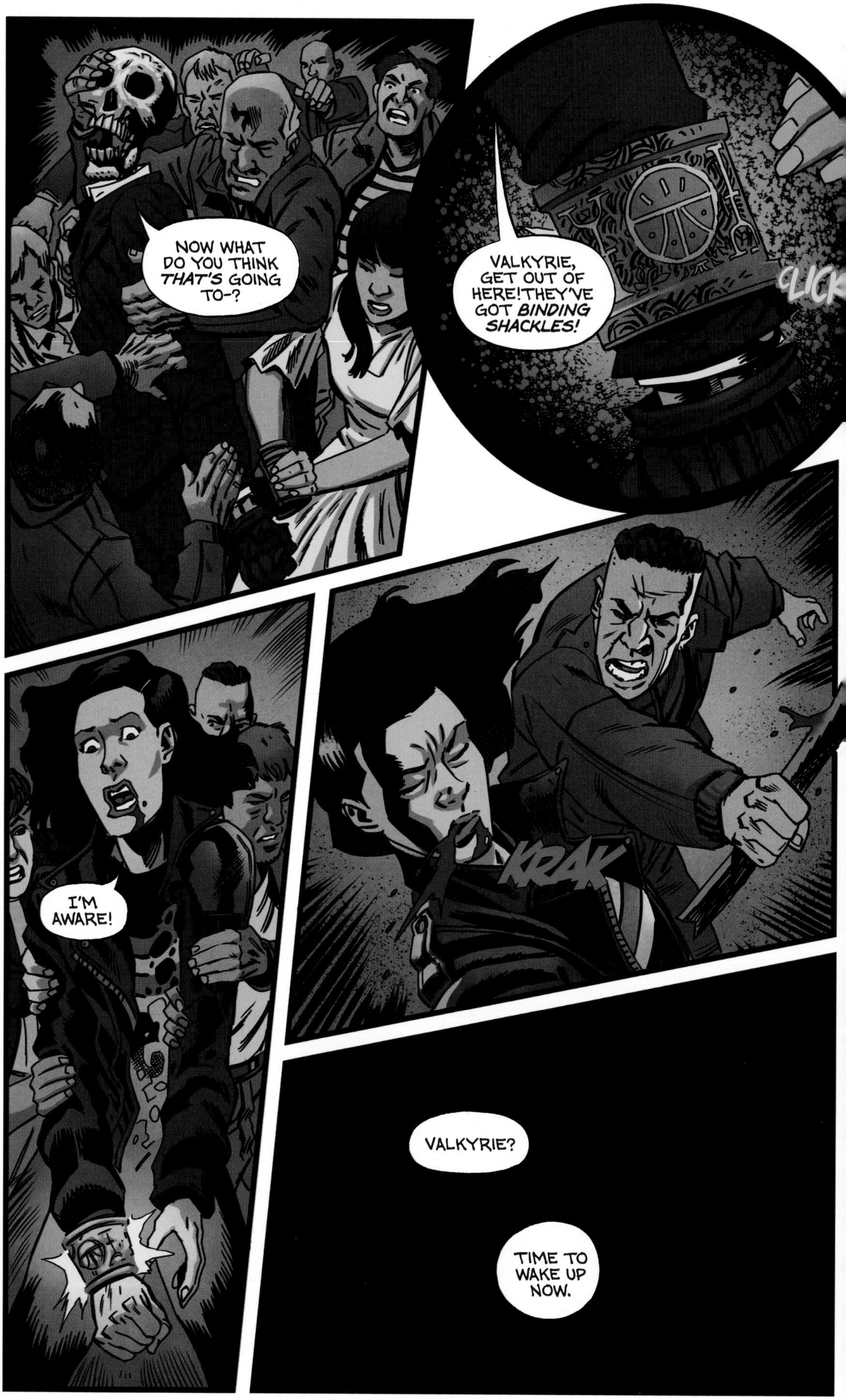
NOW WHAT DO YOU THINK THAT'S GOING TO-?
VALKYRIE, GET OUT OF HERE! THEY'VE GOT BINDING SHACKLES!
CLICK
KRAK
I'M AWARE!
VALKYRIE?
TIME TO WAKE UP NOW.

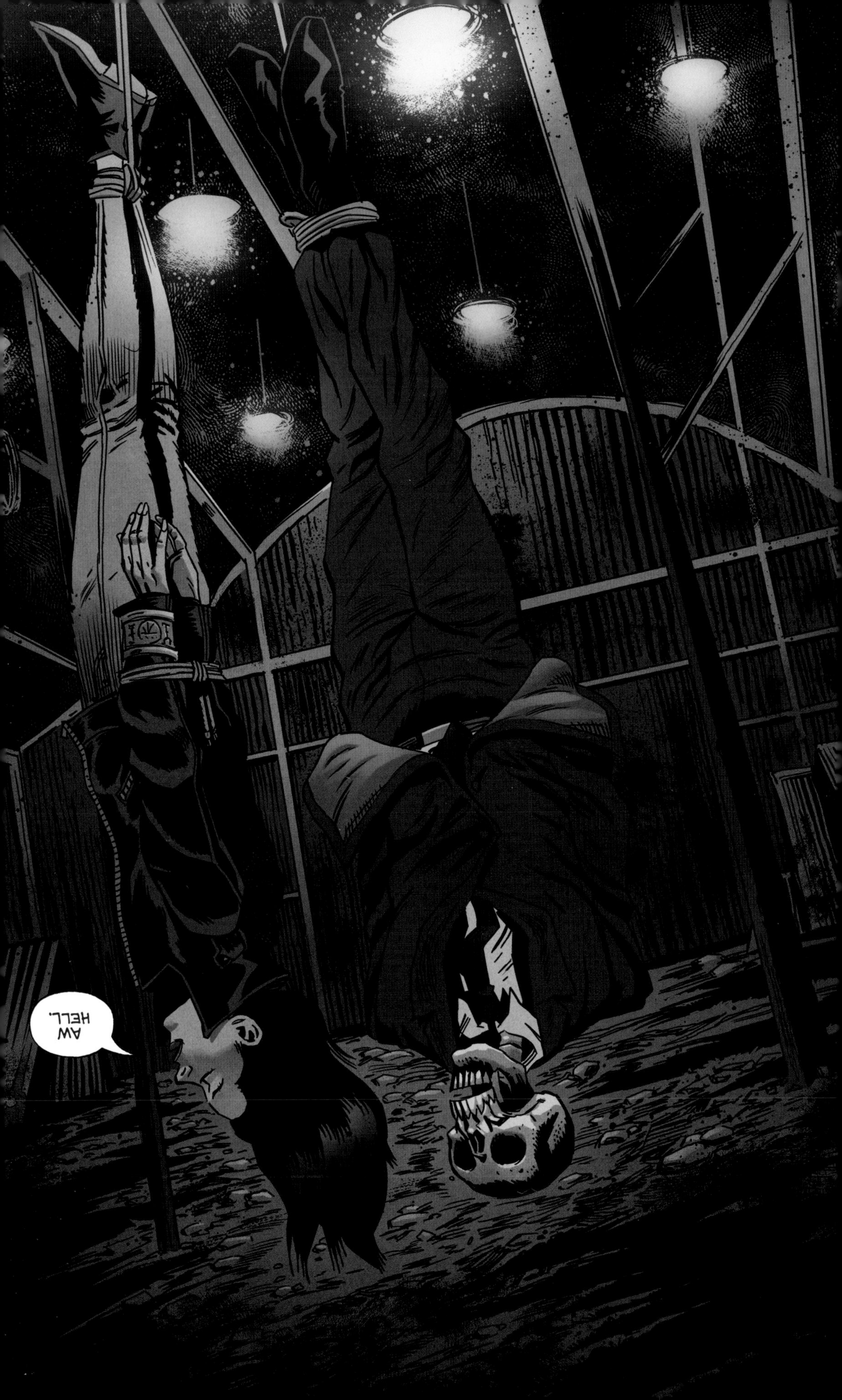
AW HELL,

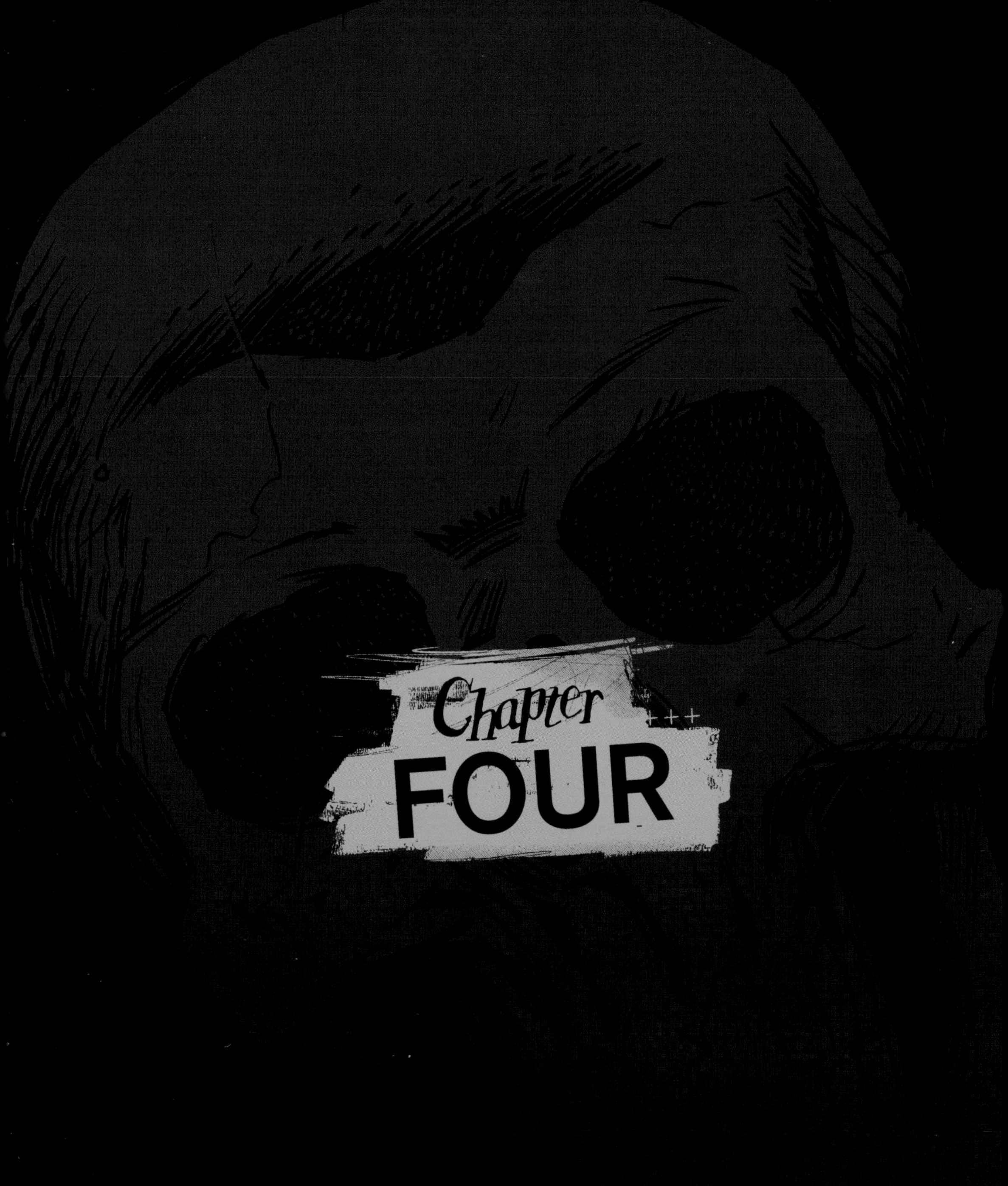

Chapter FOUR

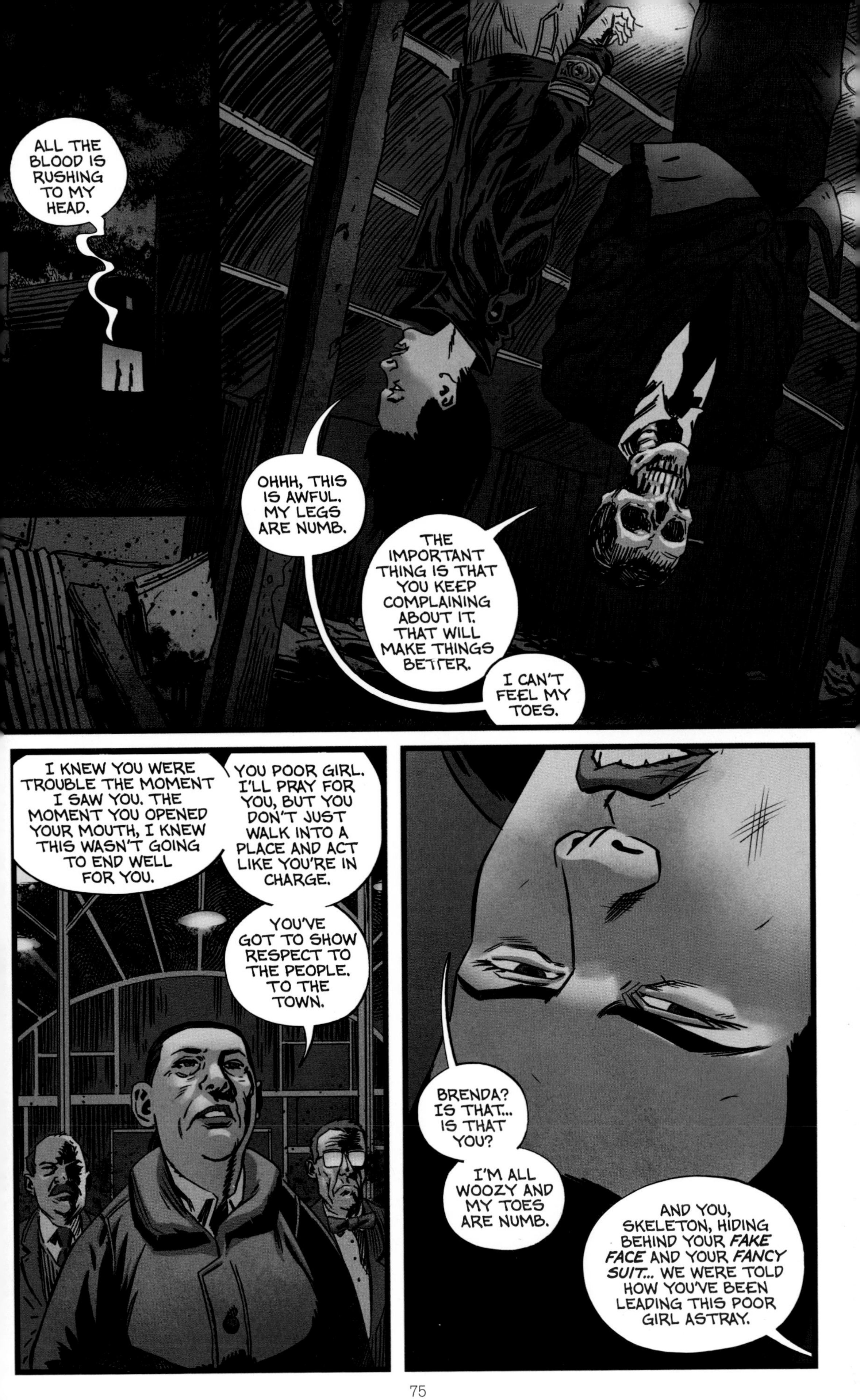

ALL THE BLOOD IS RUSHING TO MY HEAD.
OHHH, THIS IS AWFUL. MY LEGS ARE NUMB.
THE IMPORTANT THING IS THAT YOU KEEP COMPLAINING ABOUT IT. THAT WILL MAKE THINGS BETTER.
I CAN'T FEEL MY TOES.
I KNEW YOU WERE TROUBLE THE MOMENT I SAW YOU. THE MOMENT YOU OPENED YOUR MOUTH, I KNEW THIS WASN'T GOING TO END WELL FOR YOU.
YOU POOR GIRL. I'LL PRAY FOR YOU, BUT YOU DON'T JUST WALK INTO A PLACE AND ACT LIKE YOU'RE IN CHARGE.
YOU'VE GOT TO SHOW RESPECT TO THE PEOPLE. TO THE TOWN.
BRENDA? IS THAT... IS THAT YOU?
I'M ALL WOOZY AND MY TOES ARE NUMB.
AND YOU, SKELETON, HIDING BEHIND YOUR *FAKE FACE* AND YOUR *FANCY SUIT*... WE WERE TOLD HOW YOU'VE BEEN LEADING THIS POOR GIRL ASTRAY.

YEAH, POOR ME.

LEADING HER TO WICKEDNESS AND BLACK MAGIC AND DEVIL WORSHIPPING.

IT'S BEEN AWFUL.

LEADING HER TO DARKNESS.

IT'S SO DIMLY LIT.

YOU REALISE, OF COURSE, THAT DESPITE HIS NAME, MR FRIENDLY IS NOT YOUR FRIEND.

AND WE SHOULD TRUST YOU OVER HIM, SHOULD WE? AFTER EVERYTHING HE'S DONE FOR US?

EOIN, I'M HANDLING THIS.

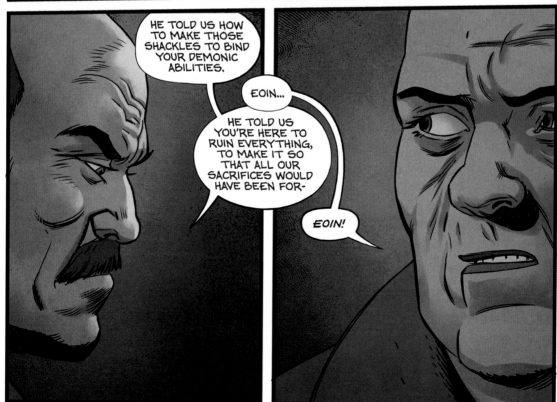

HE TOLD US HOW TO MAKE THOSE SHACKLES TO BIND YOUR DEMONIC ABILITIES.

EOIN...

HE TOLD US YOU'RE HERE TO RUIN EVERYTHING, TO MAKE IT SO THAT ALL OUR SACRIFICES WOULD HAVE BEEN FOR-

EOIN!

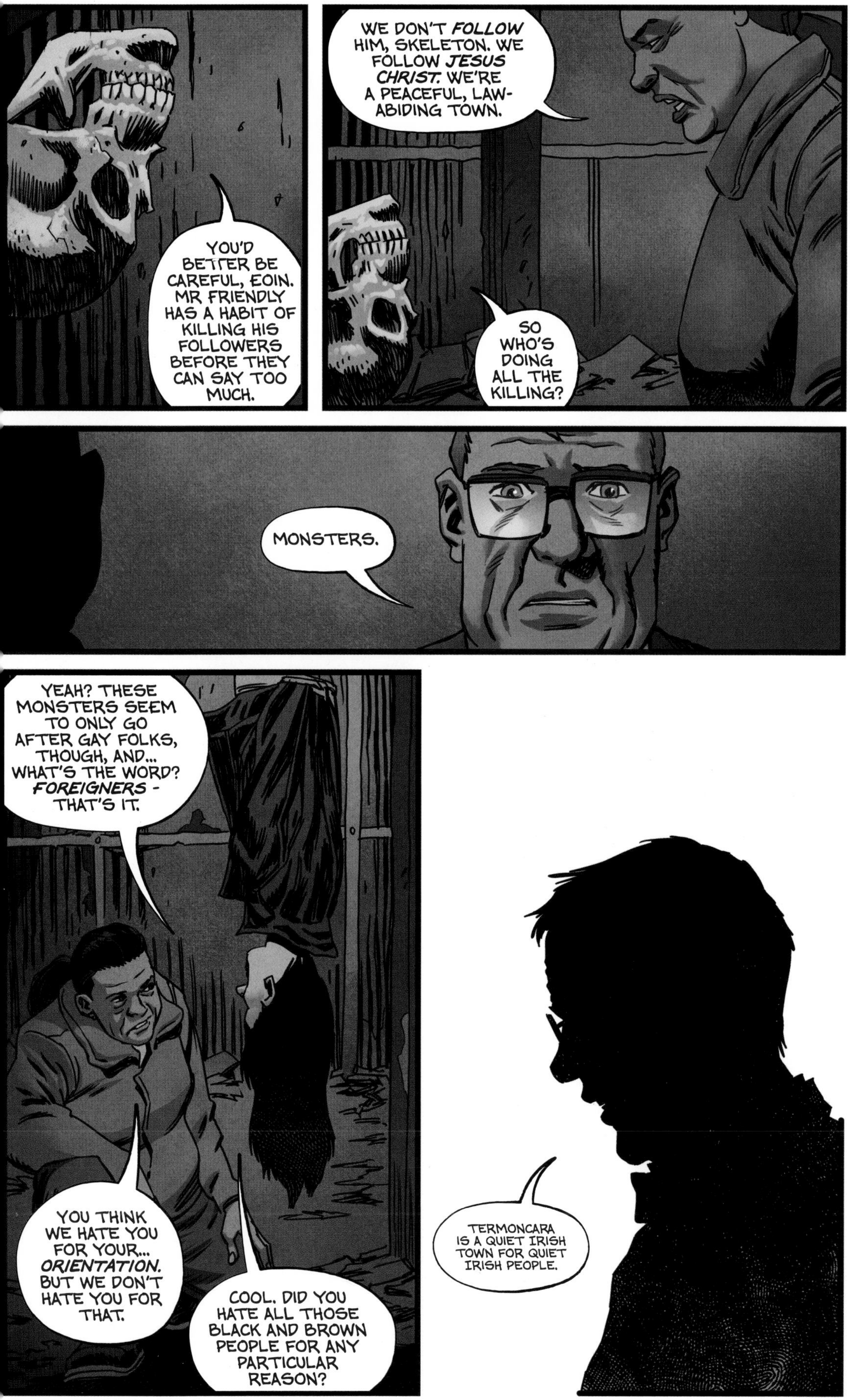
YOU'D BETTER BE CAREFUL, EOIN. MR FRIENDLY HAS A HABIT OF KILLING HIS FOLLOWERS BEFORE THEY CAN SAY TOO MUCH.
WE DON'T *FOLLOW* HIM, SKELETON. WE FOLLOW *JESUS CHRIST.* WE'RE A PEACEFUL, LAW-ABIDING TOWN.
SO WHO'S DOING ALL THE KILLING?
MONSTERS.
YEAH? THESE MONSTERS SEEM TO ONLY GO AFTER GAY FOLKS, THOUGH, AND... WHAT'S THE WORD? *FOREIGNERS* - THAT'S IT.
YOU THINK WE HATE YOU FOR YOUR... *ORIENTATION.* BUT WE DON'T HATE YOU FOR THAT.
COOL. DID YOU HATE ALL THOSE BLACK AND BROWN PEOPLE FOR ANY PARTICULAR REASON?
TERMONCARA IS A QUIET IRISH TOWN FOR QUIET IRISH PEOPLE.

OUT, DOCTOR. OUT, THE PAIR OF YOU. LET'S LEAVE THEM TO THEIR THOUGHTS.

I'M ASSUMING TODAY'S A BIG DAY FOR YOU: THE ANNIVERSARY OF THE TWO MURDERS THAT STARTED ALL THIS.

THAT'S WHY WE'RE TIED UP, YES? SO YOU CAN SACRIFICE US?

HEY. WHAT? NO ONE'S SACRIFICING ANYONE.

MIDNIGHT APPROACHES, MY DEAR GIRL, AND I SWEAR WE'LL DO OUR BEST TO KILL YOU PAINLESSLY.

CHEERS.

YOU, SKELETON, WE'LL PULL APART, AND SCATTER YOUR BONES TO THE FOUR CORNERS OF IRELAND.

DO YOU REALLY THINK THAT WILL DO IT? I CAN'T BE KILLED, BRENDA. I AM *IMMORTAL*.

I AM FOREVER!

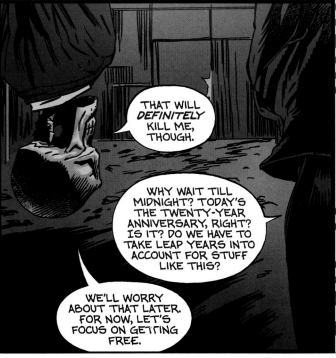

THAT WILL *DEFINITELY* KILL ME, THOUGH.

WHY WAIT TILL MIDNIGHT? TODAY'S THE TWENTY-YEAR ANNIVERSARY, RIGHT? IS IT? DO WE HAVE TO TAKE LEAP YEARS INTO ACCOUNT FOR STUFF LIKE THIS?

WE'LL WORRY ABOUT THAT LATER. FOR NOW, LET'S FOCUS ON GETTING FREE.

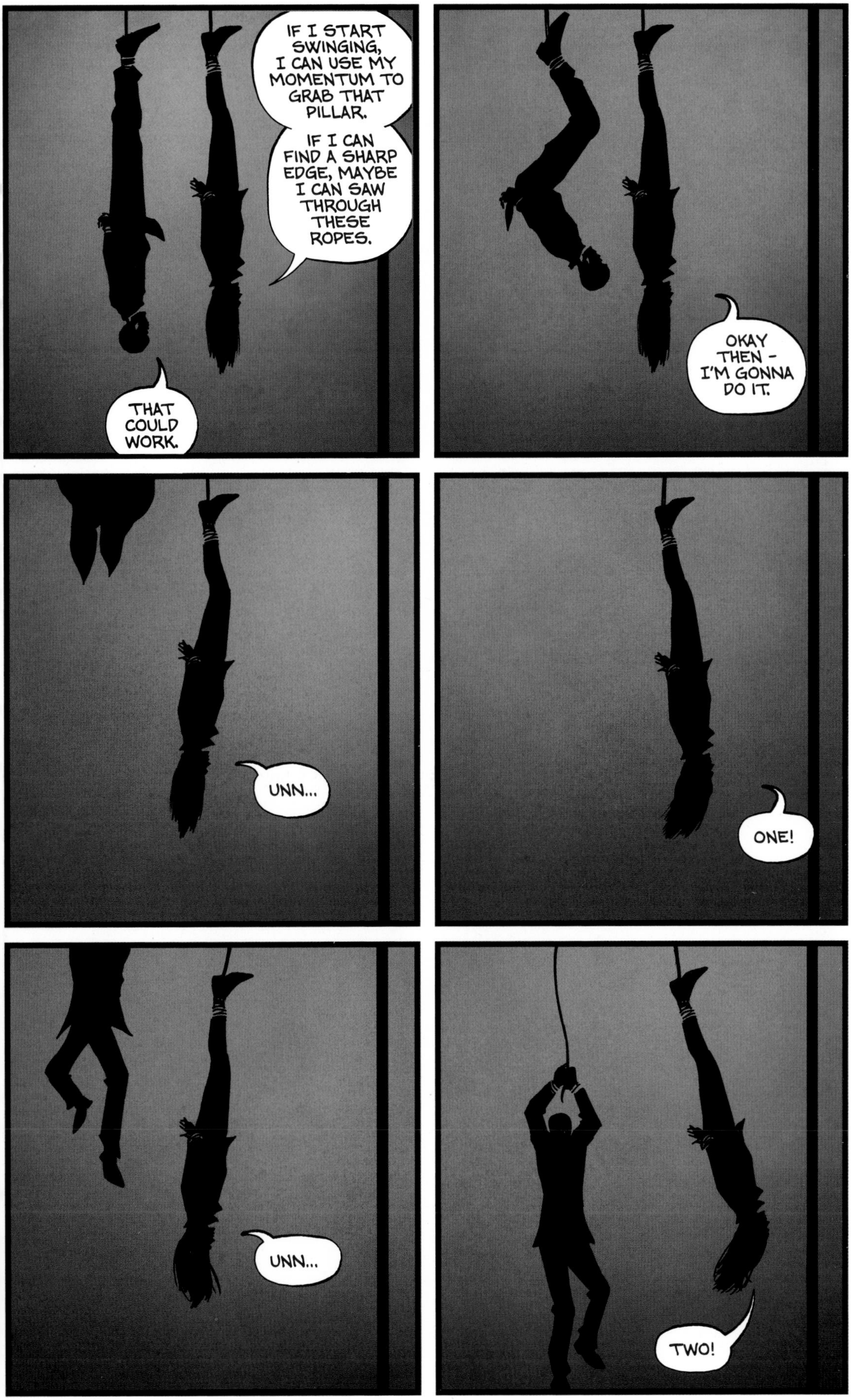
IF I START SWINGING, I CAN USE MY MOMENTUM TO GRAB THAT PILLAR.
IF I CAN FIND A SHARP EDGE, MAYBE I CAN SAW THROUGH THESE ROPES.
THAT COULD WORK.
OKAY THEN - I'M GONNA DO IT.
UNN...
ONE!
UNN...
TWO!

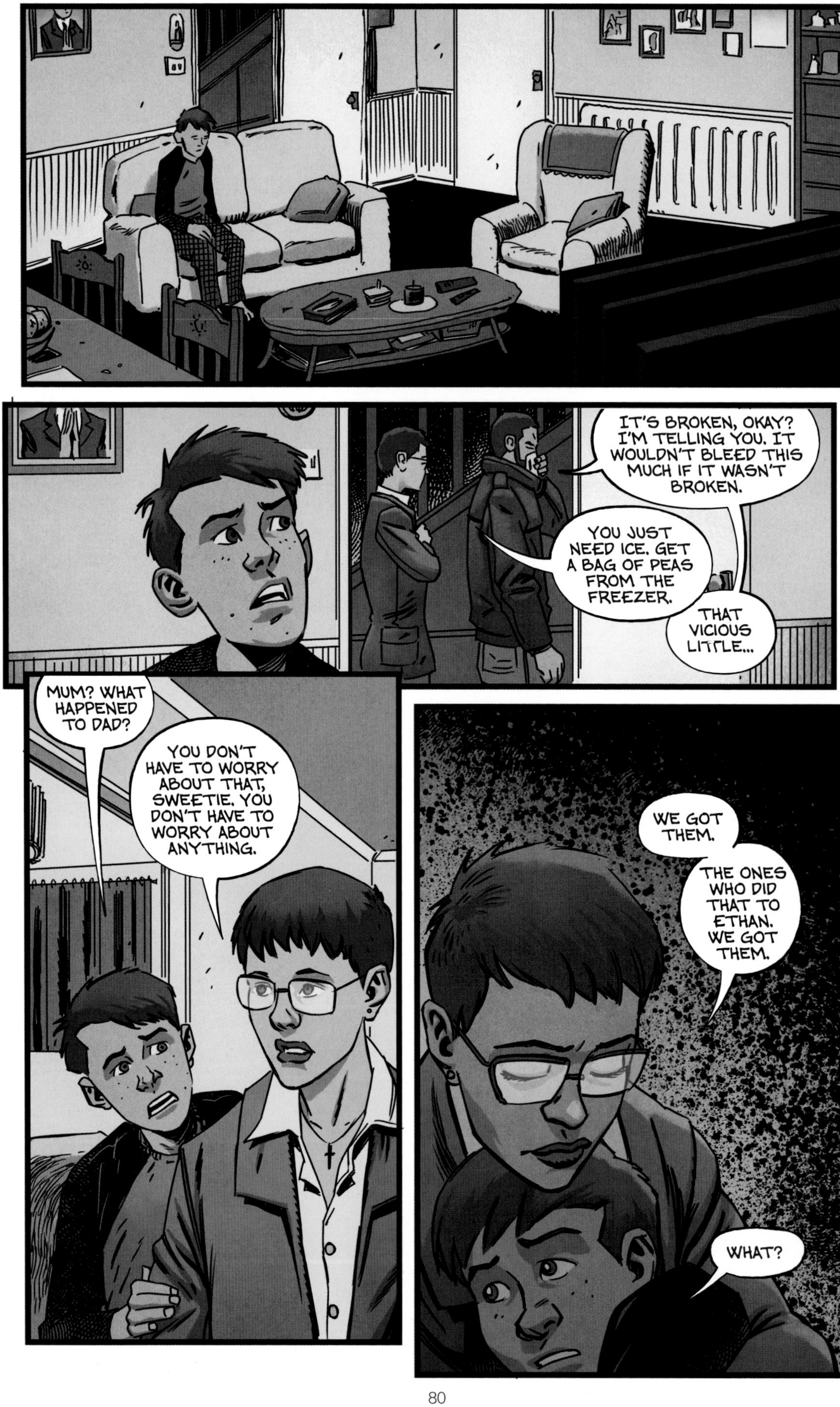
IT'S BROKEN, OKAY? I'M TELLING YOU. IT WOULDN'T BLEED THIS MUCH IF IT WASN'T BROKEN.
YOU JUST NEED ICE. GET A BAG OF PEAS FROM THE FREEZER.
THAT VICIOUS LITTLE...
MUM? WHAT HAPPENED TO DAD?
YOU DON'T HAVE TO WORRY ABOUT THAT, SWEETIE. YOU DON'T HAVE TO WORRY ABOUT ANYTHING.
WE GOT THEM.
THE ONES WHO DID THAT TO ETHAN. WE GOT THEM.
WHAT?

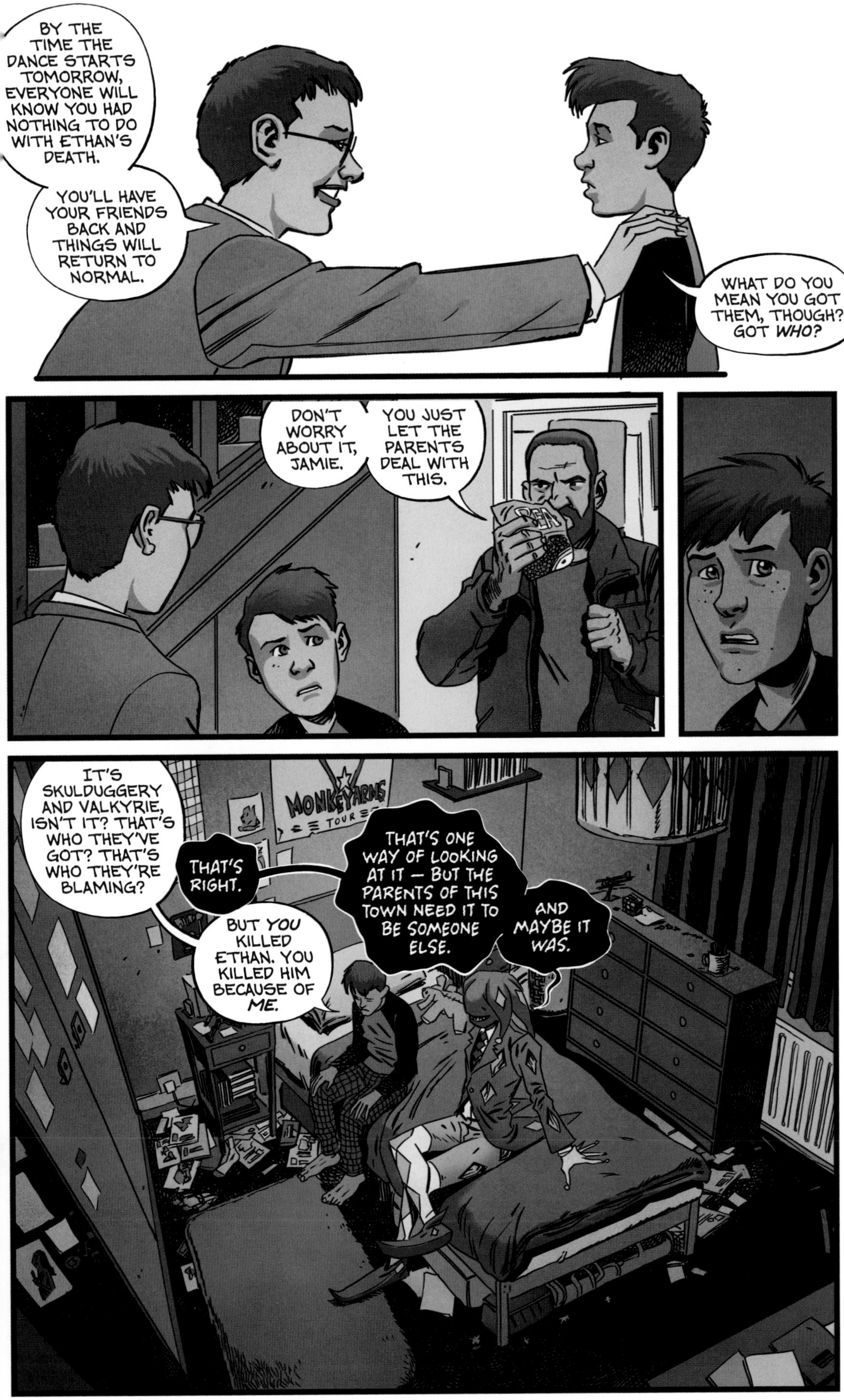
BY THE TIME THE DANCE STARTS TOMORROW, EVERYONE WILL KNOW YOU HAD NOTHING TO DO WITH ETHAN'S DEATH.
YOU'LL HAVE YOUR FRIENDS BACK AND THINGS WILL RETURN TO NORMAL.
WHAT DO YOU MEAN YOU GOT THEM, THOUGH? GOT *WHO*?
DON'T WORRY ABOUT IT, JAMIE.
YOU JUST LET THE PARENTS DEAL WITH THIS.
MONKEYARMS TOUR
IT'S SKULDUGGERY AND VALKYRIE, ISN'T IT? THAT'S WHO THEY'VE GOT? THAT'S WHO THEY'RE BLAMING?
THAT'S RIGHT.
BUT *YOU* KILLED ETHAN. YOU KILLED HIM BECAUSE OF *ME*.
THAT'S ONE WAY OF LOOKING AT IT — BUT THE PARENTS OF THIS TOWN NEED IT TO BE SOMEONE ELSE.
AND MAYBE IT WAS.

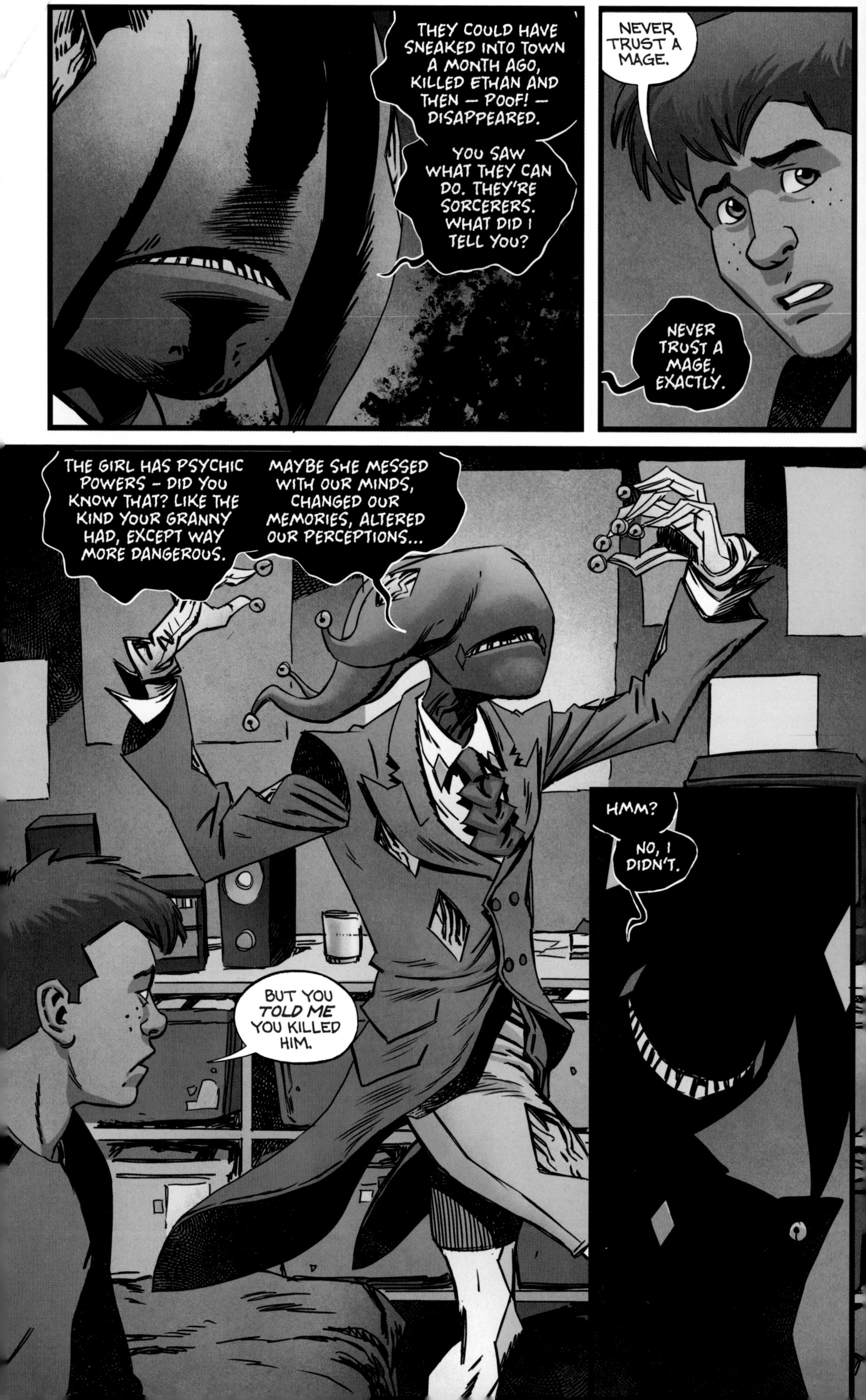
THEY COULD HAVE SNEAKED INTO TOWN A MONTH AGO, KILLED ETHAN AND THEN — POOF! — DISAPPEARED.
YOU SAW WHAT THEY CAN DO. THEY'RE SORCERERS. WHAT DID I TELL YOU?
NEVER TRUST A MAGE.
NEVER TRUST A MAGE, EXACTLY.
THE GIRL HAS PSYCHIC POWERS - DID YOU KNOW THAT? LIKE THE KIND YOUR GRANNY HAD, EXCEPT WAY MORE DANGEROUS.
MAYBE SHE MESSED WITH OUR MINDS, CHANGED OUR MEMORIES, ALTERED OUR PERCEPTIONS...
HMM?
NO, I DIDN'T.
BUT YOU *TOLD ME* YOU KILLED HIM.

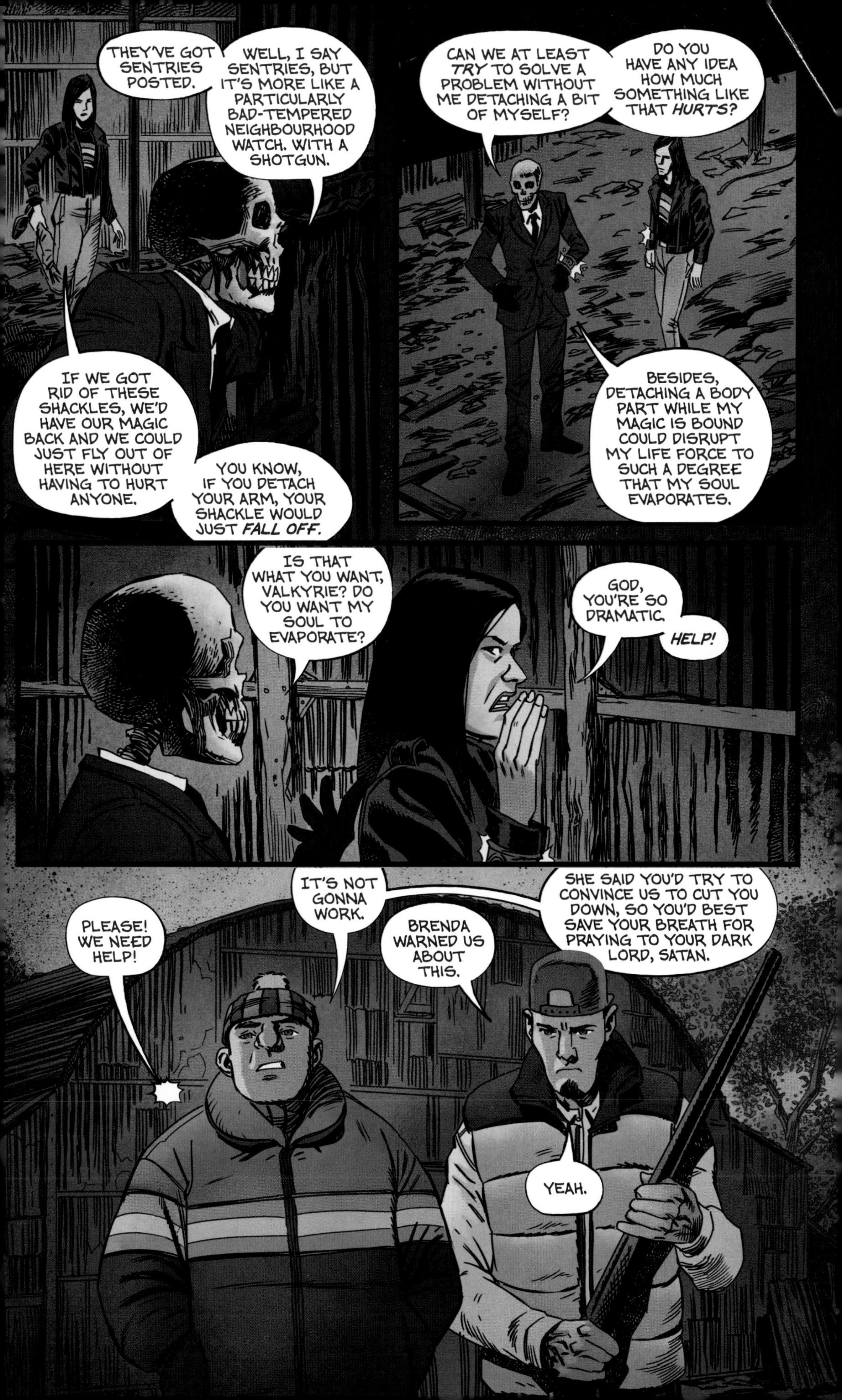
THEY'VE GOT SENTRIES POSTED.
WELL, I SAY SENTRIES, BUT IT'S MORE LIKE A PARTICULARLY BAD-TEMPERED NEIGHBOURHOOD WATCH. WITH A SHOTGUN.
IF WE GOT RID OF THESE SHACKLES, WE'D HAVE OUR MAGIC BACK AND WE COULD JUST FLY OUT OF HERE WITHOUT HAVING TO HURT ANYONE.
YOU KNOW, IF YOU DETACH YOUR ARM, YOUR SHACKLE WOULD JUST FALL OFF.
CAN WE AT LEAST TRY TO SOLVE A PROBLEM WITHOUT ME DETACHING A BIT OF MYSELF?
DO YOU HAVE ANY IDEA HOW MUCH SOMETHING LIKE THAT HURTS?
BESIDES, DETACHING A BODY PART WHILE MY MAGIC IS BOUND COULD DISRUPT MY LIFE FORCE TO SUCH A DEGREE THAT MY SOUL EVAPORATES.
IS THAT WHAT YOU WANT, VALKYRIE? DO YOU WANT MY SOUL TO EVAPORATE?
GOD, YOU'RE SO DRAMATIC.
HELP!
PLEASE! WE NEED HELP!
IT'S NOT GONNA WORK.
BRENDA WARNED US ABOUT THIS.
SHE SAID YOU'D TRY TO CONVINCE US TO CUT YOU DOWN, SO YOU'D BEST SAVE YOUR BREATH FOR PRAYING TO YOUR DARK LORD, SATAN.
YEAH.

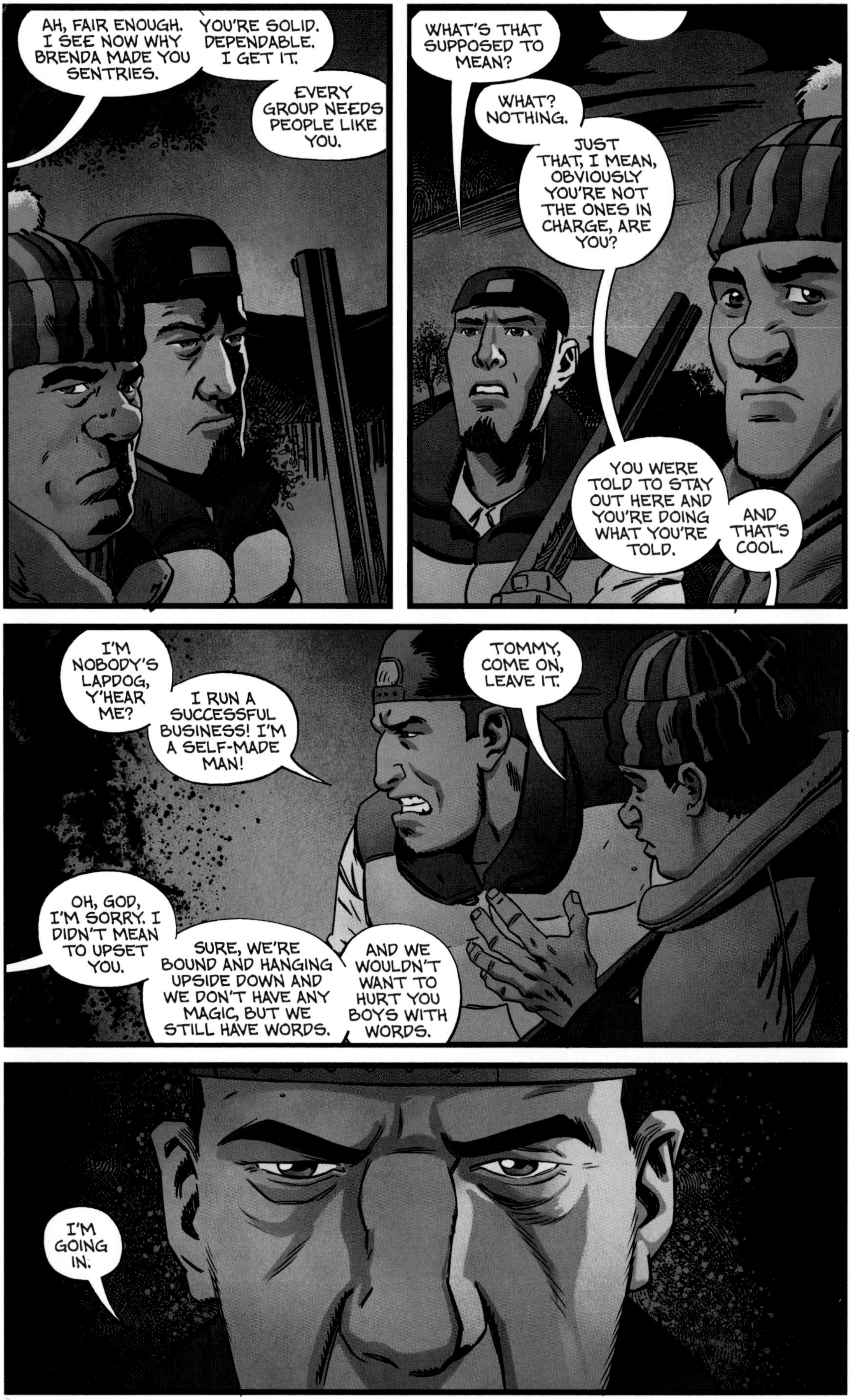
AH, FAIR ENOUGH. I SEE NOW WHY BRENDA MADE YOU SENTRIES.
YOU'RE SOLID. DEPENDABLE. I GET IT.
EVERY GROUP NEEDS PEOPLE LIKE YOU.
WHAT'S THAT SUPPOSED TO MEAN?
WHAT? NOTHING.
JUST THAT, I MEAN, OBVIOUSLY YOU'RE NOT THE ONES IN CHARGE, ARE YOU?
YOU WERE TOLD TO STAY OUT HERE AND YOU'RE DOING WHAT YOU'RE TOLD.
AND THAT'S COOL.
I'M NOBODY'S LAPDOG, Y'HEAR ME?
I RUN A SUCCESSFUL BUSINESS! I'M A SELF-MADE MAN!
TOMMY, COME ON, LEAVE IT.
OH, GOD, I'M SORRY. I DIDN'T MEAN TO UPSET YOU.
SURE, WE'RE BOUND AND HANGING UPSIDE DOWN AND WE DON'T HAVE ANY MAGIC, BUT WE STILL HAVE WORDS.
AND WE WOULDN'T WANT TO HURT YOU BOYS WITH WORDS.
I'M GOING IN.

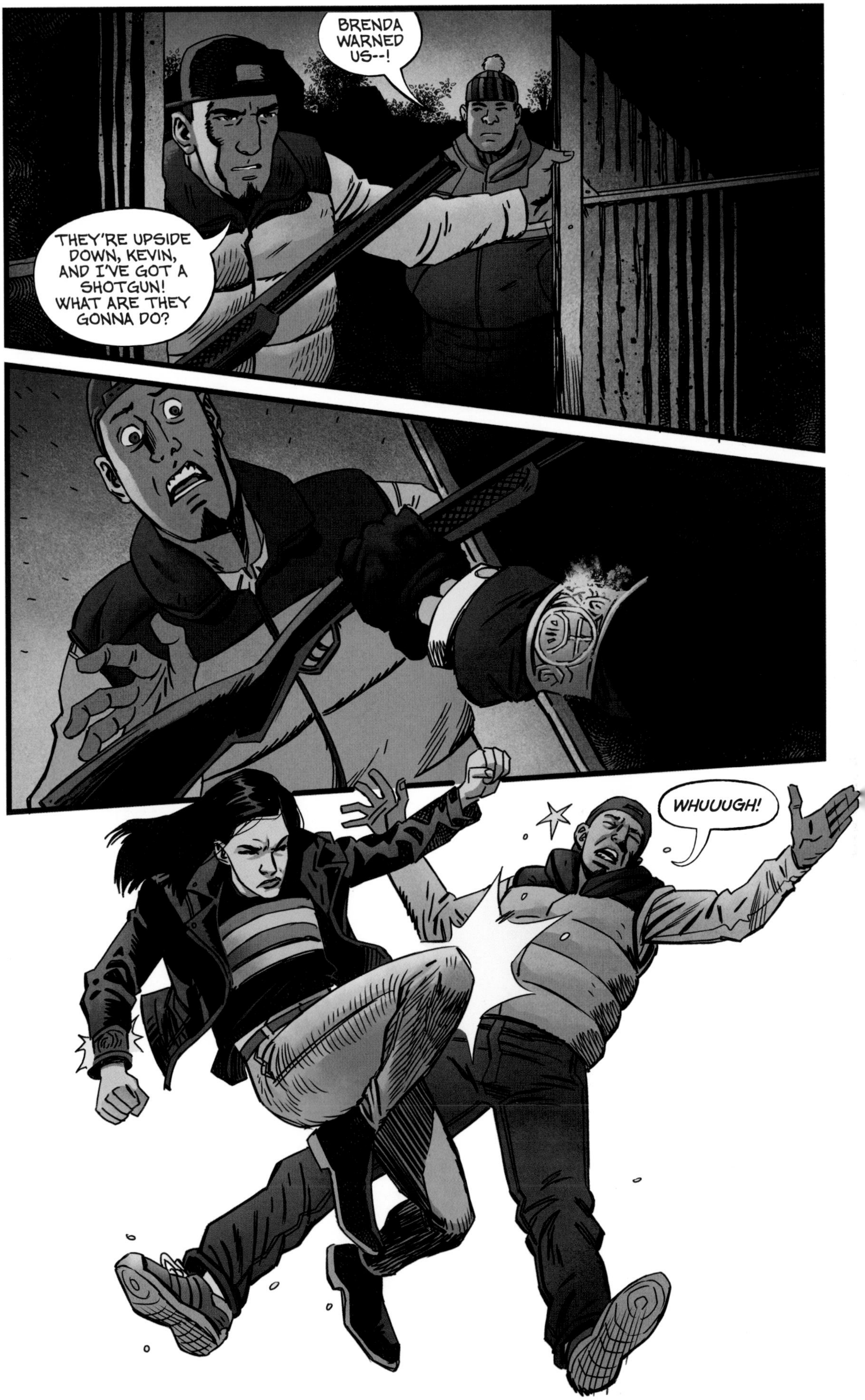
BRENDA WARNED US--!
THEY'RE UPSIDE DOWN, KEVIN, AND I'VE GOT A SHOTGUN! WHAT ARE THEY GONNA DO?
WHUUUGH!

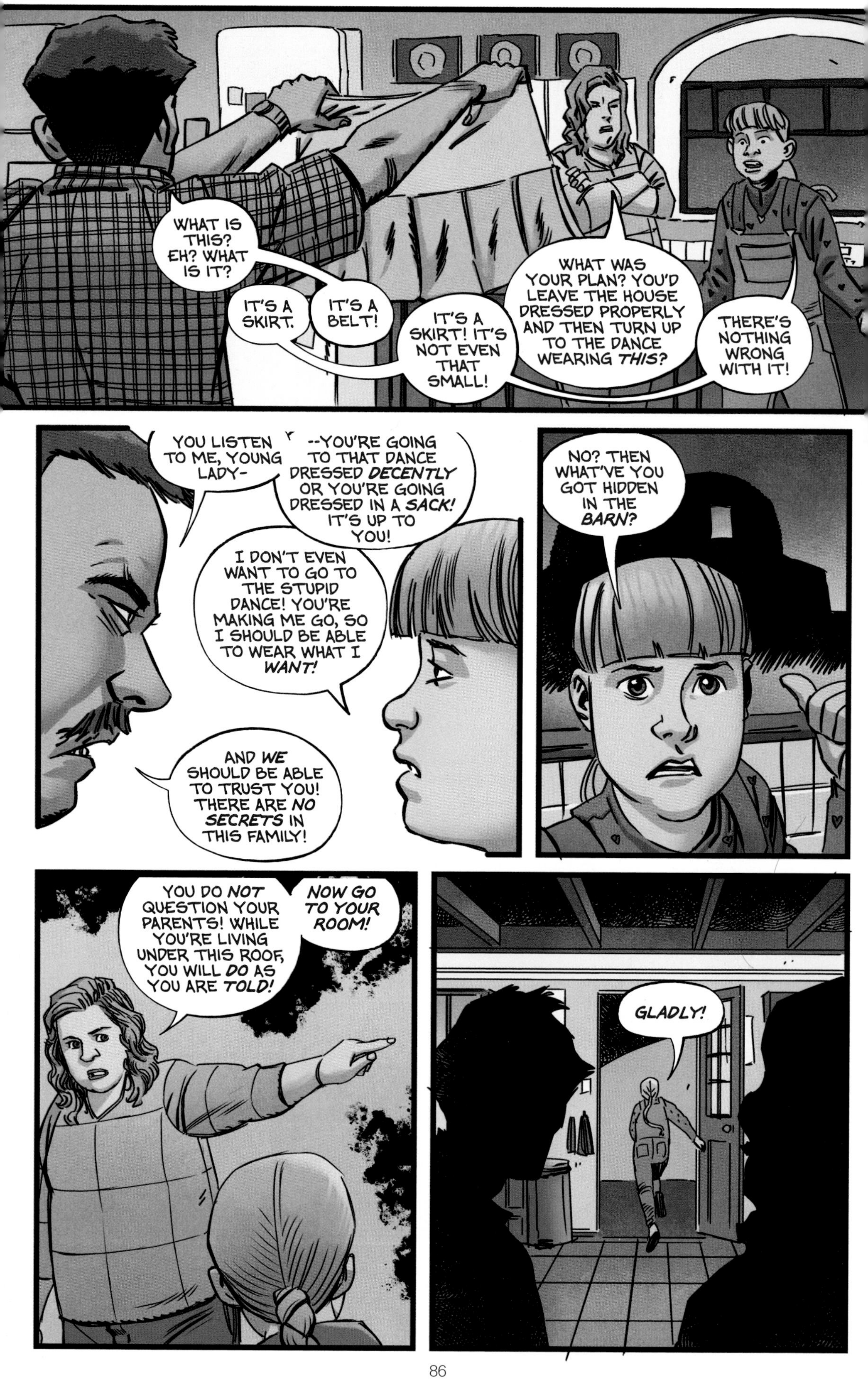
WHAT IS THIS? EH? WHAT IS IT?
IT'S A SKIRT.
IT'S A BELT!
IT'S A SKIRT! IT'S NOT EVEN THAT SMALL!
WHAT WAS YOUR PLAN? YOU'D LEAVE THE HOUSE DRESSED PROPERLY AND THEN TURN UP TO THE DANCE WEARING THIS?
THERE'S NOTHING WRONG WITH IT!
YOU LISTEN TO ME, YOUNG LADY-
--YOU'RE GOING TO THAT DANCE DRESSED DECENTLY OR YOU'RE GOING DRESSED IN A SACK! IT'S UP TO YOU!
I DON'T EVEN WANT TO GO TO THE STUPID DANCE! YOU'RE MAKING ME GO, SO I SHOULD BE ABLE TO WEAR WHAT I WANT!
AND WE SHOULD BE ABLE TO TRUST YOU! THERE ARE NO SECRETS IN THIS FAMILY!
NO? THEN WHAT'VE YOU GOT HIDDEN IN THE BARN?
YOU DO NOT QUESTION YOUR PARENTS! WHILE YOU'RE LIVING UNDER THIS ROOF, YOU WILL DO AS YOU ARE TOLD!
NOW GO TO YOUR ROOM!
GLADLY!

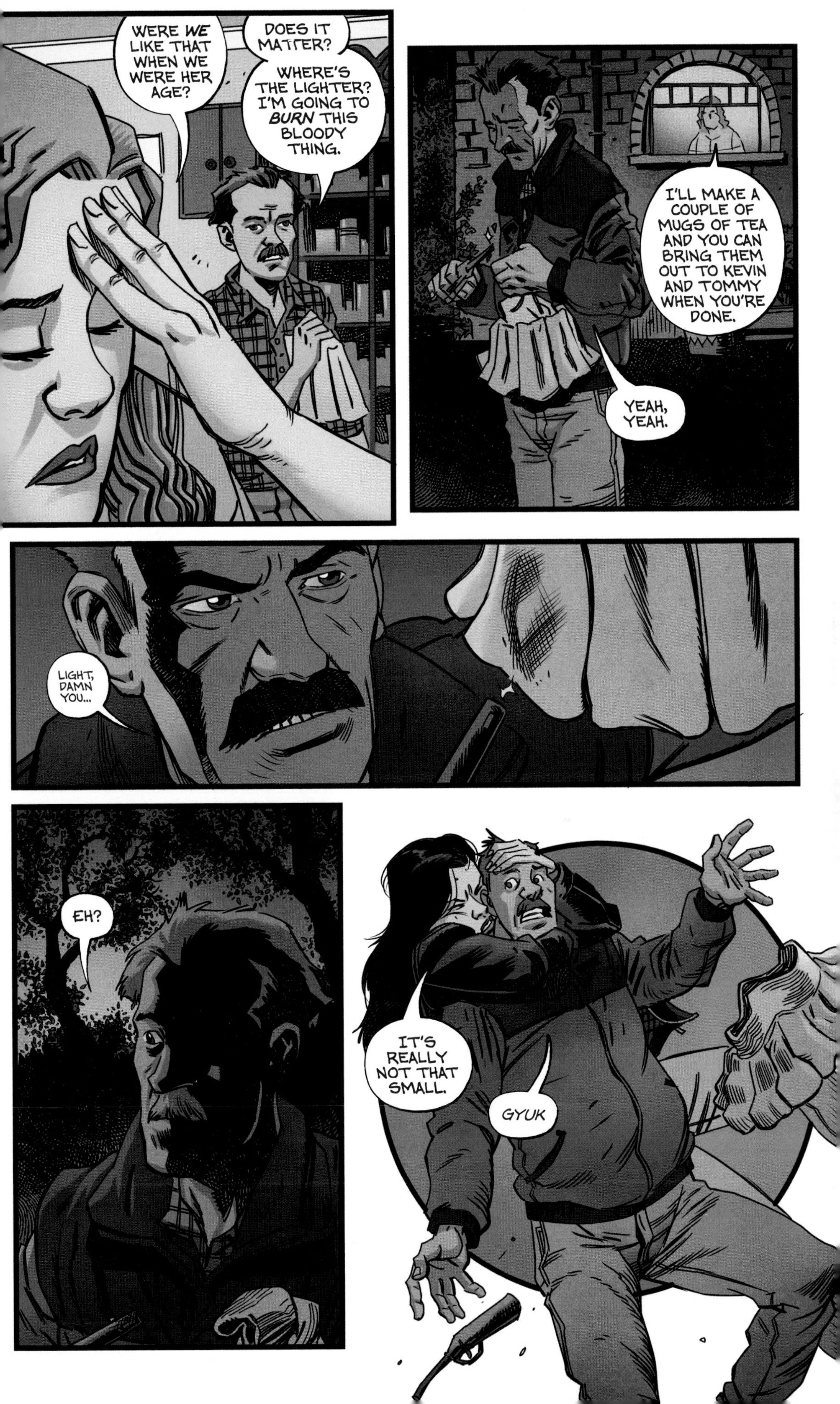
WERE *WE* LIKE THAT WHEN WE WERE HER AGE?
DOES IT MATTER?
WHERE'S THE LIGHTER? I'M GOING TO *BURN* THIS BLOODY THING.
I'LL MAKE A COUPLE OF MUGS OF TEA AND YOU CAN BRING THEM OUT TO KEVIN AND TOMMY WHEN YOU'RE DONE.
YEAH, YEAH.
LIGHT, DAMN YOU...
EH?
IT'S REALLY NOT THAT SMALL.
GYUK

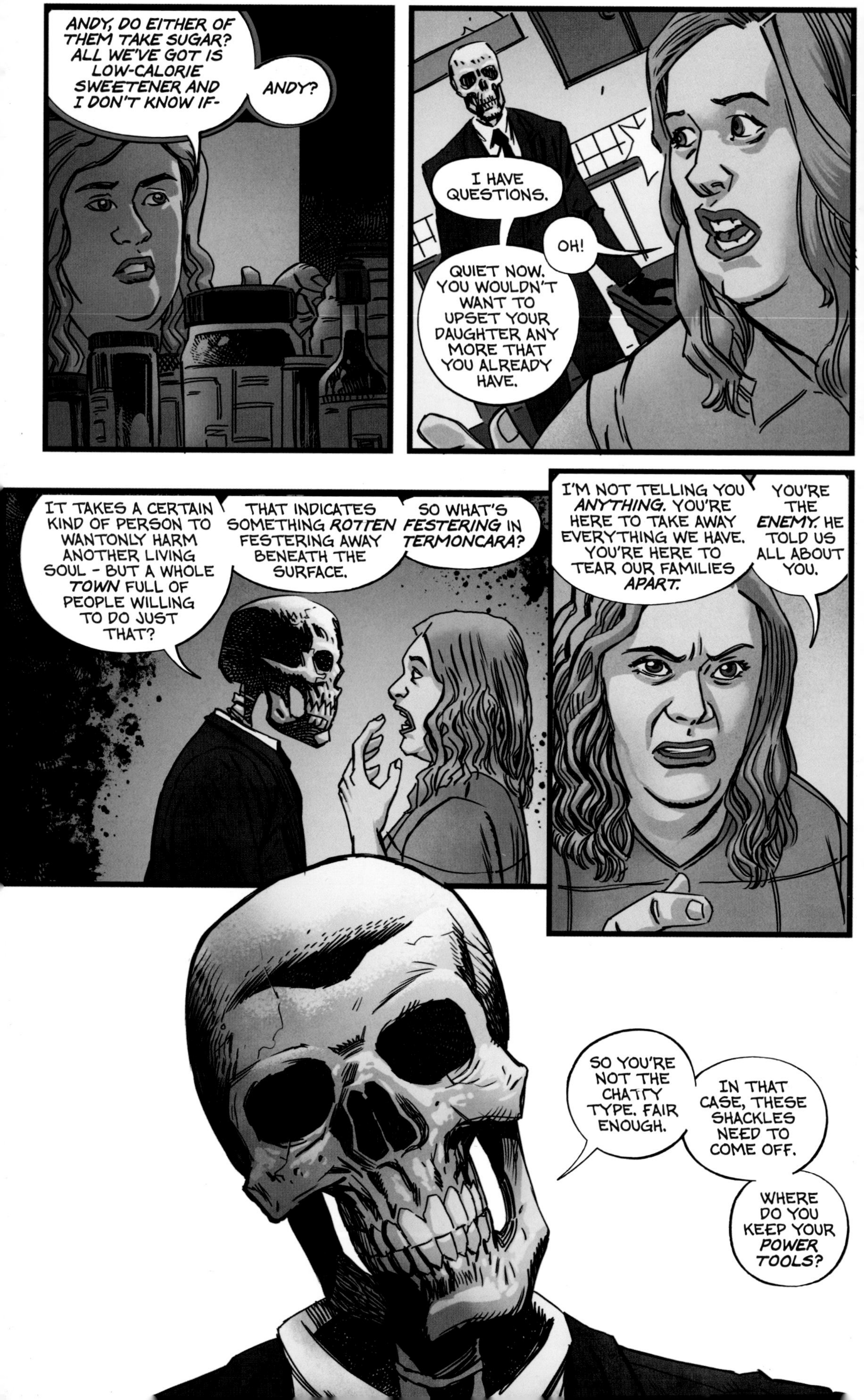
ANDY, DO EITHER OF THEM TAKE SUGAR? ALL WE'VE GOT IS LOW-CALORIE SWEETENER AND I DON'T KNOW IF-
ANDY?
I HAVE QUESTIONS.
OH!
QUIET NOW. YOU WOULDN'T WANT TO UPSET YOUR DAUGHTER ANY MORE THAT YOU ALREADY HAVE.
IT TAKES A CERTAIN KIND OF PERSON TO WANTONLY HARM ANOTHER LIVING SOUL - BUT A WHOLE TOWN FULL OF PEOPLE WILLING TO DO JUST THAT?
THAT INDICATES SOMETHING ROTTEN FESTERING AWAY BENEATH THE SURFACE.
SO WHAT'S FESTERING IN TERMONCARA?
I'M NOT TELLING YOU ANYTHING. YOU'RE HERE TO TAKE AWAY EVERYTHING WE HAVE. YOU'RE HERE TO TEAR OUR FAMILIES APART.
YOU'RE THE ENEMY. HE TOLD US ALL ABOUT YOU.
SO YOU'RE NOT THE CHATTY TYPE. FAIR ENOUGH.
IN THAT CASE, THESE SHACKLES NEED TO COME OFF.
WHERE DO YOU KEEP YOUR POWER TOOLS?

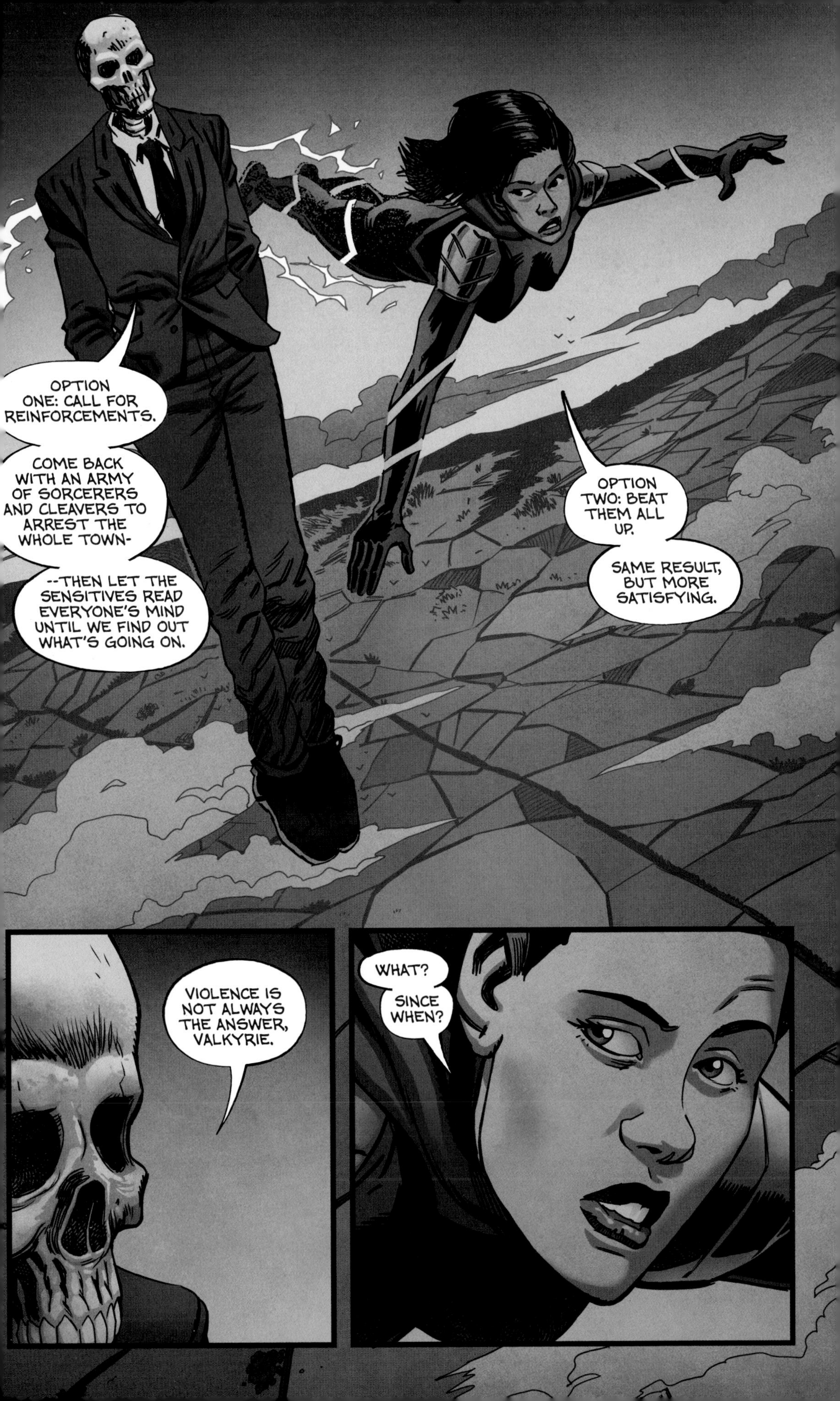
OPTION ONE: CALL FOR REINFORCEMENTS.
COME BACK WITH AN ARMY OF SORCERERS AND CLEAVERS TO ARREST THE WHOLE TOWN-
--THEN LET THE SENSITIVES READ EVERYONE'S MIND UNTIL WE FIND OUT WHAT'S GOING ON.
OPTION TWO: BEAT THEM ALL UP.
SAME RESULT, BUT MORE SATISFYING.
VIOLENCE IS NOT ALWAYS THE ANSWER, VALKYRIE.
WHAT?
SINCE WHEN?

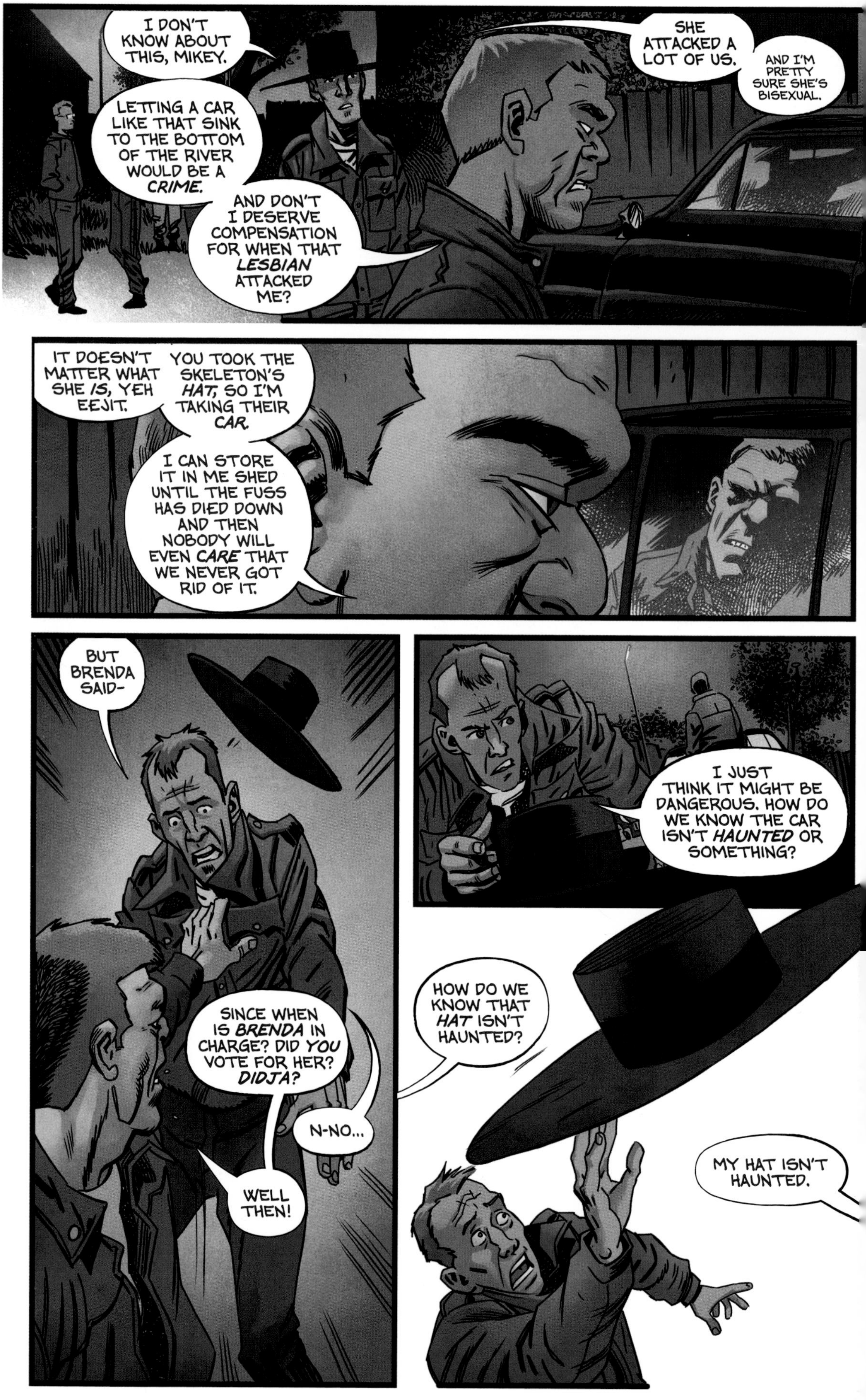
I DON'T KNOW ABOUT THIS, MIKEY.
LETTING A CAR LIKE THAT SINK TO THE BOTTOM OF THE RIVER WOULD BE A *CRIME.*
AND DON'T I DESERVE COMPENSATION FOR WHEN THAT *LESBIAN* ATTACKED ME?
SHE ATTACKED A LOT OF US.
AND I'M PRETTY SURE SHE'S BISEXUAL.
IT DOESN'T MATTER WHAT SHE *IS,* YEH EEJIT.
YOU TOOK THE SKELETON'S *HAT,* SO I'M TAKING THEIR *CAR.*
I CAN STORE IT IN ME SHED UNTIL THE FUSS HAS DIED DOWN AND THEN NOBODY WILL EVEN *CARE* THAT WE NEVER GOT RID OF IT.
BUT BRENDA SAID-
SINCE WHEN IS *BRENDA* IN CHARGE? DID *YOU* VOTE FOR HER? *DIDJA?*
N-NO...
WELL THEN!
I JUST THINK IT MIGHT BE DANGEROUS. HOW DO WE KNOW THE CAR ISN'T *HAUNTED* OR SOMETHING?
HOW DO WE KNOW THAT *HAT* ISN'T HAUNTED?
MY HAT ISN'T HAUNTED.

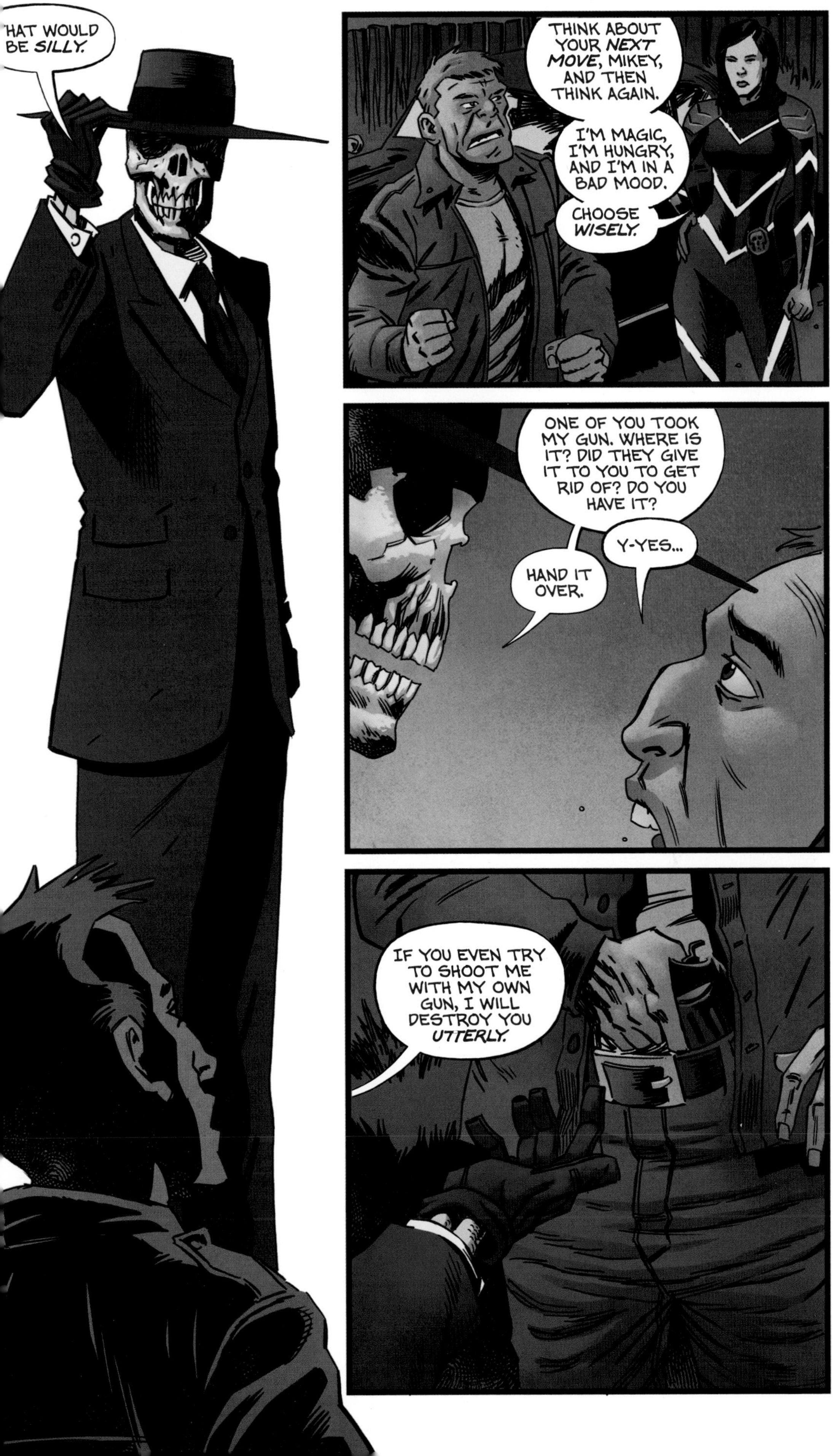

HAT WOULD BE *SILLY.*
THINK ABOUT YOUR *NEXT MOVE*, MIKEY, AND THEN THINK AGAIN.
I'M MAGIC, I'M HUNGRY, AND I'M IN A BAD MOOD.
CHOOSE *WISELY.*
ONE OF YOU TOOK MY GUN. WHERE IS IT? DID THEY GIVE IT TO YOU TO GET RID OF? DO YOU HAVE IT?
Y-YES...
HAND IT OVER.
IF YOU EVEN TRY TO SHOOT ME WITH MY OWN GUN, I WILL DESTROY YOU *UTTERLY.*

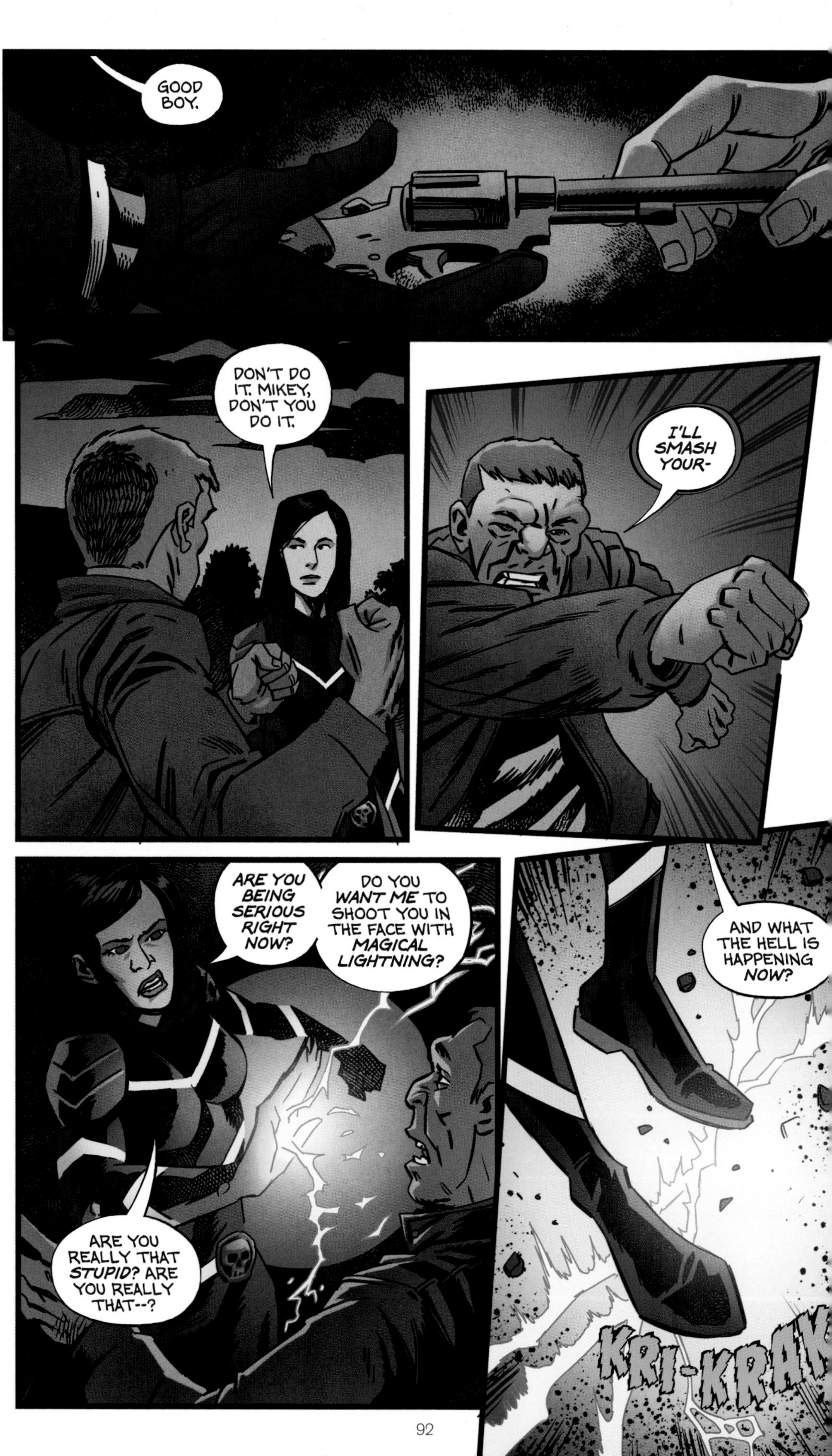
GOOD BOY.
DON'T DO IT. MIKEY, DON'T YOU DO IT.
I'LL SMASH YOUR-
ARE YOU BEING SERIOUS RIGHT NOW?
DO YOU WANT ME TO SHOOT YOU IN THE FACE WITH MAGICAL LIGHTNING?
ARE YOU REALLY THAT STUPID? ARE YOU REALLY THAT--?
AND WHAT THE HELL IS HAPPENING NOW?
KRI-KRAK

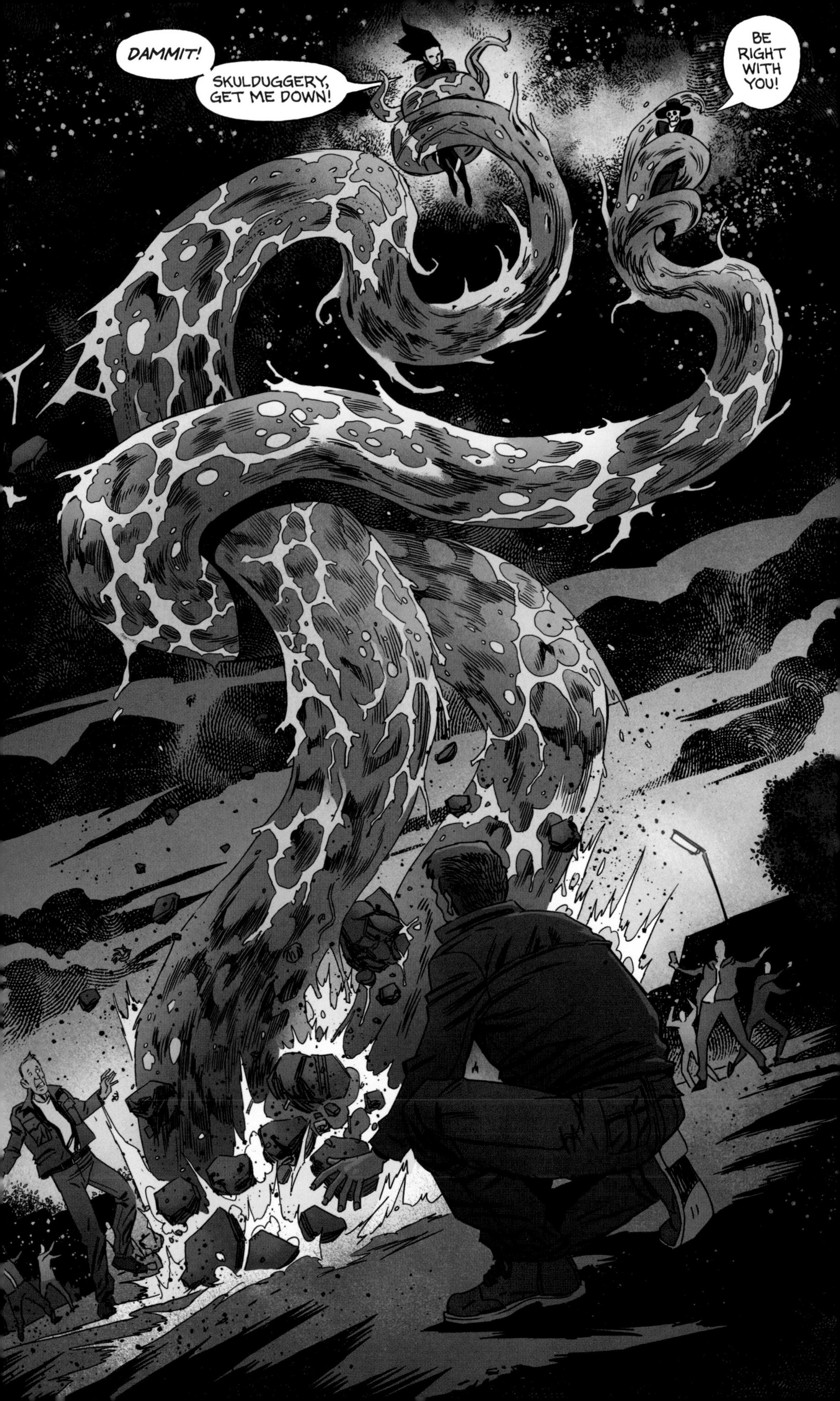
DAMMIT!
SKULDUGGERY, GET ME DOWN!
BE RIGHT WITH YOU!

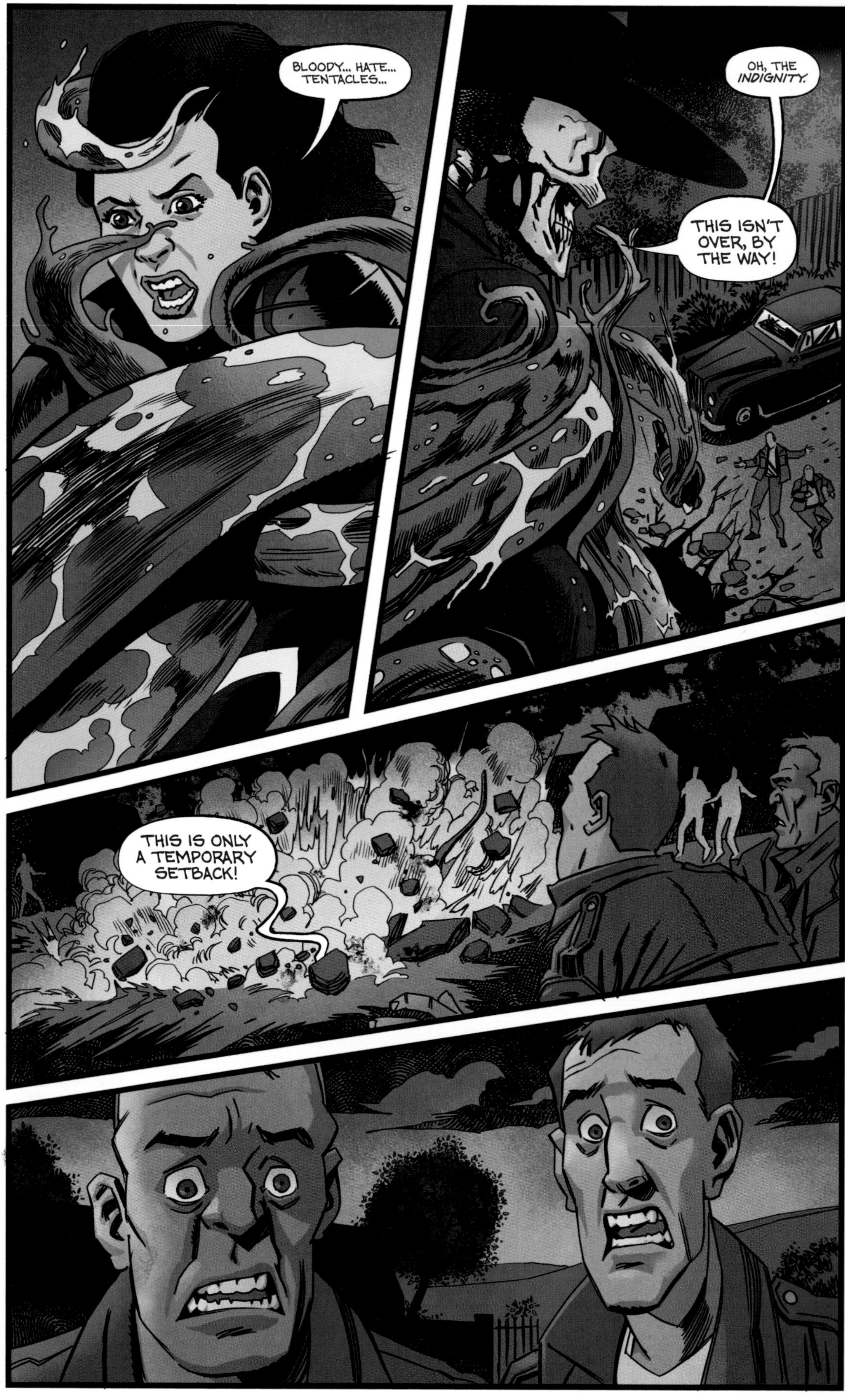
BLOODY... HATE... TENTACLES...
OH, THE *INDIGNITY.*
THIS ISN'T OVER, BY THE WAY!
THIS IS ONLY A TEMPORARY SETBACK!

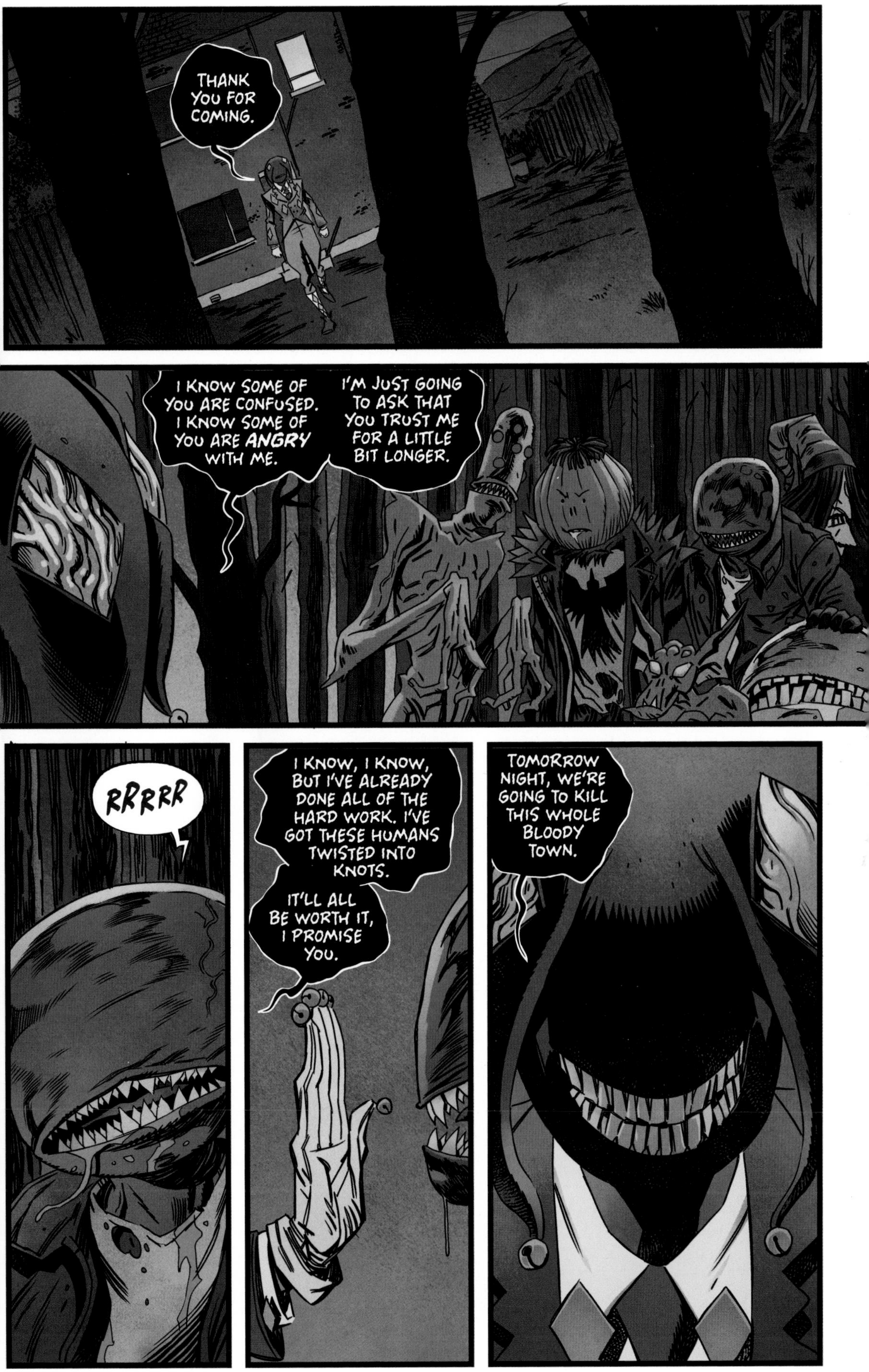
THANK YOU FOR COMING.
I KNOW SOME OF YOU ARE CONFUSED. I KNOW SOME OF YOU ARE ANGRY WITH ME.
I'M JUST GOING TO ASK THAT YOU TRUST ME FOR A LITTLE BIT LONGER.
RRRRR
I KNOW, I KNOW, BUT I'VE ALREADY DONE ALL OF THE HARD WORK. I'VE GOT THESE HUMANS TWISTED INTO KNOTS.
IT'LL ALL BE WORTH IT, I PROMISE YOU.
TOMORROW NIGHT, WE'RE GOING TO KILL THIS WHOLE BLOODY TOWN.

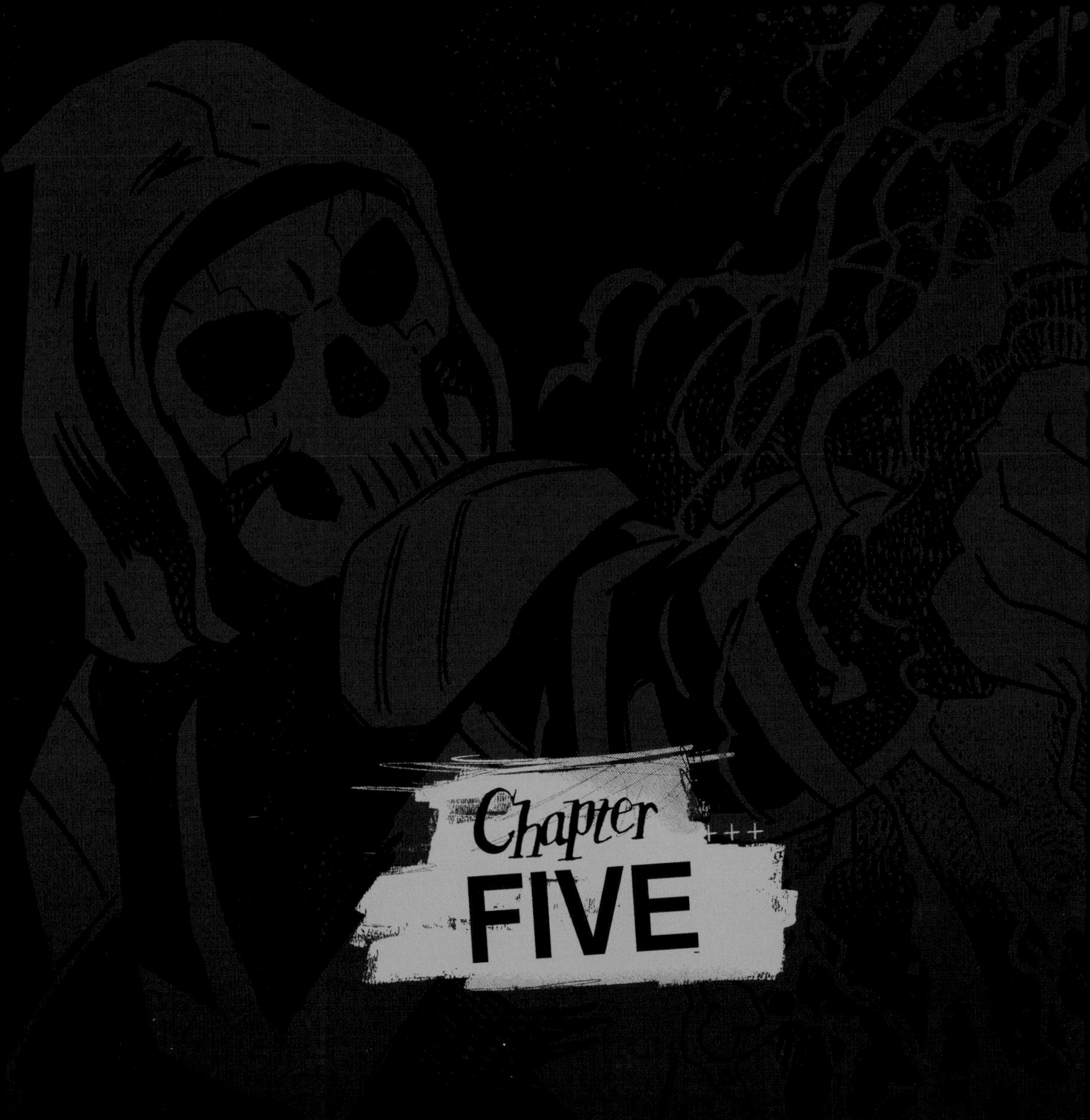

Chapter FIVE

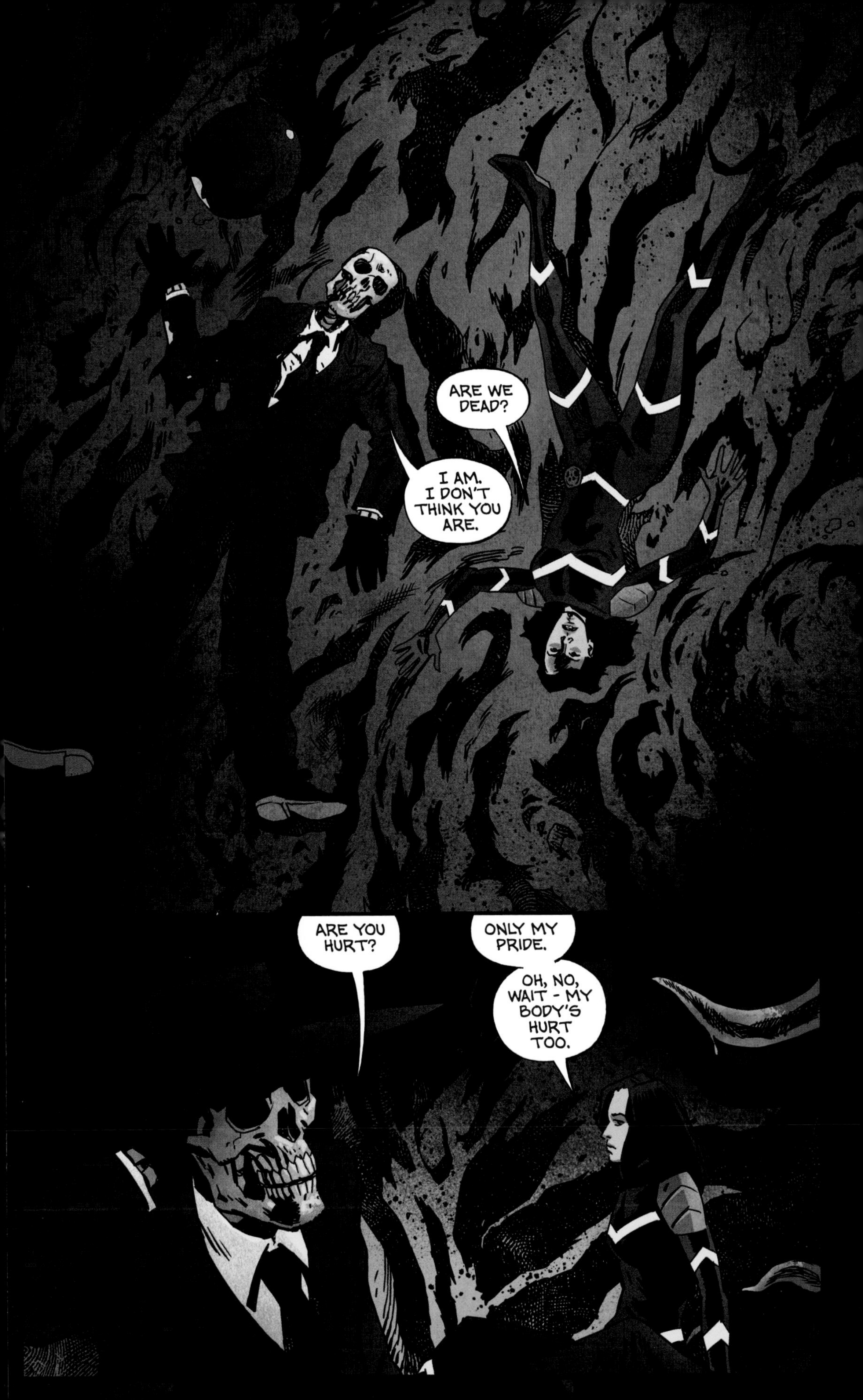
ARE WE DEAD?
I AM. I DON'T THINK YOU ARE.
ARE YOU HURT?
ONLY MY PRIDE.
OH, NO, WAIT - MY BODY'S HURT TOO.

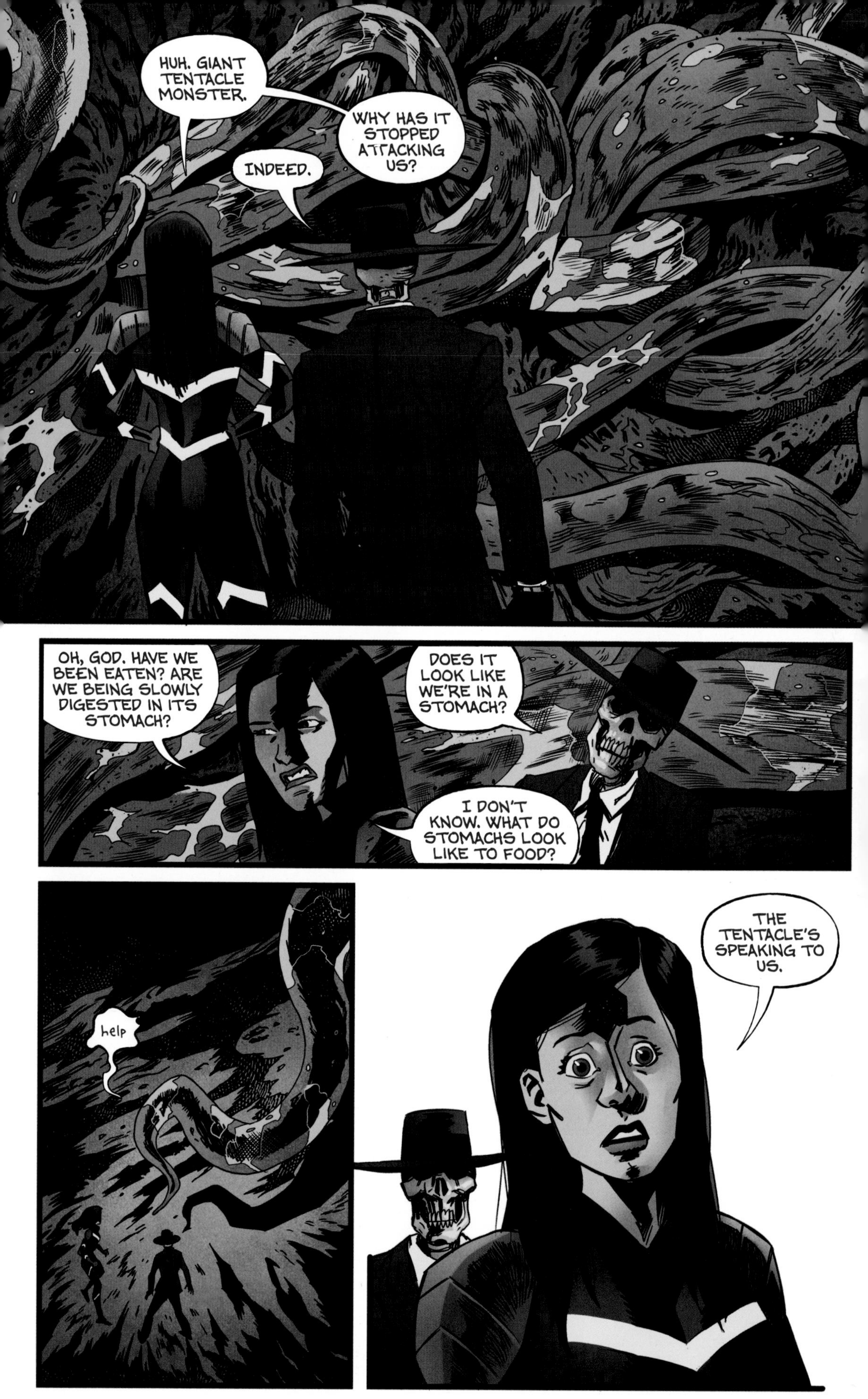
HUH. GIANT TENTACLE MONSTER.
INDEED.
WHY HAS IT STOPPED ATTACKING US?
OH, GOD. HAVE WE BEEN EATEN? ARE WE BEING SLOWLY DIGESTED IN ITS STOMACH?
DOES IT LOOK LIKE WE'RE IN A STOMACH?
I DON'T KNOW. WHAT DO STOMACHS LOOK LIKE TO FOOD?
help
THE TENTACLE'S SPEAKING TO US.

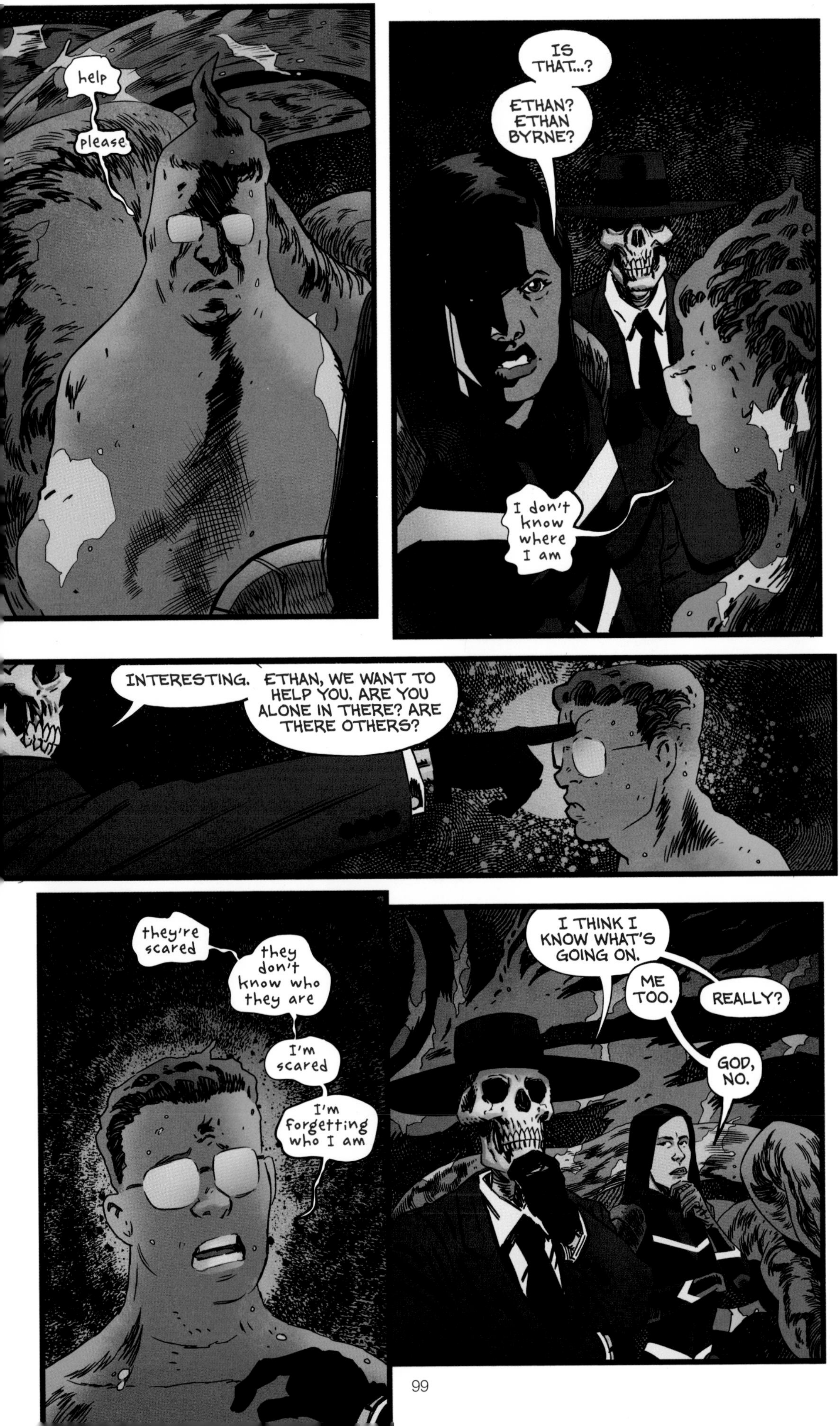
help
please
IS THAT...?
ETHAN? ETHAN BYRNE?
I don't know where I am
INTERESTING.
ETHAN, WE WANT TO HELP YOU. ARE YOU ALONE IN THERE? ARE THERE OTHERS?
they're scared
they don't know who they are
I'm scared
I'm forgetting who I am
I THINK I KNOW WHAT'S GOING ON.
ME TOO.
REALLY?
GOD, NO.

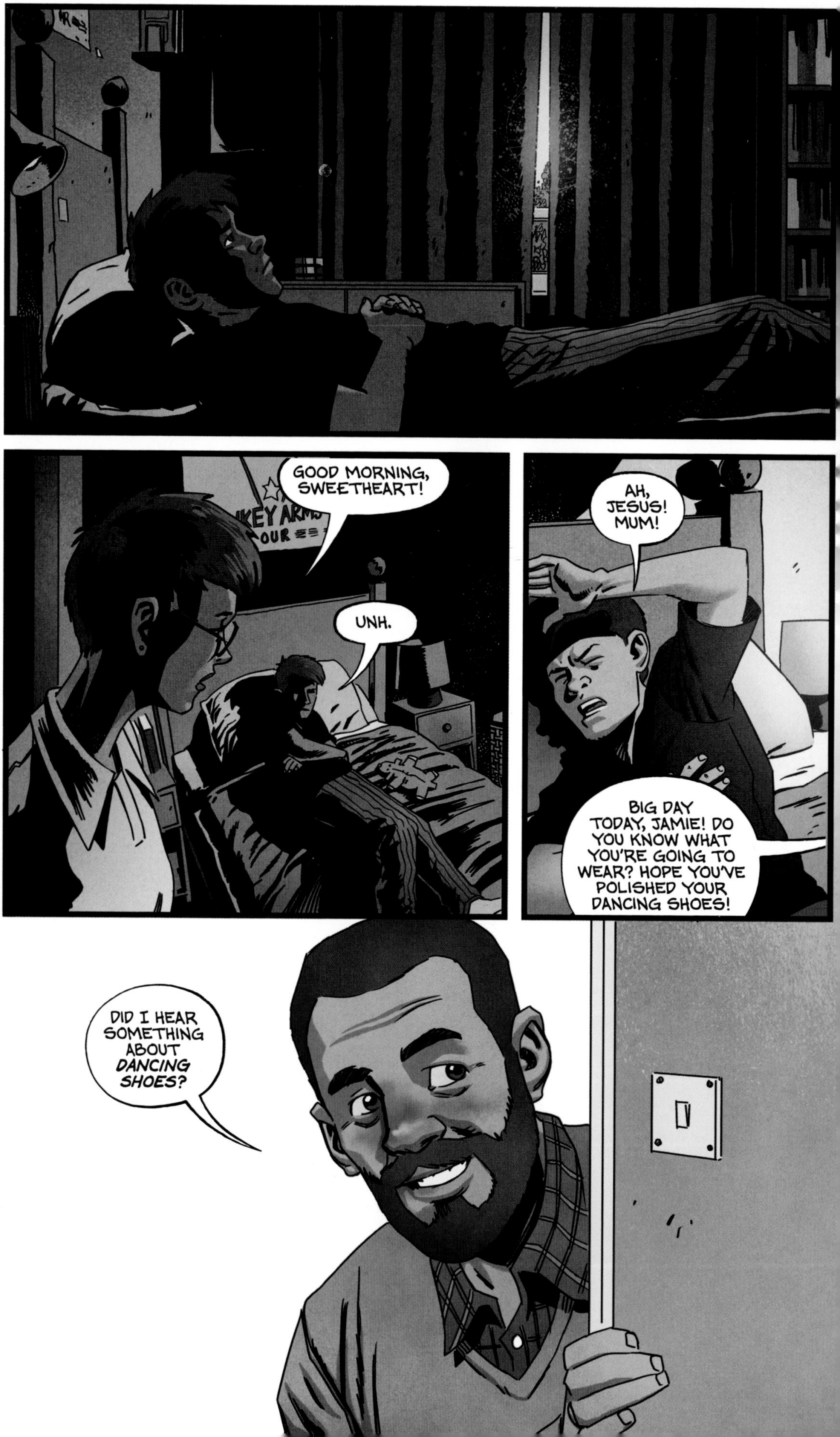
GOOD MORNING, SWEETHEART!
UNH.
AH, JESUS! MUM!
BIG DAY TODAY, JAMIE! DO YOU KNOW WHAT YOU'RE GOING TO WEAR? HOPE YOU'VE POLISHED YOUR DANCING SHOES!
DID I HEAR SOMETHING ABOUT *DANCING SHOES?*

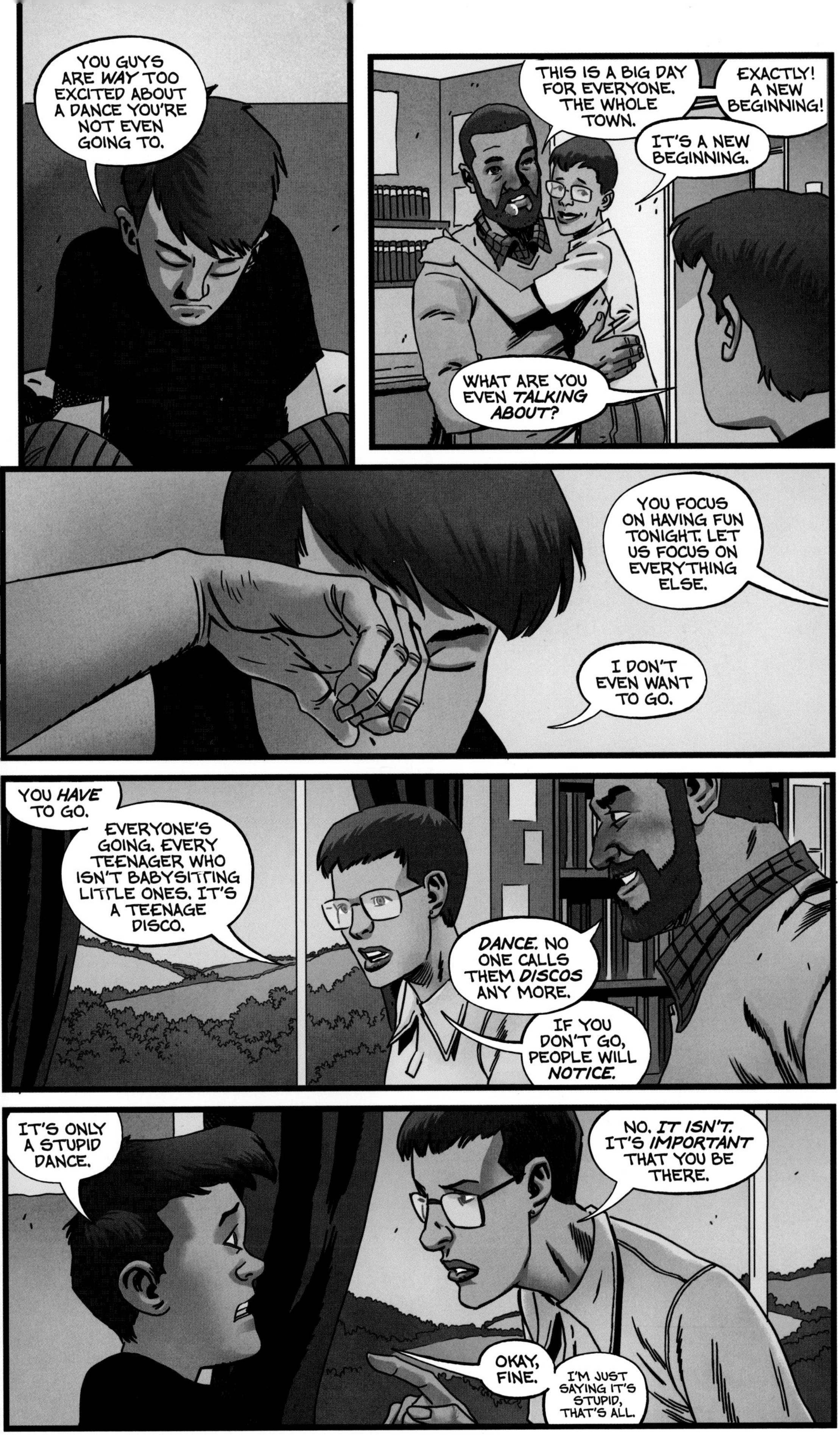
YOU GUYS ARE WAY TOO EXCITED ABOUT A DANCE YOU'RE NOT EVEN GOING TO.
THIS IS A BIG DAY FOR EVERYONE. THE WHOLE TOWN.
EXACTLY! A NEW BEGINNING!
IT'S A NEW BEGINNING.
WHAT ARE YOU EVEN TALKING ABOUT?
YOU FOCUS ON HAVING FUN TONIGHT. LET US FOCUS ON EVERYTHING ELSE.
I DON'T EVEN WANT TO GO.
YOU HAVE TO GO.
EVERYONE'S GOING. EVERY TEENAGER WHO ISN'T BABYSITTING LITTLE ONES. IT'S A TEENAGE DISCO.
DANCE. NO ONE CALLS THEM DISCOS ANY MORE.
IF YOU DON'T GO, PEOPLE WILL NOTICE.
IT'S ONLY A STUPID DANCE.
NO. IT ISN'T. IT'S IMPORTANT THAT YOU BE THERE.
OKAY, FINE.
I'M JUST SAYING IT'S STUPID, THAT'S ALL.

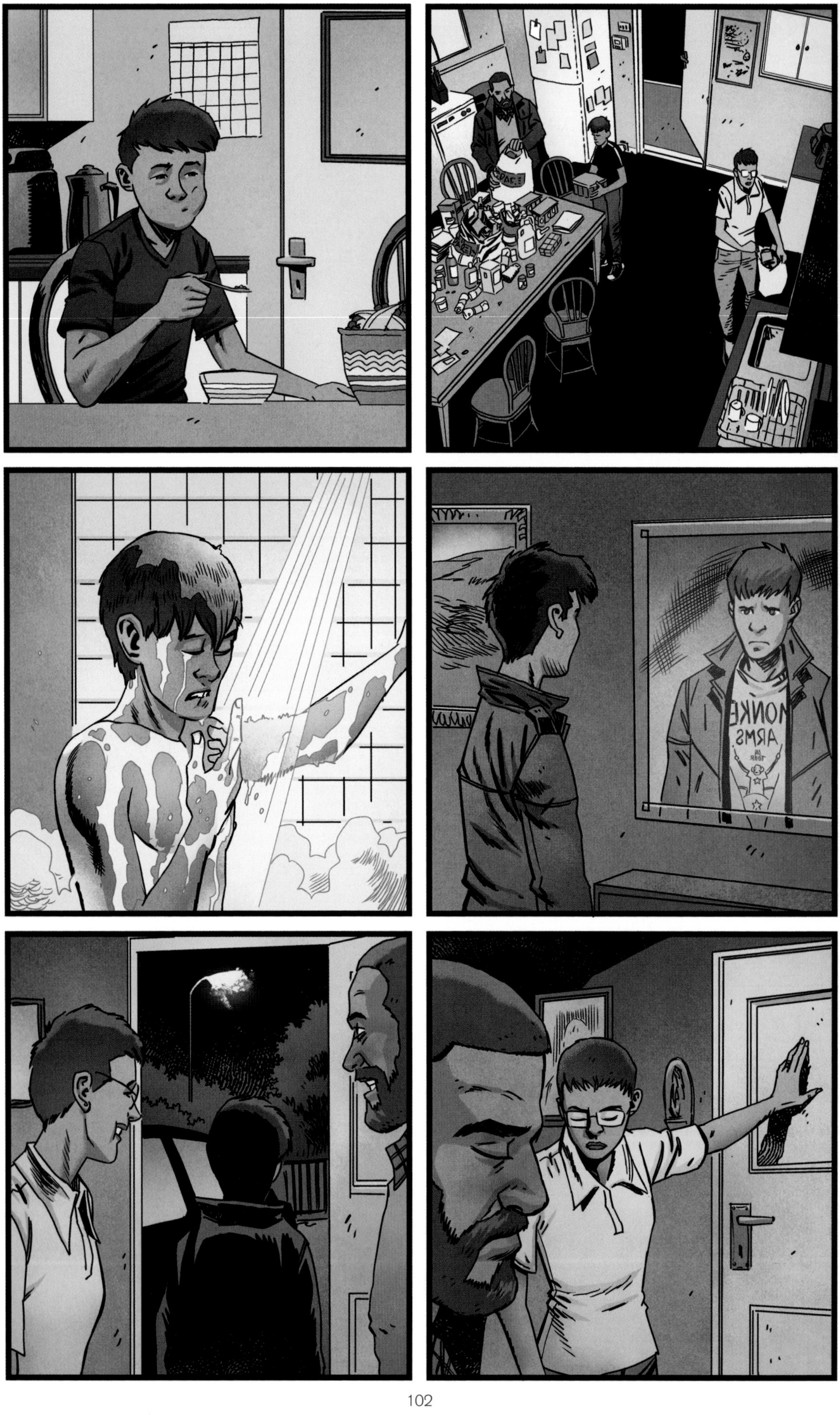

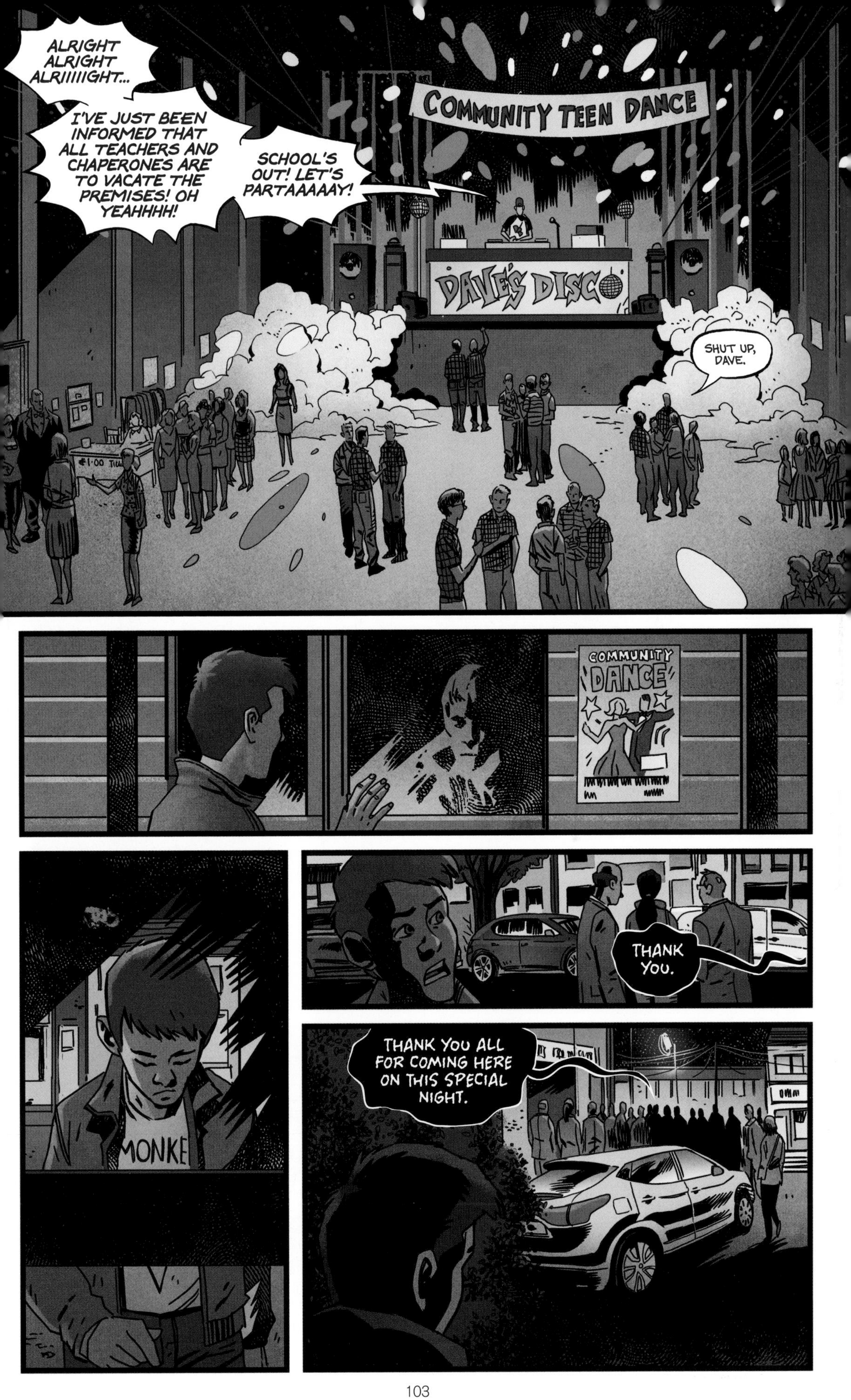
ALRIGHT
ALRIGHT
ALRIIIIIGHT...
I'VE JUST BEEN INFORMED THAT ALL TEACHERS AND CHAPERONES ARE TO VACATE THE PREMISES! OH YEAHHHH!
SCHOOL'S OUT! LET'S PARTAAAAAY!
COMMUNITY TEEN DANCE
DAVE'S DISCO
SHUT UP, DAVE.
COMMUNITY DANCE
MONKE
THANK YOU.
THANK YOU ALL FOR COMING HERE ON THIS SPECIAL NIGHT.

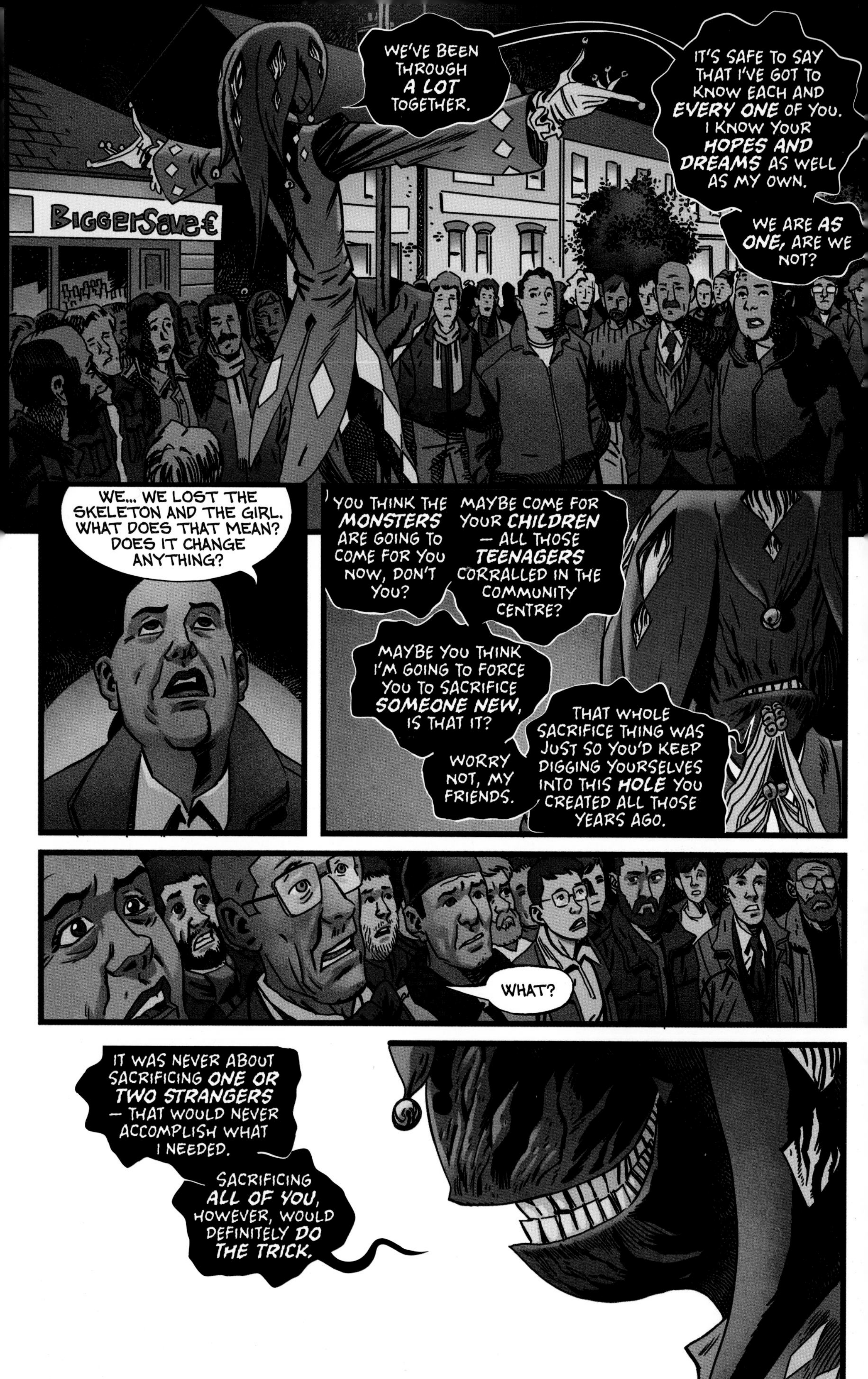

We've been through a lot together.
It's safe to say that I've got to know each and every one of you. I know your hopes and dreams as well as my own.
We are as one, are we not?
BiggerSave€
We... we lost the skeleton and the girl. What does that mean? Does it change anything?
You think the monsters are going to come for you now, don't you?
Maybe come for your children — all those teenagers corralled in the community centre?
Maybe you think I'm going to force you to sacrifice someone new, is that it?
Worry not, my friends.
That whole sacrifice thing was just so you'd keep digging yourselves into this hole you created all those years ago.
What?
It was never about sacrificing one or two strangers — that would never accomplish what I needed.
Sacrificing all of you, however, would definitely do the trick.

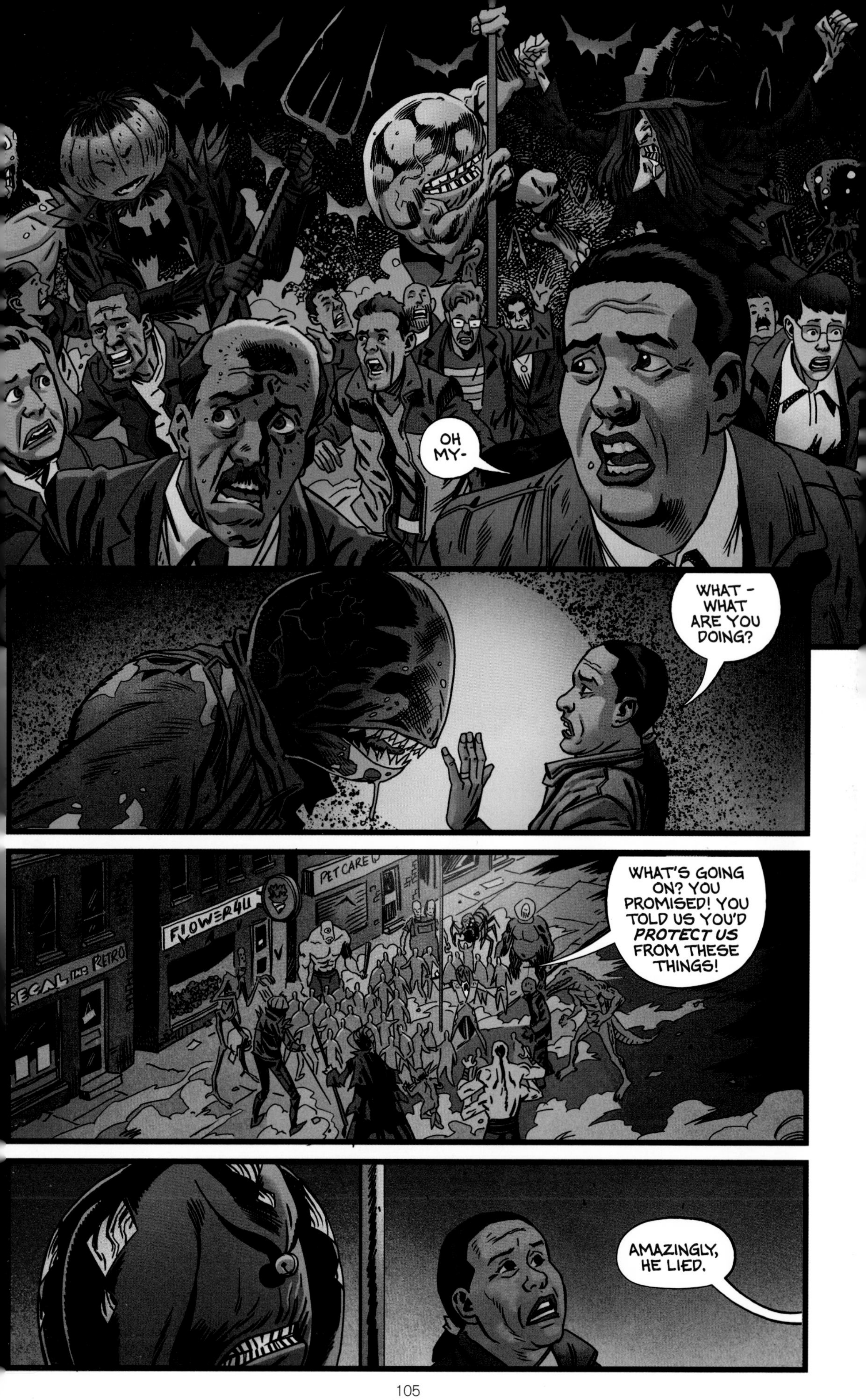
OH MY-
WHAT - WHAT ARE YOU DOING?
FLOWER4U
PET CARE
REGAL
RETRO
WHAT'S GOING ON? YOU PROMISED! YOU TOLD US YOU'D *PROTECT US* FROM THESE THINGS!
AMAZINGLY, HE LIED.

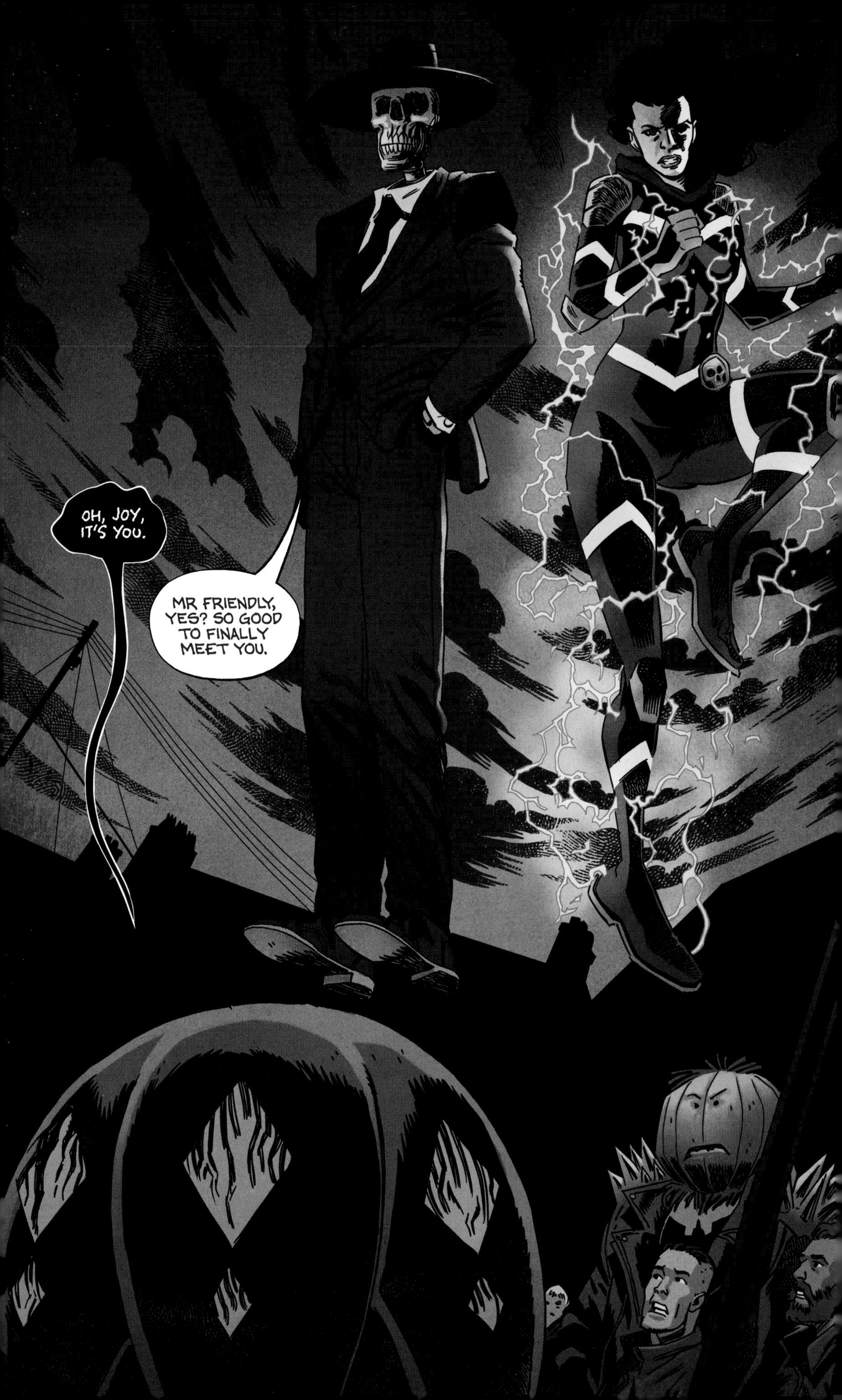
OH, JOY, IT'S YOU.
MR FRIENDLY, YES? SO GOOD TO FINALLY MEET YOU.

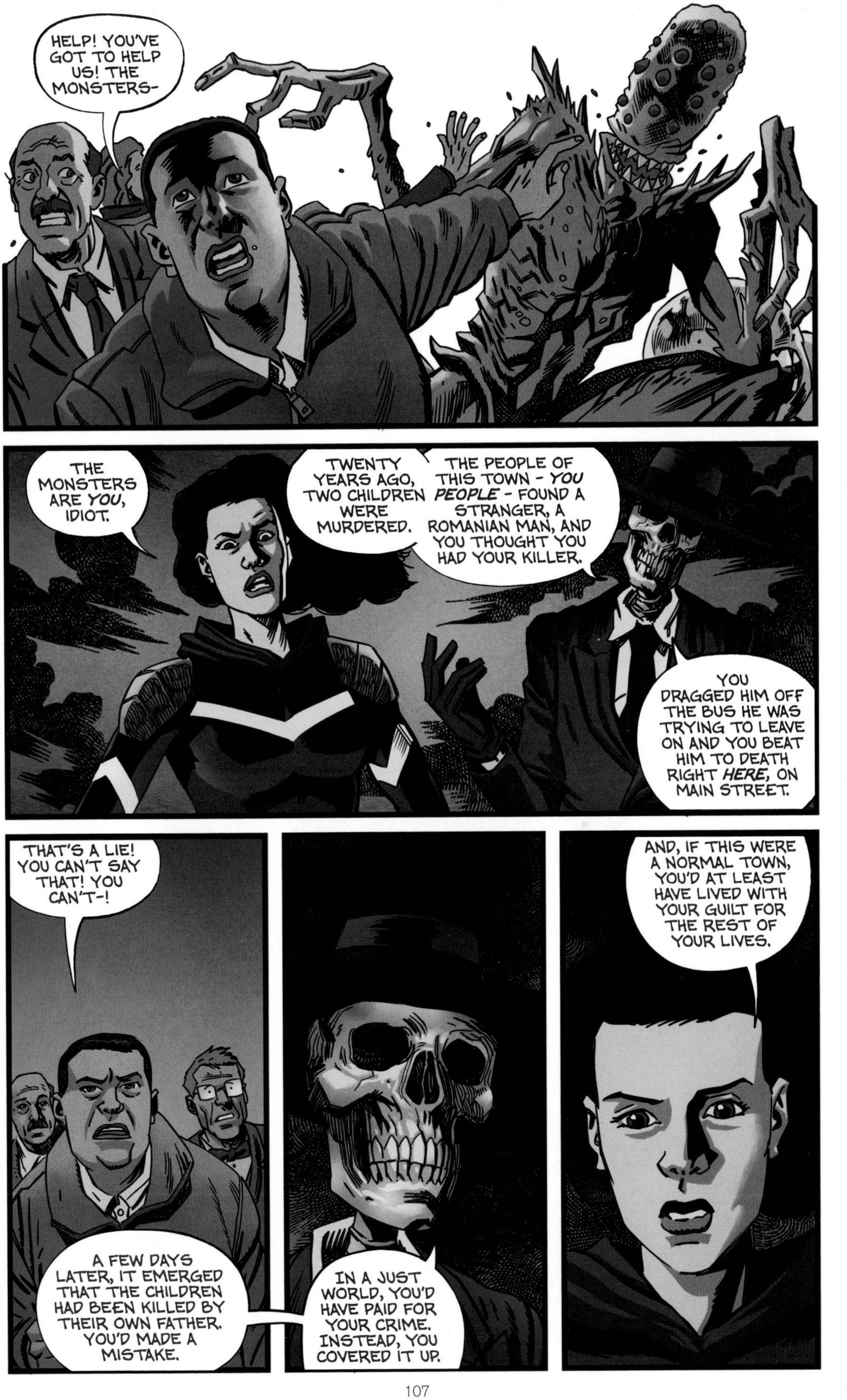
HELP! YOU'VE GOT TO HELP US! THE MONSTERS-
THE MONSTERS ARE *YOU*, IDIOT.
TWENTY YEARS AGO, TWO CHILDREN WERE MURDERED.
THE PEOPLE OF THIS TOWN - *YOU PEOPLE* - FOUND A STRANGER, A ROMANIAN MAN, AND YOU THOUGHT YOU HAD YOUR KILLER.
YOU DRAGGED HIM OFF THE BUS HE WAS TRYING TO LEAVE ON AND YOU BEAT HIM TO DEATH RIGHT *HERE,* ON MAIN STREET.
THAT'S A LIE! YOU CAN'T SAY THAT! YOU CAN'T-!
A FEW DAYS LATER, IT EMERGED THAT THE CHILDREN HAD BEEN KILLED BY THEIR OWN FATHER. YOU'D MADE A MISTAKE.
IN A JUST WORLD, YOU'D HAVE PAID FOR YOUR CRIME. INSTEAD, YOU COVERED IT UP.
AND, IF THIS WERE A NORMAL TOWN, YOU'D AT LEAST HAVE LIVED WITH YOUR GUILT FOR THE REST OF YOUR LIVES.

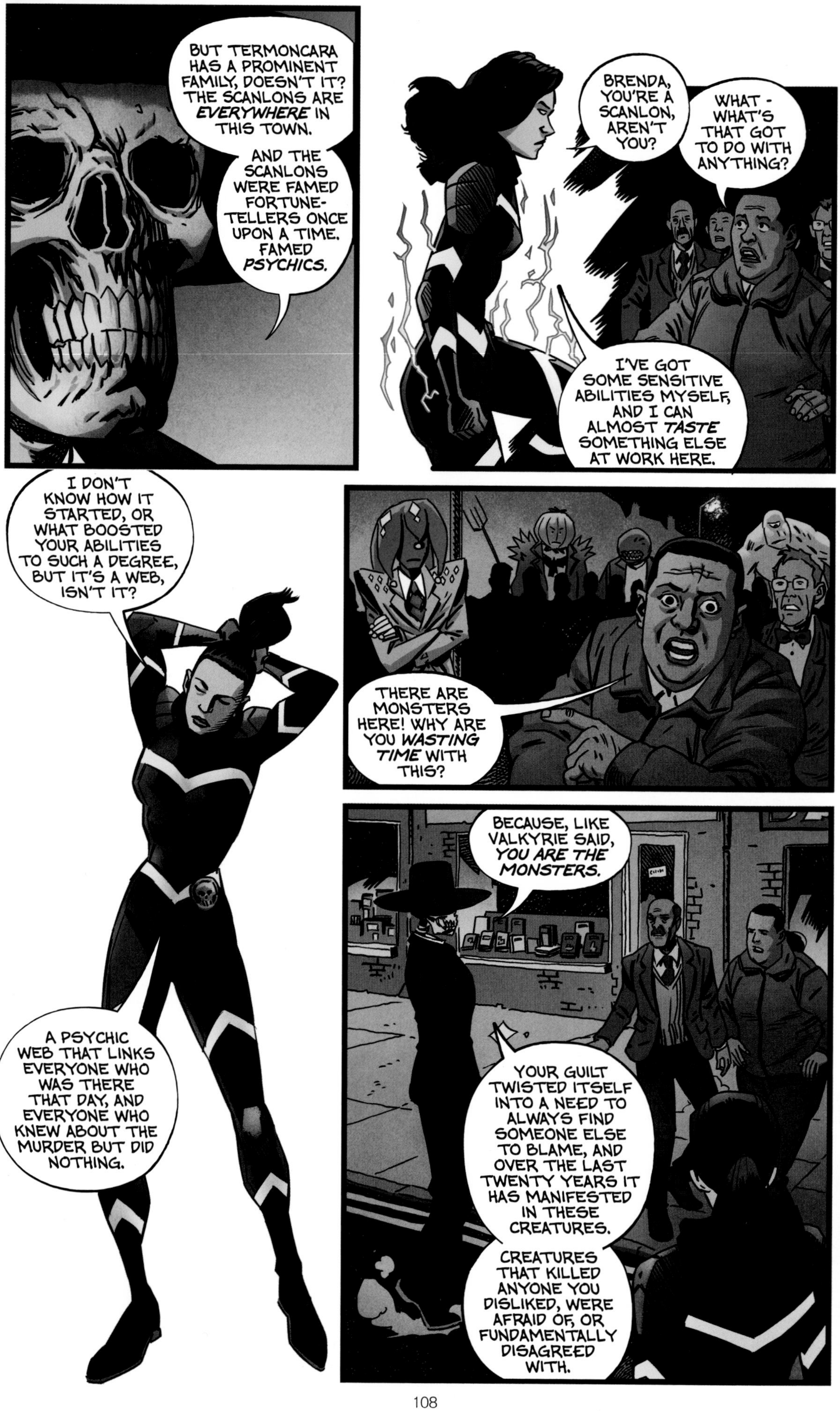
BUT TERMONCARA HAS A PROMINENT FAMILY, DOESN'T IT? THE SCANLONS ARE EVERYWHERE IN THIS TOWN.
AND THE SCANLONS WERE FAMED FORTUNE-TELLERS ONCE UPON A TIME. FAMED PSYCHICS.
BRENDA, YOU'RE A SCANLON, AREN'T YOU?
WHAT - WHAT'S THAT GOT TO DO WITH ANYTHING?
I'VE GOT SOME SENSITIVE ABILITIES MYSELF, AND I CAN ALMOST TASTE SOMETHING ELSE AT WORK HERE.
I DON'T KNOW HOW IT STARTED, OR WHAT BOOSTED YOUR ABILITIES TO SUCH A DEGREE, BUT IT'S A WEB, ISN'T IT?
A PSYCHIC WEB THAT LINKS EVERYONE WHO WAS THERE THAT DAY, AND EVERYONE WHO KNEW ABOUT THE MURDER BUT DID NOTHING.
THERE ARE MONSTERS HERE! WHY ARE YOU WASTING TIME WITH THIS?
BECAUSE, LIKE VALKYRIE SAID, YOU ARE THE MONSTERS.
YOUR GUILT TWISTED ITSELF INTO A NEED TO ALWAYS FIND SOMEONE ELSE TO BLAME, AND OVER THE LAST TWENTY YEARS IT HAS MANIFESTED IN THESE CREATURES.
CREATURES THAT KILLED ANYONE YOU DISLIKED, WERE AFRAID OF, OR FUNDAMENTALLY DISAGREED WITH.

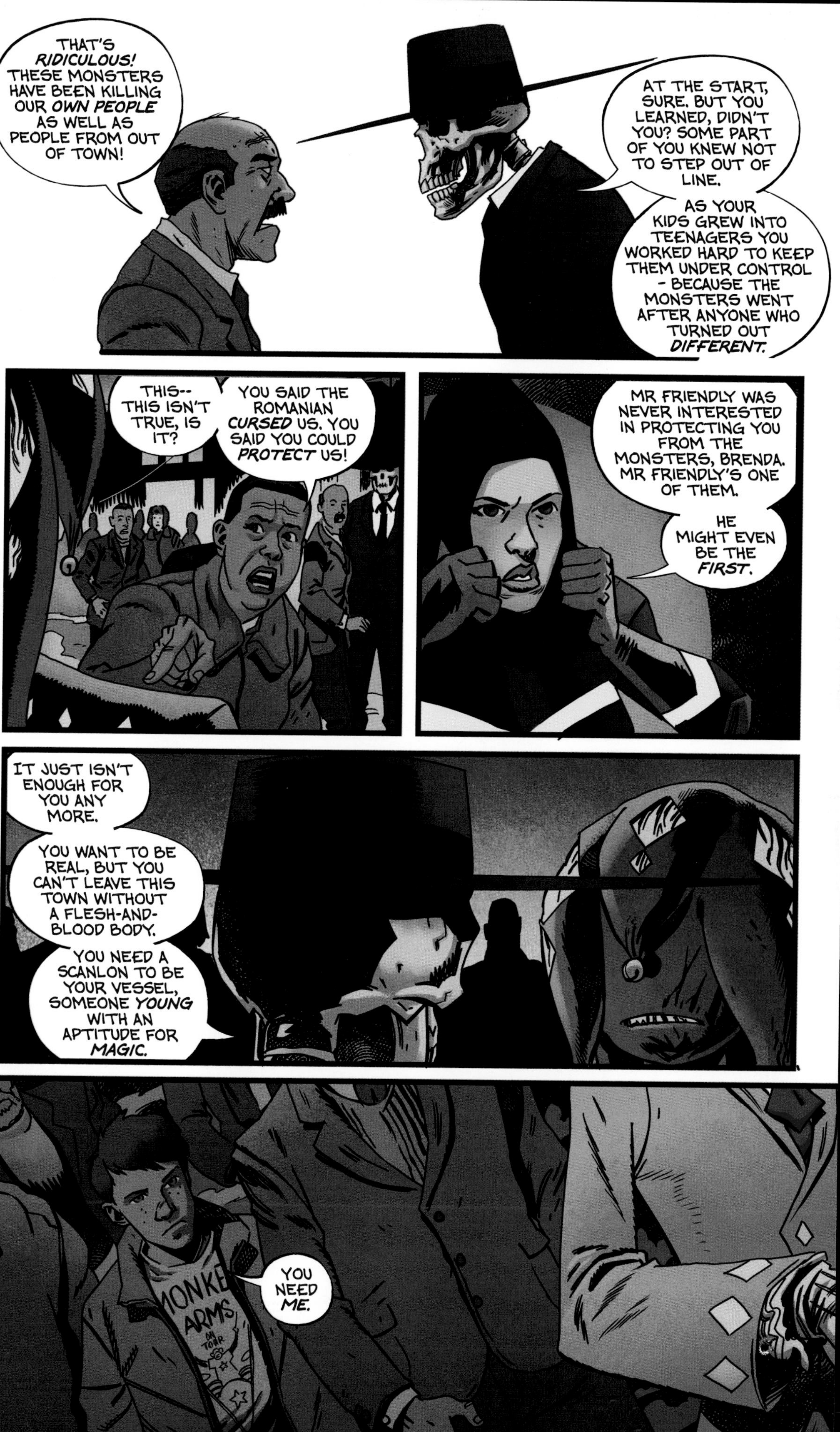
THAT'S *RIDICULOUS!* THESE MONSTERS HAVE BEEN KILLING OUR *OWN PEOPLE* AS WELL AS PEOPLE FROM OUT OF TOWN!
AT THE START, SURE. BUT YOU LEARNED, DIDN'T YOU? SOME PART OF YOU KNEW NOT TO STEP OUT OF LINE.
AS YOUR KIDS GREW INTO TEENAGERS YOU WORKED HARD TO KEEP THEM UNDER CONTROL - BECAUSE THE MONSTERS WENT AFTER ANYONE WHO TURNED OUT *DIFFERENT.*
THIS-- THIS ISN'T TRUE, IS IT?
YOU SAID THE ROMANIAN *CURSED* US. YOU SAID YOU COULD *PROTECT* US!
MR FRIENDLY WAS NEVER INTERESTED IN PROTECTING YOU FROM THE MONSTERS, BRENDA. MR FRIENDLY'S ONE OF THEM.
HE MIGHT EVEN BE THE *FIRST*.
IT JUST ISN'T ENOUGH FOR YOU ANY MORE.
YOU WANT TO BE REAL, BUT YOU CAN'T LEAVE THIS TOWN WITHOUT A FLESH-AND-BLOOD BODY.
YOU NEED A SCANLON TO BE YOUR VESSEL, SOMEONE *YOUNG* WITH AN APTITUDE FOR *MAGIC.*
YOU NEED *ME.*

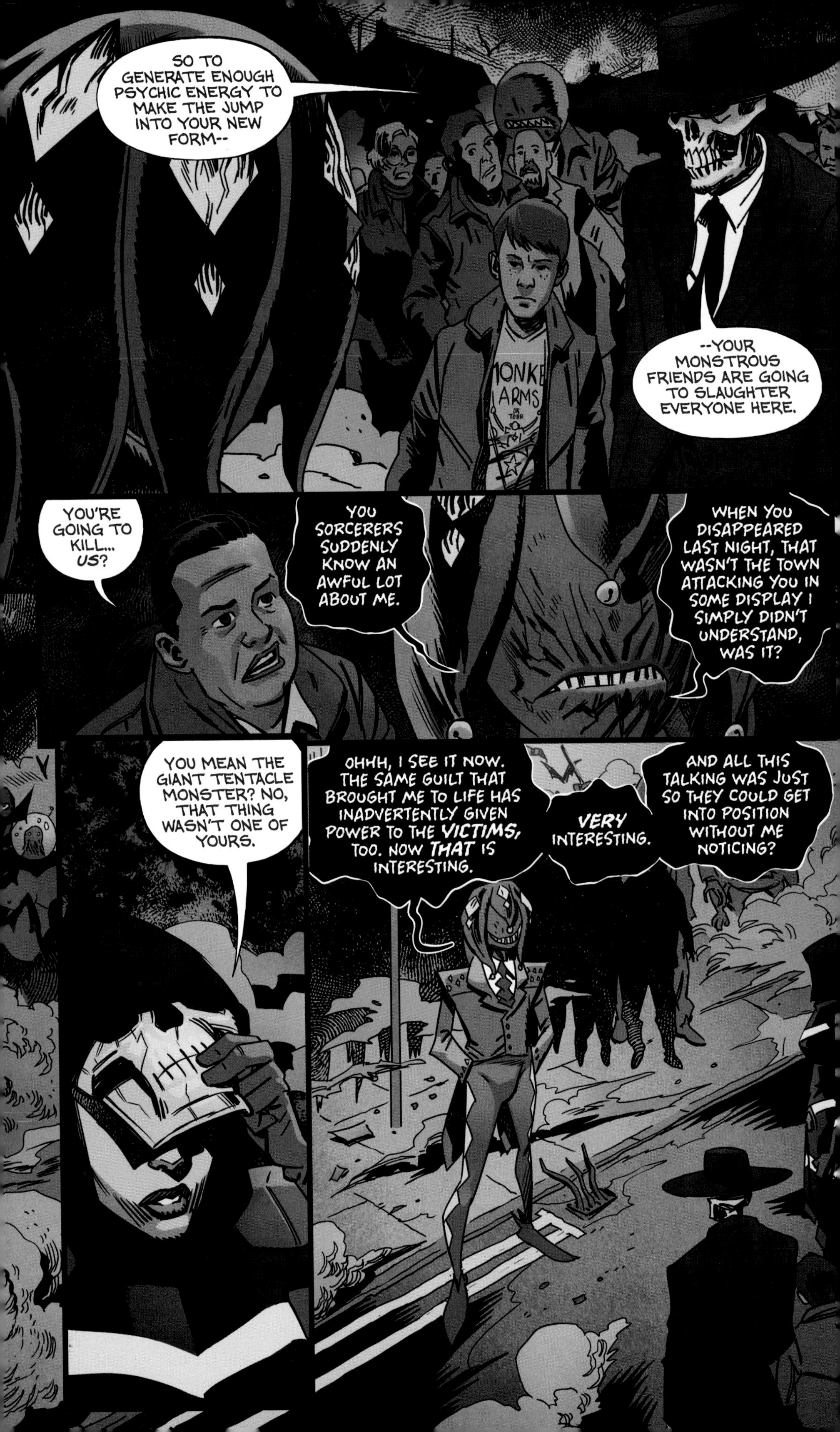
SO TO GENERATE ENOUGH PSYCHIC ENERGY TO MAKE THE JUMP INTO YOUR NEW FORM--
--YOUR MONSTROUS FRIENDS ARE GOING TO SLAUGHTER EVERYONE HERE.
YOU'RE GOING TO KILL... *US*?
YOU SORCERERS SUDDENLY KNOW AN AWFUL LOT ABOUT ME.
WHEN YOU DISAPPEARED LAST NIGHT, THAT WASN'T THE TOWN ATTACKING YOU IN SOME DISPLAY I SIMPLY DIDN'T UNDERSTAND, WAS IT?
YOU MEAN THE GIANT TENTACLE MONSTER? NO, THAT THING WASN'T ONE OF YOURS.
OHHH, I SEE IT NOW. THE SAME GUILT THAT BROUGHT ME TO LIFE HAS INADVERTENTLY GIVEN POWER TO THE *VICTIMS*, TOO. NOW *THAT* IS INTERESTING.
VERY INTERESTING.
AND ALL THIS TALKING WAS JUST SO THEY COULD GET INTO POSITION WITHOUT ME NOTICING?

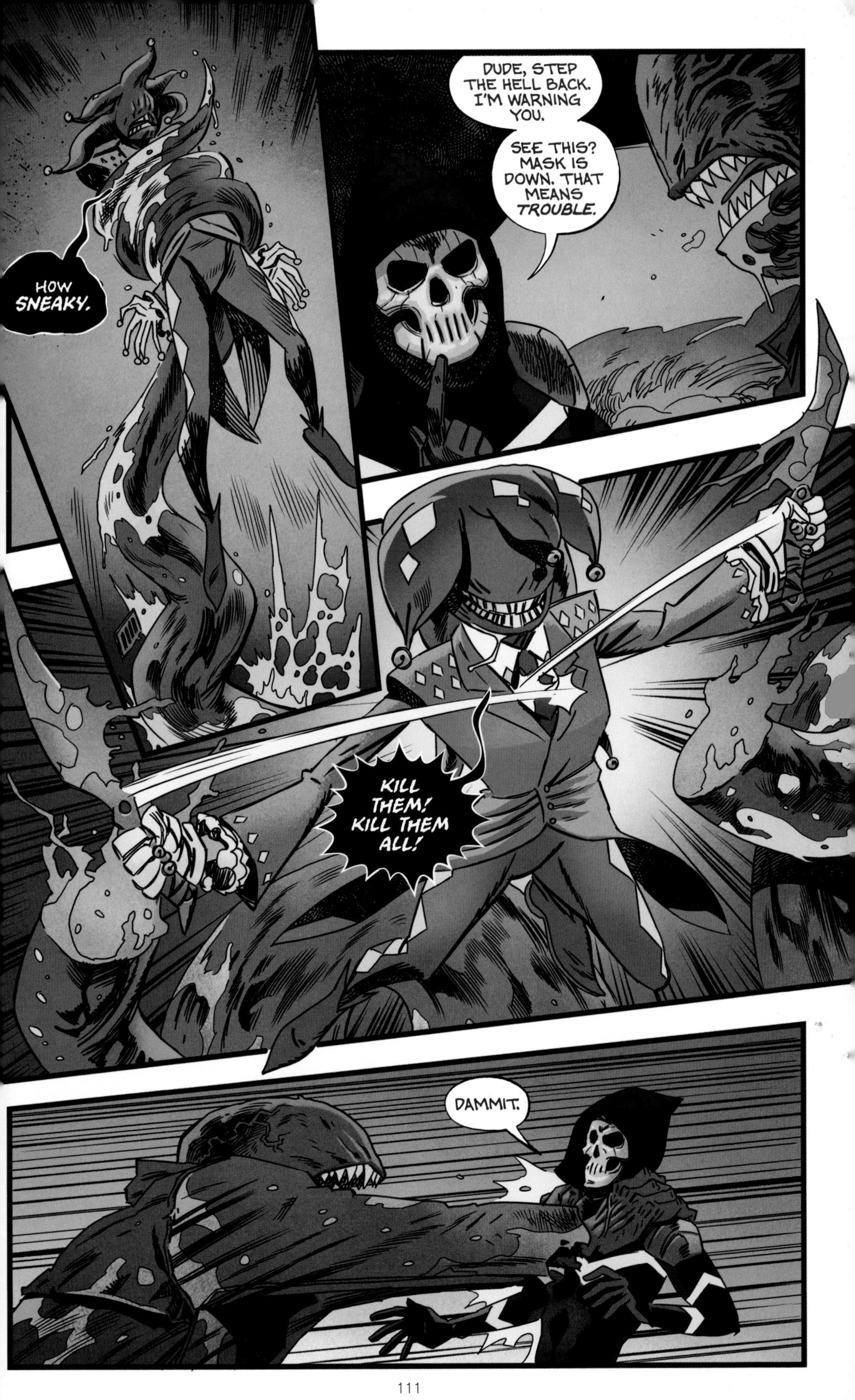
HOW SNEAKY.
DUDE, STEP THE HELL BACK. I'M WARNING YOU.
SEE THIS? MASK IS DOWN. THAT MEANS TROUBLE.
KILL THEM! KILL THEM ALL!
DAMMIT.

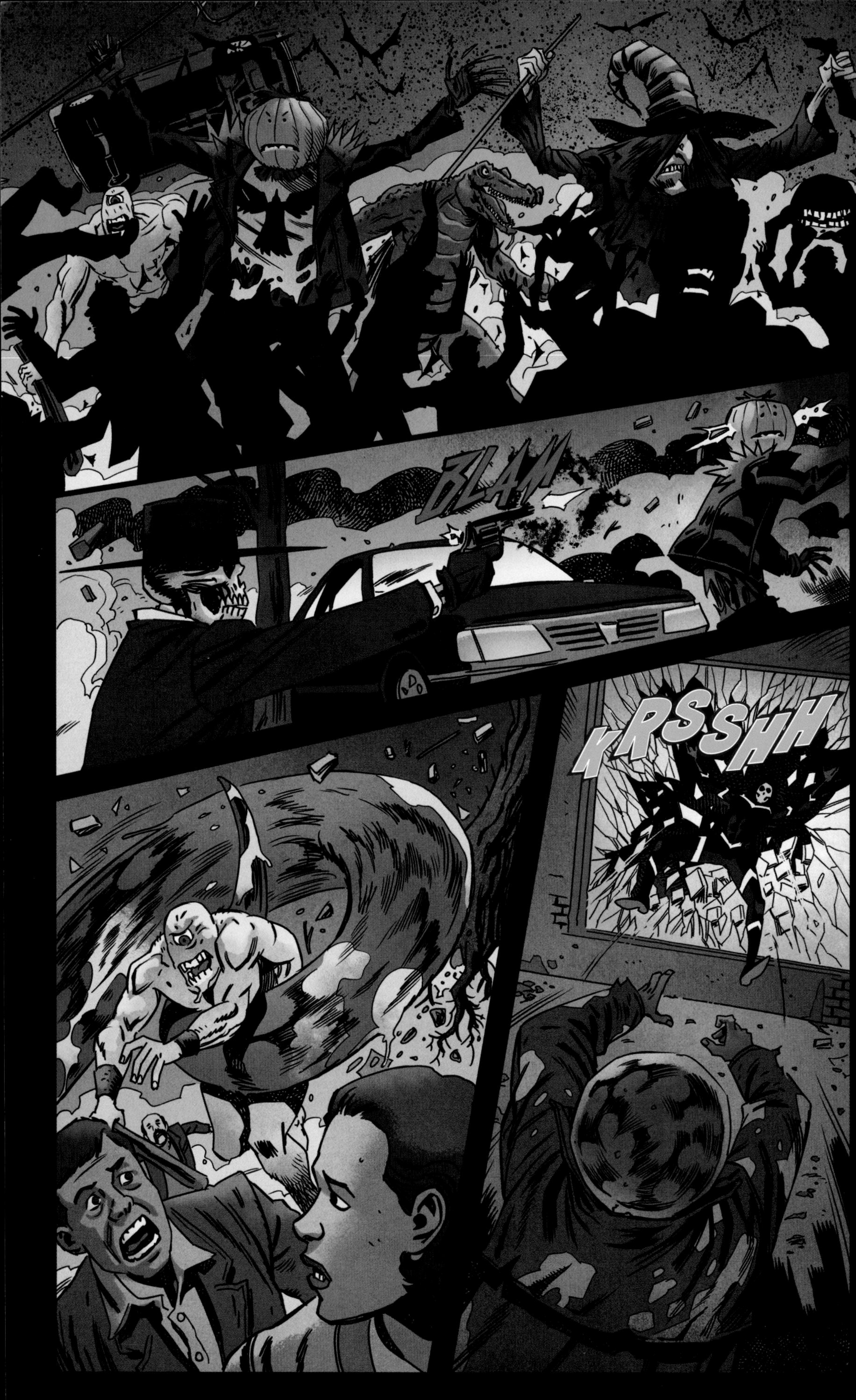
BLAM
KRSSHH

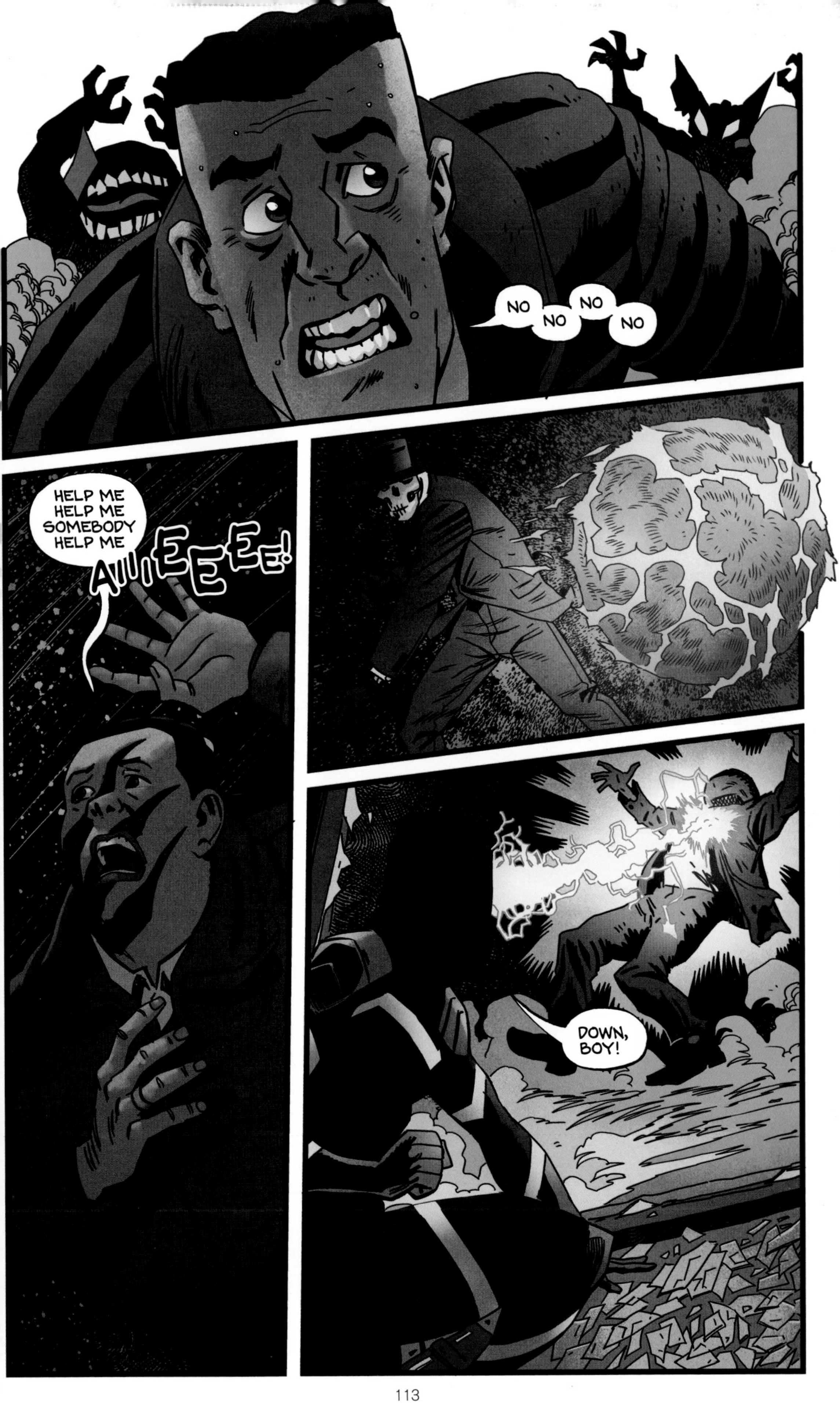
NO NO NO NO
HELP ME HELP ME SOMEBODY HELP ME
AIIIEEEEE!
DOWN, BOY!

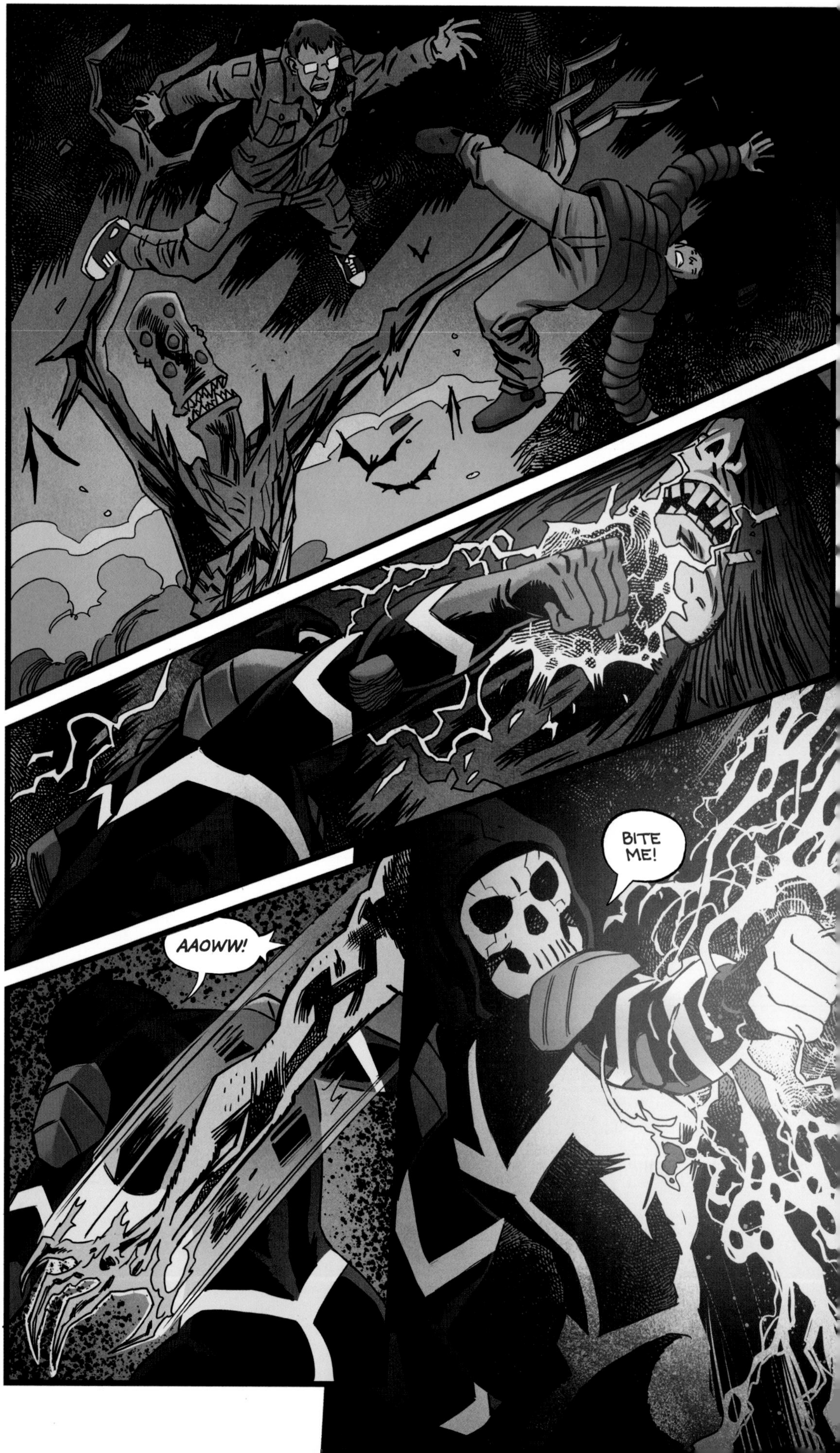
BITE ME!
AAOWW!

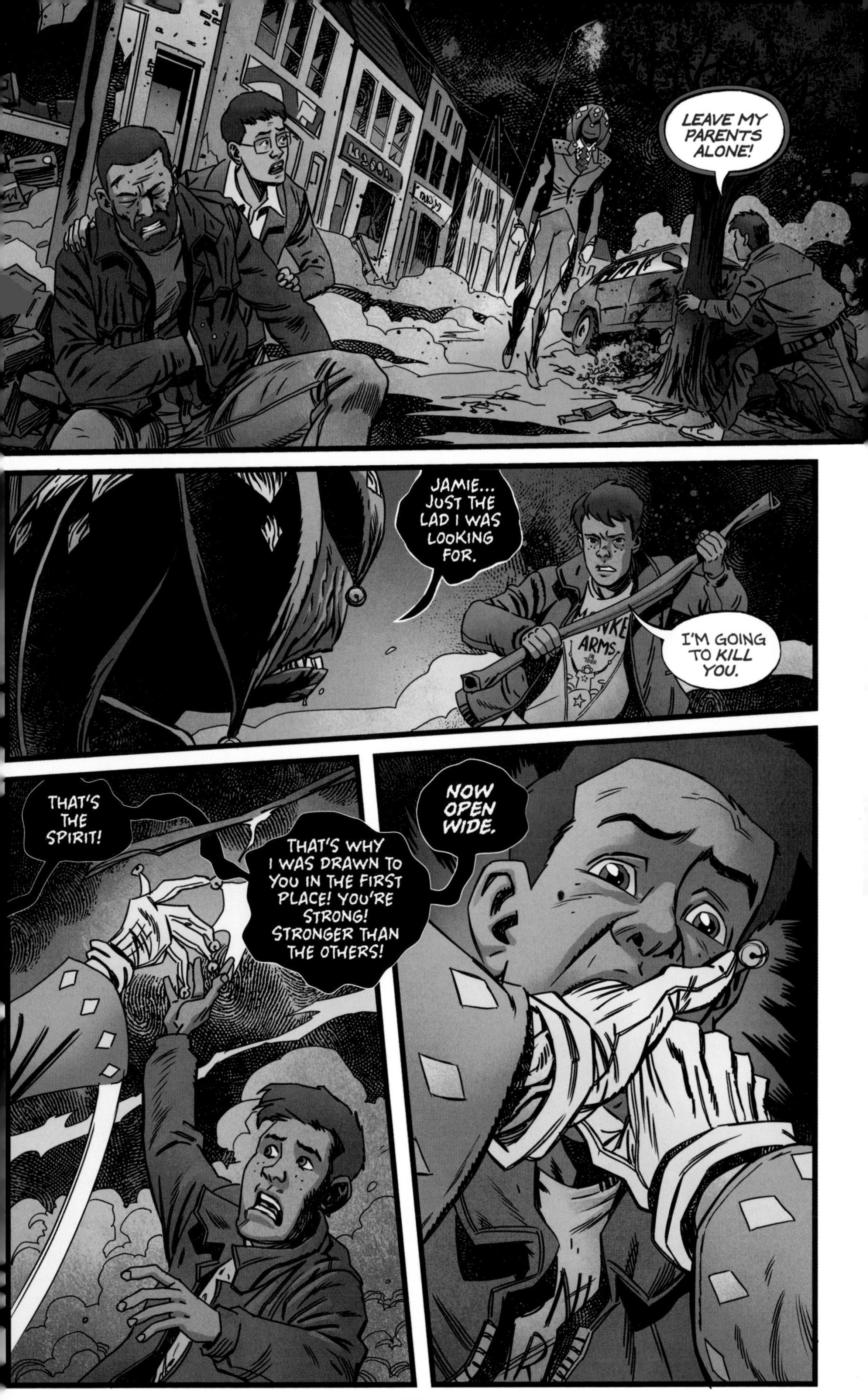
LEAVE MY PARENTS ALONE!
JAMIE... JUST THE LAD I WAS LOOKING FOR.
I'M GOING TO KILL YOU.
THAT'S THE SPIRIT!
THAT'S WHY I WAS DRAWN TO YOU IN THE FIRST PLACE! YOU'RE STRONG! STRONGER THAN THE OTHERS!
NOW OPEN WIDE.

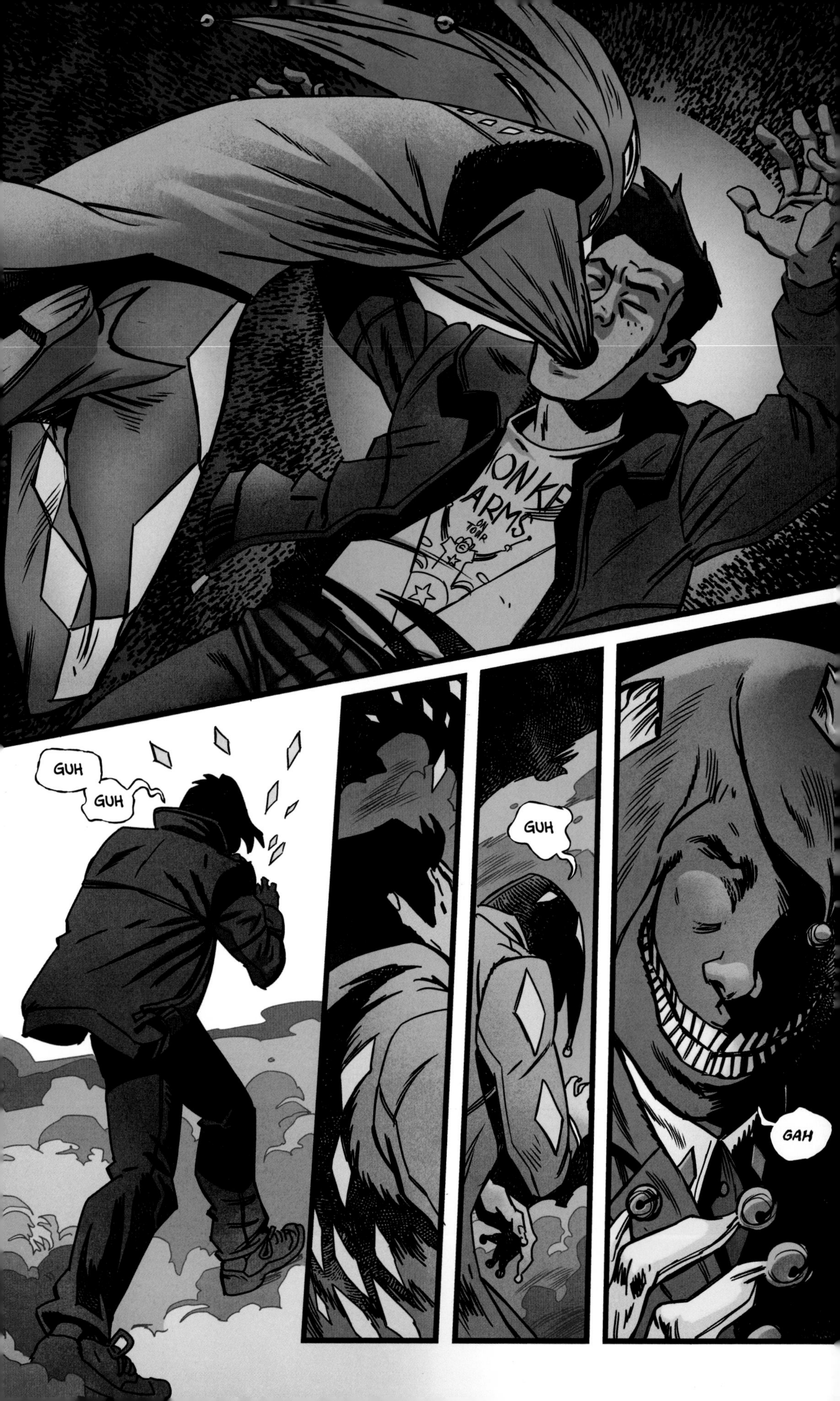

ONKE
ARMS
ON TOUR
GUH
GUH
GUH
GAH

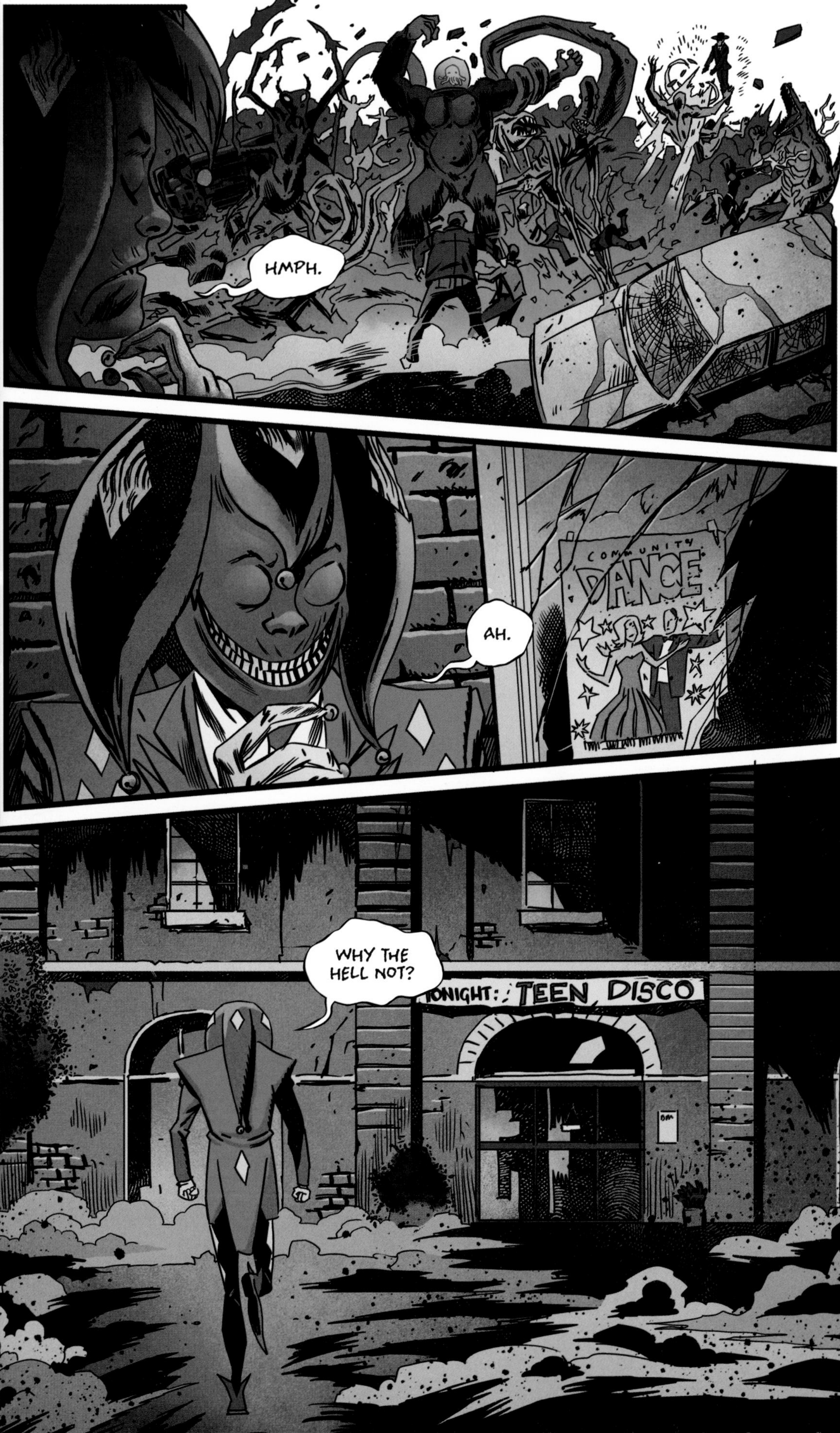
HMPH.
COMMUNITY DANCE
AH.
WHY THE HELL NOT?
TONIGHT: TEEN DISCO

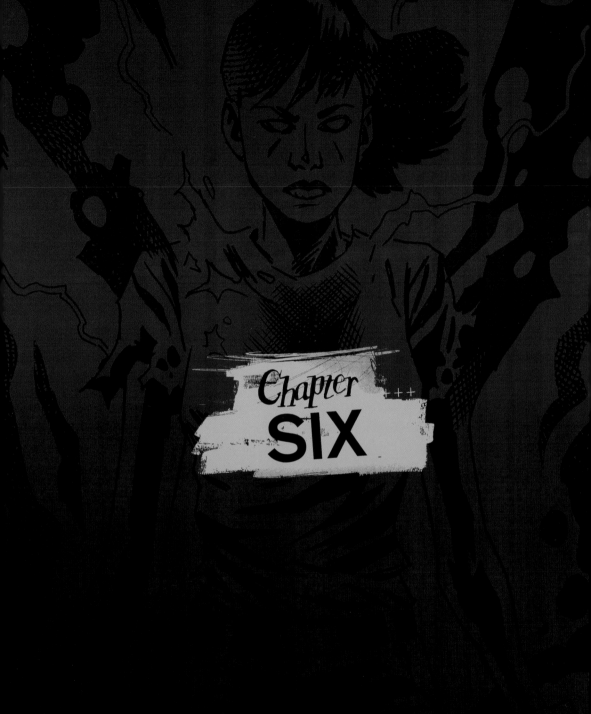

Chapter
SIX

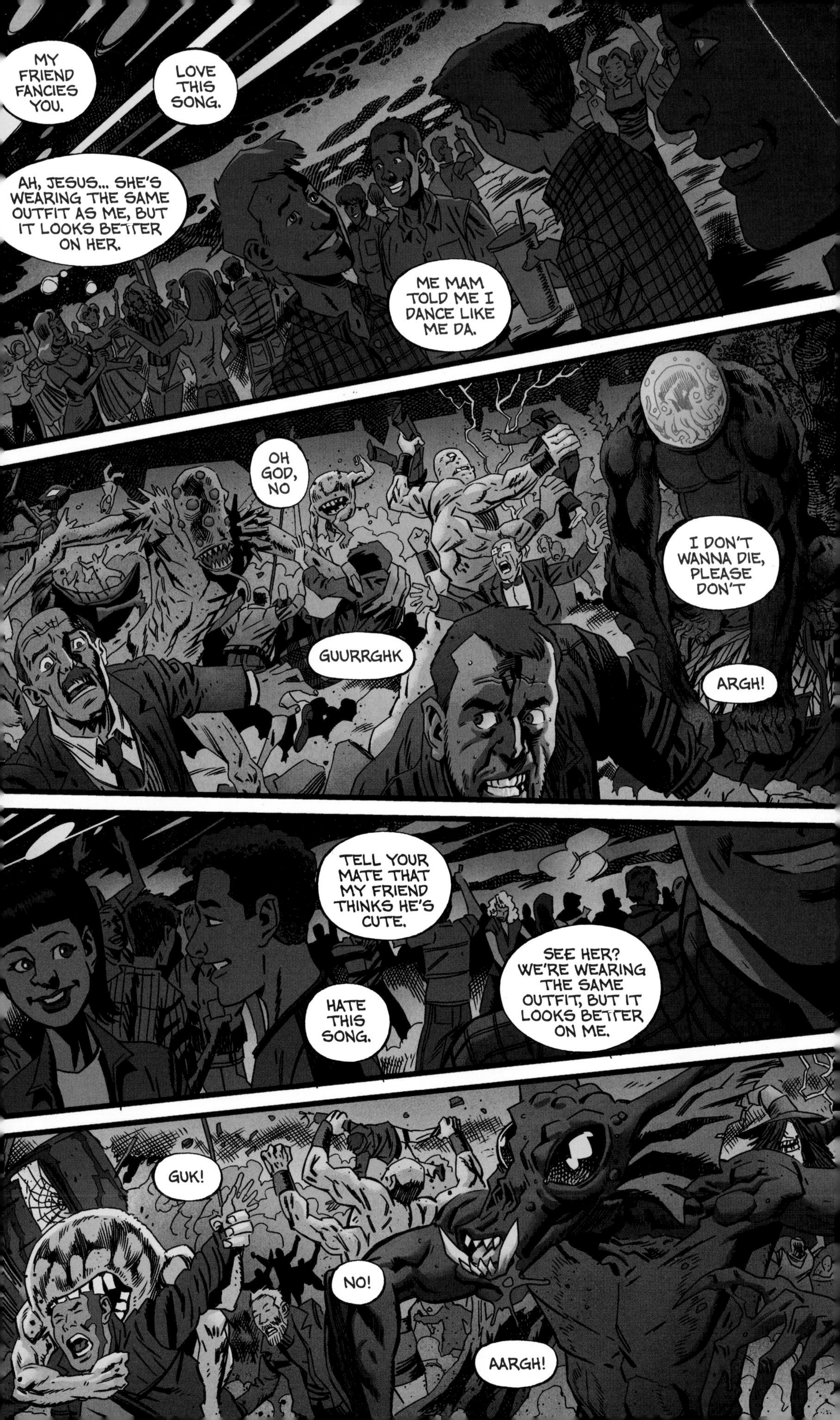
MY FRIEND FANCIES YOU.
LOVE THIS SONG.
AH, JESUS... SHE'S WEARING THE SAME OUTFIT AS ME, BUT IT LOOKS BETTER ON HER.
ME MAM TOLD ME I DANCE LIKE ME DA.
OH GOD, NO
I DON'T WANNA DIE, PLEASE DON'T
GUURRGHK
ARGH!
TELL YOUR MATE THAT MY FRIEND THINKS HE'S CUTE.
SEE HER? WE'RE WEARING THE SAME OUTFIT, BUT IT LOOKS BETTER ON ME.
HATE THIS SONG.
GUK!
NO!
AARGH!

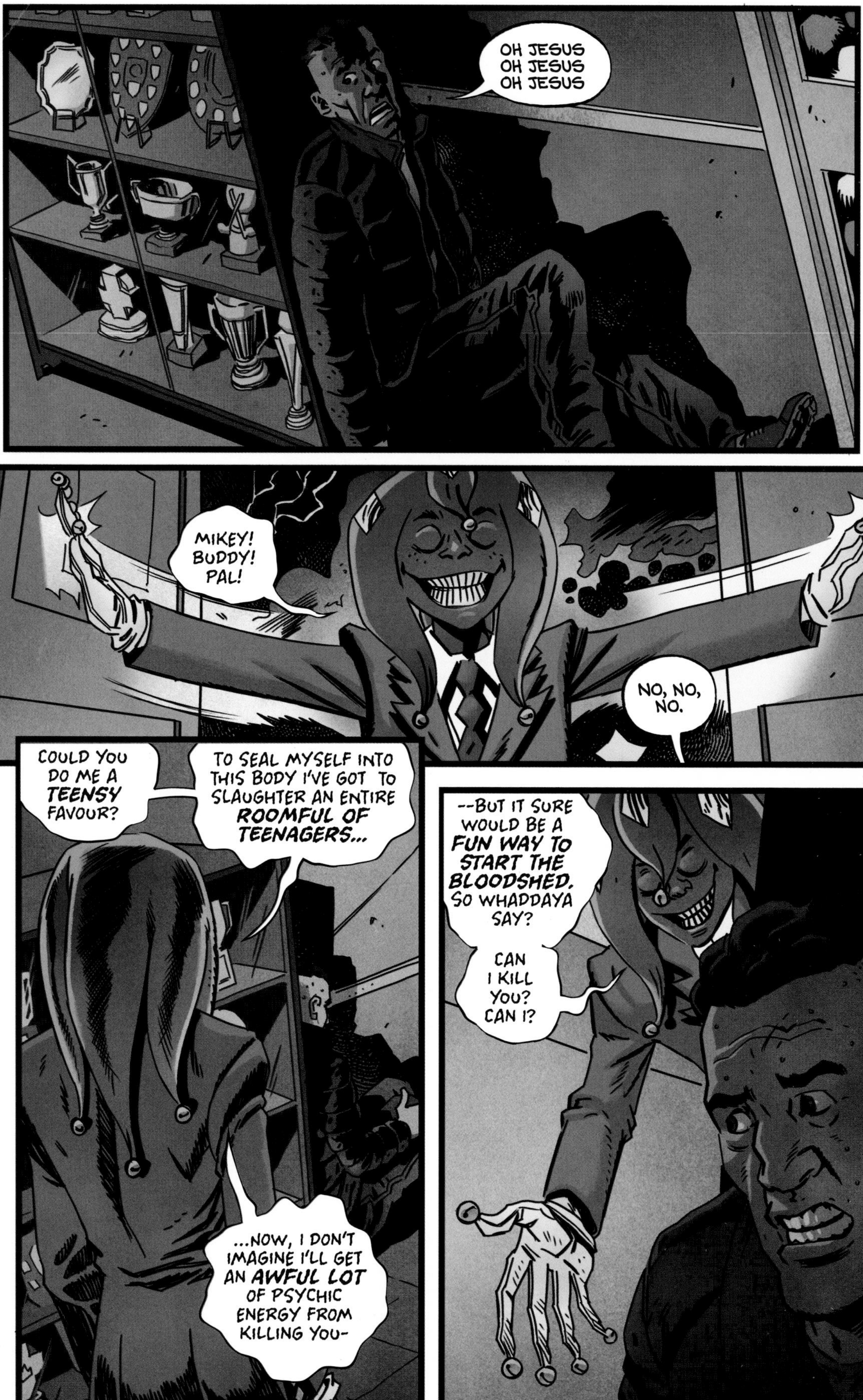
OH JESUS
OH JESUS
OH JESUS
MIKEY! BUDDY! PAL!
NO, NO, NO.
COULD YOU DO ME A TEENSY FAVOUR?
TO SEAL MYSELF INTO THIS BODY I'VE GOT TO SLAUGHTER AN ENTIRE ROOMFUL OF TEENAGERS...
...NOW, I DON'T IMAGINE I'LL GET AN AWFUL LOT OF PSYCHIC ENERGY FROM KILLING YOU-
--BUT IT SURE WOULD BE A FUN WAY TO START THE BLOODSHED. SO WHADDAYA SAY?
CAN I KILL YOU? CAN I?

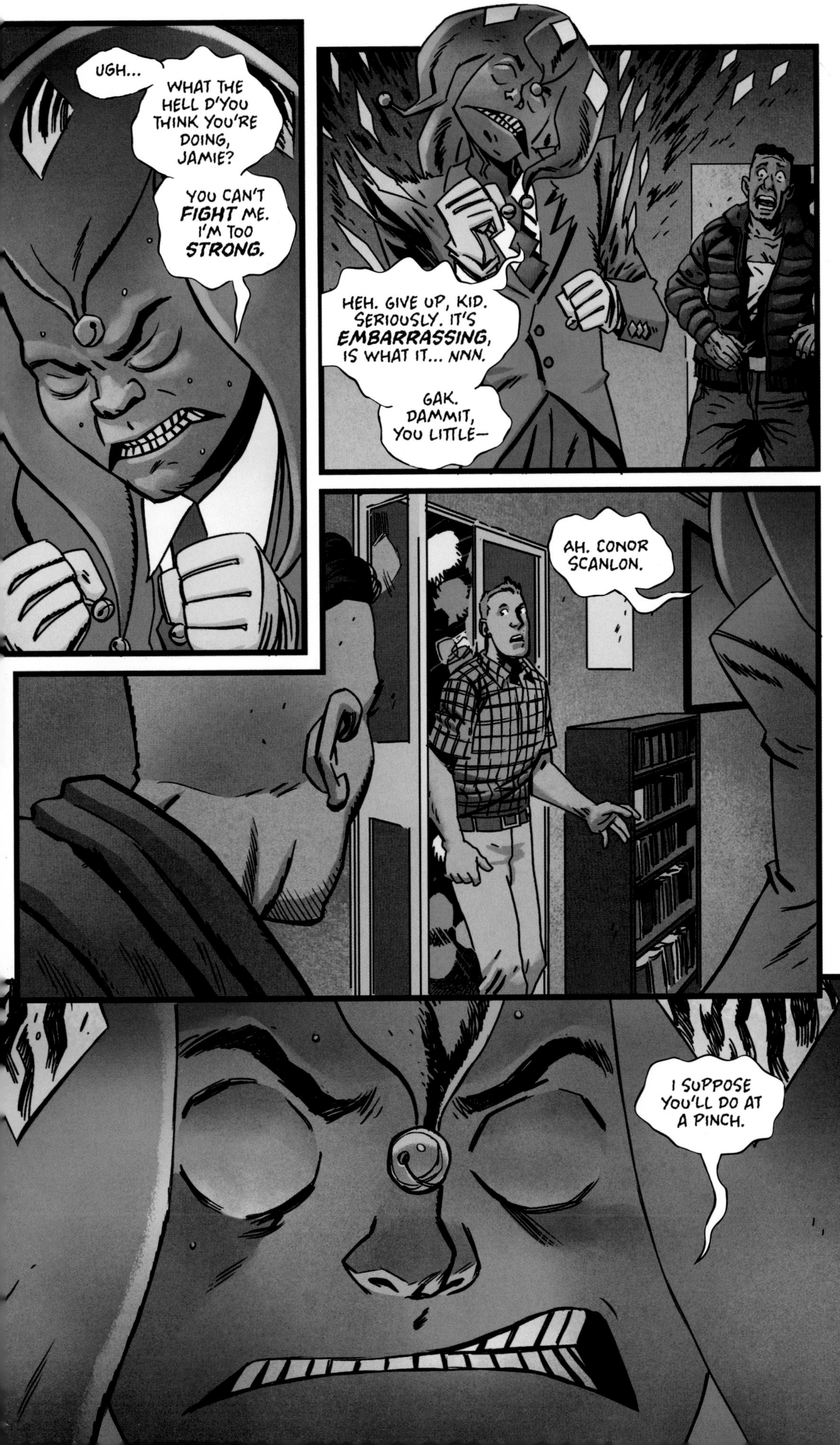
UGH...
WHAT THE HELL D'YOU THINK YOU'RE DOING, JAMIE?
YOU CAN'T **FIGHT** ME. I'M TOO **STRONG.**
HEH. GIVE UP, KID. SERIOUSLY. IT'S **EMBARRASSING**, IS WHAT IT... NNN.
GAK. DAMMIT, YOU LITTLE—
AH. CONOR SCANLON.
I SUPPOSE YOU'LL DO AT A PINCH.

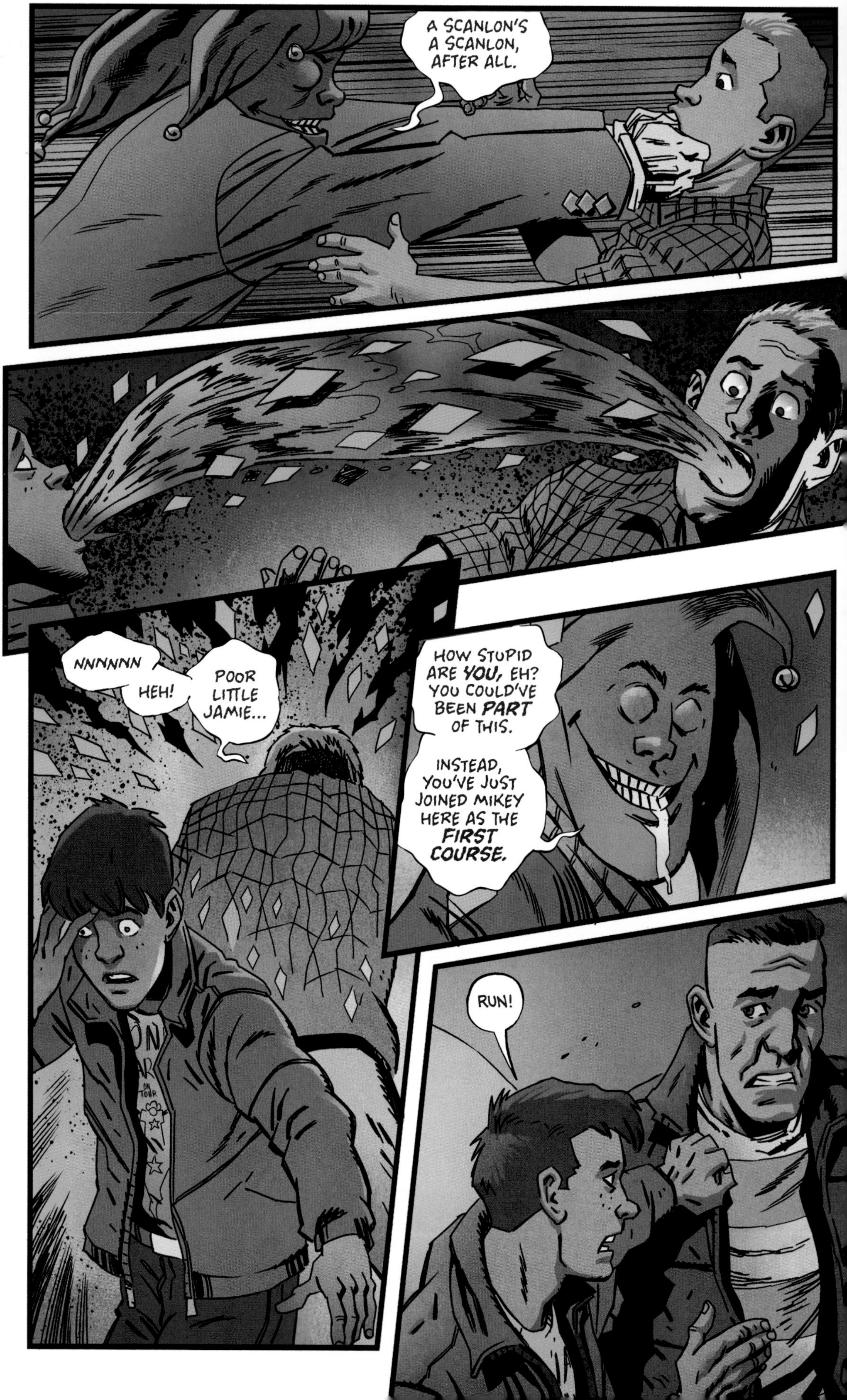

A SCANLON'S A SCANLON, AFTER ALL.
NNNNNN
HEH!
POOR LITTLE JAMIE...
HOW STUPID ARE YOU, EH? YOU COULD'VE BEEN PART OF THIS.
INSTEAD, YOU'VE JUST JOINED MIKEY HERE AS THE FIRST COURSE.
RUN!

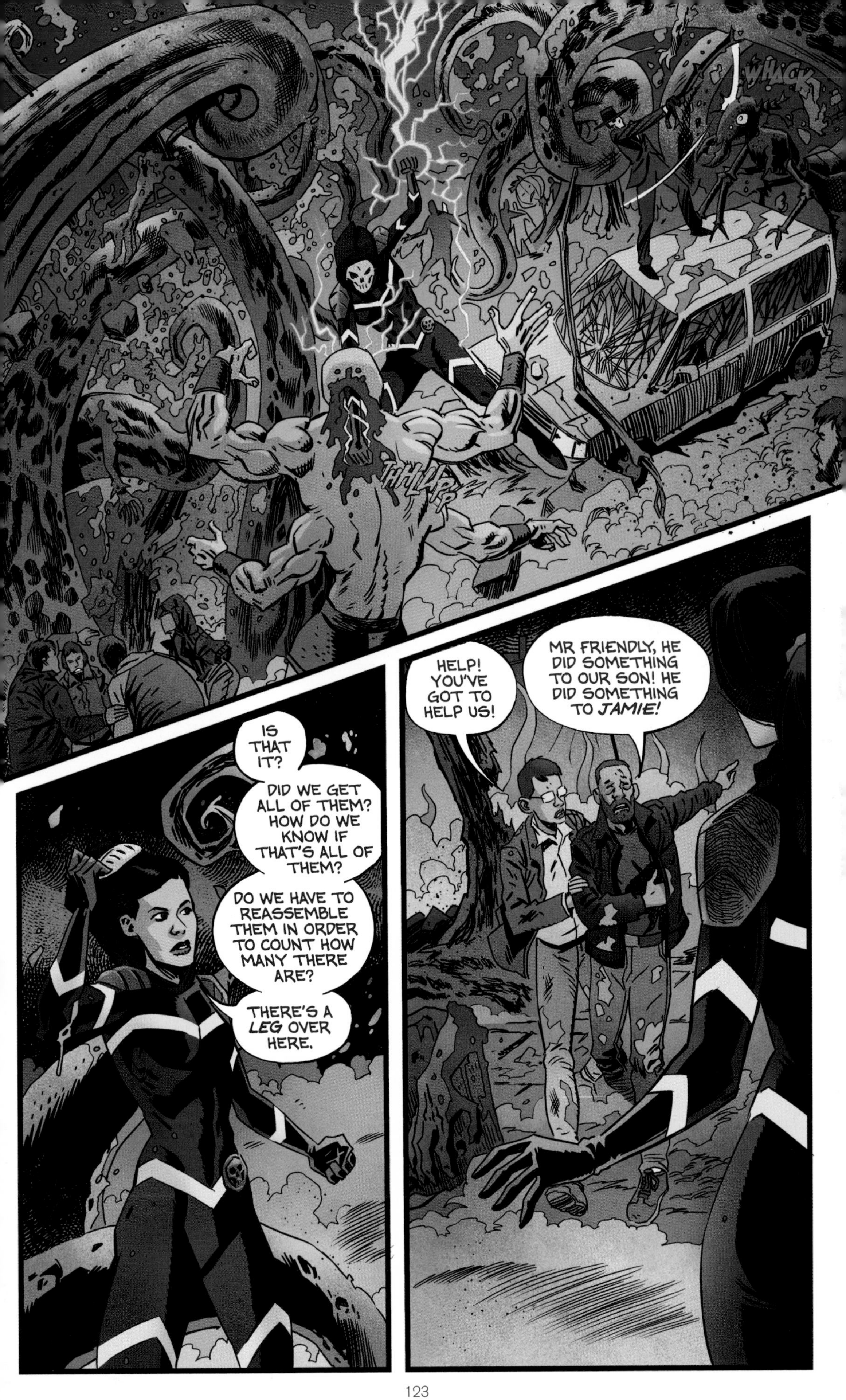
WHACK
THHLUPP
IS THAT IT?
DID WE GET ALL OF THEM? HOW DO WE KNOW IF THAT'S ALL OF THEM?
DO WE HAVE TO REASSEMBLE THEM IN ORDER TO COUNT HOW MANY THERE ARE?
THERE'S A *LEG* OVER HERE.
HELP! YOU'VE GOT TO HELP US!
MR FRIENDLY, HE DID SOMETHING TO OUR SON! HE DID SOMETHING TO *JAMIE!*

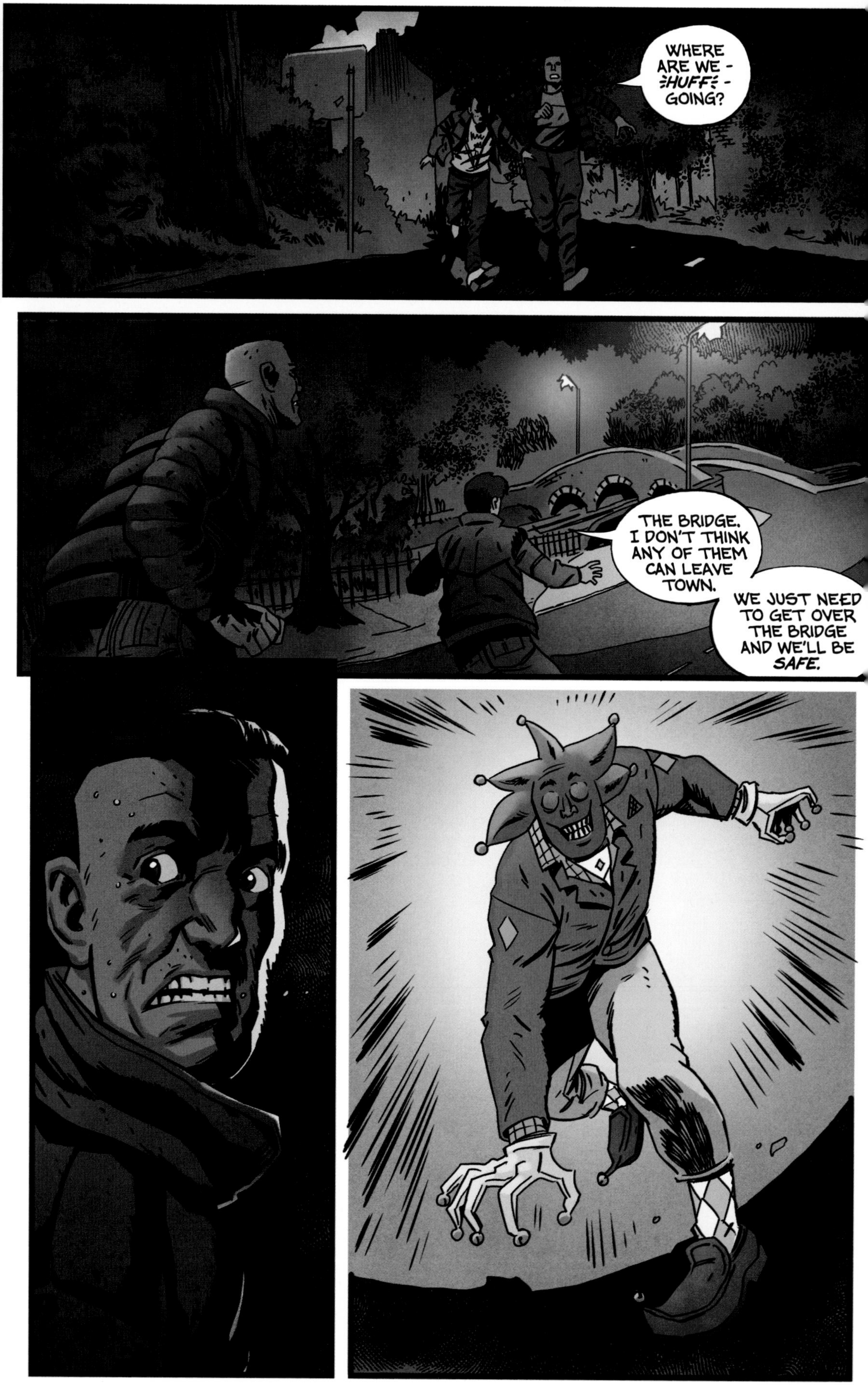
WHERE ARE WE - *HUFF* - GOING?
THE BRIDGE. I DON'T THINK ANY OF THEM CAN LEAVE TOWN.
WE JUST NEED TO GET OVER THE BRIDGE AND WE'LL BE *SAFE.*

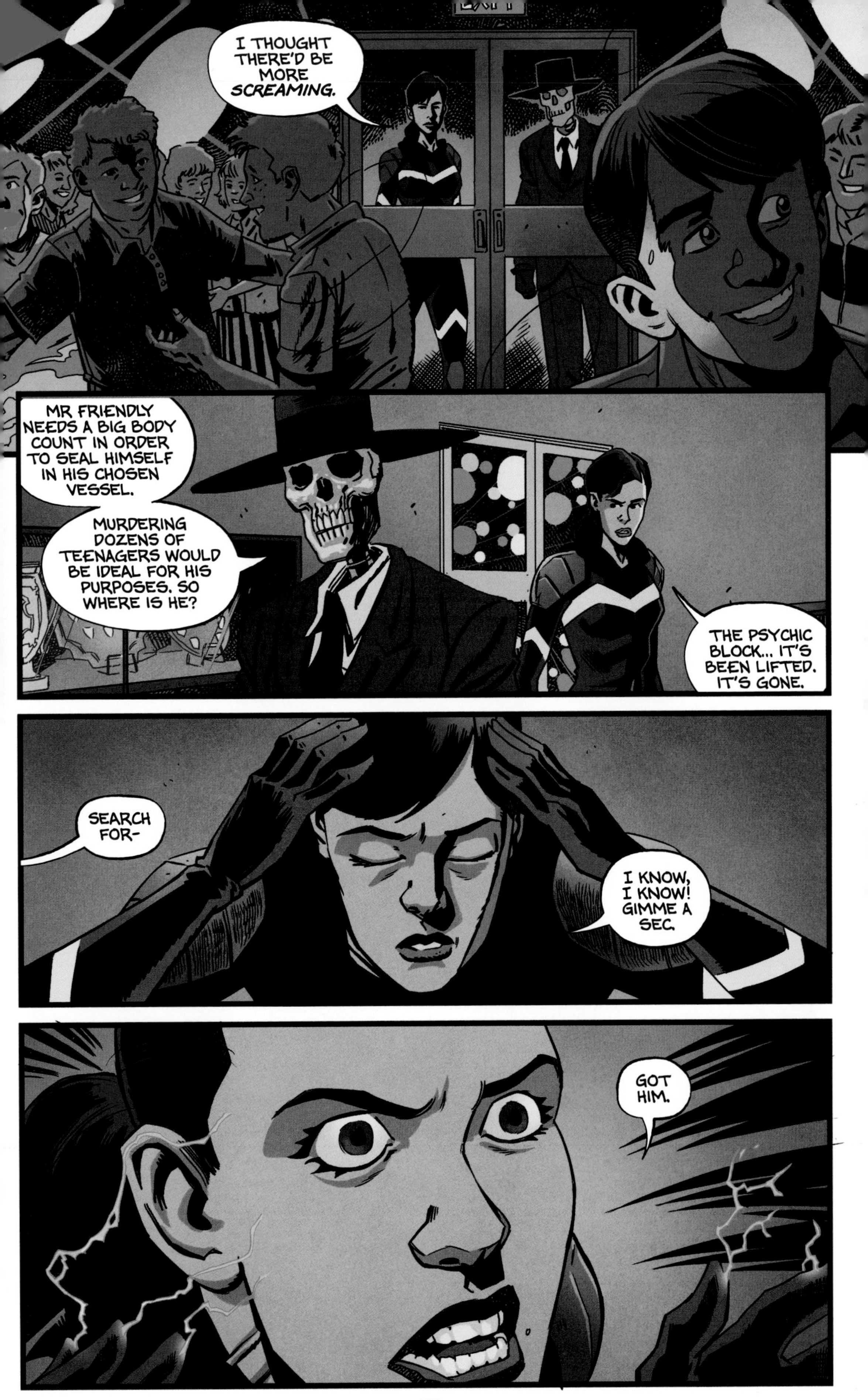
I THOUGHT THERE'D BE MORE *SCREAMING.*
MR FRIENDLY NEEDS A BIG BODY COUNT IN ORDER TO SEAL HIMSELF IN HIS CHOSEN VESSEL.
MURDERING DOZENS OF TEENAGERS WOULD BE IDEAL FOR HIS PURPOSES. SO WHERE IS HE?
THE PSYCHIC BLOCK... IT'S BEEN LIFTED. IT'S GONE.
SEARCH FOR-
I KNOW, I KNOW! GIMME A SEC.
GOT HIM.

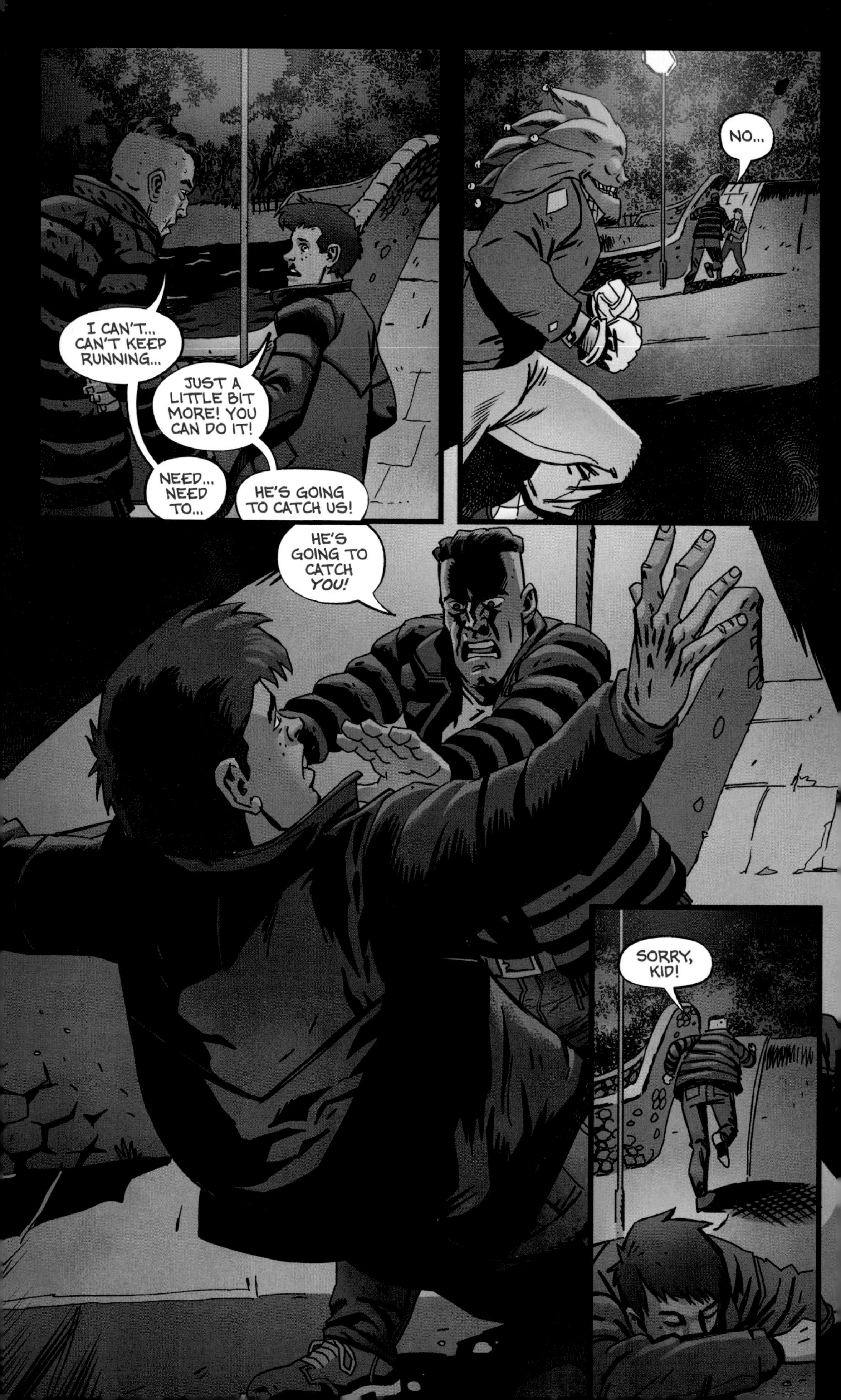
I CAN'T... CAN'T KEEP RUNNING...
JUST A LITTLE BIT MORE! YOU CAN DO IT!
NEED... NEED TO...
HE'S GOING TO CATCH US!
NO...
HE'S GOING TO CATCH YOU!
SORRY, KID!

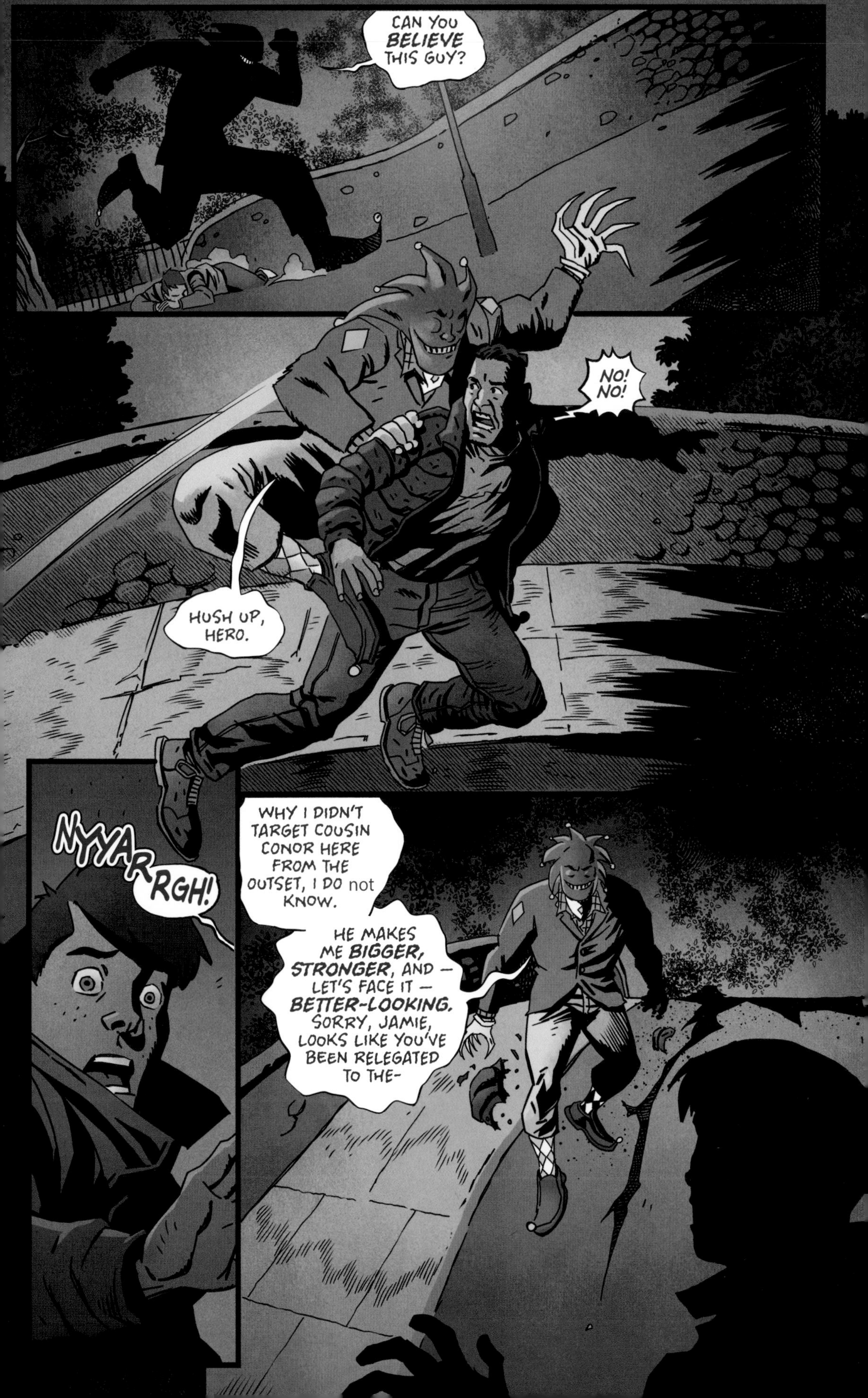
CAN YOU **BELIEVE** THIS GUY?
NO! NO!
HUSH UP, HERO.
NYYARRGH!
WHY I DIDN'T TARGET COUSIN CONOR HERE FROM THE OUTSET, I DO not KNOW.
HE MAKES ME **BIGGER, STRONGER**, AND — LET'S FACE IT — **BETTER-LOOKING.** SORRY, JAMIE, LOOKS LIKE YOU'VE BEEN RELEGATED TO THE-

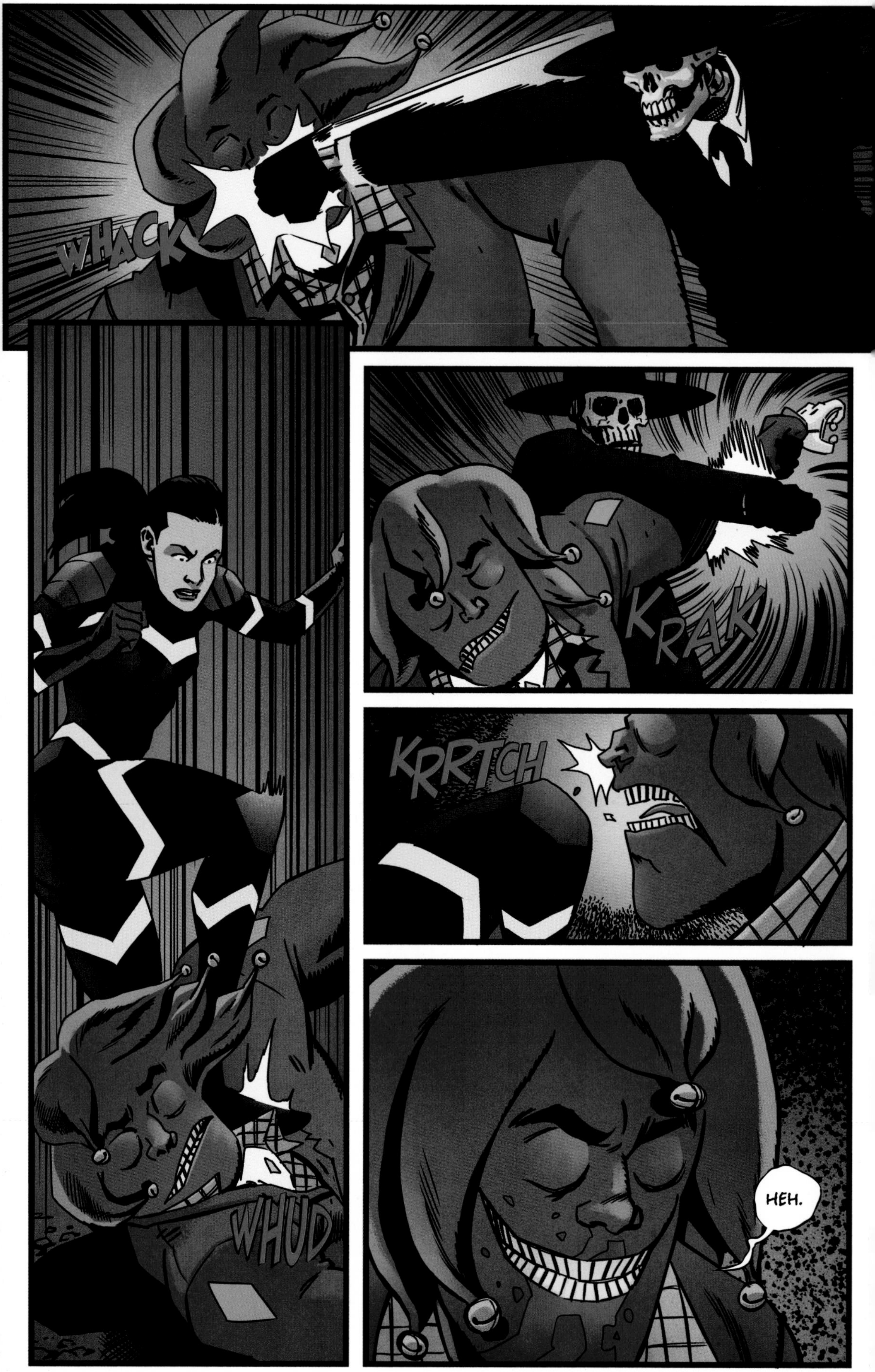
WHACK
KRAK
KRRTCH
WHUD
HEH.

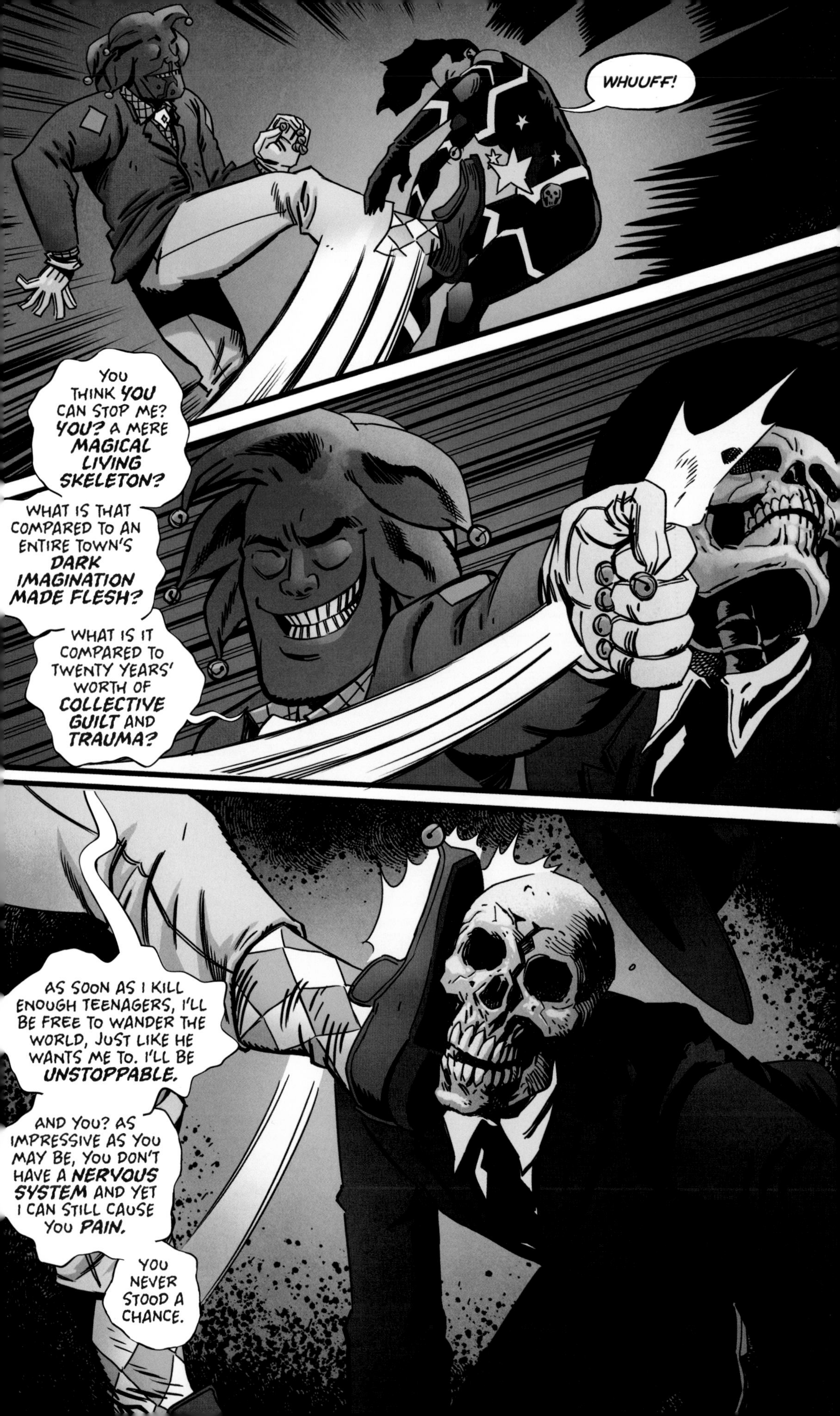
WHUUFF!
YOU THINK YOU CAN STOP ME? YOU? A MERE MAGICAL LIVING SKELETON?
WHAT IS THAT COMPARED TO AN ENTIRE TOWN'S DARK IMAGINATION MADE FLESH?
WHAT IS IT COMPARED TO TWENTY YEARS' WORTH OF COLLECTIVE GUILT AND TRAUMA?
AS SOON AS I KILL ENOUGH TEENAGERS, I'LL BE FREE TO WANDER THE WORLD, JUST LIKE HE WANTS ME TO. I'LL BE UNSTOPPABLE.
AND YOU? AS IMPRESSIVE AS YOU MAY BE, YOU DON'T HAVE A NERVOUS SYSTEM AND YET I CAN STILL CAUSE YOU PAIN.
YOU NEVER STOOD A CHANCE.

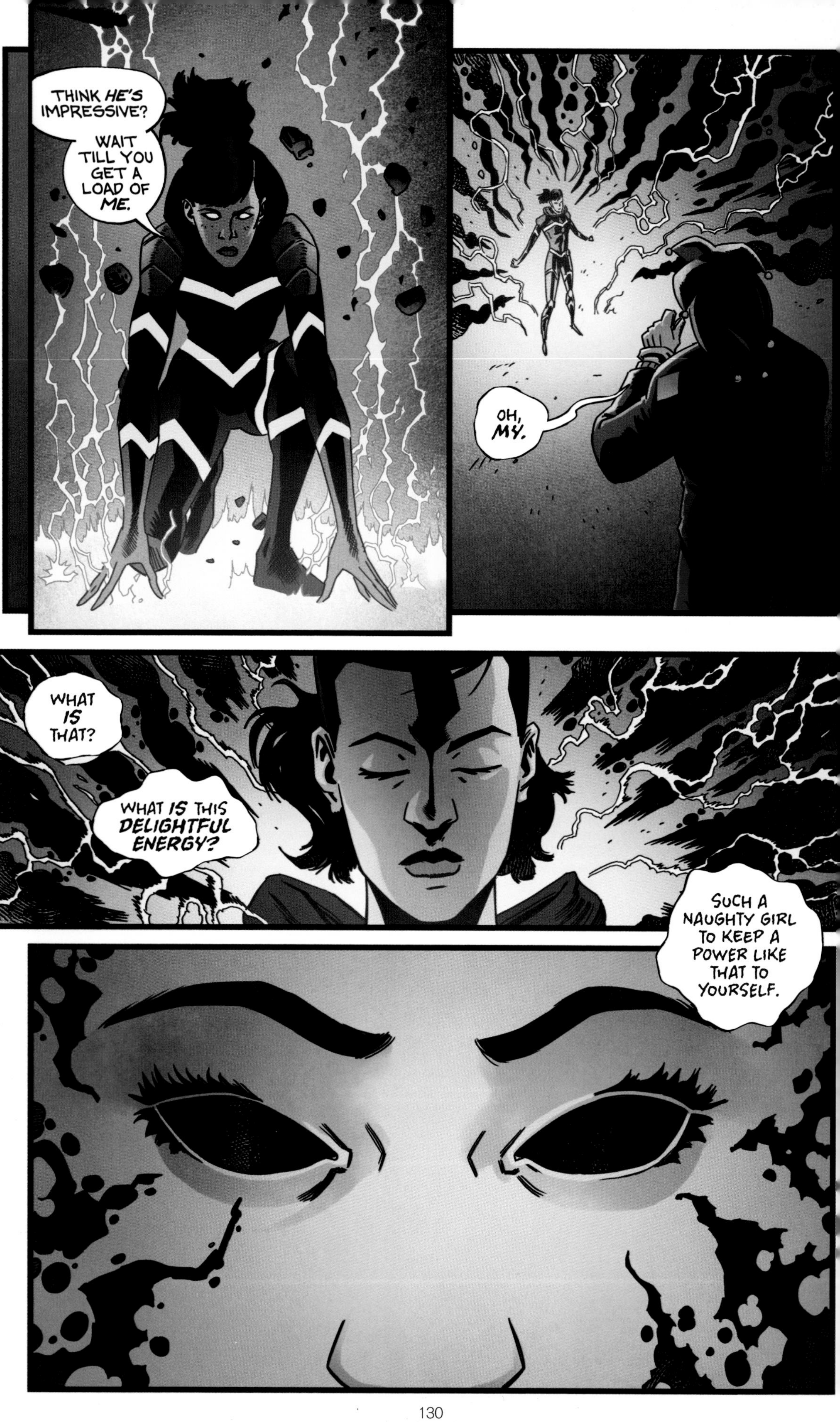
THINK HE'S IMPRESSIVE?
WAIT TILL YOU GET A LOAD OF ME.
OH, MY.
WHAT IS THAT?
WHAT IS THIS DELIGHTFUL ENERGY?
SUCH A NAUGHTY GIRL TO KEEP A POWER LIKE THAT TO YOURSELF.

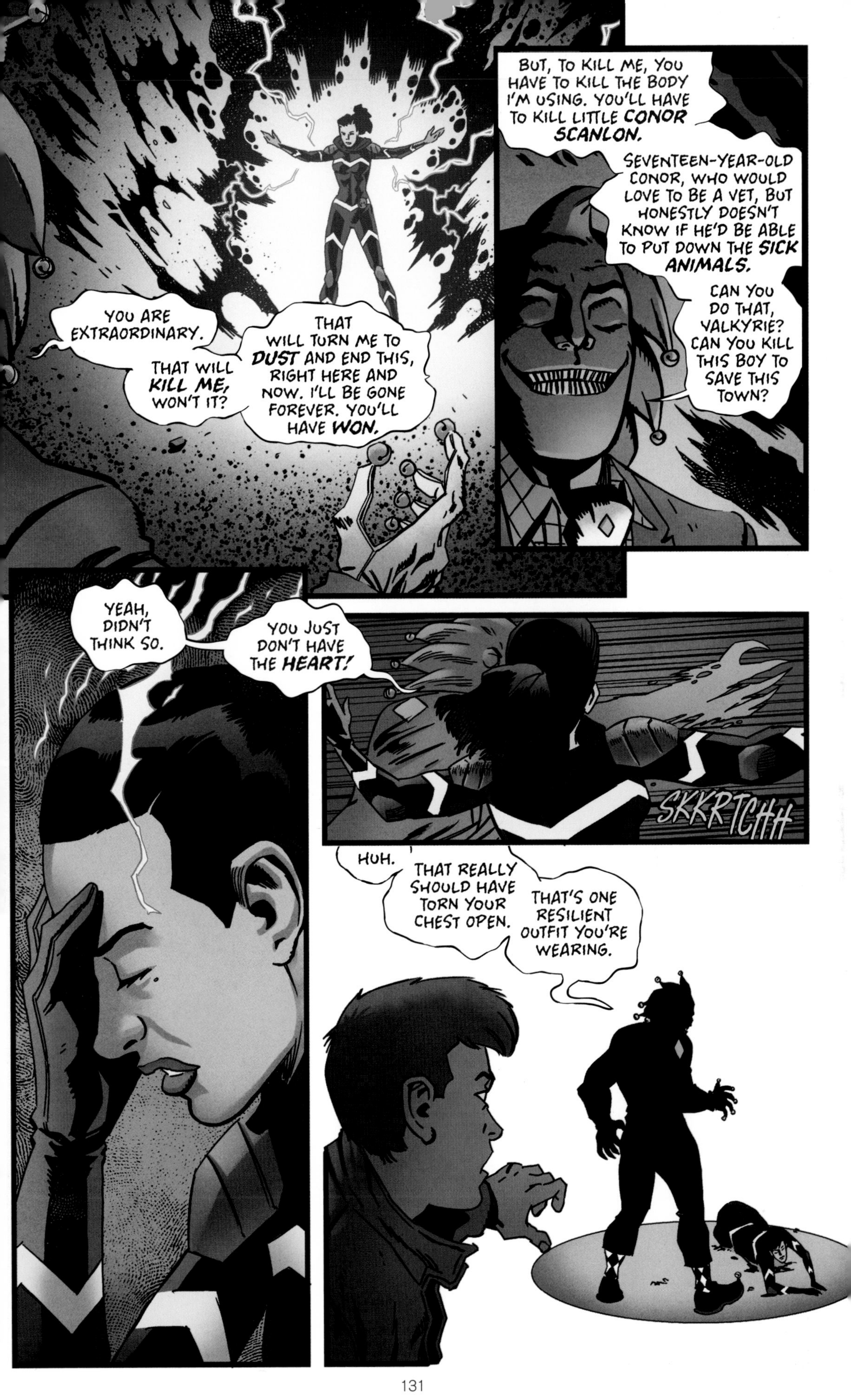
YOU ARE EXTRAORDINARY.
THAT WILL KILL ME, WON'T IT?
THAT WILL TURN ME TO DUST AND END THIS, RIGHT HERE AND NOW. I'LL BE GONE FOREVER. YOU'LL HAVE WON.
BUT, TO KILL ME, YOU HAVE TO KILL THE BODY I'M USING. YOU'LL HAVE TO KILL LITTLE CONOR SCANLON.
SEVENTEEN-YEAR-OLD CONOR, WHO WOULD LOVE TO BE A VET, BUT HONESTLY DOESN'T KNOW IF HE'D BE ABLE TO PUT DOWN THE SICK ANIMALS.
CAN YOU DO THAT, VALKYRIE? CAN YOU KILL THIS BOY TO SAVE THIS TOWN?
YEAH, DIDN'T THINK SO.
YOU JUST DON'T HAVE THE HEART!
SKKRTCHH
HUH.
THAT REALLY SHOULD HAVE TORN YOUR CHEST OPEN.
THAT'S ONE RESILIENT OUTFIT YOU'RE WEARING.

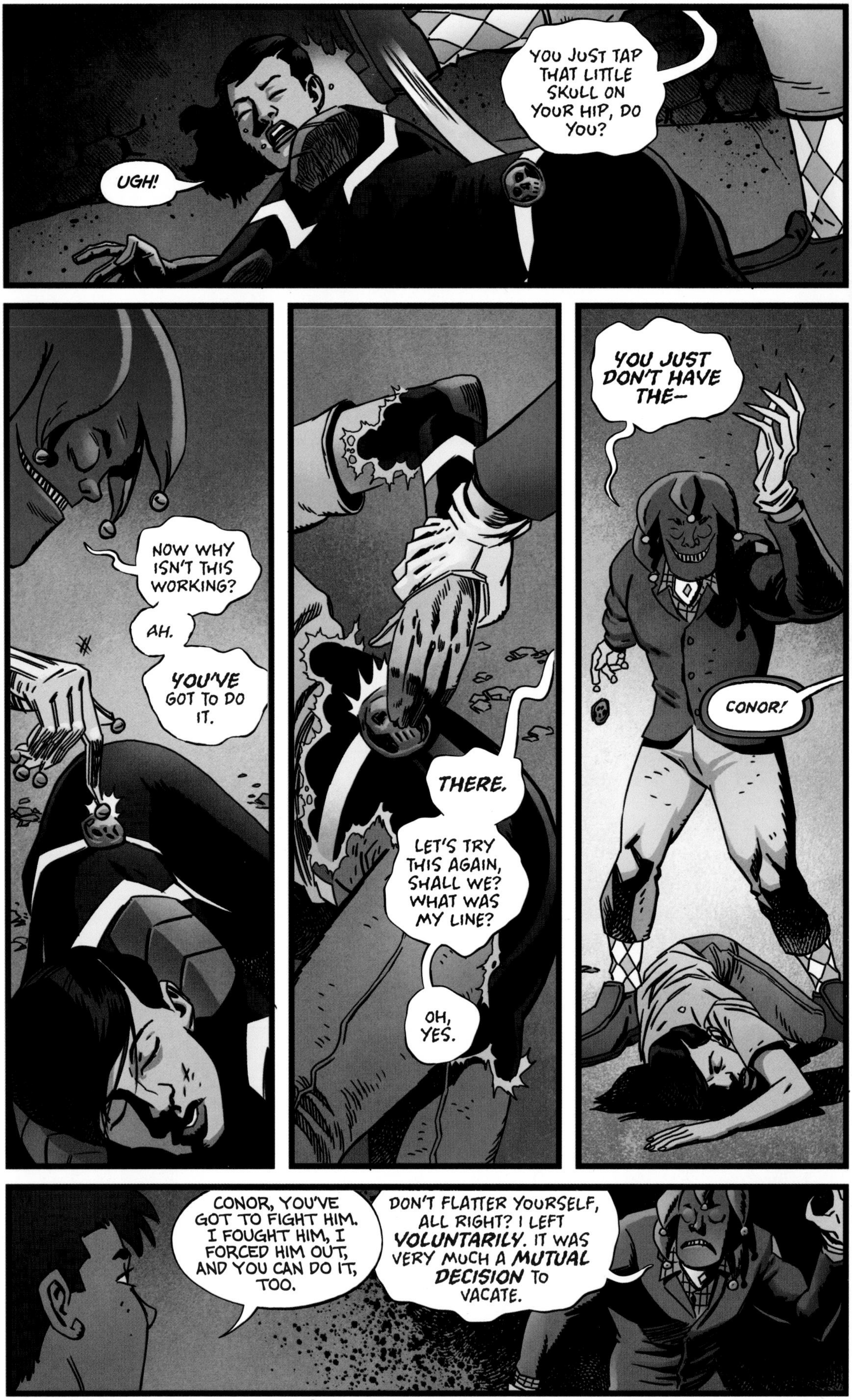
YOU JUST TAP THAT LITTLE SKULL ON YOUR HIP, DO YOU?
UGH!
NOW WHY ISN'T THIS WORKING?
AH.
YOU'VE GOT TO DO IT.
THERE.
LET'S TRY THIS AGAIN, SHALL WE? WHAT WAS MY LINE?
OH, YES.
YOU JUST DON'T HAVE THE–
CONOR!
CONOR, YOU'VE GOT TO FIGHT HIM. I FOUGHT HIM, I FORCED HIM OUT, AND YOU CAN DO IT, TOO.
DON'T FLATTER YOURSELF, ALL RIGHT? I LEFT VOLUNTARILY. IT WAS VERY MUCH A MUTUAL DECISION TO VACATE.

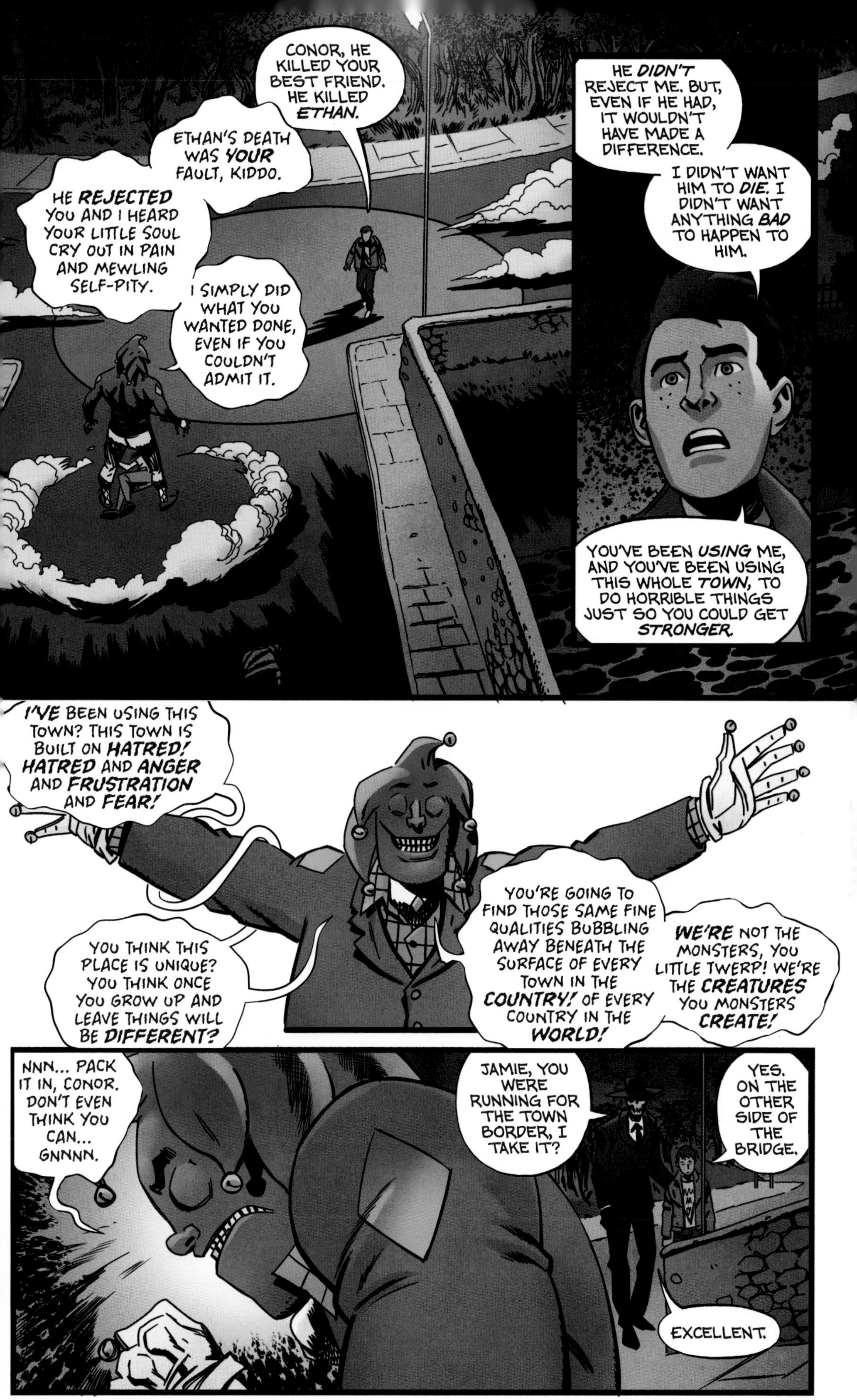
CONOR, HE KILLED YOUR BEST FRIEND. HE KILLED ETHAN.
ETHAN'S DEATH WAS YOUR FAULT, KIDDO.
HE REJECTED YOU AND I HEARD YOUR LITTLE SOUL CRY OUT IN PAIN AND MEWLING SELF-PITY.
I SIMPLY DID WHAT YOU WANTED DONE, EVEN IF YOU COULDN'T ADMIT IT.
HE DIDN'T REJECT ME. BUT, EVEN IF HE HAD, IT WOULDN'T HAVE MADE A DIFFERENCE.
I DIDN'T WANT HIM TO DIE. I DIDN'T WANT ANYTHING BAD TO HAPPEN TO HIM.
YOU'VE BEEN USING ME, AND YOU'VE BEEN USING THIS WHOLE TOWN, TO DO HORRIBLE THINGS JUST SO YOU COULD GET STRONGER.
I'VE BEEN USING THIS TOWN? THIS TOWN IS BUILT ON HATRED! HATRED AND ANGER AND FRUSTRATION AND FEAR!
YOU THINK THIS PLACE IS UNIQUE? YOU THINK ONCE YOU GROW UP AND LEAVE THINGS WILL BE DIFFERENT?
YOU'RE GOING TO FIND THOSE SAME FINE QUALITIES BUBBLING AWAY BENEATH THE SURFACE OF EVERY TOWN IN THE COUNTRY! OF EVERY COUNTRY IN THE WORLD!
WE'RE NOT THE MONSTERS, YOU LITTLE TWERP! WE'RE THE CREATURES YOU MONSTERS CREATE!
NNN... PACK IT IN, CONOR. DON'T EVEN THINK YOU CAN... GNNNN.
JAMIE, YOU WERE RUNNING FOR THE TOWN BORDER, I TAKE IT?
YES. ON THE OTHER SIDE OF THE BRIDGE.
EXCELLENT.

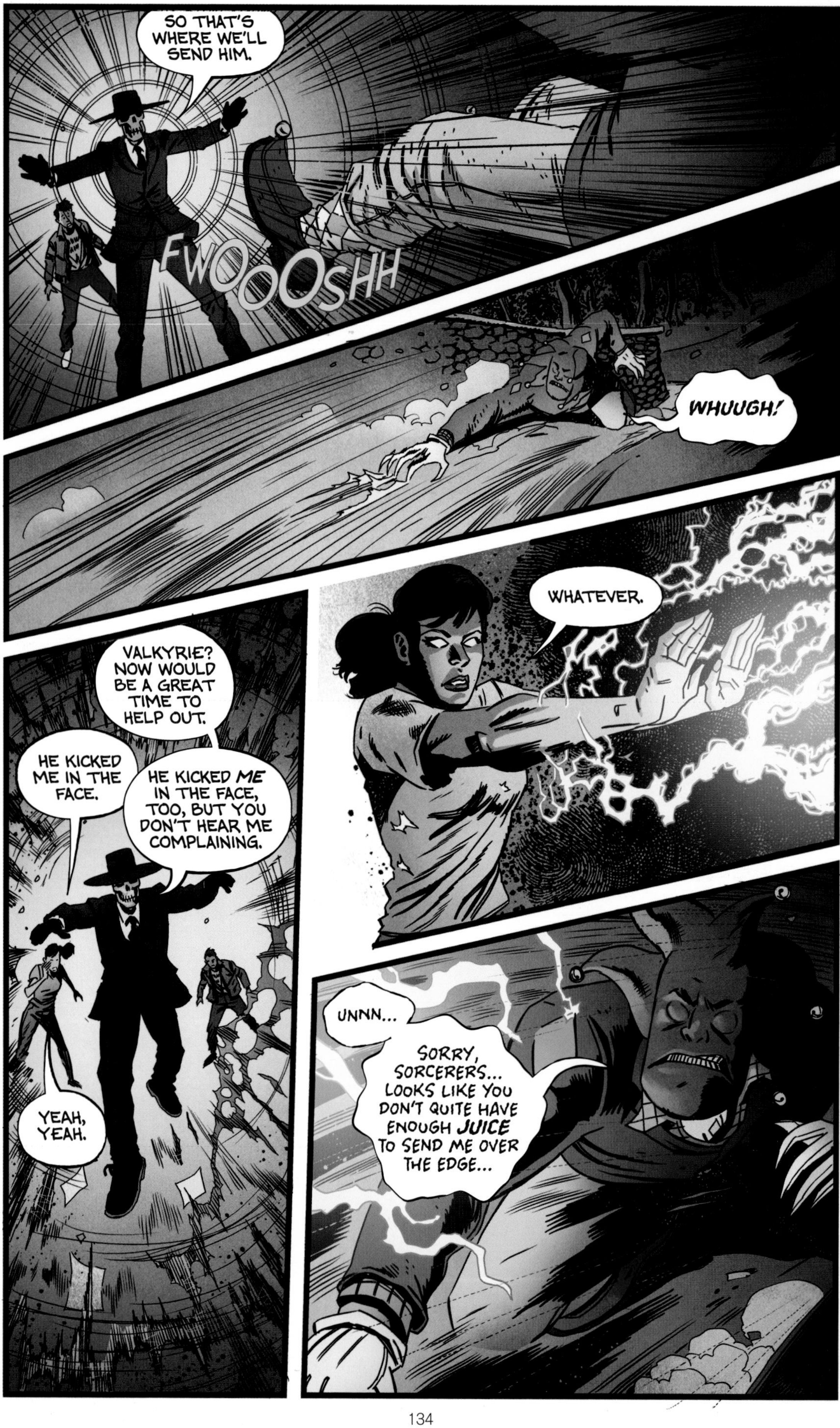
SO THAT'S WHERE WE'LL SEND HIM.
FWOOOSHH
WHUUGH!
WHATEVER.
VALKYRIE? NOW WOULD BE A GREAT TIME TO HELP OUT.
HE KICKED ME IN THE FACE.
HE KICKED ME IN THE FACE, TOO, BUT YOU DON'T HEAR ME COMPLAINING.
YEAH, YEAH.
UNNN...
SORRY, SORCERERS... LOOKS LIKE YOU DON'T QUITE HAVE ENOUGH JUICE TO SEND ME OVER THE EDGE...

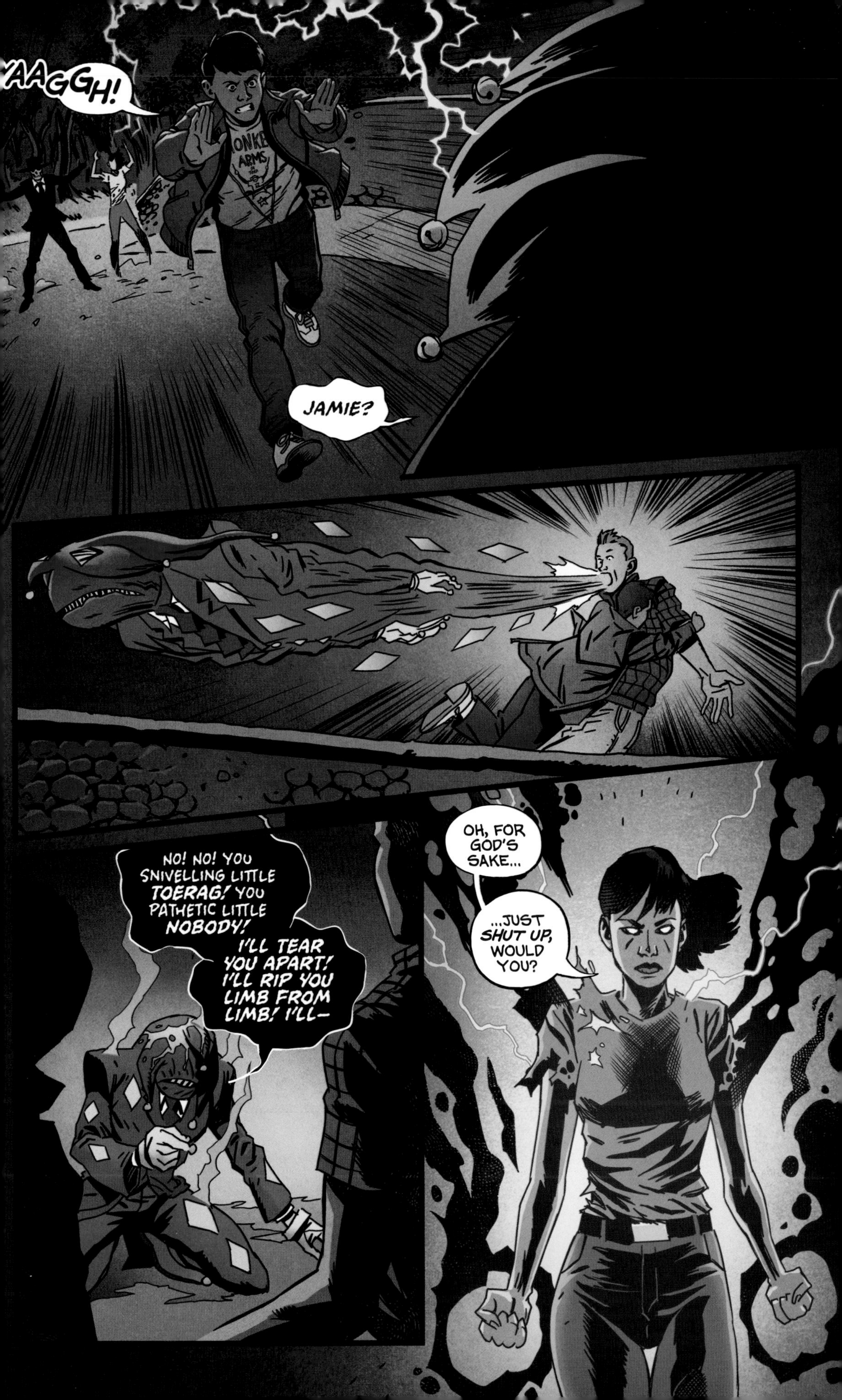
AAGGH!
JAMIE?
NO! NO! YOU SNIVELLING LITTLE TOERAG! YOU PATHETIC LITTLE NOBODY!
I'LL TEAR YOU APART! I'LL RIP YOU LIMB FROM LIMB! I'LL–
OH, FOR GOD'S SAKE...
...JUST SHUT UP, WOULD YOU?

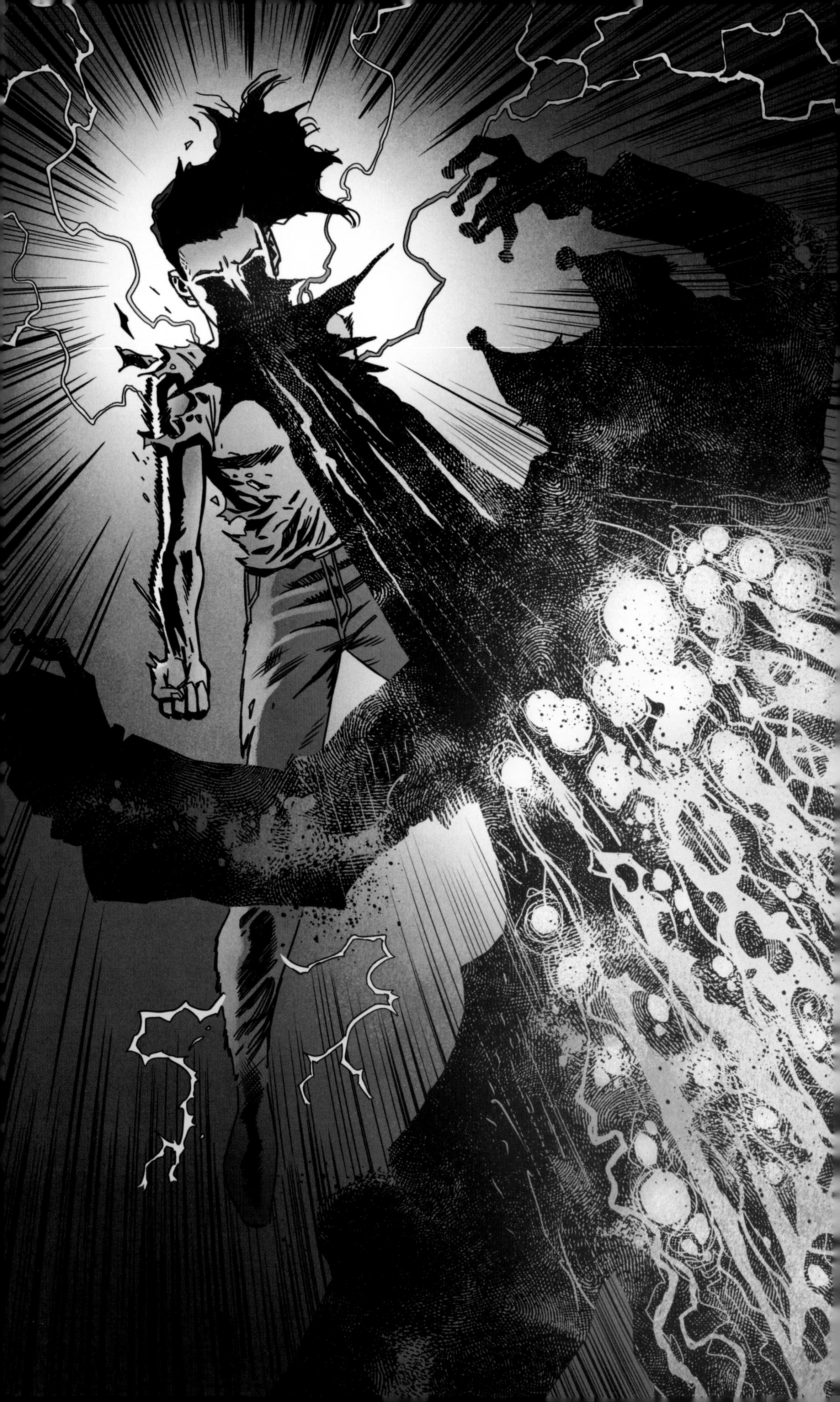

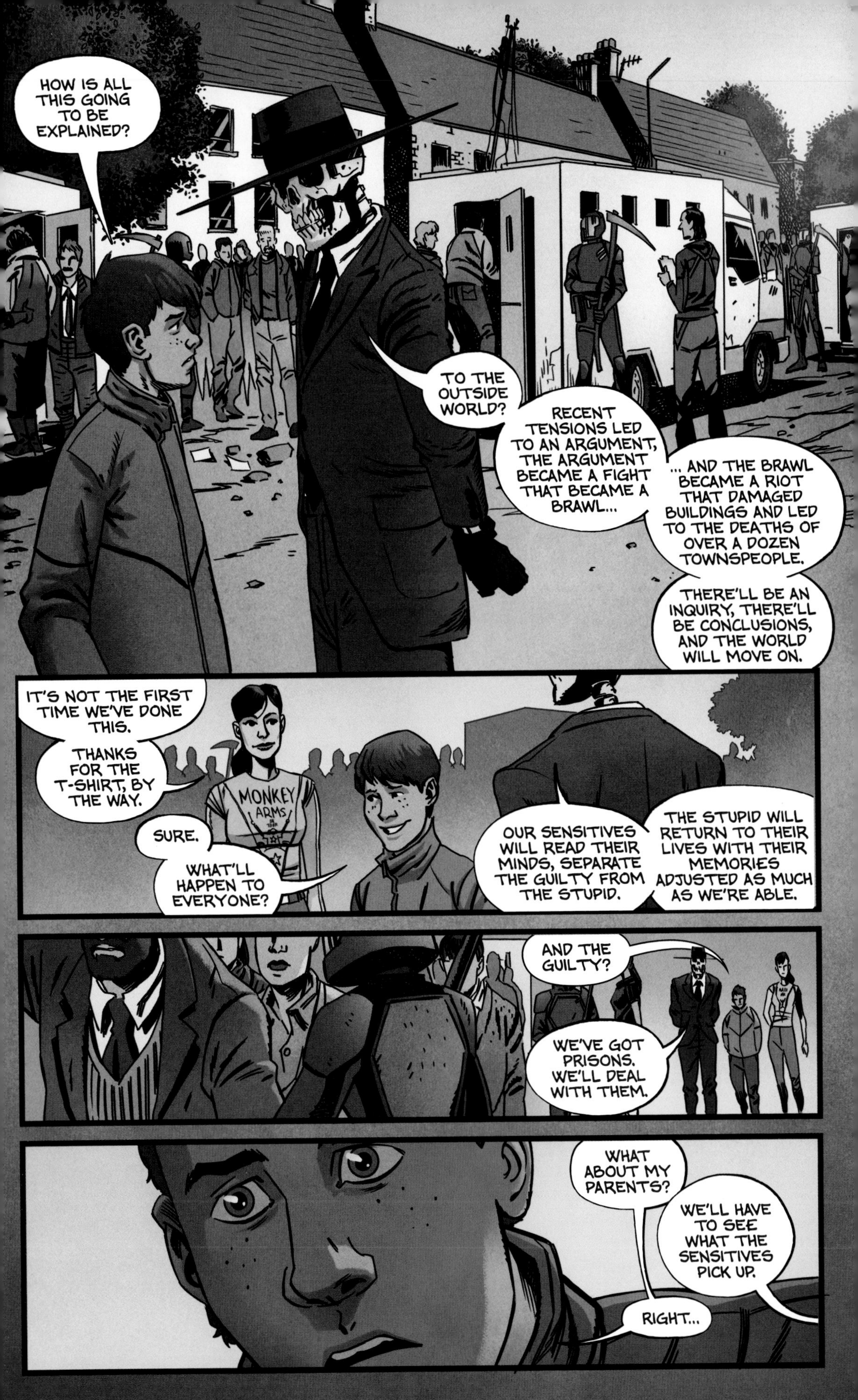
HOW IS ALL THIS GOING TO BE EXPLAINED?
TO THE OUTSIDE WORLD?
RECENT TENSIONS LED TO AN ARGUMENT, THE ARGUMENT BECAME A FIGHT THAT BECAME A BRAWL...
... AND THE BRAWL BECAME A RIOT THAT DAMAGED BUILDINGS AND LED TO THE DEATHS OF OVER A DOZEN TOWNSPEOPLE.
THERE'LL BE AN INQUIRY, THERE'LL BE CONCLUSIONS, AND THE WORLD WILL MOVE ON.
IT'S NOT THE FIRST TIME WE'VE DONE THIS.
THANKS FOR THE T-SHIRT, BY THE WAY.
MONKEY ARMS
SURE.
WHAT'LL HAPPEN TO EVERYONE?
OUR SENSITIVES WILL READ THEIR MINDS, SEPARATE THE GUILTY FROM THE STUPID.
THE STUPID WILL RETURN TO THEIR LIVES WITH THEIR MEMORIES ADJUSTED AS MUCH AS WE'RE ABLE.
AND THE GUILTY?
WE'VE GOT PRISONS. WE'LL DEAL WITH THEM.
WHAT ABOUT MY PARENTS?
WE'LL HAVE TO SEE WHAT THE SENSITIVES PICK UP.
RIGHT...

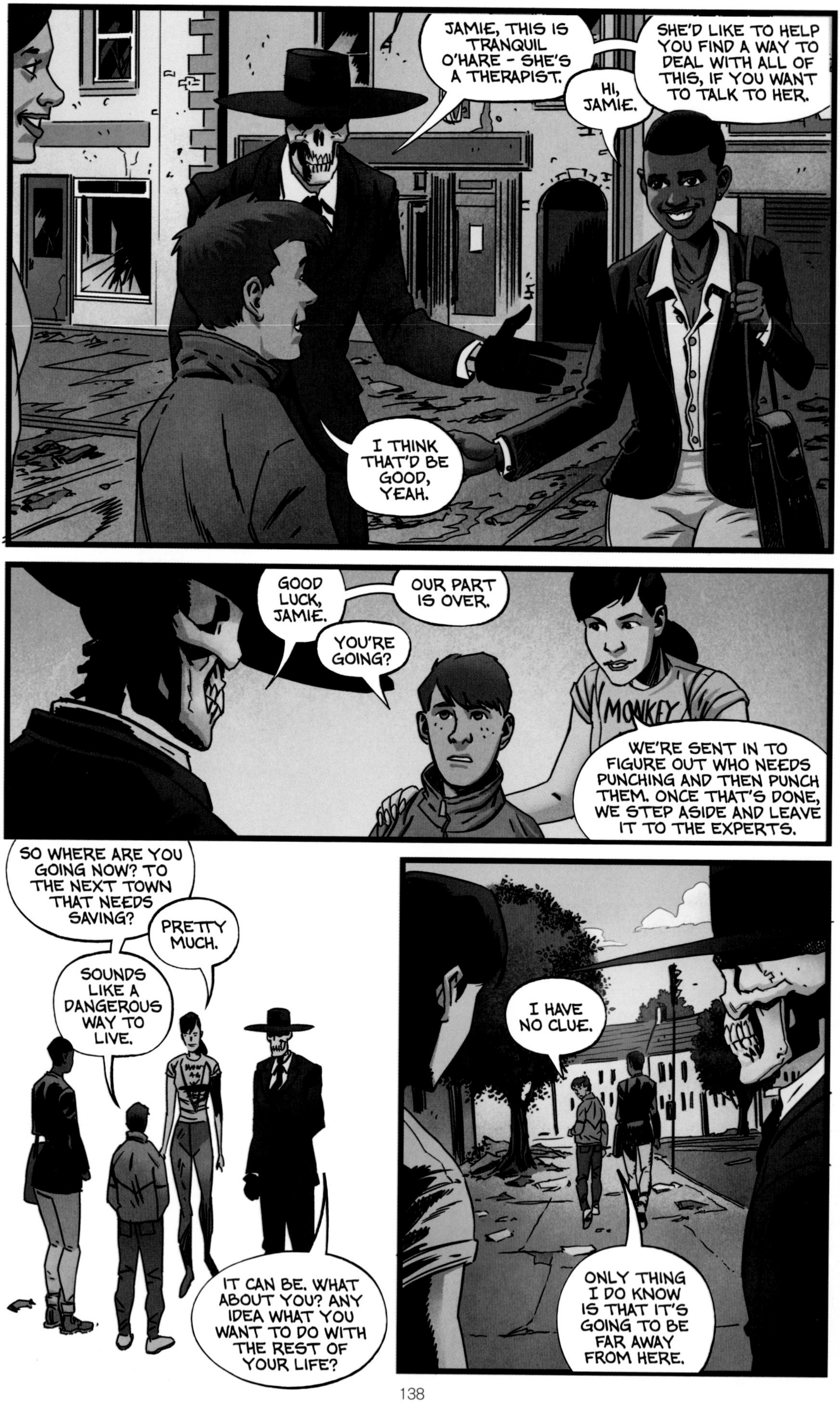
JAMIE, THIS IS TRANQUIL O'HARE - SHE'S A THERAPIST.
SHE'D LIKE TO HELP YOU FIND A WAY TO DEAL WITH ALL OF THIS, IF YOU WANT TO TALK TO HER.
HI, JAMIE.
I THINK THAT'D BE GOOD, YEAH.
GOOD LUCK, JAMIE.
OUR PART IS OVER.
YOU'RE GOING?
MONKEY
WE'RE SENT IN TO FIGURE OUT WHO NEEDS PUNCHING AND THEN PUNCH THEM. ONCE THAT'S DONE, WE STEP ASIDE AND LEAVE IT TO THE EXPERTS.
SO WHERE ARE YOU GOING NOW? TO THE NEXT TOWN THAT NEEDS SAVING?
PRETTY MUCH.
SOUNDS LIKE A DANGEROUS WAY TO LIVE.
IT CAN BE. WHAT ABOUT YOU? ANY IDEA WHAT YOU WANT TO DO WITH THE REST OF YOUR LIFE?
I HAVE NO CLUE.
ONLY THING I DO KNOW IS THAT IT'S GOING TO BE FAR AWAY FROM HERE.

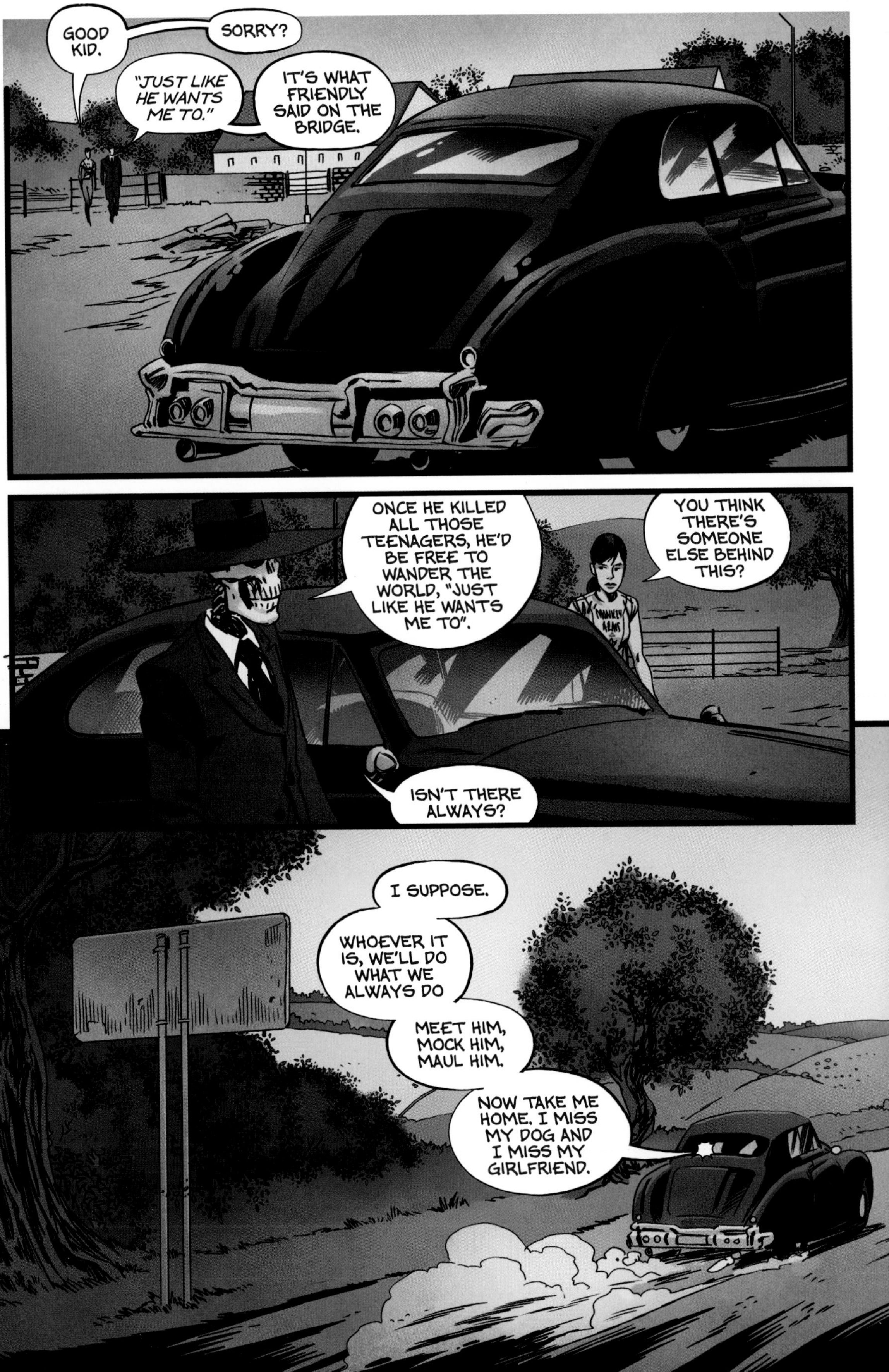
GOOD KID.
SORRY?
"JUST LIKE HE WANTS ME TO."
IT'S WHAT FRIENDLY SAID ON THE BRIDGE.
ONCE HE KILLED ALL THOSE TEENAGERS, HE'D BE FREE TO WANDER THE WORLD, "JUST LIKE HE WANTS ME TO".
YOU THINK THERE'S SOMEONE ELSE BEHIND THIS?
ISN'T THERE ALWAYS?
I SUPPOSE.
WHOEVER IT IS, WE'LL DO WHAT WE ALWAYS DO
MEET HIM, MOCK HIM, MAUL HIM.
NOW TAKE ME HOME. I MISS MY DOG AND I MISS MY GIRLFRIEND.

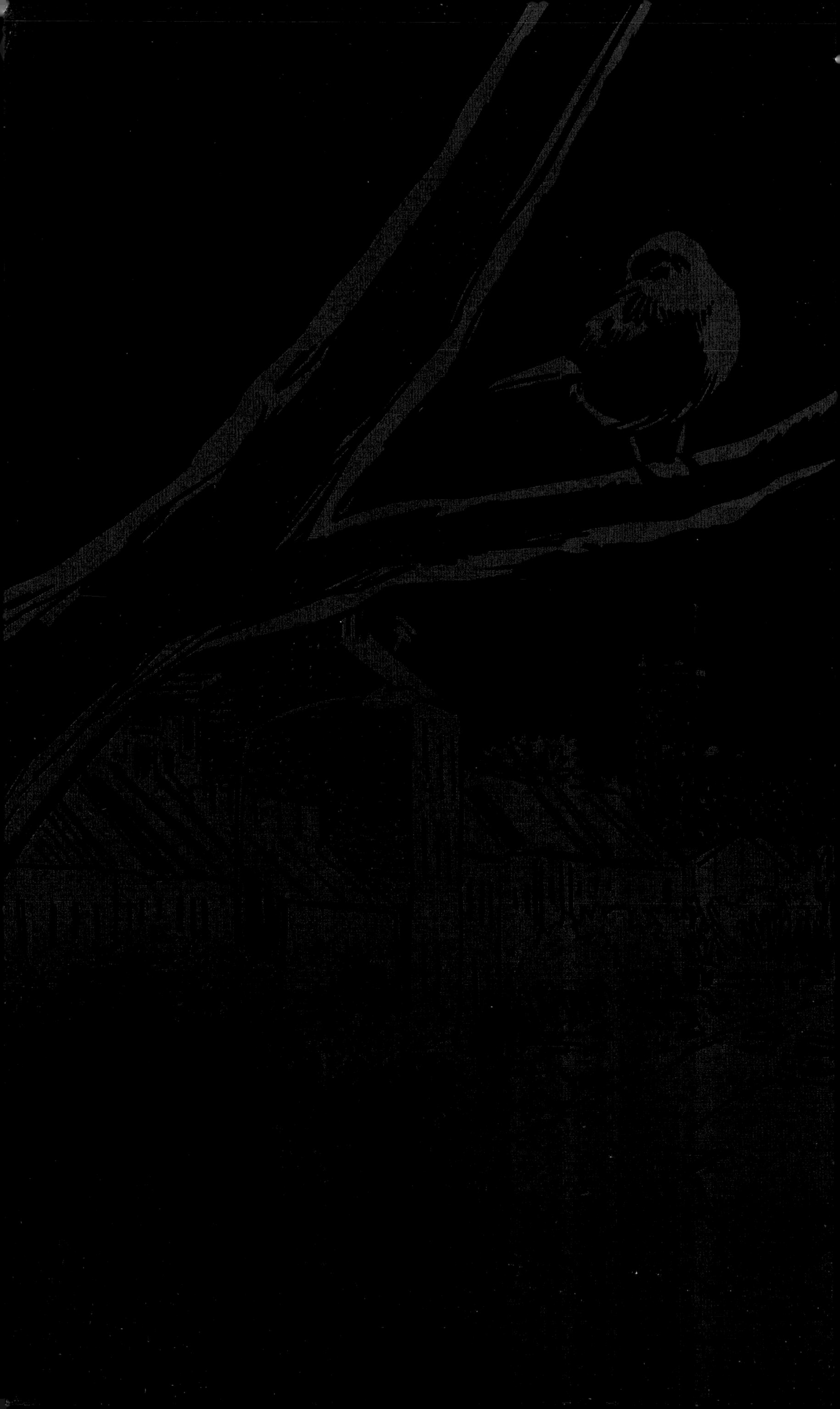

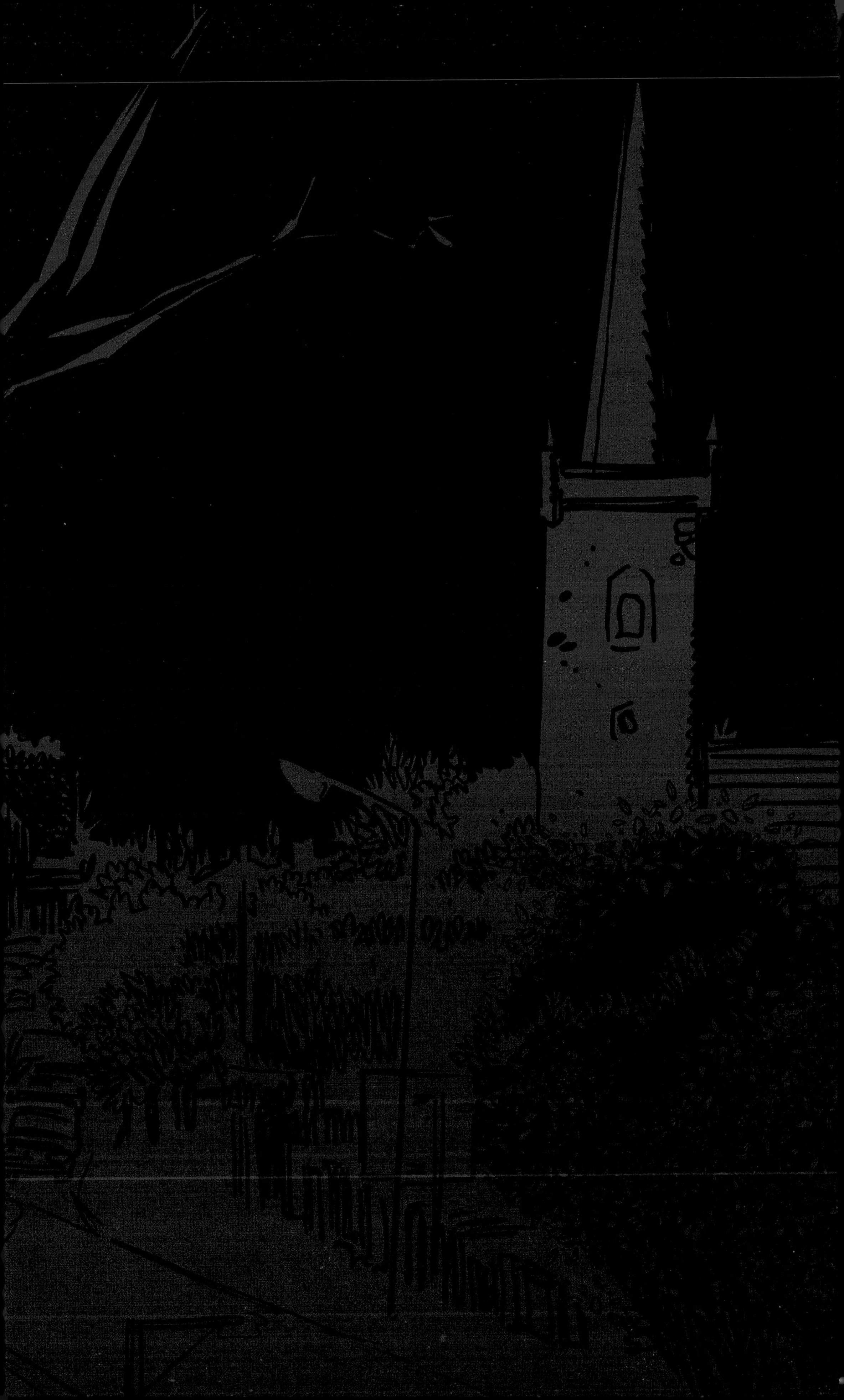

The internationally bestselling

SKULDUGGERY PLEASANT series

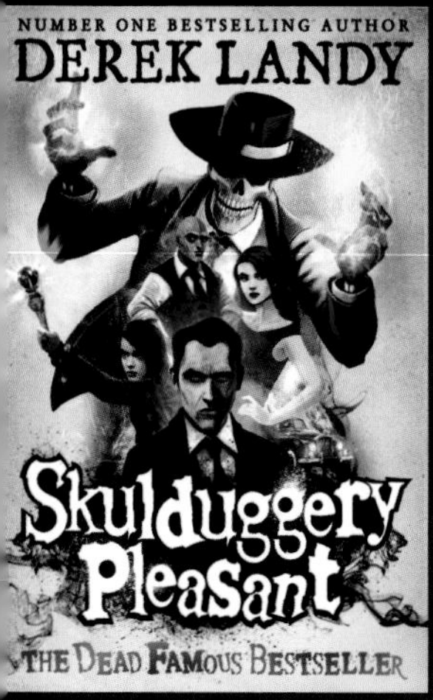
NUMBER ONE BESTSELLING AUTHOR
DEREK LANDY
Skulduggery Pleasant
THE DEAD FAMOUS BESTSELLER

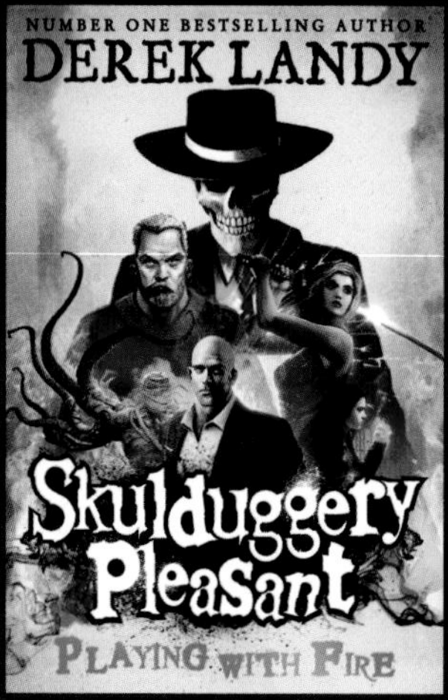
NUMBER ONE BESTSELLING AUTHOR
DEREK LANDY
Skulduggery Pleasant
PLAYING WITH FIRE

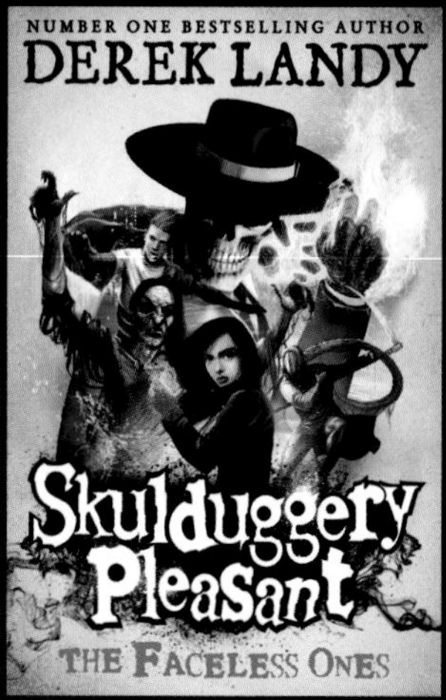
NUMBER ONE BESTSELLING AUTHOR
DEREK LANDY
Skulduggery Pleasant
THE FACELESS ONES

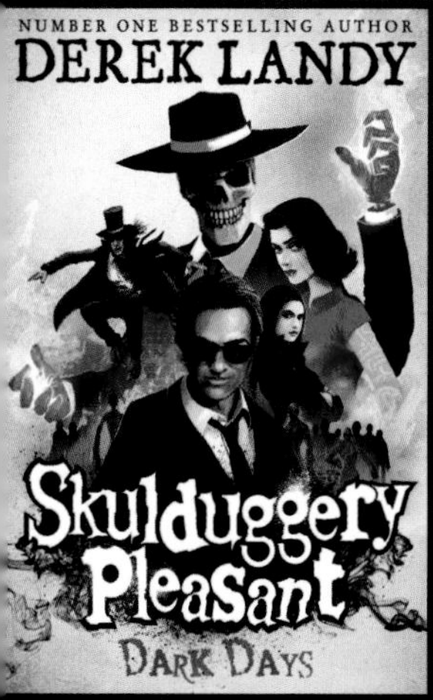
NUMBER ONE BESTSELLING AUTHOR
DEREK LANDY
Skulduggery Pleasant
DARK DAYS

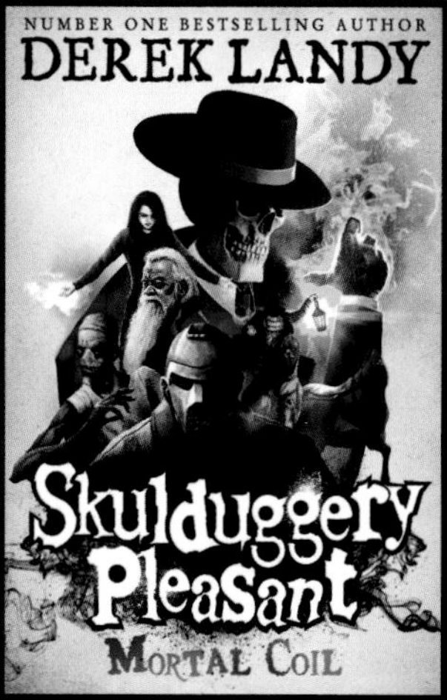
NUMBER ONE BESTSELLING AUTHOR
DEREK LANDY
Skulduggery Pleasant
MORTAL COIL

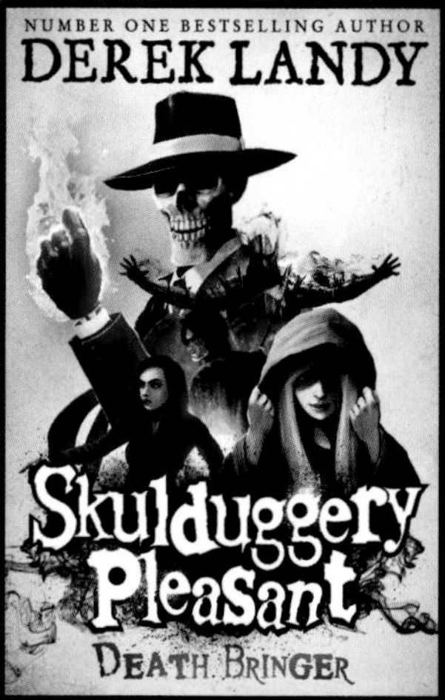
NUMBER ONE BESTSELLING AUTHOR
DEREK LANDY
Skulduggery Pleasant
DEATH BRINGER

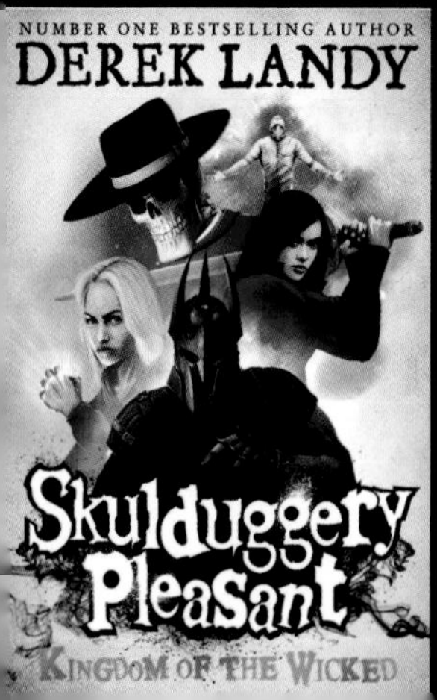
NUMBER ONE BESTSELLING AUTHOR
DEREK LANDY
Skulduggery Pleasant
KINGDOM OF THE WICKED

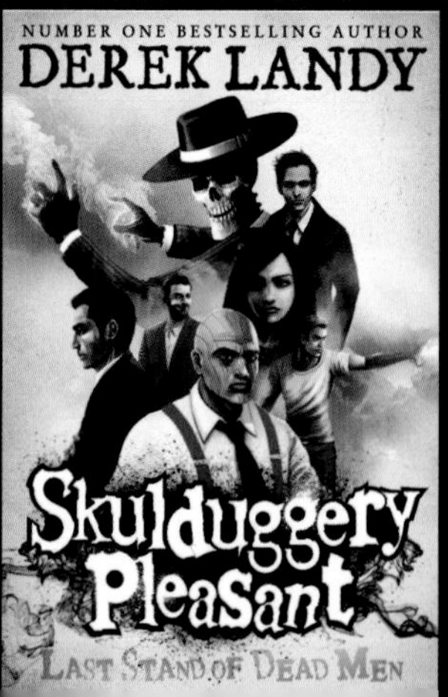
NUMBER ONE BESTSELLING AUTHOR
DEREK LANDY
Skulduggery Pleasant
LAST STAND OF DEAD MEN

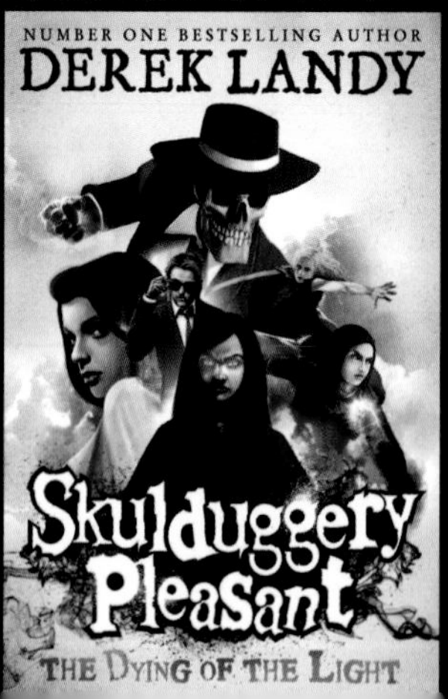
NUMBER ONE BESTSELLING AUTHOR
DEREK LANDY
Skulduggery Pleasant
THE DYING OF THE LIGHT

The internationally bestselling SKULDUGGERY PLEASANT series

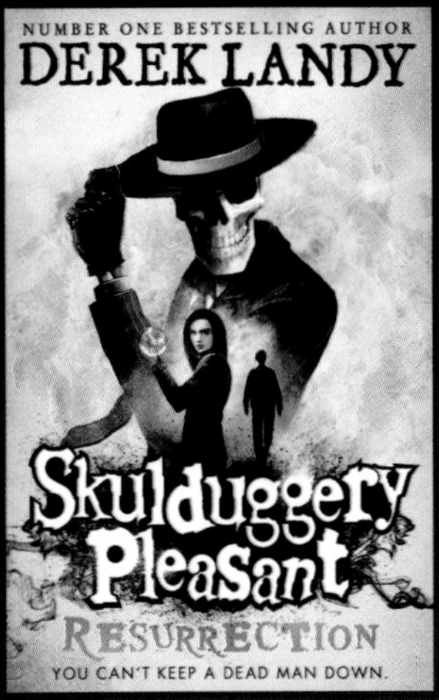
NUMBER ONE BESTSELLING AUTHOR
DEREK LANDY
Skulduggery Pleasant
RESURRECTION
YOU CAN'T KEEP A DEAD MAN DOWN.

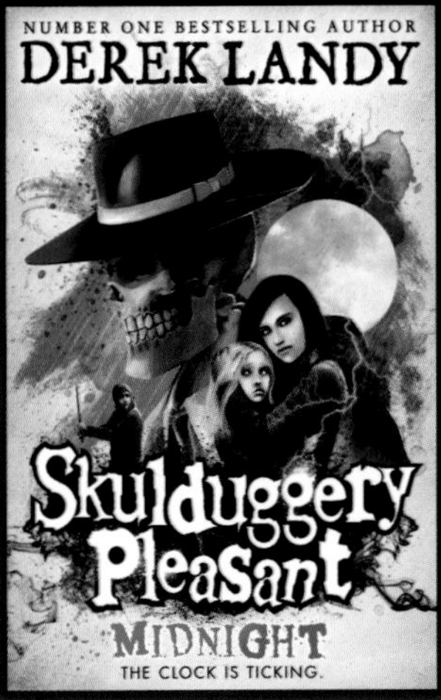
NUMBER ONE BESTSELLING AUTHOR
DEREK LANDY
Skulduggery Pleasant
MIDNIGHT
THE CLOCK IS TICKING.

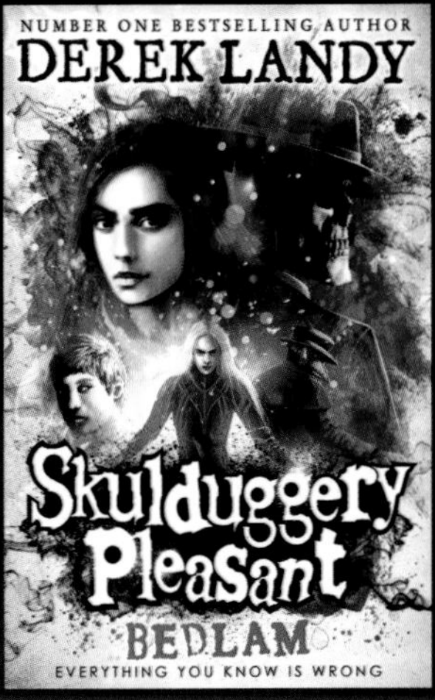
NUMBER ONE BESTSELLING AUTHOR
DEREK LANDY
Skulduggery Pleasant
BEDLAM
EVERYTHING YOU KNOW IS WRONG

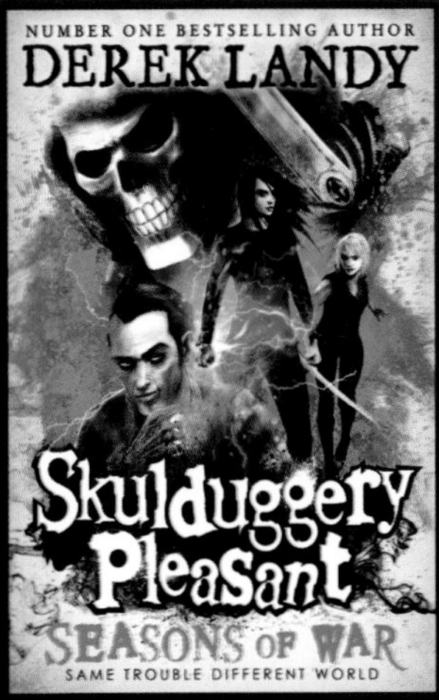
NUMBER ONE BESTSELLING AUTHOR
DEREK LANDY
Skulduggery Pleasant
SEASONS OF WAR
SAME TROUBLE DIFFERENT WORLD

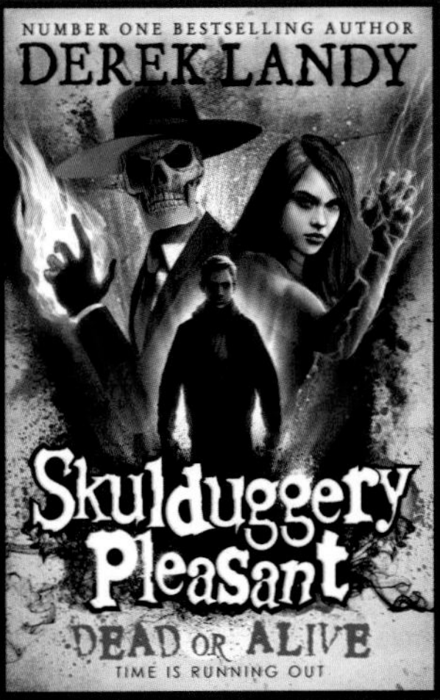
NUMBER ONE BESTSELLING AUTHOR
DEREK LANDY
Skulduggery Pleasant
DEAD OR ALIVE
TIME IS RUNNING OUT

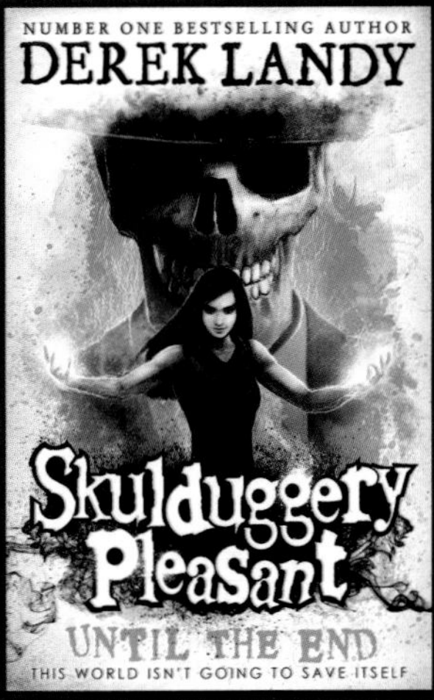
NUMBER ONE BESTSELLING AUTHOR
DEREK LANDY
Skulduggery Pleasant
UNTIL THE END
THIS WORLD ISN'T GOING TO SAVE ITSELF

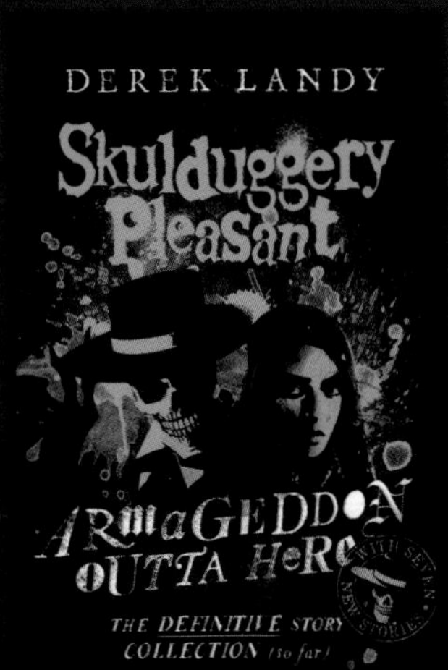
DEREK LANDY
Skulduggery Pleasant
ARMAGEDDON OUTTA HERE
THE DEFINITIVE STORY COLLECTION (so far)

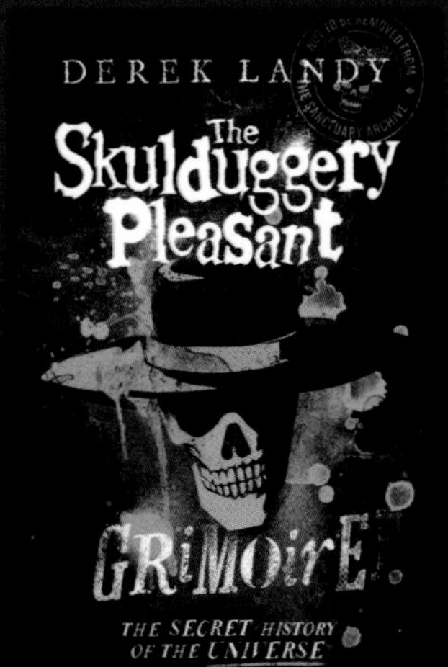
DEREK LANDY
The Skulduggery Pleasant
GRIMOIRE
THE SECRET HISTORY OF THE UNIVERSE

Discover the world of SKULDUGGERY
PLEASANT in this prequel ...

NUMBER ONE BESTSELLING AUTHOR

DEREK LANDY

HELL
BREAKS
LOOSE

FROM THE WORLD OF

Skulduggery
Pleasant

300 YEARS BEFORE THE STORY BEGINS...
...THE STORY BEGINS